HAUNTED TALES

HAUNTED TALES

Classic Stories of Ghosts and the Supernatural

EDITED BY
LISA MORTON AND
LESLIE S. KLINGER

PEGASUS BOOKS
NEW YORK LONDON

HAUNTED TALES

Pegasus Books, Ltd.
148 West 37th Street, 13th Floor
New York, NY 10018

Compilation and Introduction copyright © 2022 by Lisa Morton and Leslie S. Klinger

First Pegasus Books cloth edition August 2022

Interior design by Maria Fernandez

Library of Congress Cataloging-in-Publication Data is available.

ISBN: 978-1-63936-197-7

10 9 8 7 6 5 4 3 2 1

Printed in the United States of America
Distributed by Simon & Schuster
www.pegasusbooks.com

To Jim Riley, my sixth-grade teacher who filled me with curiosity and imagination, and to all the other teachers out there who are the inspirations for the future.
—Lisa Mortom

To my scoutmaster, whose name is lost to my memory, who first told me ghost stories around a campfire—and made me want to read them for myself!
—Leslie S. Klinger

CONTENTS

INTRODUCTION
by Lisa Morton and Leslie S. Klinger

"We are encompassed on all sides by wonders, and we can scarcely set our foot upon the ground, without trampling upon some marvellous production that our whole life and all our faculties would not suffice to comprehend."
—Catherine Crowe, from *The Night-Side of Nature*

The Industrial Revolution brought progress to Europe in many fields, including mass murder. The Napoleonic Wars killed upwards of four million people, and various wars of independence added hundreds of thousands more. As violent deaths were added to the tolls of disease and hunger, a desire to communicate with the dead and to receive some reassurance that there was a life after death sparked intense interest in ghosts and the persistence of spirits. The nineteenth century was awash in ghosts as a result.

In part, this fascination with ghosts manifested in the sudden rise of séances and the growth of Spiritualism. In addition, spooky regional lore was collected by writers like Catherine Crowe in her hugely influential *The Night-Side of Nature* (1848). Tales of ghosts and related otherworldly beings filled the pages of the magazines and books that had come about with new printing technologies such as wood engraving (replacing copperplate), lithography, and a range of photomechanical means of reproduction.

As editors working together, we have now produced four volumes of early supernatural fiction; as readers, we've been enthralled by such stories our entire lives. You might think that by now we'd have discovered every significant ghost story of the last two centuries. Instead, we are continually delighted to discover new gems that we can't wait to share. How is it possible that the larders of literary history remain so packed with hidden treasures?

During the nineteenth and early twentieth centuries, ghostly stories were as common as any other type of story; they weren't relegated to either their own periodicals or publishing's cobwebbed back corners. Pick up any major magazine from, say, 1870, whether it's an issue of *Harper's Monthly Magazine* or *All the Year Round* (founded by Charles Dickens), and it's virtually certain that you'll find a haunted tale among the serialized novels and short stories recounting adventures, mysteries, memoirs, and romances. Although some authors wrote only supernatural tales, most wrote stories about whatever interested them, unburdened by any publisher's or bookseller's demand that they confine themselves to a single type of story. When authors produced collections of their work, they sometimes gathered the ghost tales into a separate book, but quite often they simply placed them among their other nonsupernatural stories.

Ghost stories were in demand for Christmas publications, a specialized market that not only published work like Charles Dickens's *A Christmas Carol*, but also ghost stories by other authors in the Christmas issues of his magazines (at first *Household Words*, then *All the Year Round*, which was edited by Charles Dickens Jr. after the elder Dickens passed on). However, after Dickens noted in a letter dated March 8, 1855, that he had found "the best Ghost story [sent by a lady for *Household Words*] that ever was written," he didn't hold the piece until the following Christmas, as would have been customary, but instead published "A Ghost Story" (which appears in this book under its revised title "M. Anastasius") by Dinah Mulock in the March 24 issue of *Household Words*. Ghost stories, in other words, were popular all the year round (pun intended).

Why have some of these excellent spine-chillers been consigned to history's mausoleums? Certain stories—like Oscar Wilde's "The Canterville Ghost," included in this book—have been frequently anthologized and adapted to other forms. The ghost stories of M. R. James, F. Marion Crawford, and Algernon Blackwood (the latter two represented herein by "The Screaming Skull" and "The Kit-Bag," respectively) are still beloved by genre fans. But others have been undeservedly neglected. Perhaps it's simply that many were published in a disposable (i.e., magazine) form, so that contemporary readers don't know where to find them. Perhaps it's because (in the case of authors like Braddon, Wells, and Kipling) other work by the authors has overshadowed or obscured the merits of these stories.

We believe the tales we've chosen for this book (and the three volumes that came before it) remain as entertaining now as they were for readers a century or more ago. Although some include words or phrases that need footnotes and some deal with classes of society that have vanished, their emotional cores are still frightening, disturbing, tragic, moving, and even sometimes ecstatic. The best ghost stories are fundamentally about the living, and people haven't really changed much in 200 years. The mysteries of death are as impenetrable as ever, and a love for tales of supernatural dread and a longing for a glimpse of the afterlife remain part of the human condition.

It is unfortunate that the narrow categories of "genre" may consign certain great and true works of literature to the back shelves. We hope all lovers of fiction will be as drawn to these wonderful works as we were. If, after reading these, you see the world a little differently than you did before, the authors—and we—will have accomplished their purpose!

—Lisa Morton and Leslie S. Klinger

THE GHOST AND THE BONE-SETTER

by Joseph Sheridan Le Fanu

(1838)

In looking over the papers of my late valued and respected friend, Francis Purcell, who for nearly fifty years discharged the arduous duties of a parish priest in the south of Ireland, I met with the following document. It is one of many such; for he was a curious and industrious collector of old local traditions—a commodity in which the quarter where he resided mightily abounded. The collection and arrangement of such legends was, as long as I can remember him, his *hobby*; but I had never learned that his love of the marvellous and whimsical had carried him so far as to prompt him to commit the results of his enquiries to writing, until, in the character of *residuary legatee*, his will put me in possession of all his manuscript papers. To such as may think the composing of such productions as these inconsistent with the character and habits of a country priest, it is necessary to observe, that there did exist a race of priests—those of the old school, a race now nearly extinct—whose habits were from many causes more refined, and whose tastes more literary than are those of the alumni of Maynooth. [*]

It is perhaps necessary to add that the superstition illustrated by the following story, namely, that the corpse last buried is obliged, during his juniority of interment, to supply his brother tenants of the church-yard in which he lies, with fresh water to allay the burning thirst of purgatory, is prevalent throughout the south of Ireland. The writer can vouch for a case in which a respectable and wealthy farmer, on the borders of Tipperary, [†] in tenderness to the corns of his departed helpmate, enclosed in her coffin two pair of brogues, a light and a heavy, the one for dry, the other for sloppy weather; seeking thus to mitigate the fatigues of her inevitable perambulations in procuring water, and administering it to the thirsty souls of purgatory. Fierce and desperate conflicts have ensued in the case of two funeral parties approaching the same church-yard together, each endeavouring to secure to his own dead priority of sepulture, and a consequent immunity from the tax levied upon the pedestrian powers of the last comer. An instance not long since occurred, in which one of two such parties, through fear of losing to their deceased friend this inestimable advantage, made their way to the church-yard by a *short cut*, and in violation of one of their strongest prejudices, actually threw the coffin over the wall, lest time should be lost in making their entrance through the gate. Innumerable instances of the same kind might be quoted, all tending to shew how

---

[*] Maynooth College in Ireland (established in 1795 as the Royal College of St. Patrick) is the "National Seminary of Ireland." Prior to its establishment, priests-in-training had to study abroad; even after the college was opened, its library was largely composed of texts published in other countries.

[†] Tipperary can refer to either a county or a town in the southern half of Ireland.

strongly, among the peasantry of the south, this superstition is entertained.*
However, I shall not detain the reader further, by any prefatory remarks,
but shall proceed to lay before him the following—

EXTRACT FROM THE MS. PAPERS OF
THE LATE REV. FRANCIS PURCELL, OF DRUMCOOLAGH.†

I tell the following particulars, as nearly as I can recollect them,
in the words of the narrator. It may be necessary to observe
that he was what is termed a *well-spoken* man, having for a
considerable time instructed the ingenious youth of his native
parish in such of the liberal arts and sciences as he found it convenient to profess—a circumstance which may account for the
occurrence of several big words, in the course of this narrative,
more distinguished for euphonious effect, than for correctness
of application. I proceed then, without further preface, to lay
before you the wonderful adventures of Terry Neil.

"Why, thin, 'tis a quare story, an' as thrue as you're sittin'
there; and I'd make bould to say there isn't a boy in the seven
parishes could tell it better nor crickther than myself, for 'twas
my father himself it happened to, an' manys the time I heerd it
out iv his own mouth; an' I can say, an' I'm proud av that same,
my father's word was as incredible as any squire's oath in the
counthry; and so signs an' if a poor man got into any unlucky
throuble, he was the boy id go into the court an' prove; but that
doesn't signify—he was as honest and as sober a man, barrin' he
was a little bit too partial to the glass, as you'd find in a day's
walk; an' there wasn't the likes of him in the counthry round

---

* This practice was still popular by the end of the nineteenth century; it was described,
for example, in an 1895 account of the folklore of County Cork.

† This may be a regional variant spelling of Dromcolliher, a medieval town located in
County Limerick, Ireland, near the northern border of County Cork.

for nate labourin' an' *baan* diggin';* and he was mighty handy entirely for carpenther's work, and mendin' ould spudethrees, an' the likes i' that. An' so he tuck up with bone-setting, as was most nathural, for none of them could come up to him in mendin' the leg iv a stool or a table; an' sure, there never was a bone-setter got so much custom—man an' child, young an' ould—there never was such breakin' and mendin' of bones known in the memory of man. Well, Terry Neil, for that was my father's name, began to feel his heart growin' light, and his purse heavy; an' he took a bit iv a farm in Squire Phelim's† ground, just undher the ould castle, an' a pleasant little spot it was; an' day an' mornin', poor crathurs‡ not able to put a foot to the ground, with broken arms and broken legs, id be comin' ramblin' in from all quarters to have their bones spliced up. Well, yer honour, all this was as well as well could be; but it was customary when Sir Phelim id go any where out iv the country, for some iv the tinants to sit up to watch in the ould castle, just for a kind of compliment to the ould family—an' a mighty unpleasant compliment it was for the tinants, for there wasn't a man of them but knew there was some thing quare about the ould castle. The neighbours had it, that the squire's ould grandfather, as good a gintleman, God be with him, as I heer'd, as ever stood in shoe leather, used to keep walkin' about in the middle iv the night, ever sinst he bursted a blood vessel pullin' out a cork out iv a bottle, as you or I might be doin', and will too, plase God; but that doesn't signify. So, as I was sayin', the ould squire used to come down out of the frame, where his picthur was hung up, and to break the bottles and glasses, God be marciful to us all, an' dhrink all he could come at—an' small blame to him for that same; and then if any of the family id be comin' in, he id be up again

---

* "Baan" refers to coal here.

† Sir Phelim O'Neill was a real Irish nobleman in the seventeenth century.

‡ Creatures.

in his place, looking as quite an' innocent as if he didn't know any thing about it—the mischievous ould chap.

"Well, your honour, as I was sayin', one time the family up at the castle was stayin' in Dublin for a week or two; and so as usual, some of the tinants had to sit up in the castle, and the third night it kem to my father's turn. 'Oh, tare an' ouns,*" says he unto himself, 'an' must I sit up all night, and that ould vagabond of a sperit, glory be to God,' says he, 'serenading through the house, an' doin' all sorts iv mischief.' However, there was no gettin' aff, and so he put a bould face on it, an' he went up at night-fall with a bottle of pottieen,† and another of holy wather.

"It was rainin' smart enough, an' the evenin' was darksome and gloomy, when my father got in; and what with the rain he got, and the holy wather he sprinkled on himself, it wasn't long till he had to swallee a cup iv the pottieen, to keep the cowld out iv his heart. It was the ould steward, Lawrence Connor, that opened the door—and he an' my father wor always very great. So when he seen who it was, an' my father tould him how it was his turn to watch in the castle, he offered to sit up along with him; and you may be sure my father wasn't sorry for that same. So says Larry,

"'We'll have a bit iv fire in the parlour,' says he.

"'An' why not in the hall?' says my father, for he knew that the squire's picthur was hung in the parlour.

"'No fire can be lit in the hall,' says Lawrence, 'for there's an ould jackdaw's nest in the chimney.'

"'Oh thin,' says my father, "let us stop in the kitchen, for it's very unproper for the likes iv me to be sittin' in the parlour,' says he.

"'Oh, Terry, that can't be,' says Lawrence; 'if we keep up the ould custom at all, we may as well keep it up properly,' says he.

---

* "Tears and wounds," a reference to Christ on the cross.

† Illegally distilled whiskey.

"'Divil sweep the ould custom,' says my father—to himself, do ye mind, for he didn't like to let Lawrence see that he was more afeard himself.

"'Oh, very well,' says he. 'I'm agreeable, Lawrence,' says he; and so down they both went to the kitchen, until the fire id be lit in the parlour—an' that same wasn't long doin'.

"Well, your honour, they soon wint up again, an' sat down mighty comfortable by the parlour fire, and they beginn'd to talk, an' to smoke, an' to dhrink a small taste iv the pottieen; and, moreover, they had a good rousing fire of bogwood and turf, to warm their shins over.

"Well, sir, as I was sayin' they kep' convarsin' and smokin' together most agreeable, until Lawrence beginn'd to get sleepy, as was but nathural for him, for he was an ould sarvint man, and was used to a great dale iv sleep.

"'Sure it's impossible,' says my father, 'it's gettin' sleepy you are?'

"'Oh, divil a taste,' says Larry; "I'm only shuttin' my eyes,' says he, 'to keep out the parfume of the tibacky smoke, that's makin' them wather,' says he. 'So don't you mind other people's business,' says he, stiff enough, for he had a mighty high stomach av his own (rest his sowl), 'and go on,' says he, 'with your story, for I'm listenin',' says he, shuttin' down his eyes.

"Well, when my father seen spakin' was no use, he went on with his story. By the same token, it was the story of Jim Soolivan and his ould goat he was tellin'—an' a pleasant story it is—an' there was so much divarsion in it, that it was enough to waken a dormouse, let alone to pervint a Christian goin' asleep. But, faix,* the way my father tould it, I believe there never was the likes heerd sinst nor before, for he bawled out every word av it, as if the life was fairly leavin' him, thrying to keep ould Larry awake; but, faix, it was no use, for the hoorsness came an him, an' before he kem to the end of his story, Larry O'Connor beginned to snore like a bagpipes.

---

* An exclamation used to express astonishment.

"'Oh, blur an' agres,' says my father, 'isn't this a hard case,' says he, 'that ould villain, lettin' on to be my friend, and to go asleep this way, an' us both in the very room with a sperit,' says he. 'The crass o' Christ about us,' says he; and with that he was goin' to shake Lawrence to waken him, but he just remimbered if he roused him, that he'd surely go off to his bed, an' lave him complately alone, an' that id be by far worse.

"'Oh thin,' says my father, 'I'll not disturb the poor boy. It id be neither friendly nor good-nathured,' says he, 'to tormint him while he is asleep,' says he; 'only I wish I was the same way, myself,' says he.

"An' with that he beginned to walk up an' down, an' sayin' his prayers, until he worked himself into a sweat, savin' your presence. But it was all no good; so he dhrunk about a pint of sperits, to compose his mind.

"'Oh,' says he, 'I wish to the Lord I was as asy in my mind as Larry there. Maybe,' says he, 'if I thried I could go asleep;' an' with that he pulled a big arm-chair close beside Lawrence, an' settled himself in it as well as he could.

"But there was one quare thing I forgot to tell you. He couldn't help, in spite av himself, lookin' now an' thin at the picthur, an' he immediately obsarved that the eyes av it was fol-lyin' him about, an' starin' at him, an' winkin' at him, wheriver he wint. 'Oh,' says he, when he seen that, 'it's a poor chance I have,' says he; 'an' bad luck was with me the day I kem into this unforthunate place,' says he; 'but any way there's no use in bein' freckened* now,' says he; 'for if I am to die, I may as well parspire undaunted,' says he.

"Well, your honour, he thried to keep himself quite an' asy, an' he thought two or three times he might have wint asleep, but for the way the storm was groanin' and creekin' through the great heavy branches outside, an' whistlin' through the ould chimnies iv the castle. Well, afther one great roarin' blast

---

* Frightened.

iv the wind, you'd think the walls iv the castle was just goin' to fall, quite an' clane, with the shakin' iv it. All av a suddint the storm stopt, as silent an' as quite as if it was a July evenin'. Well, your honour, it wasn't stopped blowin' for three minnites, before he thought he hard a sort iv a noise over the chimney-piece; an' with that my father just opened his eyes the smallest taste in life, an' sure enough he seen the ould squire gettin' out iv the picthur, for all the world as if he was throwin' aff his ridin' coat, until he stept out clane an' complate, out av the chimly-piece, an' thrun himself down an the floor. Well, the slieveen* ould chap—an' my father thought it was the dirtiest turn iv all—before he beginned to do anything out iv the way, he stopped for a while to listen wor they both asleep; an' as soon as he thought all was quite, he put out his hand and tuck hould iv the whiskey bottle, an dhrank at laste a pint iv it. Well, your honour, when he tuck his turn out iv it, he settled it back mighty cute intirely, in the very same spot it was in before. An' he beginn'd to walk up an' down the room, lookin' as sober an' as solid as if he never done the likes at all. An' whinever he went apast my father, he thought he felt a great scent of brim-stone, an' it was that that freckened him entirely; for he knew it was brimstone that was burned in hell, savin' your presence. At any rate, he often heer'd it from Father Murphy, an' he had a right to know what belonged to it—he's dead since, God rest him. Well, your honour, my father was asy enough until the sperit kem past him; so close, God be marciful to us all, that the smell iv the sulphur tuck the breath clane out iv him; an' with that he tuck such a fit iv coughin', that it al-a-most shuck him out iv the chair he was sittin' in.

"'Ho, ho!' says the squire, stoppin' short about two steps aff, and turnin' round facin' my father, 'is it you that's in it?—an' how's all with you, Terry Neil?'

---

* Untrustworthy or devious.

"'At your honour's sarvice,' says my father (as well as the fright id let him, for he was more dead than alive), 'an' it's proud I am to see your honour to-night,' says he.

"'Terence,' says the squire, 'you're a respectable man' (an' it was thrue for him), 'an industhrious, sober man, an' an example of inebriety to the whole parish,' says he.

"'Thank your honour,' says my father, gettin' courage, 'you were always a civil spoken gintleman, God rest your honour.'

"'Rest my honour," says the sperit (fairly gettin' red in the face with the madness), 'Rest my honour?' says he. 'Why, you ignorant spalpeen," says he, 'you mane, niggarly† ignoramush,' says he, 'where did you lave your manners?' says he. 'If I *am* dead, it's no fault iv mine,' says he; 'an' it's not to be thrun in my teeth at every hand's turn, by the likes iv you,' says he, stampin' his foot an the flure, that you'd think the boords id smash undher him.

"'Oh,' says my father, 'I'm only a foolish, ignorant poor man,' says he.

"'You're nothing else,' says the squire: 'but any way,' says he, 'it's not to be listenin' to your gosther,‡ nor convarsin' with the likes iv you, that I came *up*—down I mane,' says he—(an' as little as the mistake was, my father tuck notice iv it). 'Listen to me now, Terence Neil,' says he, 'I was always a good masther to Pathrick Neil, your grandfather,' says he.

"'Tis thrue for your honour,' says my father.

"'And, moreover, I think I was always a sober, riglar gintleman,' says the squire.

"'That's your name, sure enough,' says my father (though it was a big lie for him, but he could not help it).

"'Well,' says the sperit, 'although I was as sober as most men—at laste as most gintlemen'—says he; 'an' though I was at

---

* A spalpeen is a common laborer.

† A variant spelling of "niggardly"—mean or stingy.

‡ Bragging or bravado.

different pariods a most extempory Christian, and most charitable and inhuman to the poor,' says he, 'for all that I'm not as asy where I am now,' says he, 'as I had a right to expect,' says he.

"'An' more's the pity,' says my father. 'Maybe your honour id wish to have a word with Father Murphy?'

"'Hould your tongue, you misherable bliggard,' says the squire; 'it's not iv my sowl I'm thinkin'—an' I wondher you'd have the impitence to talk to a gintleman consarnin' his sowl—and when I want *that* fixed,' says he, slappin' his thigh, 'I'll go to them that knows what belongs to the likes,' says he. 'It's not my sowl,' says he, sittin' down opposite my father; 'it's not my sowl that's annoyin' me most—I'm unasy on my right leg,' says he, 'that I bruck at Glenvarloch cover* the day I killed black Barney.'

"(My father found out afther, it was a favourite horse that fell undher him, afther leapin' the big fince that runs along by the glen.)

"'I hope,' says my father, 'your honour's not unasy about the killin' iv him?'

"'Hould your tongue, ye fool,' said the squire, "an' I'll tell you why I'm unasy on my leg,' says he. 'In the place, where I spend most iv my time,' says he, 'except the little leisure I have for lookin' about me here,' says he, 'I have to walk a great dale more than I was ever used to,' says he, 'and by far more than is good for me either,' says he; 'for I must tell you,' says he, 'the people where I am is ancommonly fond iv could wather, for there is nothin' betther to be had; an', moreover, the weather is hotter than is altogether plisint," says he; 'and I'm appinted,' says he, 'to assist in carryin' the wather, an' gets a mighty poor share iv it myself,' says he, 'an' a mighty throublesome, warin' job it is, I can tell you,' says he; 'for they're all iv them surprisingly dhry,

---

* The name "Glenvarloch" may be an homage to a character from Sir Walter Scott's novel *The Fortunes of Nigel* (Scott's work had a great influence on Le Fanu's historical novels). "Cover" refers to a wooded area.

an' dhrinks it as fast as my legs can carry it,' says he; 'but what kills me intirely,' says he, 'is the wakeness in my leg,' says he, 'an' I want you to give it a pull or two to bring it to shape,' says he, 'and that's the long an' the short iv it,' says he.

"'Oh, plase your honour,' says my father (for he didn't like to handle the sperit at all), 'I wouldn't have the impitence to do the likes to your honour,' says he; 'it's only to poor crathurs like myself I'd do it to,' says he.

"'None iv your blarney,' says the squire, 'here's my leg,' says he, cockin' it up to him, 'pull it for the bare life,' says he; 'an' if you don't, by the immortial powers I'll not lave a bone in your carcish I'll not powdher,' says he.

"When my father heerd that, he seen there was no use in purtendin', so he tuck hould iv the leg, an' he kep' pullin' an' pullin', till the sweat, God bless us, beginned to pour down his face.

"'Pull, you divil,' says the squire.

"'At your sarvice, your honour,' says my father.

"'Pull harder,' says the squire.

"My father pulled like the divil.

"'I'll take a little sup,' says the squire, rachin' over his hand to the bottle, 'to keep up my courage,' says he, lettin' an to be very wake in himself intirely. But, as cute as he was, he was out here, for he tuck the wrong one. 'Here's to your good health, Terence,' says he; 'an' now pull like the very divil,' an' with that he lifted the bottle of holy wather, but it was hardly to his mouth, whin he let a screech out, you'd think the room id fairly split with it, an' made one chuck that sent the leg clane aff his body in my father's hands; down wint the squire over the table, an' bang wint my father half way across the room on his back, upon the flure. Whin he kem to himself the cheerful mornin' sun was shinin' through the windy shutthers, an' he was lying flat an his back, with the leg iv one of the great ould chairs pulled clane out iv the socket an' tight in his hand, pintin' up to the ceilin', an' ould Larry fast asleep, an' snorin' as loud as ever. My father wint that mornin' to Father Murphy, an' from that to the day of his death, he never neglected confission nor mass, an' what he tould was betther believed that he spake av it but seldom. An', as for the squire, that is the sperit, whether it was that he did not like his liquor, or by rason iv the loss iv his leg, he was never known to walk again.'

On March 8, 1855, Charles Dickens wrote a letter to his friend Angela Burdett-Coutts in which he noted, "I think I have just got the best Ghost story (sent by a lady for Household Words*) that ever was written . . ." Dickens published "A Ghost Story" two weeks later in his magazine* Household Words*; the "lady" was author* **DINAH MULOCK**. *Born in 1826, by 1855 she had already published several novels and enough short stories for a collection called* Avillion and Other Tales *(1853). In 1856, she published her most famous work, the novel* John Halifax, Gentleman*; in 1865, she married George Lillie Craik, a partner in the Macmillan publishing company. When she reprinted "A Ghost Story" in her 1857 collection* Nothing New*, she changed the title to "M. Anastasius" and slightly rewrote it. She was still one of England's most popular authors when she died in 1887.*

M. ANASTASIUS

by Dinah Mulock

(1857)

CHAPTER I

I will relate to you, my friend, the whole history, from the beginning to—nearly—the end.

The first time that—*that it happened*, was on this wise.

My husband and myself were sitting in a private box at the theatre—one of the two large London theatres. The performance was, I remember well, an Easter piece, in which were introduced live dromedaries and an elephant, at whose clumsy feats we were considerably amused. I mention this to show how calm and even gay was the state of both our minds that evening, and how little there was in any of the circumstances of the place or time to cause, or render us liable to—what I am about to describe.

I liked this Easter piece better than any serious drama. My life had contained enough of the tragic element to make me turn with a sick distaste from all imitations thereof in books or plays. For months, ever since our marriage, Alexis and I had striven to lead a purely childish, commonplace existence, eschewing all stirring events and strong emotions, mixing little in society, and then, with one exception, making no associations beyond the moment.

It was easy to do this in London; for we had no relations—we two were quite alone and free. Free—free! How wildly I sometimes grasped Alexis's hand as I repeated that word.

He was young—so was I. At times, as on this night, we would sit together and laugh like children. It was so glorious to know of a surety that now we could think, feel, speak, act—above all, love one another—haunted by no counteracting spell, responsible to no living creature for our life and our love.

But this had been our lot only for a year—I had recollected the date, shuddering, in the morning—for one year, from this same day.

We had been laughing very heartily, cherishing mirth, as it were, like those who would caress a lovely bird that had been frightened out of its natural home and grown wild and rare in its visits, only tapping at the lattice for a minute, and then gone. Suddenly, in the pause between the acts, when the house was half darkened, our laughter died away.

"How cold it is!" said Alexis, shivering. I shivered too; but not with cold—it was more like the involuntary sensation at which people say, "Some one is walking over my grave." I said so, jestingly.

"Hush, Isbel," whispered my husband, and again the draft of cold air seemed to blow right between us.

I should describe the position in which we were sitting; both in front of the box, but he in full view of the audience, while I was half hidden by the curtain. Between us, where the cold draft blew, was a vacant chair. Alexis tried to move this chair, but it was fixed to the floor. He passed behind it, and wrapped a mantle over my shoulders.

"This London winter is cold for you, my love. I half wish we had taken courage, and sailed once more for Hispaniola."*

"Oh, no—oh, no! No more of the sea!" said I, with another and stronger shudder.

He took his former position, looking round indifferently at the audience. But neither of us spoke. The mere word "Hispaniola" was enough to throw a damp and a silence over us both.

"Isbel," he said at last, rousing himself, with a half smile, "I think you must have grown remarkably attractive. Look! Half the glasses opposite are lifted to our box. It can not be to gaze at me, you know. Do you remember telling me I was the ugliest fellow you ever saw?"

"Oh, Alex!" Yet it was quite true—I had thought him so, in far back, strange, awful times, when I, a girl of sixteen, had my mind wholly filled with one ideal—one insane, exquisite dream; when I brought my innocent child's garlands, and sat me down under one great spreading magnificent tree, which seemed to me the king of all the trees of the field, until I felt its dews dropping death upon my youth, and my whole soul withering under its venomous shade.

"Oh, Alex!" I cried once more, looking fondly on his beloved face, where no unearthly beauty dazzled, no unnatural calm repelled; where all was simple, noble, manly, true. "Husband, I thank Heaven for that dear 'ugliness' of yours. Above all, though blood runs strong, they say, I thank Heaven that I see in you no likeness to—"

Alexis knew what name I meant, though for a whole year past—since God's mercy made it to us only a name—we had ceased to utter it, and let it die wholly out of the visible world. We dared not breathe to ourselves, still less to one another, how much brighter, holier, happier, that world was, now that the Divine wisdom had taken—*him*—into another. For he had been my husband's uncle; likewise, once my guardian. He was now dead.

I sat looking at Alexis, thinking what a strange thing it was that his dear face should not have always been as beautiful to me as it was now. That loving my husband now so deeply, so wholly, clinging to him heart to heart,

---

* Hispaniola is the second largest (after Cuba) island in the West Indies. It is now divided into two nations: Haiti and the Dominican Republic.

in the deep peace of satisfied, all-trusting, and all-dependent human affection, I could ever have felt that emotion, first as an exquisite bliss, then as an ineffable terror, which now had vanished away, and become—nothing.

"They are gazing still, Isbel."

"Who, and where?" For I had quite forgotten what he said about the people staring at me.

"And there is Colonel Hart. He sees us. Shall I beckon him?"

"As you will."

Colonel Hart came up into our box. He shook hands with my husband, bowed to me, then looked round, half curiously, half uneasily.

"I thought there was a friend with you."

"None. We have been alone all evening."

"Indeed? How strange!"

"What! That my wife and I should enjoy a play alone together?" said Alexis, smiling.

"Excuse me, but really I was surprised to find you alone. I have certainly seen for the last half hour a third person sitting on the chair, between you both."

We could not help starting; for, as I stated before, the chair had, in truth, been left between us, empty.

"Truly our unknown friend must have been invisible. Nonsense, Colonel; how can you turn Mrs. Saltram pale, by thus peopling with your fancies the vacant air?"

"I tell you, Alexis," said the Colonel (he was my husband's old friend, and had been present at our hasty and private marriage), "nothing could be more unlike a fancy, even were I given to such. It was a very remarkable person who sat here. Even strangers noticed him."

"Him?" I whispered.

"It was a man, then," said my husband, rather angrily.

"A very peculiar-looking, and extremely handsome man. I saw many glasses leveled at him."

"What was he like?" said Alexis, rather sarcastically. "Did he speak? Or we to him?"

"No—neither. He sat quite still, in this chair."

My husband turned away. If the Colonel had not been his friend, and so very simple-minded, honest, and sober a gentleman, I think Alexis would have suspected some drunken hoax, and turned him out of the box immediately. As it was, he only said:

"My dear fellow, the third act is beginning. Come up again at its close, and tell me if you again see my invisible friend, who must find so great an attraction in viewing, gratis, a dramatic performance."

"I perceive—you think it a mere hallucination of mine. We shall see. I suspect the trick is on your side, and that you are harboring some proscribed Hungarian.* But I'll not betray him. Adieu!"

"The ghostly Hungarian shall not sit next you, love, this time," said Alexis, trying once more to remove the chair. But possibly, though he jested, he was slightly nervous, and his efforts were in vain. "What nonsense this is! Isbel, let us forget it. I will stand behind you, and watch the play."

He stood—I clasping his hand secretly and hard; then, I grew quieter; until, as the drop-scene fell, the same cold air swept past us. It was as if some one, fresh from the sharp sea-wind, had entered the box. And just at that moment, we saw Colonel Hart's and several other glasses leveled as before.

"It is strange," said Alexis.

"It is horrible," I said. For I had been cradled in Scottish, and then filled with German superstition; besides, the events of my own life had been so wild, so strange, that there was nothing too ghastly or terrible for my imagination to conjure up.

"I will summon the Colonel. We must find out this," said my husband, speaking beneath his breath, and looking round, as if he thought he was overheard.

Colonel Hart came up. He looked very serious; so did a young man who was with him.

"Captain Elmore, let me introduce you to Mrs. Saltram. Saltram, I have brought my friend here to attest that I have played off on you no unworthy jest. Not ten minutes since, he, and I, and some others saw the same gentleman whom I described to you half an hour ago, sitting as I described—in this chair."

---

* Hungarians fleeing revolution and the Crimean War were in fact largely welcomed in Britain in the 1850s, so the source for this reference is unknown.

"Most certainly—in this chair," added the young captain.

My husband bowed; he kept a courteous calmness, but I felt his hand grow clammy in mine.

"Of what appearance, sir, was this unknown acquaintance of my wife's and mine, whom everybody appears to see except ourselves?"

"He was of middle-age, dark-haired, pale. His features were very still, and rather hard in expression. He had on a cloth cloak with a fur collar, and wore a long, pointed Charles-the-First beard."

My husband and I clung hand to hand with an inexpressible horror. Could there be another man—a living man, who answered this description?

"Pardon me," Alexis said, faintly. "The portrait is rather vague; may I ask you to repaint it as circumstantially as you can?"

"He was, I repeat, a pale, or rather a sallow-featured man. His eyes were extremely piercing, cold, and clear. The mouth close-set—a very firm but passionless mouth. The hair dark, seamed with gray—bald on the brow—"

"Oh, Heaven!" I groaned in an anguish of terror. For I saw again—clear as if he had never died—the face over which, for twelve long months, had swept the merciful sea waves off the shores of Hispaniola.

"Can you, Captain Elmore," said Alexis, "mention no other distinguishing mark? This countenance might resemble many men."

"I think not. It was a most remarkable face. It struck me the more—because—" and the young man grew almost as pale as we—"I once saw another very like it."

"You see—a chance resemblance only. Fear not, my darling," Alexis breathed in my ear. "Sir, have you any reluctance to tell me who was the gentleman?"

"It was no living man, but a corpse that we last year picked up off a wreck, and again committed to the deep—in the Gulf of Mexico. It was exactly the same face, and had the same mark—a scar, cross-shape, over one temple."

"'Tis he! He can follow and torture us still; I knew he could!"

Alexis smothered my shriek on his breast.

"My wife is ill. This description resembles slightly a—a person we once knew. Hart, will you leave us? But no, we must probe this mystery. Gentlemen, will you once more descend to the lower part of the house, while we remain here, and tell me if you still see the—the figure, sitting in this chair?"

They went. We held our breaths. The lights in the theatre were being extinguished, the audience moving away. No one came near our box; it was perfectly empty. Except our two selves, we were conscious of no sight, no sound. A few minutes after Colonel Hart knocked.

"Come in," said Alexis, cheerily.

But the Colonel—the bold soldier—shrank back like a frightened child.

"I have seen him—I saw him but this minute, sitting there!"

I swooned away.

CHAPTER II

It is right I should briefly give you my history up to this night's date.

I was a West Indian heiress*—a posthumous, and, soon after birth, an orphan child. Brought up in my mother's country until I was sixteen years old, I never saw my guardian. Then he met me in Paris, with my governess, and for the space of two years we lived under the same roof, seeing one another daily.

I was very young; I had no father or brother; I wished for neither lover nor husband; my guardian became to me the one object of my existence.

It was no love-passion; he was far too old for that, and I comparatively too young, at least too childish. It was one of those insane, rapturous adorations which young maidens sometimes conceive, mingling a little of the tenderness of the woman with the ecstatic enthusiasm of the devotee. There is hardly a prophet or leader noted in the world's history who has not been followed and worshiped by many such women.

So was my guardian, M. Anastasius—not his true name, but it sufficed then, and will now.

---

* The British began to move into the West Indies in the 17th century, originally to gain a foothold against the Spanish. By the time of this story, most of the islands were part of a federation controlled by a single British governor.

Many may recognize him as a known leader in the French political and moral world—as one who, by the mere force of intellect, wielded the most irresistible and silently complete power of any man I ever knew, in every circle into which he came; women he won by his polished gentleness—men by his equally polished strength. He would have turned a compliment and signed a death-warrant with the same exquisitely calm grace. Nothing was to him too great or too small. I have known him, on his way to advise that the President's soldiers should sweep a cannonade down the thronged street, stop to pick up a strayed canary-bird, stroke its broken wing, and confide it with beautiful tenderness to his bosom.

Oh, how tender! How mild! How pitiful he could be!

When I say I loved him, I use, for want of a better, a word which ill expresses that feeling. It was—Heaven forgive me if I err in using the similitude!—the sort of feeling the Shunamite woman might have had for Elisha.* Religion added to its intensity, for I was brought up a devout Catholic; and he, whatever his private opinions might have been, adhered strictly to the forms of the same Church. He was unmarried, and most people supposed him to belong to that Order called—though often, alas! how unlike Him from whom they assume their name—the Society of Jesus.†

We lived thus—I entirely worshiping, he guiding, fondling, watching, and ruling by turns, for two whole years. I was mistress of a large fortune, and, though not beautiful, had, I believe, a tolerable intellect, and a keen wit. With both he used to play, according as it suited his whim—just as a boy plays with fire-works, amusing himself with their glitter—sometimes directing them against others, and smiling as they flashed or scorched—knowing that against himself they were utterly powerless and harmless. Knowing, too, perhaps, that were it otherwise, he had

---

* The Biblical book 2 Kings 4:8-37 tells the story of Elisha, a holy man who is given food and shelter by a wealthy woman of Shunem. He prophesizes that she will soon give birth to a son; years later, the son dies abruptly, the woman throws herself at Elisha's feet, and he restores the boy to life.

† Also known as the Jesuits, the society was founded in 1540 by Ignatius of Loyola, a military man who structured the society along military lines; Jesuits have been occasionally referred to as "God's soldiers."

only to tread them out under foot, and step aside from the ashes, with the same unmoved, easy smile.

I never knew—nor know I to this day—whether I was in the smallest degree dear to him. Useful I was, I think, and pleasant, I believe. Possibly he liked me a little, as the potter likes his clay and the skillful mechanician his tools—until the clay hardened, and the fine tools refused to obey the master's hand.

I was the brilliant West Indian heiress. I did not marry. Why should I? At my house—at least it was called mine—all sorts and societies met, carrying on their separate games; the quiet, soft hand of M. Anastasius playing his game—in, and under, and through them all. Mingled with this grand game of the world was a lesser one—to which he turned sometimes, just for amusement, or because he could not cease from his *métier*—a simple, easy, domestic game, of which the battledore was that same ingenious hand, and the shuttlecock my foolish child's heart.*

Thus much have I dilated on him, and on my own life, during the years when all its strong wild current flowed toward him; that, in what followed when the tide turned, no one may accuse me of fickleness, or causeless aversion, or insane terror of one who after all was only man, "whose breath is in his nostrils."

At seventeen I was wholly passive in his hands; he was my sole arbiter of right and wrong—my conscience—almost my God. As my character matured, and in a few things I began to judge for myself, we had occasional slight differences—begun, on my part, in shy humility, continued with vague doubt, but always ending in penitence and tears. Since one or other erred, of course it must be I. These differences were wholly on abstract points of truth or justice.

It was his taking me, by a persuasion that was like compulsion, to the ball at the Tuileries,† which was given after Louis Napoleon Bonaparte‡ had seized the Orleans property—and it was my watching my cousin's conduct

---

* The game "battledore and shuttlecock" was an early version of badminton.

† The Tuileries was the imperial French palace in Paris, until it was burned down in 1871 by the democratic Paris Communes.

‡ Charles Louis Napoléon Bonaparte—also known as Napoleon III—served as France's president from 1848 to 1852, but when he was not reelected he seized power, declared himself emperor, and served in that capacity until 1870, when he lost a war to Prussia, fled to England, and died there in 1873.

there, his diplomatic caution of speech, his smooth smiling reverence to men whom I knew, and fancied he knew, to be either knaves or fools—that first startled me concerning him. Then it was I first began to question, in a trembling, terrified way—like one who catches a glimpse of the miracle-making priest's hands behind the robe of the worshiped idol—whether, great as M. Anastasius was, as a political ruler, as a man of the world, as a faithful member of the Society of Jesus, he was altogether so great when viewed beside any one of those whose doctrines he disseminated, whose faith he professed.

He had allowed me the New Testament, and I had been reading it a good deal lately. I placed him, my spiritual guide, at first in adoring veneration, afterward with an uneasy comparison, beside the Twelve Fishermen of Galilee*—beside the pattern of perfect manhood, as set forth in the preaching of their Divine Lord, and ours.

There was a difference.

The next time we came to any argument—always on abstract questions, for my mere individual will never had any scruple in resigning itself to his—instead of yielding I ceased open contest, and brought the matter afterward privately to the one infallible rule of right and wrong.

The difference grew.

Gradually, I began to take my cousin's wisdom—perhaps, even his virtues—with certain reservations, feeling that there was growing in me some antagonistic quality which prevented my full understanding or sympathizing with the idiosyncrasies of his character.

"But," I thought, "he is a Jesuit; he only follows the law of his Order, which allows temporizing, and diplomatizing, for noble ends. He merely dresses up the truth, and puts it in the most charming and safest light, even as we do our images of the Holy Virgin, adorning them for the adoration of the crowd, but ourselves spiritually worshiping them still. I do believe, much as he will dandle and play with the truth, that not for his hope of Heaven would Anastasius stoop to a lie."

One day, he told me he should bring to my saloons an Englishman, his relative, who had determined on leaving the world and entering the priesthood.

---

* The twelve Apostles, four of whom were fishermen when called by Jesus, and who were sometimes called "fishers of men."

"Is he of our faith?" asked I, indifferently.

"He is, from childhood. He has a strong, fine intellect; this, under fit guidance, may accomplish great things. Once of our Society, he might be my right hand in every Court in Europe. You will receive him?"

"Certainly."

But I paid very little heed to the stranger. There was nothing about him striking or peculiar. He was the very opposite of M. Anastasius. Besides, he was young, and I had learned to despise youth—my guardian was fifty years old.

Mr. Saltram (you will already have guessed that it was he) showed equal indifference to me. He watched me sometimes, did little kindnesses for me, but always was quiet and silent—a mere cloud floating in the brilliant sky, which M. Anastasius lit up as its gorgeous sun. For me, I became moonlike, appearing chiefly at my cousin's set and rise.

I was not happy. I read more in my Holy Book, and less in my breviary;* I watched with keener, harder eyes my cousin Anastasius, weighed all his deeds, listened to and compared his words. My intellect worshiped him, my memoried tenderness clung round him still, but my conscience had fled out of his keeping, and made for itself a higher and purer ideal. Measured with common men, he was godlike yet—above all passions, weaknesses, crimes; but viewed by the one perfect standard of Christian man—in charity, humility, single-mindedness, guilelessness, truth—my idol was no more. I came to look for it, and found only the empty shrine.

He went on a brief mission to Rome. I marveled that, instead as of yore, wandering sadly through the empty house, from the moment he quitted it, I breathed freer, as if a weight were taken out of the air. His absence used to be like wearisome ages—now it seemed hardly a week before he came back.

I happened to be sitting with his nephew Alexis when I heard his step down the corridor—the step which had once seemed at every touch to draw music from the chords of my prostrate heart, but which now made it shrink into itself, as if an iron-shod footfall had passed along its strings.

Anastasius looked slightly surprised at seeing Alexis and myself together, but his welcome was very kind to both.

---

* A breviary is a Catholic prayer book.

I could not altogether return it. I had just found out two things which, to say the least, had startled me. I determined to prove them at once.

"My cousin, I thought you were aware that, though a Catholic myself, my house is open and my friendship likewise, to honest men of every creed. Why did you give your relative so hard an impression of me, as to suppose I would dislike him on account of his faith? And why did you not tell me that Mr. Saltram has, for some years, been a Protestant?"

I know not what reply he made; I know only that it was ingenious, lengthy, gentle, courteous, that for the time being it seemed entirely satisfactory, that we spent all three together a most pleasant evening. It was only when I lay down on my bed, face to face with the solemn Dark, in which dwelt conscience, truth, and God, that I discovered how Anastasius had, for some secret—doubtless blameless, nay, even justifiable purpose, told of me, and to me, two absolute Lies!

Disguise it as he might, excuse it as I might, and did, they were Lies. They haunted me—flapping their black wings like a couple of fiends, mopping and mowing behind him when he came—sitting on his shoulders and mocking his beautiful, calm, majestic face—for days. That was the beginning of sorrows; gradually they grew until they blackened my whole world.

Anastasius was bent, as he had (for once truly) told me, on winning his young nephew back into the true fold, making him an instrument of that great purpose which was to bring all Europe, the Popedom itself, under the power of the Society of Jesus. Not thus alone—a man may be forgiven, nay, respected, who sells his soul for an abstract cause, in which he himself is to be absorbed and forgotten; but in this case it was not—though I long believed it, it was not so. Carefully as he disguised it, I slowly found out that the centre of all things—the one grand pivot upon which this vast machinery for the improvement, or rather government, of the world, was to be made to turn, was M. Anastasius.

Alexis Saltram might be of use to him. He was rich, and money is power; an Englishman, and Englishmen are usually honorable and honored. Also there was in him a dogged directness of purpose that would make him a strong, if carefully guided, tool.

However, the young man resisted. He admired and revered his kinsman; but he himself was very single-hearted, stanch, and true. Something in that truth, which was the basis of his character, struck sympathy with mine. He was far inferior in most things to Anastasius—he knew it, I knew it—but, through all, this divine element of truth was patent, beautifully clear. It was the one quality I had ever worshiped, ever sought for, and never found.

Alexis and I became friends—equal, earnest friends. Not in the way of wooing or marriage—at least, he never spoke of either; and both were far, oh, how far! from my thought—but there was a great and tender bond between us, which strengthened day by day.

The link which riveted it was religion. He was, as I said, a Protestant, not adhering to any creed, but simply living—not preaching, but living—the faith of our Saviour. He was not perfect—he had his sins and shortcomings, even as I. We were both struggling on toward the glimmering light. So, after a season, we clasped hands in friendship, and with eyes steadfastly upward, determined to press on together toward the one goal, and along the self-same road.

I put my breviary aside, and took wholly to the New Testament, assuming no name either of Catholic or Protestant, but simply that of Christian.

When I decided on this, of course I told Anastasius. He had ceased to be my spiritual confessor for some time; yet I could see he was surprised.

"Who has done this?" was all he said.

Was I a reed, then, to be blown about with every wind? Or a toy, to be shifted about from hand to hand, and set in motion just as my chance master chose? Had I no will, no conscience of my own?

He knew where he could sting me—and did it—but I let the words pass.

"Cousin, I'll answer like Desdemona.

"'Nobody; I myself.'"

"I have had no book but this—which you gave me; no priest, except the inward witness of my own soul."

"And Alexis Saltram."

Not said in any wrath, or suspicion, or inquiry—simply as the passive statement of a fact. When I denied it, he accepted my denial; when I

---

* This is part of Desdemona's final words in Shakespeare's *Othello*, spoken to deny that her husband Othello has murdered her.

protested, he suffered me to protest. My passionate arguments he took in his soft passionless hold—melted and moulded them—turned and twisted them—then reproduced them to me so different that I failed to recognize either my own meaning or even my own words.

After that, on both sides the only resource was silence.

CHAPTER III

"I wish," said I to my guardian one day, "as I shall be twenty-one next year, to have more freedom. I with even"—for since the discovery of my change of faith he had watched me so closely, so quietly, so continually, that I had conceived a vague fear of him, and a longing to get away—to put half the earth between me and his presence—"I wish even, if possible this summer, to visit my estates in Hispaniola?"

"Alone?"

"No; Madame Gradelle will accompany me. And Mr. Saltram will charter one of his ships for my use."

"I approve the plan. Alexis is going too, I believe?" How could he have known that which Alexis had never told me? But he knew everything. "Madame Gradelle is not sufficient escort. I, as your guardian, will accompany and protect you."

A cold dread seized me. Was I never to be free? Already I began to feel my guardian's influence surrounding me—an influence once of love, now of intolerable distaste, and even fear. Not that he was ever harsh or cruel—not that I could accuse him of any single wrong toward me or others; but I knew I had thwarted him, and through him his cause—that cause whose strongest dogma is, that any means are sacred, any evil consecrated to good, if furthering the one great end—Power.

I had opposed him, and I was in his hand—that hand which I had once believed to have almost superhuman strength. In my terror I half believed so still.

"He will go with us—we cannot escape from him," I said to Alexis. "He will make you a priest and me a nun, as he once planned—I know he did. Our very souls are not our own."

"What, when the world is so wide, and life so long, and God's kindness over all—when, too, I am free, and you will be free in a year—when—"

"I shall never be free. He is my evil genius. He will haunt me till my death."

It was a morbid feeling I had, consequent on the awful struggle which had so shaken body and mind. The very sound of his step made me turn sick and tremble; the very sight of his grand face—perhaps the most beautiful I ever saw, with its faultless features, and the half-melancholy cast given by the high bald forehead and the pointed beard—was to me more terrible than any monster of ugliness the world ever produced.

He held my fortune—he governed my house. All visitors there came and went under his control, except Alexis. Why this young man still came—or how—I could not tell. Probably because, in his pure singleness of heart and purpose, he was stronger even than M. Anastasius.

The time passed. We embarked on board the ship *Argo*, for Hispaniola.

My guardian told me, at the last minute, that business relating to his order would probably detain him in Europe—that we were to lie at anchor for twelve hours off Havre*—and, if he then came not, sail.

He came not—we sailed

It was a glorious evening. The sun, as he went down over the burning seas, beckoned us with a finger of golden fire, westward—to the free, safe, happy West.

I say *us*, because on that evening we first began unconsciously to say it too—as if vaguely binding our fates together—Alexis and I. We talked for a whole hour—till long after France, with all our old life therein, had become a mere line, a cloudy speck on the horizon—of the new life we should lead in Hispaniola. Yet all the while, if we had been truly the priest and nun Anastasius wished to make us, our words, and I believe our thoughts, could not have been more angel-pure, more free from any bias of human passion.

Yet, as the sun went down, and the sea-breeze made us draw nearer together, both began, I repeat, instinctively to say "we," and talk of our future as if it had been the future of one.

"Good-evening, friends!"

---

* Le Havre ("the harbor") is a major port located on the northwestern shore of France.

He was there—M. Anastasius!

I stood petrified. That golden finger of hope had vanished. I shuddered, a captive on his courteously compelling arm—seeing nothing but his terrible smiling face and the black wilderness of sea. For the moment I felt inclined to plunge therein—as I had often longed to plunge penniless into the equally fearsome wilderness of Paris—only I felt sure he would follow me still. He would track me, it seemed, through the whole world.

"You see I have been able to accomplish the voyage; men mostly can achieve any fixed purpose—at least some men. Isbel, this sea-air will bring you back your bloom. And Alexis, my friend, despite those clear studies you told me of, I hope you will bestow a little of your society at times on my ward and me. We will bid you a good-evening now."

He transferred to his nephew my powerless hand; that of Alexis, too, felt cold and trembling. It seemed as if he likewise were succumbing to the fate which, born out of one man's indomitable will, dragged us asunder. Ere my guardian consigned me to Madame Gradelle, he said, smiling, but looking me through and through,

"Remember, my fair cousin, that Alexis is to be—must be—a priest."

"It is impossible!" said I, stung to resistance. "You know he has altogether seceded from the Catholic creed; he will never return to it. His conscience is his own."

"But not his passions. He is young—I am old. He will be a priest yet."

With a soft hand-pressure, M. Anastasius left me.

Now began the most horrible phase of my existence. For four weeks we had to live in the same vessel, bounded and shut up together—Anastasius, Alexis, and I; meeting continually in the soft bland atmosphere of courteous calm; always in public—never alone.

From various accidental circumstances, I discovered how M. Anastasius was now bending all the powers of his enormous intellect, his wonderful moral influence, to compass his cherished ends with regard to Alexis Saltram.

An overwhelming dread took possession of me. I ceased to think of myself at all—my worldly hopes, prospects, or joys—over which this man's influence had long hung like an accursed shadow, a sun turned into darkness, the more terrible because it had once been a sun. I seemed to see

M. Anastasius only with relation to this young man, over whom I knew he once had so great power. Would it return—and in what would it result? Not merely in the breaking off any feeble tie to me. I scarcely trembled for that, since, could it be so broken, it was not worth trembling for. No! I trembled for Alexis's soul.

It was a soul I had gradually learned—more than ever, perhaps, in this voyage, of which every day seemed a life, full of temptation, contest, trial—a soul pure as God's own Heaven, that hung over us hour by hour in its steady tropic blue; and deep as the seas that rolled everlastingly around us. Like them, stirring with the lightest breath, often tempest-tossed, liable to adverse winds and currents; yet keeping far, far below the surface a divine tranquility, diviner than any mere stagnant calm. And this soul, full of all rich impulses, emotions, passions—a soul which, because it could strongly sympathize with, might be able to regenerate its mind, M. Anastasius wanted to make into a Catholic Jesuit priest—a mere machine, to work as he, the head machine, chose!

This was why (the thought suddenly struck me, like lightning) he had told each of us severally concerning one another, those two lies. Because we were young; we might love—we might marry; there was nothing externally to prevent us. And then what would become of his scheme?

I think there was born in me—while the most passive slave to lawful, loving rule—a faculty of savage resistance to all unlawful and unjust power. Also, a something of the female wild-beast, which, if alone, will lie tame and cowed in her solitary den, to be shot at by any daring hunter; whereas if she be *not* alone—if she have any love-instinct at work for cubs or mate—her whole nature changes from terror to daring, from cowardice to fury.

When, as we neared the tropics, I saw Alexis's cheek growing daily paler, and his eye more sunken and restless with some secret struggle, in the which M. Anastasius never left him for a day, an hour, a minute, I became not unlike that poor wild-beast mother. It had gone ill with the relentless hunter of souls if he had come near me then.

But he did not. For the last week of our voyage, M. Anastasius kept altogether out of my way.

It was nearly over—we were in sight of the shores of Hispaniola. Then we should land. My estates lay in this island. Mr. Saltram's business, I was aware, called him to Barbadoes;* thence again beyond seas. Once parted, I well knew that if the power and will of my guardian could compass anything—and it seemed to me that they were able to compass everything in the whole wide earth—Alexis and I should never meet again.

In one last struggle after life—after the fresh, wholesome, natural life which contact with this young man's true spirit had given me—I determined to risk all.

It was a rich tropic twilight. We were all admiring it, just as three ordinary persons might do who were tending peacefully to their voyage-end.

Yet Alexis did not seem at peace. A settled, deadly pallor dwelt on his face—a restless anxiety troubled his whole mien.

M. Anastasius said, noticing the glowing tropic scenery which already dimly appeared in our shoreward view, "It is very grand; but Europe is more suited to us grave Northerns. You will think so, Alexis, when you are once again there."

"Are you returning?" I asked of Mr. Saltram.

My cousin answered for him, "Yes, immediately."

Alexis started; then leaned over the poop in silence, and without denial.

I felt profoundly sad. My interest in Alexis Saltram was at this time—and but for the compulsion of opposing power might have ever been—entirely apart from love. We might have gone on merely as tender friends for years and years—at least I might. Therefore no maidenly consciousness warned me from doing what my sense of right impelled toward one who held the same faith as I did, and whose life seemed strangled in the same mesh of circumstances which had nearly paralyzed my own.

"Alexis, this is our last evening; you will sail for Europe—and we shall be friends no more. Will you take one twilight stroll with me?" and I extended my hand.

If he had hesitated, or shrunk back from me, I would have flung him to the winds, and fought my own battle alone; I was strong enough now. But he sprang to me, clung to my hand, looked wildly in my face, as if there were the sole light of truth and trust left in the world; and as if even there, he had begun—or been taught—to doubt. He did not, now.

---

* Although also in the West Indies, Barbados is more than 900 miles from Hispaniola.

"Isbel, tell me! You still hold our faith—you are not going to become a nun?"

"Never! I will offer myself to Heaven as Heaven gave me to myself—free, bound by no creed, subservient to no priest. What is he, but a man that shall die, whom the worms shall cover?"

I said the words out loud. I meant M. Anastasius to hear. But he looked as if he heard not; only when we turned up the deck, he slowly followed.

I stood at bay. "Cousin, leave me. I wish to speak to Mr. Saltram. Cannot I have any friend but you?"

"None, whom I believe you would harm and receive harm from."

"Dare you—"

"I myself dare nothing; but there is nothing which my Church does not dare. Converse, my children. I hinder you not. The deck is free for all."

He bowed, and let us pass; then followed. Every sound of that slow, smooth step seemed to strike on my heart like the tracking tread of doom.

Alexis and I said little or nothing. A leaden despair seemed to bind us closely round, allowing only one consciousness, that for a little, little time it bound us together! He held my arm so fast that I felt every throbbing of his heart. My sole thought was now to say some words that should be fixed eternally there, so that no lure, no power might make him swerve from his faith. That faith, which was my chief warranty of meeting him—never, oh never in this world! but in the world everlasting.

Once or twice in turning we came face to face with M. Anastasius. He was walking at his usual slow pace, his hands loosely clasped behind him, head bent; a steely repose—even pensiveness, which was his natural look—settled in his grave eyes. He was a man of intellect too great to despise, of character too spotless to loathe. The one sole feeling he inspired was that of unconquerable fear. Because you saw at once that *he* feared nothing either in earth or heaven, that he owned but one influence, and was amenable but to one law, which he called "the Church," but which was himself.

Men like M. Anastasius, one-idea'd, all-engrossed men, are, according to slight variations in their temperaments, the salvation, the laughing-stock, or the terror of the world.

He appeared in the latter form to Alexis and me. Slowly, surely came the conviction that there was no peace for us on this earth while he stood on it; so strong, so powerful, that at times I almost yielded to a vague belief in his immortality. On this night, especially, I was stricken with a horrible—curiosity, I think it was—to see whether he *could* die—whether the grave could open her mouth to swallow him, and death have power upon his flesh, like that of other men.

More than once, as he passed under a huge beam, I thought—should it fall? as he leaned against the ship's side—should it give way? But only, I declare solemnly, out of a frenzied speculative curiosity, which I would not for words have breathed to a human soul! I never once breathed it to Alexis Saltram, who was his sister's son, and whom he had been kind to as a child.

Night darkened, and our walk ceased. We had said nothing—nothing; except that on parting, with a kind of desperation, Alexis buried my hand tightly in his bosom, and whispered, "To-morrow?"

That midnight a sudden hurricane came on. In half an hour all that was left of the good ship *Argo* was a little boat, filled almost to sinking with half-drowned passengers, and a few sailors clinging to spars and fragments of the wreck.

Alexis was lashed to a mast, holding me partly fastened to it, and partly sustained in his arms. How he had found and rescued me I know not; but love is very strong. It has been sweet to me afterward to think that I owed my life to him—and him alone. I was the only woman saved.

He was at the extreme end of the mast; we rested, face to face, my head against his shoulder. All along to its slender point, the sailors were clinging to the spar like flies; but we two did not see anything in the world, save one another.

Life was dim, death was near, yet I think we were not unhappy. Our heaven was clear; for between us and Him to whom we were going came no threatening image, holding in its remorseless hand life, faith, love. Death itself was less terrible than M. Anastasius.

We had seen him among the saved passengers swaying in the boat; then we thought of him no more. We clung together, with closed eyes, satisfied to die.

"No room—off there! No room!" I heard shouted, loud and savage, by the sailor lashed behind me.

I opened my eyes. Alexis was gazing on me only. I gazed, transfixed, over his shoulder, into the breakers beyond.

There, in the trough of a wave, I saw, clear as I see my own right hand now, the upturned face of Anastasius, and his two white, stretched-out hands, on one finger of which was his well-known diamond-ring—for it flashed that minute in the moon.

"Off!" yelled the sailor, striking at him with an oar. "One man's life's as good as another's. Off!"

The drowning face rose above the wave, the eyes fixed themselves full on me, without any entreaty in them, or wrath, or terror—the long-familiar, passionless, relentless eyes.

I see them now; I shall see them till I die. Oh, would I had died!

For one brief second I thought of tearing off the lashings and giving him my place; for I had loved him. But youth and life were strong within me, and my head was pressed to Alexis's breast.

A full minute, or it seemed so, was that face above the water; then I watched it sink slowly, down, down.

CHAPTER IV

We, and several others, were picked up from the wreck of the *Argo* by a homeward-bound ship. As soon as we reached London I became Alexis's wife.

That which happened at the theatre was exactly twelve months after—as we believed—Anastasius died.

I do not pretend to explain, I doubt if any reason can explain, a circumstance so singular—so impossible to be attributed to either imagination or illusion; for, as I must again distinctly state, we ourselves saw nothing. The apparition, or whatever it was, was visible only to other persons, all total strangers.

I had a fever. When I arose from it, and things took their natural forms and relations, this strange occurrence became mingled with the rest of my delirium, of which my husband persuaded me it was a part. He took me abroad—to Italy—Germany. He loved me dearly! He was, and he made me, entirely happy.

In our happiness we strove to live, not merely for one another, but for all the world; all who suffered and had need. We did—nor shrunk from the doing—many charities which had first been planned by Anastasius, with what motives we never knew. While carrying them out, we learned to utter his name without trembling; remembering only that which was beautiful in him and his character, and which we had both so worshiped once.

In the furtherance of these schemes of good it became advisable that we should go to Paris, to my former hotel, which still remained empty there.

"But not, dear wife, if any uneasiness or lingering pain rests in your mind in seeing the old spot. For me, I love it! Since there I loved Isbel, before Isbel knew it, long."

So I smiled; and went to Paris.

My husband proposed, and I was not sorry, that Colonel Hart and his newly-married wife should join us there, and remain as our guests. I shrunk a little from reinhabiting the familiar rooms, long shut up from the light of day; and it was with comfort I heard my husband arranging that a portion of the hotel should be made ready for us, namely, two salons *en suite*, leading out of the farther one of which were a chamber and dressing-room for our own use—opposite two similar apartments for the Colonel and his lady.

I am thus minute for reasons that will appear.

Mrs. Hart had been traveling with us some weeks. She was a mild, sweet-faced English girl, who did not much like the Continent, and was half shocked at some of my reckless foreign ways on board steamboats and on railways. She said I was a little—just a little—too free. It might have seemed so to her; for my southern blood rushed bright and warm, and my manner of life in France had completely obliterated early impressions. Faithful and tender woman and true wife as I was, I believe I was in some things unlike an English woman or an English wife, and that Mrs. Hart thought so.

Once—for being weak of nature and fast of tongue, she often said things she should not—there was even some hint of the kind dropped before my husband. He flashed up—but laughed the next minute; for I was his, and he loved me!

Nevertheless, that quick glow of anger pained me—bringing back the recollection of many things his uncle had said to me of him, which then I heard as one that heareth not. The sole saying which remained on my mind was one which, in a measure, I had credited—that his conscience was in his hand—"but not his passions."

I had known always—and rather rejoiced in the knowledge—that Alexis Saltram could not boast the frozen calm of M. Anastasius.

But I warned tame Eliza Hart, half jestingly, to take heed, and not lightly blame me before my husband again.

Reaching Paris, we were all very gay and sociable together. Colonel Hart was a grave, honorable man; my husband and I both loved him.

We dined together—a lively *partie quarreé*,* I shut my eyes to the familiar objects about us, and tried to believe the rooms had never echoed familiar foot-steps save those of Mrs. Hart and the Colonel's soldiery tread. Once or so, while silence fell over us, I would start, and feel my heart beating; but Alexis was near me, and altogether mine. Therefore I feared not, even here.

After coffee, the gentlemen went out to some evening amusement. We, the weary wives, contented ourselves with lounging about, discussing toi-lettes† and Paris sights. Especially the fair Empress Eugénie‡—the wifely crown which my old aversion Louis Bonaparte had chosen to bind about his ugly brows. Mrs. Hart was anxious to see all, and then fly back to her beloved London.

"How long is it since you left London, Mrs. Saltram?"

"A year, I think. What is to-day?"

"The twenty-fifth—no, the twenty-sixth of May."

I dropped my head on the cushion. Then, that date—the first she mentioned—had passed over unthought of by us. That night—the night of mortal horror when the *Argo* went down—lay thus far buried in the past, parted from us by two blessed years.

---

* A party of four, especially one comprising two men and two women.

† Clothing.

‡ Eugénie de Montijo (1826–1920) was fair enough that Napoleon III married her even though most did not consider her to have enough social standing to become his empress.

But I found it impossible to converse longer with Mrs. Hart; so about ten o'clock I left her reading, and went to take half an hour's rest in my chamber, which, as I have explained, was divided from the salon by a small boudoir or dressing-room. Its only other entrance was from a door near the head of my bed, which I went and locked.

It seemed uncourteous to retire for the night; so I merely threw my dressing-gown over my evening toilette, and lay down outside the bed, dreamily watching the shadows which the lamp threw. This lamp was in my chamber; but its light extended faintly into the boudoir, showing the tall mirror there, and a sofa which was placed opposite. Otherwise, the little room was half in gloom, save for a narrow glint streaming through the not quite closed door of the salon.

I lay broad awake, but very quiet, contented and happy. I was thinking of Alexis. In the midst of my reverie, I heard, as I thought, my maid trying the handle of the door behind me.

"It is locked," I said; "come another time."

The sound ceased; yet I almost thought Fanchon* had entered, for there came a rift of wind, which made the lamp sway in its socket. But when I looked, the door was closely shut, and the bolt still fast.

I lay, it might be, half an hour longer. Then, with a certain compunction at my own discourtesy in leaving her, I saw the salon door open, and Mrs. Hart appear.

She looked into the boudoir, drew back hurriedly, and closed the door after her.

Of course I immediately rose to follow her. Ere doing so, I remember particularly standing with the lamp in my hand, arranging my dress before the mirror in the boudoir, and seeing reflected in the glass, with my cashmere lying over its cushions, the sofa, unoccupied.

Eliza was standing thoughtful.

"I ought to ask pardon for my long absence, my dear Mrs. Hart."

"Oh, no—but I of you, for intruding in your apartment; I did not know Mr. Saltram had returned. Where is my husband?"

---

* Fanchon, we will learn, is the maid.

"With mine, no doubt! We need not expect them for an hour yet, the renegades."

"You are jesting," said Mrs. Hart, half-offended. "I know they are come home. I saw Mr. Saltram in your boudoir not two minutes since."

"How?"

"In your boudoir, I repeat. He was lying on the sofa."

"Impossible!" and I burst out laughing. "Unless he has suddenly turned into a cashmere shawl. Come and look."

I flung the folding doors open, and poured a blaze of light into the little room.

"It is very odd," fidgeted Mrs. Hart; "very odd, indeed. I am sure I saw a gentleman here. His face was turned aside; but of course I concluded it was Mr. Saltram. Very odd, indeed!"

I still laughed at her, though an uneasy feeling was creeping over me. To dismiss it, I showed her how the door was fastened, and how it was impossible my husband could have entered.

"No; I distinctly heard you say, 'It is locked—come another time.' What did you mean by that?"

"I thought it was Fanchon."

To change the subject, I began showing her some *parures** my husband had just brought me. Eliza Hart was very fond of jewels. We remained looking at them some time longer in the inner-room where I had been lying on my bed; and then she bade me good-night.

"No light, thank you. I can find my way back through the boudoir. Good-night. Do not look so pale to-morrow, my dear."

She kissed me in the friendly English fashion, and danced lightly away, out at my bedroom door and into the boudoir adjoining—but instantly I saw her reappear, startled and breathless, covered with angry blushes.

"Mrs. Saltram, you have deceived me! You are a wicked French woman."

"Eliza!"

"You know it—you knew it all along. I will go and seek my husband. He will not let me stay another night in your house!"

"As you will"—for I was sick of her follies. "But explain yourself."

---

* A set of several pieces of jewelry, meant to be worn together.

"Have you no shame? Have you foreign women never any shame? But I have found you out at last."

"Indeed!"

"There is—I have seen him twice with my own eyes—there is a man lying this minute in your boudoir—and he is—*not* Mr. Saltram!"

Then, indeed, I sickened. A deadly horror came over me. No wonder the young thing, convinced of my guilt, fled from me, appalled.

For I knew now *whom* she had seen.

❦

Hour after hour I must have lain where I fell. There was some confusion in the house—no one came near me. It was early daylight when I woke and saw Fanchon leaning over me, and trying to lift me from the floor.

"Fanchon—is it morning?"

"Yes, madame."

"What day is it?"

"The twenty-sixth of May."

It had been *he*, then. He followed us still.

Shudder after shudder convulsed me. I think Fanchon thought I was dying.

"Oh, madame! Oh, poor madame! And monsieur not yet come home."

I uttered a terrible cry—for my heart foreboded what either had happened or assuredly would happen.

Alexis never came home again.

An hour after, I was sent for to the little woodcutter's hut, outside Paris gates, where he lay dying.

Anastasius had judged clearly; my noble generous husband had in him but one thing lacking—his passions were "not in his hand." When Colonel Hart, on the clear testimony of his wife, impugned *his* wife's honor, Alexis challenged him—fought, and fell.

It all happened in an hour or two, when their blood was fiery hot. By daylight, the colonel stood, cold as death, pale as a shadow, by Alexis's bedside. He had killed him, and he loved him!

No one thought of me. They let me weep near my husband—unconscious as he was—doubtless believing them the last contrite tears of an adulteress. I did not heed nor deny that horrible name—Alexis was dying.

Toward evening he revived a little, and his senses returned. He opened his eyes and saw me—they closed with a shudder.

"Alexis—Alexis!"

"Isbel, I am dying. You know the cause. In the name of God—are you—"

"In the name of God, I am your pure wife, who never loved any man but you."

"I am satisfied. I thought it was so."

He looked at Colonel Hart, faintly smiling; then opened his arms and took me into them, as if to protect me with his last breath.

"Now," he said, still holding me, "my friends, we must make all clear. Nothing must harm her when I am gone. Hart, fetch your wife here."

Mrs. Hart came, trembling violently. My husband addressed her.

"I sent for you to ask a question. Answer, as to a dying person, who to-morrow will know all secrets. Who was the man you saw in my wife's chamber?"

"He was a stranger to me. I never met him before, any where. He lay on the sofa, wrapped in a fur cloak."

"Did you see his face?"

"Not the first time. The second time I did."

"What was he like? Be accurate, for the sake of more than life—honor."

My husband's voice sank. There was terror in his eyes, but not *that* terror—he held me to his bosom still.

"What was he like, Eliza?" repeated Colonel Hart.

"He was middle-aged; of a pale, grave countenance, with keen, large eyes, high forehead, and a pointed beard."

"Heaven save us! I have seen him too," cried the Colonel, horror-struck. "It was no living man."

"It was M. Anastasius!"

My husband died that night. He died, his lips on mine, murmuring how dearly he loved me, and how happy he had been.

For many months after then I was quite happy, too; for my wits wandered, and I thought I was again a little West Indian girl, picking gowans* in the meadows about Dumfries.†

The Colonel and Mrs. Hart were, I believe, very kind to me. I always took her for a little playfellow I had, who was called Eliza. It is only lately, as the year has circled round again to the spring, that my head has become clear, and I have found out who she is, and—ah, me!—who I am.

This coming to my right senses does not give me so much pain as they thought it would; because great weakness of body has balanced and soothed my mind.

I have but one desire: to go to my own Alexis; and before the twenty-fifth of May.

Now I have been able nearly to complete our story, which is well. My friend, judge between us—and *him*. Farewell.

ISBEL SALTRAM.

CHAPTER V

I think it necessary that I, Eliza Hart, should relate, as simply as veraciously, the circumstances of Mrs. Saltram's death, which happened on the night of the twenty-fifth of May.

She was living with us at our house, some miles out of London. She had been very ill and weak during May, but toward the end of the month she revived. We thought if she could live till June she might even recover. My husband desired that on no account might she be told the day of the month; she was, indeed, purposely deceived on the subject. When the twenty-fifth came, she thought it was only the twenty-second.

For some weeks she had kept her bed, and Fanchon never left her—Fanchon, who knew the whole history, and was strictly charged, whatever delusions might occur, to take no notice whatever of the subject

---

* A small yellow flower, like a daisy.

† Dumfries is in Jamaica, located to the west of Hispaniola.

to her mistress. For my husband and myself were again persuaded that it must be some delusion. So was the physician, who nevertheless determined to visit us himself on the night of the twenty-fifth of May.

It happened that the Colonel was unwell, and I could not remain constantly in Mrs. Saltram's room. It was a large but very simple suburban bedchamber, with white curtains and modern furniture, all of which I myself arranged in such a manner that there should be no dark corners, no shadows thrown by hanging draperies, or anything of the kind.

About ten o'clock at night Fanchon accidentally quitted her mistress for a few minutes, sending in her place a nursemaid who had lately come into our family.

This girl tells me that she entered the room quickly, but stopped, seeing, as she believed, the physician sitting by the bed, on the further side, at Mrs. Saltram's right hand. She thought Mrs. Saltram did not see him, for she turned and asked her, the nursemaid—"Susan, what o'clock is it?"

The gentleman did not speak. She says he appeared sitting with his elbows resting on his knees, and his face partly concealed in his hands. He wore a long coat or cloak—she could not distinguish which, for the room was rather dark, but she could plainly see on his little finger the sparkle of a diamond ring.

She is quite certain that Mrs. Saltram did not see the gentleman at all, which rather surprised her, for the poor lady moved from time to time and spoke, complainingly, of its being "very cold." At length she called Susan to sit by her side, and chafe her hands.

Susan acquiesced—"But did not Mrs. Saltram see the gentleman?"

"What gentleman?"

"He was sitting beside you not a minute since. I thought he was the doctor, or the clergyman. He is gone now."

And the girl, much terrified, saw that there was no one in the room.

She says Mrs. Saltram did not seem terrified at all. She only pressed her hands on her forehead, her lips slightly moving—then whispered: "Go, call Fanchon and them all, tell them what you saw."

"But I must leave you. Are you not afraid?"

"No. Not now—not now."

She covered her eyes, and again her lips began moving.

Fanchon entered, and I too, immediately.

I do not expect to be credited. I can only state on my honor what we both then beheld.

Mrs. Saltram lay, her eyes open, her face quite calm, as that of a dying person; her hands spread out on the counterpane. Beside her sat erect the same figure I had seen lying on the sofa in Paris exactly a year ago. It appeared more lifelike than she. Neither looked at each other. When we brought a bright lamp into the room the appearance vanished.

Isbel said to me, "Eliza, he is come."

"Impossible! You have not seen him?"

"No, but you have?" She looked me steadily in the face. "I knew it. Take the light away, and you will see him again. He is here, I want to speak to him. Quick, take the light away."

Alarmed as I was, I could not refuse, for I saw by her features that her last hour was at hand.

As surely as I write this, I, Eliza Hart, saw, when the candles were removed, that figure grow again, as out of air, and become plainly distinguishable, sitting by her bedside.

She turned herself with difficulty, and faced it. "Eliza, is he there? I see nothing but the empty chair. Is he there?"

"Yes."

"Does he look angry or terrible?"

"No."

"Anastasius." She extended her hand toward the vacant chair. "Cousin Anastasius!"

Her voice was sweet, though the cold drops stood on her brow.

"Cousin Anastasius, I do not see you, but you can see and hear me. I am not afraid of you now. You know, once, I loved you very much."

Here, overcome with terror, I stole back toward the lighted stair-case. Thence I still heard Isbel speaking.

"We erred, both of us, cousin. You were too hard upon me—I had too great love first, too great terror afterward of you. Why should I be afraid of a man that shall die, and of the son of man, whose breath is in his nostrils? I should have worshiped, have feared, not you, but only God."

She paused—drawing twice or thrice, heavily, the breath that could not last.

"I forgive you—forgive me also! I loved you. Have you anything to say to me, Anastasius?"

Silence.

"Shall we ever meet in the boundless spheres of Heaven?"

Silence—a long silence. We brought in candles, for she was evidently dying.

"Eliza—thank you for all! Your hand. It is so dark—and"—shivering— "I am afraid of going into the dark. I might meet Anastasius there. I wish my husband would come."

She was wandering in her mind, I saw. Her eyes turned to the vacant chair.

"Is there any one sitting by me?"

"No, dear Isbel; can you see any one?"

"No one—yes"—and with preternatural strength she started right up in bed, extending her arms. "Yes! There—close behind you—I see—my husband. I am quite safe—now!"

So, with a smile upon her face, she died.

FITZ-JAMES O'BRIEN *was born and raised in Ireland but immigrated to the United States at the age of twenty-five. He enjoyed a bohemian lifestyle that often led to debt; before leaving the British Isles, he spent a substantial inheritance in three years. Although he wrote poetry and plays, as well as editing periodicals, he is now considered to be one of the earliest science fiction writers due to his frequently anthologized stories "The Diamond Age," about a man who uses a super-microscope to discover a tiny woman in a drop of water, and "What Was It?: A Mystery," in which an invisible being confounds the residents of a boarding house. Although "The Lost Room" (which first appeared in the September 1855 issue of* Harpers New Monthly Magazine) *could be read as a forerunner of alternate-dimension fiction, its pervasive terrors align more with surreal horror. O'Brien died at only thirty-five from wounds received as a soldier in the Civil War, but his reputation has grown with each passing decade.*

THE LOST ROOM

by Fitz-James O'Brien

(1858)

It was oppressively warm. The sun had long disappeared, but seemed to have left its vital spirit of heat behind it. The air rested; the leaves of the acacia-trees that shrouded my windows hung plumb-like on their delicate stalks. The smoke of my cigar scarce rose above my head, but hung about me in a pale blue cloud, which I had to dissipate with languid waves of my hand. My shirt was open at the throat, and my chest heaved laboriously in the effort to catch some breaths of fresher air. The noises of the city seemed to be wrapped in slumber, and the shrilling of the mosquitos was the only sound that broke the stillness.

As I lay with my feet elevated on the back of a chair, wrapped in that peculiar frame of mind in which thought assumes a species of lifeless motion, the strange fancy seized me of making a languid inventory of the principal articles of furniture in my room. It was a task well suited to the mood in which I found myself. Their forms were duskily defined in the dim twilight that floated shadowily through the chamber; it was no labour to note and particularize each, and from the place where I sat I could command a view of all my possessions without even turning my head.

There was, *imprimis,*[*] that ghostly lithograph by Calame.[†] It was a mere black spot on the white wall, but my inner vision scrutinized every detail of the picture. A wild, desolate, midnight heath, with a spectral oak-tree in the centre of the foreground. The wind blows fiercely, and the jagged branches, clothed scantily with ill-grown leaves, are swept to the left continually by its giant force.

A formless wrack of clouds streams across the awful sky, and the rain sweeps almost parallel with the horizon. Beyond, the heath stretches off into endless blackness, in the extreme of which either fancy or art has conjured up some undefinable shapes that seem riding into space. At the base of the huge oak stands a shrouded figure. His mantle is wound by the blast in tight folds around his form, and the long cock's feather in his hat is blown upright, till it seems as if it stood on end with fear. His features are not visible, for he has grasped his cloak with both hands, and drawn it from either side across his face. The picture is seemingly objectless. It tells no tale, but there is a weird power about it that haunts one, and it was for that I bought it.

Next to the picture comes the round blot that hangs below it, which I know to be a smoking-cap. It has my coat of arms embroidered on the front, and for that reason I never wear it; though, when properly arranged on my head, with its long blue silken tassel hanging down by my cheek, I believe it becomes me well. I remember the time when it was in the course

---

[*] The first item in a list.

[†] Alexandre Calame (1810–1864) was a prolific Swiss landscape painter whose works often featured a lone tree framed by a desolate wilderness; it's unknown what specific work (if any) is described here.

of manufacture. I remember the tiny little hands that pushed the coloured silks so nimbly through the cloth that was stretched on the embroidery-frame—the vast trouble I was put to get a coloured copy of my armorial bearings for the heraldic work which was to decorate the front of the band—the pursings up of the little mouth, and the contractions of the young fore-head, as their possessor plunged into a profound sea of cogitation touching the way in which the cloud should be represented from which the armed hand, that is my crest, issues—the heavenly moment when the tiny hands placed it on my head, in a position that I could not bear for more than a few seconds, and I, kinglike, immediately assumed my royal prerogative after the coronation, and instantly levied a tax on my only subjects which was, however, not paid unwillingly. Ah! the cap is there, but the embroiderer has fled; for Atropos* was severing the web of life above her head while she was weaving that silken shelter for mine!

How uncouthly the huge piano that occupies the corner at the left of the door looms out in the uncertain twilight! I neither play nor sing, yet I own a piano. It is a comfort to me to look at it, and to feel that the music is there, although I am not able to break the spell that binds it. It is pleasant to know that Bellini and Mozart, Cimarosa, Porpora, Glück† and all such—or at least their souls—sleep in that unwieldy case. There lie embalmed, as it were, all operas, sonatas, oratorios, nocturnos, marches, songs and dances, that ever climbed into existence through the four bars that wall in melody. Once I was entirely repaid for the investment of my funds in that instrument which I never use. Blokeeta,‡ the composer, came to see me. Of course his instincts urged him as irresistibly to my piano as if some magnetic power lay within it compelling him to approach. He tuned it, he played on it. All night long, until the gray and spectral dawn rose out of the depths of the midnight, he sat and played, and I lay smoking by the window listening. Wild, unearthly, and sometimes insufferably painful, were the improvisations of Blokeeta. The chords of the instrument seemed breaking

---

* In Greek mythology, Atropos is the oldest of the three Fates and the one who severs the thread of a mortal's life.

† All noted operatic composers of the early Classical period.

‡ Unlike the others, a fictional composer.

with anguish. Lost souls shrieked in his dismal preludes; the half-heard utterances of spirits in pain, that groped at inconceivable distances from anything lovely or harmonious, seemed to rise dimly up out of the waves of sound that gathered under his hands. Melancholy human love wandered out on distant heaths, or beneath dank and gloomy cypresses, murmuring its unanswered sorrow, or hateful gnomes sported and sang in the stagnant swamps triumphing in unearthly tones over the knight whom they had lured to his death. Such was Blokeeta's night's entertainment; and when he at length closed the piano, and hurried away through the cold morning, he left a memory about the instrument from which I could never escape.

Those snow-shoes that hang in the space between the mirror and the door recall Canadian wanderings—a long race through the dense forests, over the frozen snow through whose brittle crust the slender hoofs of the caribou that we were pursuing sank at every step, until the poor creature despairingly turned at bay in a small juniper coppice, and we heartlessly shot him down. And I remember how Gabriel, the *habitant*,[*] and François, the half-breed,[†] cut his throat, and how the hot blood rushed out in a torrent over the snowy soil; and I recall the snow *cabane*[‡] that Gabriel built, where we all three slept so warmly; and the great fire that glowed at our feet, painting all kinds of demoniac shapes on the black screen of forest that lay without; and the deer-steaks that we roasted for our breakfast; and the savage drunkenness of Gabriel in the morning, he having been privately drinking out of my brandy-flask all the night long.

That long haftless dagger that dangles over the mantelpiece makes my heart swell. I found it, when a boy, in a hoary old castle in which one of my maternal ancestors once lived. That same ancestor—who, by the way, yet lives in history—was a strange old sea-king, who dwelt on the extremest point of the southwestern coast of Ireland. He owned the whole of that

---

[*] A Canadian native of French descent.

[†] The correct term today is Metís. Canada's treatment of people of mixed European and Indigenous ancestry has a long and complex history, and while they were marginalized and disdained in the late 19th century, the Metís Nation is now recognized as an Aboriginal people with rights enshrined in the Constitution of Canada.

[‡] A cabin.

fertile island called Inniskeiran, which directly faces Cape Clear,* where between them the Atlantic rolls furiously, forming what the fishermen of the place call "the Sound." An awful place in winter is that same Sound. On certain days no boat can live there for a moment, and Cape Clear is frequently cut off for days from any communication with the mainland.

This old sea-king—Sir Florence O'Driscoll[†] by name—passed a stormy life. From the summit of his castle he watched the ocean, and when any richly laden vessels bound from the South to the industrious Galway merchants, hove in sight, Sir Florence hoisted the sails of his galley, and it went hard with him if he did not tow into harbor ship and crew. In this way he lived; not a very honest mode of livelihood, certainly, according to our modern ideas, but quite reconcilable with the morals of the time. As may be supposed, Sir Florence got into trouble. Complaints were laid against him at the English court by the plundered merchants, and the Irish Viking set out for London, to plead his own cause before good Queen Bess,[‡] as she was called. He had one powerful recommendation: he was a marvellously handsome man. Not Celtic by descent, but half Spanish, half Danish in blood, he had the great northern stature with the regular features, flashing eyes, and dark hair of the Iberian race. This may account for the fact that his stay at the English court was much longer than was necessary, as also for the tradition, which a local historian mentions, that the English Queen evinced a preference for the Irish chieftain, of other nature than that usually shown by monarch to subject.

Previous to his departure, Sir Florence had intrusted the care of his property to an Englishman named Hull. During the long absence of the knight, this person managed to ingratiate himself with the local authorities, and gain their favour so far that they were willing to support him in almost any scheme. After a protracted stay, Sir Florence, pardoned of all his misdeeds, returned to his home. Home no longer. Hull was in possession,

---

* Cape Clear *Island* is off the southwest coast of County Cork; Inniskeiran is fictional.

† O'Brien is playing with his own family history here: Florence O'Driscoll was the name of O'Brien's great-great-grandfather, who was shot as a rebel by the English. The real O'Driscoll resided in Cloghan Castle on an island of Lough (Lake) Hyne in Ireland.

‡ Elizabeth I (1533–1603).

and refused to yield an acre of the lands he had so nefariously acquired. It was no use appealing to the law, for its officers were in the opposite interest. It was no use appealing to the Queen, for she had another lover, and had forgotten the poor Irish knight by this time; and so the Viking passed the best portion of his life in unsuccessful attempts to reclaim his vast estates, and was eventually, in his old age, obliged to content himself with his castle by the sea and the island of Inniskeiran, the only spot of which the usurper was unable to deprive him. So this old story of my kinsman's fate looms up out of the darkness that enshrouds that haftless dagger hanging on the wall.

It was somewhat after the foregoing fashion that I dreamily made the inventory of my personal property. As I turned my eyes on each object, one after the other—or the places where they lay, for the room was now so dark that it was almost impossible to see with any distinctness—a crowd of memories connected with each rose up before me, and, perforce, I had to indulge them. So I proceeded but slowly, and at last my cigar shortened to a hot and bitter morsel that I could barely hold between my lips, while it seemed to me that the night grew each moment more insufferably oppressive. While I was revolving some impossible means of cooling my wretched body, the cigar stump began to burn my lips. I flung it angrily through the open window, and stooped out to watch it falling. It first lighted on the leaves of the acacia, sending out a spray of red sparkles, then, rolling off, it fell plump on the dark walk in the garden, faintly illuminating for a moment the dusky trees and breathless flowers. Whether it was the contrast between the red flash of the cigar-stump and the silent darkness of the garden, or whether it was that I detected by the sudden light a faint waving of the leaves, I know not; but something suggested to me that the garden was cool. I will take a turn there, thought I, just as I am; it cannot be warmer than this room, and however still the atmosphere, there is always a feeling of liberty and spaciousness in the open air, that partially supplies one's wants. With this idea running through my head, I arose, lit another cigar, and passed out into the long, intricate corridors that led to the main staircase. As I crossed the threshold of my room, with what a different feeling I should have passed it had I known that I was never to set foot in it again!

I lived in a very large house, in which I occupied two rooms on the second floor. The house was old-fashioned, and all the floors communicated by a huge circular staircase that wound up through the centre of the building, while at every landing long, rambling corridors stretched off into mysterious nooks and corners. This palace of mine was very high, and its resources, in the way of crannies and windings, seemed to be interminable. Nothing seemed to stop anywhere. Cul-de-sacs were unknown on the premises. The corridors and passages, like mathematical lines, seemed capable of indefinite extension, and the object of the architect must have been to erect an edifice in which people might go ahead forever. The whole place was gloomy, not so much because it was large, but because an unearthly nakedness seemed to pervade the structure. The staircases, corridors, halls, and vestibules all partook of a desert-like desolation. There was nothing on the walls to break the sombre monotony of those long vistas of shade. No carvings on the wainscoting, no moulded masks peering down from the simply severe cornices, no marble vases on the landings. There was an eminent dreariness and want of life—so rare in an American establishment—all over the abode. It was Hood's haunted house* put in order and newly painted. The servants, too, were shadowy, and chary of their visits. Bells rang three times before the gloomy chambermaid could be induced to present herself; and the negro waiter, a ghoul-like looking creature from Congo, obeyed the summons only when one's patience was exhausted or one's want satisfied in some other way. When he did come, one felt sorry that he had not stayed away altogether, so sullen and savage did he appear.† He moved along the echoless floors with a slow, noiseless shamble, until his dusky figure, advancing from the gloom, seemed like some reluctant afreet,‡ compelled by the superior power of his master to disclose himself. When the doors of all the chambers were closed, and no light illuminated the long corridor save the red, unwholesome glare of a

---

* "The Haunted House" by Thomas Hood is a long poem from 1844 describing someone entering a half-ruined house.

† The narrator here reflects the typical racial prejudices of the day.

‡ An evil spirit in Muslim lore.

small oil lamp on a table at the end, where late lodgers lit their candles, one could not by any possibility conjure up a sadder or more desolate prospect.

Yet the house suited me. Of meditative and sedentary habits, I enjoyed the extreme quiet. There were but few lodgers, from which I infer that the landlord did not drive a very thriving trade; and these, probably oppressed by the sombre spirit of the place, were quiet and ghost-like in their movements. The proprietor I scarcely ever saw. My bills were deposited by unseen hands every month on my table, while I was out walking or riding, and my pecuniary response was intrusted to the attendant afreet. On the whole, when the bustling, wide-awake spirit of New York is taken into consideration, the sombre, half-vivified character of the house in which I lived was an anomaly that no one appreciated better than I who lived there.

I felt my way down the wide, dark staircase in my pursuit of zephyrs. The garden, as I entered it, did feel somewhat cooler than my own room, and I puffed my cigar along the dim, cypress-shrouded walks with a sensation of comparative relief. It was very dark. The tall-growing flowers that bordered the path were so wrapped in gloom as to present the aspect of solid pyramidal masses, all the details of leaves and blossoms being buried in an embracing darkness, while the trees had lost all form, and seemed like masses of overhanging cloud. It was a place and time to excite the imagination; for in the impenetrable cavities of endless gloom there was room for the most riotous fancies to play at will. I walked and walked, and the echoes of my footsteps on the ungravelled and mossy path suggested a double feeling. I felt alone and yet in company at the same time. The solitariness of the place made itself distinct enough in the stillness, broken alone by the hollow reverberations of my step, while those very reverberations seemed to imbue me with an undefined feeling that I was not alone. I was not, therefore, much startled when I was suddenly accosted from beneath the solid darkness of an immense cypress by a voice saying, "Will you give me a light, sir?"

"Certainly," I replied, trying in vain to distinguish the speaker amidst the impenetrable dark.

Somebody advanced, and I held out my cigar. All I could gather defini-tively about the individual who thus accosted me was that he must have been of extremely small stature; for I, who am by no means an overgrown man, had to stoop considerably in handing him my cigar. The vigorous puff that he gave his own lighted up my Havana for a moment, and I fancied that I caught a glimpse of long, wild hair. The flash was, however, so momentary that I could not even say certainly whether this was an actual impression or the mere effort of imagination to embody that which the senses had failed to distinguish.

"Sir, you are out late," said this unknown to me, as he, with half-uttered thanks, handed me back my cigar, for which I had to grope in the gloom.

"Not later than usual," I replied, dryly.

"Hum! you are fond of late wanderings, then?"

"That is just as the fancy seizes me."

"Do you live here?"

"Yes."

"Queer house, isn't it?"

"I have only found it quiet."

"Hum! But you *will* find it queer, take my word for it." This was earnestly uttered; and I felt at same time a bony finger laid on my arm, that cut it sharply like a blunted knife.

"I cannot take your word for any such assertion," I replied rudely, shaking off the bony finger with an irrepressible motion of disgust.

"No offence, no offence," muttered my unseen companion rapidly, in a strange, subdued voice, that would have been shrill had it been louder; "your being angry does not alter the matter. You will find it a queer house. Everybody finds it a queer house. Do you know who live there?"

"I never busy myself, sir, about other people's affairs," I answered sharply, for the individual's manner, combined with my utter uncertainty as to his appearance, oppressed me with an irksome longing to be rid of him.

"O, you don't? Well, I do. I know what they are—well, well, well!" and as he pronounced the three last words his voice rose with each, until, with the last, it reached a shrill shriek that echoed horribly among the lonely walks. "Do you know what they eat?" he continued.

"No, sir—nor care."

"O, but you will care. You must care. You shall care. I'll tell you what they are. They are enchanters. They are ghouls. They are cannibals. Did you never remark their eyes, and how they gloated on you when you passed? Did you never remark the food that they served up at your table? Did you never in the dead of night hear muffled and unearthly footsteps gliding along the corridors, and stealthy hands turning the handle of your door? Does not some magnetic influence fold itself continually around you when they pass, and send a thrill through spirit and body, and a cold shiver that no sunshine will chase away? O, you have! You have felt all these things! I know it!"

The earnest rapidity, the subdued tones, the eagerness of accent, with which all this was uttered, impressed me most uncomfortably. It really seemed as if I could recall all those weird occurrences and influences of which he spoke; and I shuddered in spite of myself in the midst of the impenetrable darkness that surrounded me.

"Hum!" said I, assuming, without knowing it, a confidential tone, "may I ask you how you know these things?"

"How I know them? Because I am their enemy; because they tremble at my whisper; because I hang upon their track with the perseverance of a bloodhound and the stealthiness of a tiger; because—because—I was *of* them once!"

"Wretch!" I cried excitedly, for involuntarily his eager tones had wrought me up to a high pitch of spasmodic nervousness, "then you mean to say that you—"

As I uttered this word, obeying an uncontrollable impulse, I stretched forth my hand in the direction of the speaker and made a blind clutch. The tips of my fingers seemed to touch a surface as smooth as glass, that glided suddenly from under them. A sharp, angry hiss sounded through the gloom, followed by a whirring noise, as if some projectile passed rapidly by, and the next moment I felt instinctively that I was alone.

A most disagreeable feeling instantly assailed me—a prophetic instinct that some terrible misfortune menaced me; an eager and overpowering anxiety to get back to my own room without loss of time. I turned and ran blindly along the dark cypress alley, every dusky clump of flowers that rose blackly in the borders making my heart each moment cease to beat. The echoes of my own footsteps seemed to redouble and assume the sounds of unknown pursuers following fast upon my track. The boughs of lilac-bushes

and syringas,* that here and there stretched partly across the walk, seemed
to have been furnished suddenly with hooked hands that sought to grasp
me as I flew by, and each moment I expected to behold some awful and
impassable barrier fall across my track and wall me up forever.

At length I reached the wide entrance. With a single leap I sprang up
the four or five steps that formed the stoop, and dashed along the hall,
up the wide, echoing stairs, and again along the dim, funereal corridors
until I paused, breathless and panting, at the door of my room. Once so
far, I stopped for an instant and leaned heavily against one of the panels,
panting lustily after my late run. I had, however, scarcely rested my whole
weight against the door, when it suddenly gave way, and I staggered in
head-foremost. To my utter astonishment the room I had left in profound
darkness was now a blaze of light. So intense was the illumination that,
for a few seconds while the pupils of my eyes were contracting under the
sudden change, I saw absolutely nothing save the dazzling glare. This fact in
itself, coming on me with such utter suddenness, was sufficient to prolong
my confusion, and it was not until after several minutes had elapsed that
I perceived the room was not only illuminated, but occupied. And such
occupants! Amazement at the scene took such possession of me that I was
incapable of either moving or uttering a word. All that I could do was to
lean against the wall, and stare blankly at the strange picture.

It might have been a scene out of Faublas,† or Gramont's Memoirs,‡ or
happened in some palace of Minister Foucque.§

Round a large table in the centre of the room, where I had left a student-
like litter of books and papers, were seated half a dozen persons. Three

---

* Also known as a mock-orange, a pipe tree, and sometimes a lilac, the syringa is a shrub
  bearing white, aromatic flowers.

† Faublas is the protagonist of a trio of novels by Jean-Baptiste Louvet de Couvray, all
  published about the time of the French Revolution and exploring the decadent notions
  of eighteenth-century "libertinage."

‡ Philibert de Gramont (1621–1707) was a French nobleman whose memoirs, apparently
  dictated to his brother-in-law Anthony Hamilton when he was eighty, painted an
  especially decadent portrait of the court of Charles II.

§ This may be a reference to A. Foucques de Vagnonville, who was principally know for
  collecting the written works of sculptor Jean Bologne.

were men and three were women. The table was heaped with a prodigality of luxuries. Luscious eastern fruits were piled up in silver filigree vases, through whose meshes their glowing rinds shone in the contrasts of a thousand hues. Small silver dishes that Benvenuto* might have designed, filled with succulent and aromatic meats, were distributed upon a cloth of snowy damask. Bottles of every shape, slender ones from the Rhine, stout fellows from Holland, sturdy ones from Spain, and quaint basket-woven flasks from Italy, absolutely littered the board. Drinking-glasses of every size and hue filled up the interstices, and the thirsty German flagon stood side by side with the aërial bubbles of Venetian glass that rest so lightly on their threadlike stems. An odour of luxury and sensuality floated through the apartment. The lamps that burned in every direction seemed to diffuse a subtle incense on the air, and in a large vase that stood on the floor I saw a mass of magnolias, tuberoses, and jasmines grouped together, stifling each other with their honeyed and heavy fragrance.

The inhabitants of my room seemed beings well suited to so sensual an atmosphere. The women were strangely beautiful, and all were attired in dresses of the most fantastic devices and brilliant hues. Their figures were round, supple, and elastic; their eyes dark and languishing; their lips full, ripe, and of the richest bloom. The three men wore half-masks, so that all I could distinguish were heavy jaws, pointed beards, and brawny throats that rose like massive pillars out of their doublets. All six lay reclining on Roman couches about the table, drinking down the purple wines in large draughts, and tossing back their heads and laughing wildly.

I stood, I suppose, for some three minutes, with my back against the wall staring vacantly at the bacchanal vision, before any of the revellers appeared to notice my presence. At length, without any expression to indicate whether I had been observed from the beginning or not, two of the women arose from their couches, and, approaching, took each a hand and led me to the table. I obeyed their motions mechanically. I sat on a couch, between them as they indicated. I unresistingly permitted them to wind their arms about my neck.

---

* Benvenuto Cellini was both the author of a famous autobiography and a celebrated sixteenth-century goldsmith.

"You must drink," said one, pouring out a large glass of red wine, "here is Clos Vougeout* of a rare vintage; and here," pushing a flask of amber-hued wine before me, "is Lachryma Christi.†"

"You must eat," said the other, drawing the silver dishes toward her. "Here are cutlets stewed with olives, and here are slices of a *filet* stuffed with bruised sweet chestnuts"—and as she spoke, she, without waiting for a reply, proceeded to help me.

The sight of the food recalled to me the warnings I had received in the garden. This sudden effort of memory restored to me my other faculties at the same instant. I sprang to my feet, thrusting the women from me with each hand.

"Demons!" I almost shouted. "I will have none of your accursed food. I know you. You are cannibals, you are ghouls, you are enchanters. Begone, I tell you! Leave my room in peace!"

A shout of laughter from all six was the only effect that my passionate speech produced. The men rolled on their couches, and their half-masks quivered with the convulsions of their mirth. The women shrieked, and tossed the slender wine-glasses wildly aloft, and turned to me and flung themselves on my bosom fairly sobbing with laughter.

"Yes," I continued, as soon as the noisy mirth had subsided, "yes, I say, leave my room instantly! I will have none of your unnatural orgies here!"

"His room!" shrieked the woman on my right.

"His room!" echoed she on my left.

"His room! He calls it his room!" shouted the whole party, as they rolled once more into jocular convulsions.

"How know you that it is your room?" said one of the men who sat opposite to me, at length, after the laughter had once more somewhat subsided.

"How do I know?" I replied indignantly. "How do I know my own room? How could I mistake it, pray? There's my furniture—my piano—"

---

* Clos de Vougeot is the name of both a famous vineyard in Burgundy and the high-quality wines produced from there.

† Lacryma Christi is a famous Italian wine produced in both white and red varieties from grapes grown on Mount Vesuvius. The name—meaning "tears of Christ"—stems from a legend that Christ cried when Satan fell from Heaven, and wherever his tears fell, grape vines sprang up.

"He calls that a piano," shouted my neighbours, again in convulsions as I pointed to the corner where my huge piano, sacred to the memory of Blokeeta, used to stand. "O, yes! It is his room. There—there is his piano!"

The peculiar emphasis they laid on the word "piano" caused me to scrutinize the article I was indicating more thoroughly. Up to this time, though utterly amazed at the entrance of these people into my chamber, and connecting them somewhat with the wild stories I had heard in the garden, I still had a sort of indefinite idea that the whole thing was a masquerading freak got up in my absence, and that the bacchanalian orgie I was witnessing was nothing more than a portion of some elaborate hoax of which I was to be the victim. But when my eyes turned to the corner where I had left a huge and cumbrous piano, and beheld a vast and sombre organ lifting its fluted front to the very ceiling, and convinced myself, by a hurried process of memory, that it occupied the very spot in which I had left my own instrument, the little self-possession that I had left forsook me. I gazed around me bewildered.

In like manner everything was changed. In the place of that old haftless dagger, connected with so many historic associations personal to myself, I beheld a Turkish yataghan* dangling by its belt of crimson silk, while the jewels in the hilt blazed as the lamplight played upon them. In the spot where hung my cherished smoking cap, memorial of a buried love, a knightly casque was suspended on the crest of which a golden dragon stood in the act of springing. That strange lithograph of Calame was no longer a lithograph, but it seemed to me that the portion of the wall which it covered, of the exact shape and size, had been cut out, and, in place of the picture, a *real* scene on the same scale, and with real actors, was distinctly visible. The old oak was there, and the stormy sky was there; but I saw the branches of the oak sway with the tempest, and the clouds drive before the wind. The wanderer in his cloak was gone; but in his place I beheld a circle of wild figures, men and women, dancing with linked hands around the hole of the great tree, chanting some wild fragment of a song, to which the winds roared an unearthly chorus. The snow-shoes, too, on whose sinewy woof I had sped for many days amidst

---

* A short sabre.

Canadian wastes, had vanished, and in their place lay a pair of strange up-curled Turkish slippers, that had, perhaps, been many a time shuffled off at the doors of mosques, beneath the steady blaze of an orient sun.

All was changed. Wherever my eyes turned they missed familiar objects, yet encountered strange representatives. Still, in all the substitutes there seemed to me a reminiscence of what they replaced. They seemed only for a time transmuted into other shapes, and there lingered around them the atmosphere of what they once had been. Thus I could have sworn the room to have been mine, yet there was nothing in it that I could rightly claim. Everything reminded me of some former possession that it was not. I looked for the acacia at the window, and lo! long silken palm-leaves swayed in through the open lattice; yet they had the same motion and the same air of my favourite tree, and seemed to murmur to me, "Though we seem to be palm-leaves, yet are we acacia-leaves; yea, those very ones on which you used to watch the butterflies alight and the rain patter while you smoked and dreamed!" So in all things; the room was, yet was not, mine; and a sickening consciousness of my utter inability to reconcile its identity with its appearance overwhelmed me, and choked my reason.

"Well, have you determined whether or not this is your room?" asked the girl on my left, proffering me a huge tumbler creaming over with champagne, and laughing wickedly as she spoke.

"It is mine," I answered, doggedly, striking the glass rudely with my hand, and dashing the aromatic wine over the white cloth. "I know that it is mine; and ye are jugglers and enchanters who want to drive me mad."

"Hush! hush!" she said, gently, not in the least angered by my rough treatment. "You are excited. Alf shall play something to soothe you."

At her signal, one of the men sat down at the organ. After a short, wild, spasmodic prelude, he began what seemed to me to be a symphony of recollections. Dark and sombre, and all through full of quivering and intense agony, it appeared to recall a dark and dismal night, on a cold reef, around which an unseen but terribly audible ocean broke with eternal fury. It seemed as if a lonely pair were on the reef, one living, the other dead; one clasping his arms around the tender neck and naked bosom of the other, striving to warm her into life, when his own vitality was being each moment sucked from him by the icy breath of the storm. Here and there a terrible wailing minor key would tremble through the chords like the shriek of sea-birds, or the warning of advancing death. While the man played I could scarce restrain myself. It seemed to be Blokeeta whom I listened to, and on whom I gazed. That wondrous night of pleasure and pain that I had once passed listening to him seemed to have been taken up again at the spot where it had broken off, and the same hand was continuing it. I stared at the man called Alf. There he sat with his cloak and doublet, and long rapier and mask of black velvet. But there was something in the air of the peaked beard, a familiar mystery in the wild mass of raven hair that fell as if wind-blown over his shoulders, which riveted my memory.

"Blokeeta! Blokeeta!" I shouted, starting up furiously from the couch on which I was lying, and bursting the fair arms that were linked around my neck as if they had been hateful chains—"Blokeeta! my friend! speak to me, I entreat you! Tell these horrid enchanters to leave me. Say that I hate them. Say that I command them to leave my room."

The man at the organ stirred not in answer to my appeal. He ceased playing, and the dying sound of the last note he had touched faded off into a melancholy moan. The other men and the women burst once more into peals of mocking laughter.

"Why will you persist in calling this your room?" said the woman next me, with a smile meant to be kind, but to me inexpressibly loathsome. "Have we not shown you by the furniture, by the general appearance of the place, that you are mistaken, and that this cannot be your apartment? Rest content, then, with us. You are welcome here, and need no longer trouble yourself about your room."

"Rest content!" I answered madly; "live with ghosts, eat of awful meats, and see awful sights! Never! never! You have cast some enchantment over the place that has disguised it; but for all that I know it to be my room. You shall leave it!"

"Softly, softly!" said another of the sirens. "Let us settle this amicably. This poor gentleman seems obstinate and inclined to make an uproar. Now we do not want an uproar. We love the night and its quiet; and there is no night that we love so well as that on which the moon is coffined in clouds. Is it not so, my brothers?"

An awful and sinister smile gleamed on the countenances of her unearthly audience, and seemed to glide visibly from underneath their masks.

"Now," she continued, "I have a proposition to make. It would be ridiculous for us to surrender this room simply because this gentleman states that it is his; and yet I feel anxious to gratify, as far as may be fair, his wild assertion of ownership. A room, after all, is not much to us; we can get one easily enough, but still we should be loath to give this apartment up to so imperious a demand. We are willing, however, to *risk* its loss. That is to say,"—turning to me—"I propose that we play for the room. If you win, we will immediately surrender it to you just as it stands; if, on the contrary, you lose, you shall bind yourself to depart and never molest us again."

Agonized at the ever-darkening mysteries that seemed to thicken around me, and despairing of being able to dissipate them by the mere exercise of my own will, I caught almost gladly at the chance thus presented to me. The idea of my loss or my gain scarce entered into my calculations. All I felt was an indefinite knowledge that I might, in the way proposed, regain in an instant, that quiet chamber and that peace of mind of which I had so strangely been deprived.

"I agree!" I cried eagerly; "I agree. Anything to rid myself of such unearthly company!"

The woman touched a small golden bell that stood near her on the table, and it had scarce ceased to tinkle when a negro dwarf entered with a silver tray on which were dice-boxes and dice. A shudder passed over me as I thought in this stunted African I could trace a resemblance to the ghoul-like black servant to whose attendance I had been accustomed.

"Now," said my neighbour, seizing one of the dice-boxes and giving me the other, "the highest wins. Shall I throw first?"

I nodded assent. She rattled the dice, and I felt an inexpressible load lifted from my heart as she threw fifteen.

"It is your turn," she said, with a mocking smile; "but before you throw, I repeat the offer I made you before. Live with us. Be one of us. We will initiate you into our mysteries and enjoyments—enjoyments of which you can form no idea unless you experience them. Come; it is not too late yet to change your mind. Be with us!"

My reply was a fierce oath, as I rattled the dice with spasmodic nervousness and flung them on the board. They rolled over and over again, and during that brief instant I felt a suspense, the intensity of which I have never known before or since. At last they lay before me. A shout of the same horrible, maddening laughter rang in my ears. I peered in vain at the dice, but my sight was so confused that I could not distinguish the amount of the cast. This lasted for a few moments. Then my sight grew clear, and I sank back almost lifeless with despair as I saw that I had thrown but *twelve*!

"Lost! lost!" screamed my neighbour, with a wild laugh. "Lost! lost!" shouted the deep voices of the masked men. "Leave us, coward!" they all cried; "you are not fit to be one of us. Remember your promise; leave us!"

Then it seemed as if some unseen power caught me by the shoulders and thrust me toward the door. In vain I resisted. In vain I screamed and shouted for help. In vain I implored them for pity. All the reply I had was those mocking peals of merriment, while, under the invisible influence, I staggered like a drunken man toward the door. As I reached the threshold the organ pealed out a wild triumphal strain. The power that impelled me concentrated itself into one vigorous impulse that sent me blindly staggering out into the echoing corridor, and as the door closed swiftly behind me, I caught one glimpse of the apartment I had left forever. A change passed like a shadow over it. The lamps died out, the siren women and masked men vanished, the flowers, the fruits, the bright silver and bizarre furniture faded swiftly, and I saw again, for the tenth of a second, my own old chamber restored. There was the acacia waving darkly; there was the table littered with books; there was the ghostly lithograph, the dearly beloved smoking-cap, the Canadian snow-shoes, the ancestral dagger. And there, at the piano, organ no longer, sat Blokeeta playing.

The next instant the door closed violently, and I was left standing in the corridor stunned and despairing.

As soon as I had partially recovered my comprehension I rushed madly to the door, with the dim idea of beating it in. My fingers touched a cold and solid wall. There was no door! I felt all along the corridor for many yards on both sides. There was not even a crevice to give me hope. I rushed downstairs shouting madly. No one answered. In the vestibule I met the negro; I seized him by the collar and demanded my room. The demon showed his white and awful teeth, which were filed into a saw-like shape, and extricating himself from my grasp with a sudden jerk, fled down the passage with a gibbering laugh. Nothing but echo answered to my despairing shrieks. The lonely garden resounded with my cries as I strode madly through the dark walls, and the tall funereal cypresses seemed to bury me beneath their heavy shadows. I met no one—could find no one. I had to bear my sorrow and despair alone.

Since that awful hour I have never found my room. Everywhere I look for it, yet never see it. Shall I ever find it?

MARY ELIZABETH BRADDON *(1835–1915), who frequently wrote as M. E. Braddon, was one of the literary celebrities of the Victorian age. Author of more than eighty novels, she is best remembered for* Lady Audley's Secret *(1862), a huge bestseller. Braddon also wrote one of the earliest detective novels in England, variously known as* Three Times Dead *or* Trail of the Serpent *(1860), as well as countless historical and sensational tales. This story—her first published work—initially appeared in the* Welcome Guest Magazine's *September 29, 1860, issue, and was reprinted two years later in her collection* Ralph the Bailiff and Other Tales.

THE COLD EMBRACE

by Mary Elizabeth Braddon

(1860)

H e was an artist—such things as happened to him happen sometimes to artists.

He was a German—such things as happened to him happen sometimes to Germans.

He was young, handsome, studious, enthusiastic, metaphysical, reckless, unbelieving, heartless.

And being young, handsome and eloquent, he was beloved.

He was an orphan, under the guardianship of his dead father's brother, his uncle Wilhelm, in whose house he had been brought up from a little child; and she who loved him was his cousin—his cousin Gertrude, whom he swore he loved in return.

Did he love her? Yes, when he first swore it. It soon wore out, this passionate love; how threadbare and wretched a sentiment it became at last in the selfish heart of the student! But in its first golden dawn, when he was only nineteen, and had just returned from his apprenticeship to a great painter at Antwerp, and they wandered together in the most romantic outskirts of the city at rosy sunset, by holy moonlight, or bright and joyous morning, how beautiful a dream!

They keep it a secret from Wilhelm, as he has the father's ambition of a wealthy suitor for his only child—a cold and dreary vision beside the lover's dream.

So they are betrothed; and standing side by side when the dying sun and the pale rising moon divide the heavens, he puts the betrothal ring upon her finger, the white and tapered finger whose slender shape he knows so well. This ring is a peculiar one, a massive golden serpent, its tail in its mouth, the symbol of eternity; it had been his mother's, and he would know it amongst a thousand. If he were to become blind tomorrow, he could select it from amongst a thousand by the touch alone.

He places it on her finger, and they swear to be true to each other for ever and ever—through trouble and danger—sorrow and change—in wealth or poverty. Her father must needs be won to consent to their union by-and-by, for they were now betrothed, and death alone could part them.

But the young student, the scoffer at revelation, yet the enthusiastic adorer of the mystical asks:

"Can death part us? I would return to you from the grave, Gertrude. My soul would come back to be near my love. And you—you, if you died before me—the cold earth would not hold you from me; if you loved me, you would return, and again these fair arms would be clasped round my neck as they are now."

But she told him, with a holier light in her deep-blue eyes than had ever shone in his—she told him that the dead who die at peace with God are happy in heaven, and cannot return to the troubled earth; and that it is only the suicide—the lost wretch on whom sorrowful angels shut the door of Paradise—whose unholy spirit haunts the footsteps of the living.

The first year of their betrothal is passed, and she is alone, for he has gone to Italy, on a commission for some rich man, to copy Raphaels, Titians, Guidos, in a gallery at Florence. He has gone to win fame, perhaps; but it is not the less bitter—he is gone!

Of course her father misses his young nephew, who has been as a son to him; and he thinks his daughter's sadness no more than a cousin should feel for a cousin's absence.

In the meantime, the weeks and months pass. The lover writes—often at first, then seldom—at last, not at all.

How many excuses she invents for him! How many times she goes to the distant little post-office, to which he is to address his letters! How many times she hopes, only to be disappointed!

How many times she despairs, only to hope again!

But real despair comes at last, and will not be put off any more. The rich suitor appears on the scene, and her father is determined. She is to marry at once. The wedding-day is fixed—the fifteenth of June.

The date seems burnt into her brain.

The date, written in fire, dances for ever before her eyes.

The date, shrieked by the Furies, sounds continually in her ears.

But there is time yet—it is the middle of May—there is time for a letter to reach him at Florence; there is time for him to come to Brunswick,* to take her away and marry her, in spite of her father—in spite of the whole world.

But the days and weeks fly by, and he does not write—he does not come. This is indeed despair which usurps her heart, and will not be put away.

It is the fourteenth of June. For the last time she goes to the little post-office; for the last time she asks the old question, and they give her for the last time the dreary answer, "No; no letter."

For the last time—for tomorrow is the day appointed for her bridal. Her father will hear no entreaties; her rich suitor will not listen to her prayers. They will not be put off a day—an hour; tonight alone is hers—this night, which she may employ as she will.

She takes another path than that which leads home; she hurries through some by-streets of the city, out on to a lonely bridge, where he and she had stood so often in the sunset, watching the rose-coloured light glow, fade, and die upon the river.

---

* Brunswick is the English name for the German city of Braunschweig, which is about 788 miles from Florence.

He returns from Florence. He had received her letter. That letter, blotted with tears, entreating, despairing—he had received it, but he loved her no longer. A young Florentine, who has sat to him for a model, had bewitched his fancy—that fancy which with him stood in place of a heart—and Gertrude had been half-forgotten. If she had a rich suitor, good; let her marry him; better for her, better far for himself. He had no wish to fetter himself with a wife. Had he not his art always?—his eternal bride, his unchanging mistress.

Thus he thought it wiser to delay his journey to Brunswick, so that he should arrive when the wedding was over—arrive in time to salute the bride.

And the vows—the mystical fancies—the belief in his return, even after death, to the embrace of his beloved? O, gone out of his life; melted away for ever, those foolish dreams of his boyhood.

So on the fifteenth of June he enters Brunswick, by that very bridge on which she stood, the stars looking down on her, the night before. He strolls across the bridge and down by the water's edge, a great rough dog at his heels, and the smoke from his short meerschaum-pipe curling in blue wreaths fantastically in the pure morning air. He has his sketch-book under his arm, and attracted now and then by some object that catches his artist's eye, stops to draw: a few weeds and pebbles on the river's brink—a crag on the opposite shore—a group of pollard willows in the distance. When he has done, he admires his drawing, shuts his sketch-book, empties the ashes from his pipe, refills from his tobacco-pouch, sings the refrain of a gay drinking-song, calls to his dog, smokes again, and walks on. Suddenly he opens his sketch-book again; this time that which attracts him is a group of figures: but what is it? It is not a funeral, for there are no mourners.

It is not a funeral, but a corpse lying on a rough bier, covered with an old sail, carried between two bearers.

It is not a funeral, for the bearers are fishermen—fishermen in their everyday garb.

About a hundred yards from him they rest their burden on a bank—one stands at the head of the bier, the other throws himself down at the foot of it.

And thus they form a perfect group; he walks back two or three paces, selects his point of sight, and begins to sketch a hurried outline. He has finished it before they move; he hears their voices, though he cannot hear their words, and wonders what they can be talking of. Presently he walks on and joins them.

"You have a corpse there, my friends?" he says.

"Yes; a corpse washed ashore an hour ago."

"Drowned?"

"Yes, drowned. A young girl, very handsome."

"Suicides are always handsome," says the painter; and then he stands for a little while idly smoking and meditating, looking at the sharp outline of the corpse and the stiff folds of the rough canvas covering.

Life is such a golden holiday for him—young, ambitious, clever—that it seems as though sorrow and death could have no part in his destiny.

At last he says that, as this poor suicide is so handsome, he should like to make a sketch of her.

He gives the fishermen some money, and they offer to remove the sail-cloth that covers her features.

No; he will do it himself. He lifts the rough, coarse, wet canvas from her face. What face?

The face that shone on the dreams of his foolish boyhood; the face which once was the light of his uncle's home. His cousin Gertrude—his betrothed!

He sees, as in one glance, while he draws one breath, the rigid features—the marble arms—the hands crossed on the cold bosom; and, on the third finger of the left hand, the ring which had been his mother's—the golden serpent; the ring which, if he were to become blind, he could select from a thousand others by the touch alone.

But he is a genius and a metaphysician—grief, true grief, is not for such as he. His first thought is flight—flight anywhere out of that accursed city—anywhere far from the brink of that hideous river—anywhere away from remorse—anywhere to forget.

He is miles on the road that leads away from Brunswick before he knows that he has walked a step.

It is only when his dog lies down panting at his feet than he feels how exhausted he is himself, and sits down upon a bank to rest. How the land-scape spins round and round before his dazzled eyes, while his morning's sketch of the two fishermen and the canvas-covered bier glares redly at him out of the twilight!

At last, after sitting a long time by the roadside, idly playing with his dog, idly smoking, idly lounging, looking as any idle, light-hearted travelling student might look, yet all the while acting over that morning's scene in his burning brain a hundred times a minute; at last he grows a little more composed, and tries presently to think of himself as he is, apart from his cousin's suicide.

Apart from that, he was no worse off than he was yesterday. His genius was not gone; the money he had earned at Florence still lined his pocket-book; he was his own master, free to go whither he would.

And while he sits on the roadside, trying to separate himself from the scene of that morning—trying to put away the image of the corpse covered with the damp canvas sail—trying to think of what he should do next, where he should go, to be farthest away from Brunswick and remorse, the old diligence comes rumbling and jingling along. He remembers it; it goes from Brunswick to Aix-la-Chapelle.*

He whistles to his dog, shouts to the postillion† to stop, and springs into the coupé.

During the whole evening, through the long night, though he does not once close his eyes, he never speaks a word; but when morning dawns, and the other passengers awake and begin to talk to each other, he joins in the conversation. He tells them that he is an artist, that he is going to Cologne and to Antwerp to copy Rubenses, and the great picture by Quentin Matsys,‡ in the museum. He remembered afterwards that he talked and laughed boisterously, and that when he was talking and laughing loudest, a passenger, older and graver than the rest, opened the window near him, and told him to put his head out. He remembered the fresh air blowing in his face, the singing of the birds in his ears, and the flat fields and roadside

---

* The English name for the German city Aachen, which is about 260 miles from Braunschweig.

† The postillion rides the leading horse on the left, normally serving as the driver in this fashion.

‡ Quentin Matsys (1466–1530) was a Flemish painter who founded the Antwerp school of painting and is probably best known for his portrait *A Grotesque Old Woman* (or *The Ugly Duchess*).

reeling before his eyes. He remembered this, and then falling in a lifeless heap on the floor of the diligence.

It is a fever that keeps him for six long weeks on a bed at a hotel in Aix-la-Chapelle.

He gets well, and, accompanied by his dog, starts on foot for Cologne. By this time he is his former self once more. Again the blue smoke from his short meerschaum curls upwards in the morning air—again he sings some old university drinking-song—again stops here and there, meditating and sketching.

He is happy, and has forgotten his cousin—and so on to Cologne.

It is by the great cathedral he is standing, with his dog at his side. It is night, the bells have just chimed the hour, and the clocks are striking eleven; the moonlight shines full upon the magnificent pile, over which the artist's eye wanders, absorbed in the beauty of form.

He is not thinking of his drowned cousin, for he has forgotten her and is happy.

Suddenly some one, something from behind him, puts two cold arms round his neck, and clasps its hands on his breast.

And yet there is no one behind him, for on the flags bathed in the broad moonlight there are only two shadows, his own and his dog's. He turns quickly round—there is no one—nothing to be seen in the broad square but himself and his dog; and though he feels, he cannot see the cold arms clasped round his neck.

It is not ghostly, this embrace, for it is palpable to the touch—it cannot be real, for it is invisible.

He tries to throw off the cold caress. He clasps the hands in his own to tear them asunder, and to cast them off his neck. He can feel the long delicate fingers cold and wet beneath his touch, and on the third finger of the left hand he can feel the ring which was his mother's—the golden serpent—the ring which he has always said he would know among a thousand by the touch alone. He knows it now!

His dead cousin's cold arms are round his neck—his dead cousin's wet hands are clasped upon his breast. He asks himself if he is mad. "Up, Leo!" he shouts. "Up, up, boy!" and the Newfoundland leaps to his shoulders—the dog's paws are on the dead hands, and the animal utters a terrific howl, and springs away from his master.

The student stands in the moonlight, the dead arms around his neck, and the dog at a little distance moaning piteously.

Presently a watchman, alarmed by the howling of the dog, comes into the square to see what is wrong.

In a breath the cold arms are gone.

He takes the watchman home to the hotel with him and gives him money; in his gratitude he could have given that man half his little fortune.

Will it ever come to him again, this embrace of the dead?

He tries never to be alone; he makes a hundred acquaintances, and shares the chamber of another student. He starts up if he is left by himself in the public room at the inn where he is staying, and runs into the street. People notice his strange actions, and begin to think that he is mad.

But, in spite of all, he is alone once more; for one night the public room being empty for a moment, when on some idle pretence he strolls into the street, the street is empty too, and for the second time he feels the cold arms round his neck, and for the second time, when he calls his dog, the animal slinks away from him with a piteous howl.

After this he leaves Cologne, still travelling on foot—of necessity now, for his money is getting low. He joins travelling hawkers, he walks side by side with labourers, he talks to every foot-passenger he falls in with, and tries from morning till night to get company on the road.

At night he sleeps by the fire in the kitchen of the inn at which he stops; but do what he will, he is often alone, and it is now a common thing for him to feel the cold arms around his neck.

Many months have passed since his cousin's death—autumn, winter, early spring. His money is nearly gone, his health is utterly broken, he is the shadow of his former self, and he is getting near to Paris. He will reach that city at the time of the Carnival.* To this he looks forward. In Paris, in Carnival time, he need never, surely, be alone, never feel that deadly caress; he may even recover his lost gaiety, his lost health, once more resume his profession, once more earn fame and money by his art.

---

* Carnival, celebrated in February or early March, is a time of excess and indulgence that precedes Lent in the Christian calendar.

How hard he tries to get over the distance that divides him from Paris, while day by day he grows weaker, and his step slower and more heavy!

But there is an end at last; the long dreary roads are passed. This is Paris, which he enters for the first time—Paris, of which he has dreamed so much—Paris, whose million voices are to exorcise his phantom.

To him tonight Paris seems one vast chaos of lights, music, and confusion—lights which dance before his eyes and will not be still—music that rings in his ears and deafens him—confusion which makes his head whirl round and round.

But, in spite of all, he finds the opera-house, where there is a masked ball. He has enough money left to buy a ticket of admission, and to hire a domino* to throw over his shabby dress. It seems only a moment after his entering the gates of Paris that he is in the very midst of all the wild gaiety of the opera-house ball.

No more darkness, no more loneliness, but a mad crowd, shouting and dancing, and a lovely Débardeuse† hanging on his arm.

The boisterous gaiety he feels surely is his old light-heartedness come back. He hears the people round him talking of the outrageous conduct of some drunken student, and it is to him they point when they say this to him, who has not moistened his lips since yesterday at noon, for even now he will not drink; though his lips are parched, and his throat burning, he cannot drink.

His voice is thick and hoarse, and his utterance indistinct; but still this must be his old light-heartedness come back that makes him so wildly gay.

The little Débardeuse is wearied out—her arm rests on his shoulder heavier than lead—the other dancers one by one drop off.

The lights in the chandeliers one by one die out.

The decorations look pale and shadowy in that dim light which is neither night nor day.

A faint glimmer from the dying lamps, a pale streak of cold grey light from the new-born day, creeping in through half-opened shutters.

---

* A long, hooded cloak worn at masquerade balls.

† A traditional female Carnival character.

And by this light the bright-eyed Débardeuse fades sadly. He looks her in the face. How the brightness of her eyes dies out! Again he looks her in the face. How white that face has grown!

Again—and now it is the shadow of a face alone that looks in his.

Again—and they are gone—the bright eyes, the face, the shadow of the face. He is alone; alone in that vast saloon.

Alone, and, in the terrible silence, he hears the echoes of his own footsteps in that dismal dance which has no music.

No music but the beating of his breast. For the cold arms are round his neck—they whirl him round, they will not be flung off, or cast away; he can no more escape from their icy grasp than he can escape from death. He looks behind him—there is nothing but himself in the great empty salle;* but he can feel—cold, deathlike, but O, how palpable!—the long slender fingers, and the ring which was his mother's.

He tries to shout, but he has no power in his burning throat. The silence of the place is only broken by the echoes of his own footsteps in the dance from which he cannot extricate himself.

Who says he has no partner? The cold hands are clasped on his breast, and now he does not shun their caress. No! One more polka, if he drops down dead.

The lights are all out, and, half an hour after, the gendarmes come in with a lantern to see that the house is empty; they are followed by a great dog that they have found seated howling on the steps of the theatre. Near the principal entrance they stumble over—The body of a student, who has died from want of food, exhaustion, and the breaking of a blood-vessel.

---

* A salle is a large room like a concert hall or auditorium.

London-born **AMELIA B. EDWARDS** *(1831–1892) was a true renaissance woman, skilled in art, music, history, public speaking, and mathematics. However, it was as a writer that she found her greatest fame, producing both acclaimed novels like* Barbara's History *(1864) and the classic travelogue* A Thousand Miles Up the Nile *(1877), which she also illustrated (Edwards's interest in Egypt earned her the nickname "the god-mother of Egyptology"). She is best remembered now as an early figure in LGBTQ history—she never married, but had lasting relationships with women throughout her life—and for her ghost stories, especially those produced for Christmas issues of magazines edited by Charles Dickens. "The Phantom Coach" first appeared in the Christmas 1864 issue of Dickens's* All the Year Round, *where it was presented under the title "Another Past Lodger Relates His Own Ghost Story" as Chapter V of a multiauthor story called "Mrs. Lirriper's Legacy." It has since become one of the most popular ghost stories of all time.*

THE PHANTOM COACH

by Amelia B. Edwards

(1864)

The circumstances I am about to relate to you have truth to recommend them. They happened to myself, and my recollection of them is as vivid as if they had taken place only yesterday. Twenty years, however, have gone by since that night. During those twenty years I have told the story to but one other person. I tell it now with a reluctance which I find it difficult to overcome. All I entreat, meanwhile, is that you will abstain from forcing your own conclusions upon me. I want nothing explained away. I desire no arguments. My mind on this subject is quite made up, and, having the testimony of my own senses to rely upon, I prefer to abide by it.

Well! It was just twenty years ago, and within a day or two of the end of the grouse season. I had been out all day with my gun, and had had no sport to speak of. The wind was due east; the month, December; the place, a bleak wide moor in the far north of England. And I had lost my way. It was not a pleasant place in which to lose one's way, with the first feathery flakes of a coming snowstorm just fluttering down upon the heather, and the leaden evening closing in all around. I shaded my eyes with my hand, and stared anxiously into the gathering darkness, where the purple moorland melted into a range of low hills, some ten or twelve miles distant. Not the faintest smoke-wreath, not the tiniest cultivated patch, or fence, or sheep-track, met my eyes in any direction. There was nothing for it but to walk on, and take my chance of finding what shelter I could, by the way. So I shouldered my gun again, and pushed wearily forward; for I had been on foot since an hour after daybreak, and had eaten nothing since breakfast.

Meanwhile, the snow began to come down with ominous steadiness, and the wind fell. After this, the cold became more intense, and the night came rapidly up. As for me, my prospects darkened with the darkening sky, and my heart grew heavy as I thought how my young wife was already watching for me through the window of our little inn parlour, and thought of all the suffering in store for her throughout this weary night. We had been married four months, and, having spent our autumn in the Highlands, were now lodging in a remote little village situated just on the verge of the great English moorlands. We were very much in love, and, of course, very happy. This morning, when we parted, she had implored me to return before dusk, and I had promised her that I would. What would I not have given to have kept my word!

Even now, weary as I was, I felt that with a supper, an hour's rest, and a guide, I might still get back to her before midnight, if only guide and shelter could be found.

And all this time, the snow fell and the night thickened. I stopped and shouted every now and then, but my shouts seemed only to make the silence deeper. Then a vague sense of uneasiness came upon me, and I began to remember stories of travellers who had walked on and on in the falling snow until, wearied out, they were fain to lie down and sleep their lives away. Would it be possible, I asked myself, to keep on thus through all the long dark night? Would there not come a time when my limbs must fail, and my resolution give way? When I, too, must sleep the sleep of death. Death! I shuddered. How hard to die just now, when life lay all so bright before me! How hard for my darling, whose whole loving heart—but that thought was not to be borne! To banish it, I shouted again, louder and longer, and then listened eagerly. Was my shout answered, or did I only fancy that I heard a far-off cry? I halloed again, and again the echo followed. Then a wavering speck of light came suddenly out of the dark, shifting, disappearing, growing momentarily nearer and brighter. Running towards it at full speed, I found myself, to my great joy, face to face with an old man and a lantern.

"Thank God!" was the exclamation that burst involuntarily from my lips.

Blinking and frowning, he lifted his lantern and peered into my face.

"What for?" growled he, sulkily.

"Well—for you. I began to fear I should be lost in the snow."

"Eh, then, folks do get cast away hereabouts fra' time to time, an' what's to hinder you from bein' cast away likewise, if the Lord's so minded?"

"If the Lord is so minded that you and I shall be lost together, friend, we must submit," I replied; "but I don't mean to be lost without you. How far am I now from Dwolding?"*

"A gude twenty mile, more or less."

"And the nearest village?"

"The nearest village is Wyke,† an' that's twelve mile t'other side."

"Where do you live, then?"

"Out yonder," said he, with a vague jerk of the lantern.

"You're going home, I presume?"

"Maybe I am."

---

* This is a fictitious place name.

† Wyke is a real village located in the moors of West Yorkshire.

"Then I'm going with you."

The old man shook his head, and rubbed his nose reflectively with the handle of the lantern.

"It ain't o' no use," growled he. "He 'ont let you in—not he."

"We'll see about that," I replied, briskly. "Who is He?"

"The master."

"Who is the master?"

"That's nowt to you," was the unceremonious reply.

"Well, well; you lead the way, and I'll engage that the master shall give me shelter and a supper to-night."

"Eh, you can try him!" muttered my reluctant guide; and, still shaking his head, he hobbled, gnome-like, away through the falling snow. A large mass loomed up presently out of the darkness, and a huge dog rushed out, barking furiously.

"Is this the house?" I asked.

"Ay, it's the house. Down, Bey!" And he fumbled in his pocket for the key.

I drew up close behind him, prepared to lose no chance of entrance, and saw in the little circle of light shed by the lantern that the door was heavily studded with iron nails, like the door of a prison. In another minute he had turned the key and I had pushed past him into the house.

Once inside, I looked round with curiosity, and found myself in a great raftered hall, which served, apparently, a variety of uses. One end was piled to the roof with corn, like a barn. The other was stored with flour-sacks, agricultural implements, casks, and all kinds of miscellaneous lumber; while from the beams overhead hung rows of hams, flitches,* and bunches of dried herbs for winter use. In the centre of the floor stood some huge object gauntly dressed in a dingy wrapping-cloth, and reaching half way to the rafters. Lifting a corner of this cloth, I saw, to my surprise, a telescope of very considerable size, mounted on a rude movable platform, with four small wheels. The tube was made of painted wood, bound round with bands of metal rudely fashioned; the speculum,†

---

* An unsliced side of bacon.

† A metal mirror used in telescopes through the mid-nineteenth century.

so far as I could estimate its size in the dim light, measured at least fifteen inches in diameter. While I was yet examining the instrument, and asking myself whether it was not the work of some self-taught optician, a bell rang sharply.

"That's for you," said my guide, with a malicious grin. "Yonder's his room."

He pointed to a low black door at the opposite side of the hall. I crossed over, rapped somewhat loudly, and went in, without waiting for an invitation. A huge, white-haired old man rose from a table covered with books and papers, and confronted me sternly.

"Who are you?" said he. "How came you here? What do you want?"

"James Murray, barrister-at-law. On foot across the moor. Meat, drink, and sleep."

He bent his bushy brows into a portentous frown.

"Mine is not a house of entertainment," he said, haughtily. "Jacob, how dared you admit this stranger?"

"I didn't admit him," grumbled the old man. "He followed me over the muir, and shouldered his way in before me. I'm no match for six foot two."

"And pray, sir, by what right have you forced an entrance into my house?"

"The same by which I should have clung to your boat, if I were drowning. The right of self-preservation."

"Self-preservation?"

"There's an inch of snow on the ground already," I replied, briefly; "and it would be deep enough to cover my body before daybreak."

He strode to the window, pulled aside a heavy black curtain, and looked out.

"It is true," he said. "You can stay, if you choose, till morning. Jacob, serve the supper."

With this he waved me to a seat, resumed his own, and became at once absorbed in the studies from which I had disturbed him.

I placed my gun in a corner, drew a chair to the hearth, and examined my quarters at leisure. Smaller and less incongruous in its arrangements than the hall, this room contained, nevertheless, much to awaken my curiosity.

The floor was carpetless. The whitewashed walls were in parts scrawled over with strange diagrams, and in others covered with shelves crowded with philosophical instruments, the uses of many of which were unknown to me. On one side of the fireplace, stood a bookcase filled with dingy folios; on the other, a small organ, fantastically decorated with painted carvings of mediæval saints and devils. Through the half-opened door of a cupboard at the further end of the room, I saw a long array of geological specimens, surgical preparations, crucibles, retorts, and jars of chemicals; while on the mantelshelf beside me, amid a number of small objects, stood a model of the solar system, a small galvanic battery, and a microscope. Every chair had its burden. Every corner was heaped high with books. The very floor was littered over with maps, casts, papers, tracings, and learned lumber of all conceivable kinds.

I stared about me with an amazement increased by every fresh object upon which my eyes chanced to rest. So strange a room I had never seen; yet seemed it stranger still, to find such a room in a lone farmhouse amid those wild and solitary moors! Over and over again, I looked from my host to his surroundings, and from his surroundings back to my host, asking myself who and what he could be? His head was singularly fine; but it was more the head of a poet than of a philosopher. Broad in the temples, prominent over the eyes, and clothed with a rough profusion of perfectly white hair, it had all the ideality and much of the rugged-ness that characterises the head of Louis von Beethoven.* There were the same deep lines about the mouth, and the same stern furrows in the brow. There was the same concentration of expression. While I was yet observing him, the door opened, and Jacob brought in the supper. His master then closed his book, rose, and with more courtesy of manner than he had yet shown, invited me to the table.

A dish of ham and eggs, a loaf of brown bread, and a bottle of admirable sherry, were placed before me.

"I have but the homeliest farmhouse fare to offer you, sir," said my entertainer. "Your appetite, I trust, will make up for the deficiencies of our larder."

---

* The great composer Ludwig van Beethoven is sometimes referred to by this name.

I had already fallen upon the viands, and now protested, with the enthusiasm of a starving sportsman, that I had never eaten anything so delicious.

He bowed stiffly, and sat down to his own supper, which consisted, primitively, of a jug of milk and a basin of porridge. We ate in silence, and, when we had done, Jacob removed the tray. I then drew my chair back to the fireside. My host, somewhat to my surprise, did the same, and turning abruptly towards me, said:

"Sir, I have lived here in strict retirement for three-and-twenty years. During that time, I have not seen as many strange faces, and I have not read a single newspaper. You are the first stranger who has crossed my threshold for more than four years. Will you favour me with a few words of information respecting that outer world from which I have parted company so long?"

"Pray interrogate me," I replied. "I am heartily at your service."

He bent his head in acknowledgment; leaned forward, with his elbows resting on his knees and his chin supported in the palms of his hands; stared fixedly into the fire; and proceeded to question me.

His inquiries related chiefly to scientific matters, with the later progress of which, as applied to the practical purposes of life, he was almost wholly unacquainted. No student of science myself, I replied as well as my slight information permitted; but the task was far from easy, and I was much relieved when, passing from interrogation to discussion, he began pouring forth his own conclusions upon the facts which I had been attempting to place before him. He talked, and I listened spellbound. He talked till I believe he almost forgot my presence, and only thought aloud. I had never heard anything like it then; I have never heard anything like it since. Familiar with all systems of all philosophies, subtle in analysis, bold in generalisation, he poured forth his thoughts in an uninterrupted stream, and, still leaning forward in the same moody attitude with his eyes fixed upon the fire, wandered from topic to topic, from speculation to speculation, like an inspired dreamer. From practical science to mental philosophy; from electricity in the wire to electricity in the nerve; from Watts to Mesmer, from Mesmer to Reichenbach, from Reichenbach to Swedenborg, Spinoza, Condillac,

Descartes, Berkeley, Aristotle, Plato,* and the Magi and mystics of the East, were transitions which, however bewildering in their variety and scope, seemed easy and harmonious upon his lips as sequences in music. By-and-by—I forget now by what link of conjecture or illustration—he passed on to that field which lies beyond the boundary line of even conjectural philosophy, and reaches no man knows whither. He spoke of the soul and its aspirations; of the spirit and its powers; of second sight; of prophecy; of those phenomena which, under the names of ghosts, spectres, and super-natural appearances, have been denied by the sceptics and attested by the credulous, of all ages.

"The world," he said, "grows hourly more and more sceptical of all that lies beyond its own narrow radius; and our men of science foster the fatal tendency. They condemn as fable all that resists experiment. They reject as false all that cannot be brought to the test of the laboratory or the dissecting-room. Against what superstition have they waged so long and obstinate a war, as against the belief in apparitions? And yet what superstition has maintained its hold upon the minds of men so long and so firmly? Show me any fact in physics, in history, in archæology, which is supported by testimony so wide and so various. Attested by all races of men, in all ages, and in all climates, by the soberest sages of antiquity, by the rudest savage of to-day, by the Christian, the Pagan,

---

* James Watt (1736–1819; Edwards has misspelled the name as "Watts") was a Scottish inventor who perfected the steam engine (the "watt" is named for him); Franz Anton Mesmer (1734–1815) was a German physician whose theories of magnetic poles in the body were named "animal magnetism" or "mesmerism"; Carl Reichenbach (1788–1869) was a German chemist who believed that all living things possessed an energy field he called the Odic force; Emanuel Swedenborg (1688–1772) was a Swedish mystic whose work *The Heavenly Doctrine* was the result of visions he'd experienced and which was hugely influential in the development of Spiritualism (as was mesmerism); Baruch Spinoza (1632–1677) was a Dutch philosopher who espoused rationalism; Étienne Bonnot de Condillac (1714–1780) was a French philosopher who was also influential in the early development of psychology; René Descartes (1596–1650) was the French thinker now regarded as one of the founders of modern philosophy; George Berkeley (1685–1753) was an Irish philosopher whose theory "immaterialism" argued that material objects lacked substance unless they were perceived by a human mind; Aristotle (384 BCE–322 BCE) was the great Greek philosopher and polymath whose ideas formed the basis for much of Western thought; Plato (approx. 428 BCE–348 BCE) is the Greek philosopher who is considered to be one of the founders of Western philosophy.

the Pantheist, the Materialist, this phenomenon is treated as a nursery tale by the philosophers of our century. Circumstantial evidence weighs with them as a feather in the balance. The comparison of causes with effects, however valuable in physical science, is put aside as worthless and unreliable. The evidence of competent witnesses, however conclusive in a court of justice, counts for nothing. He who pauses before he pronounces, is condemned as a trifler. He who believes, is a dreamer or a fool."

He spoke with bitterness, and, having said thus, relapsed for some minutes into silence. Presently he raised his head from his hands, and added, with an altered voice and manner, "I, sir, paused, investigated, believed, and was not ashamed to state my convictions to the world. I, too, was branded as a visionary, held up to ridicule by my contemporaries, and hooted from that field of science in which I had laboured with honour during all the best years of my life. These things happened just three-and-twenty years ago. Since then, I have lived as you see me living now, and the world has forgotten me, as I have forgotten the world. You have my history."

"It is a very sad one," I murmured, scarcely knowing what to answer.

"It is a very common one," he replied. "I have only suffered for the truth, as many a better and wiser man has suffered before me."

He rose, as if desirous of ending the conversation, and went over to the window.

"It has ceased snowing," he observed, as he dropped the curtain, and came back to the fireside.

"Ceased!" I exclaimed, starting eagerly to my feet. "Oh, if it were only possible—but no! it is hopeless. Even if I could find my way across the moor, I could not walk twenty miles to-night."

"Walk twenty miles to-night!" repeated my host. "What are you thinking of?"

"Of my wife," I replied, impatiently. "Of my young wife, who does not know that I have lost my way, and who is at this moment breaking her heart with suspense and terror."

"Where is she?"

"At Dwolding, twenty miles away."

"At Dwolding," he echoed, thoughtfully. "Yes, the distance, it is true, is twenty miles; but—are you so very anxious to save the next six or eight hours?"

"So very, very anxious, that I would give ten guineas at this moment for a guide and a horse."

"Your wish can be gratified at a less costly rate," said he, smiling. "The night mail from the north, which changes horses at Dwolding, passes within five miles of this spot, and will be due at a certain cross-road in about an hour and a quarter. If Jacob were to go with you across the moor, and put you into the old coach-road, you could find your way, I suppose, to where it joins the new one?"

"Easily—gladly."

He smiled again, rang the bell, gave the old servant his directions, and, taking a bottle of whisky and a wineglass from the cupboard in which he kept his chemicals, said:

"The snow lies deep, and it will be difficult walking to-night on the moor. A glass of usquebaugh* before you start?"

I would have declined the spirit, but he pressed it on me, and I drank it. It went down my throat like liquid flame, and almost took my breath away.

"It is strong," he said; "but it will help to keep out the cold. And now you have no moments to spare. Good night!"

I thanked him for his hospitality, and would have shaken hands, but that he had turned away before I could finish my sentence. In another minute I had traversed the hall, Jacob had locked the outer door behind me, and we were out on the wide white moor.

Although the wind had fallen, it was still bitterly cold. Not a star glimmered in the black vault overhead. Not a sound, save the rapid crunching of the snow beneath our feet, disturbed the heavy stillness of the night. Jacob, not too well pleased with his mission, shambled on before in sullen silence, his lantern in his hand, and his shadow at his feet. I followed, with my gun over my shoulder, as little inclined for conversation as himself. My thoughts were full of my late host. His voice yet rang in my ears. His eloquence yet held my imagination captive. I remember to this day, with

---

* A Scottish/Irish word for whiskey (the literal translation is "water of life").

surprise, how my over-excited brain retained whole sentences and parts of sentences, troops of brilliant images, and fragments of splendid reasoning, in the very words in which he had uttered them. Musing thus over what I had heard, and striving to recall a lost link here and there, I strode on at the heels of my guide, absorbed and unobservant. Presently—at the end, as it seemed to me, of only a few minutes—he came to a sudden halt, and said:

"Yon's your road. Keep the stone fence to your right hand, and you can't fail of the way."

"This, then, is the old coach-road?"

"Ay, 'tis the old coach-road."

"And how far do I go, before I reach the cross-roads?"

"Nigh upon three mile."

I pulled out my purse, and he became more communicative.

"The road's a fair road enough," said he, "for foot passengers; but 'twas over steep and narrow for the northern traffic. You'll mind where the parapet's broken away, close again the sign-post. It's never been mended since the accident."

"What accident?"

"Eh, the night mail pitched right over into the valley below—a gude fifty feet an' more—just at the worst bit o' road in the whole county."

"Horrible! Were many lives lost?"

"All. Four were found dead, and t'other two died next morning."

"How long is it since this happened?"

"Just nine year."

"Near the sign-post, you say? I will bear it in mind. Good night."

"Gude night, sir, and thankee." Jacob pocketed his half-crown, made a faint pretence of touching his hat, and trudged back by the way he had come.

I watched the light of his lantern till it quite disappeared, and then turned to pursue my way alone. This was no longer matter of the slightest difficulty, for, despite the dead darkness overhead, the line of stone fence showed distinctly enough against the pale gleam of the snow. How silent it seemed now, with only my footsteps to listen to; how silent and how solitary! A strange disagreeable sense of loneliness stole over me. I walked faster. I hummed a fragment of a tune. I cast up enormous sums in my head, and accumulated them at compound interest. I did my best, in short, to forget the startling speculations to which I had but just been listening, and, to some extent, I succeeded.

Meanwhile the night air seemed to become colder and colder, and though I walked fast I found it impossible to keep myself warm. My feet were like ice. I lost sensation in my hands, and grasped my gun mechanically. I even breathed with difficulty, as though, instead of traversing a quiet north country highway, I were scaling the uppermost heights of some gigantic Alp. This last symptom became presently so distressing, that I was forced to stop for a few minutes, and lean against the stone fence. As I did so, I chanced to look back up the road, and there, to my infinite relief, I saw a distant point of light, like the gleam of an approaching lantern. I at first concluded that Jacob had retraced his steps and followed me; but even as the conjecture presented itself, a second light flashed into sight—a light evidently parallel with the first, and approaching at the same rate of motion. It needed no second thought to show me that these must be the carriage-lamps of some private vehicle, though it seemed strange that any private vehicle should take a road professedly disused and dangerous.

There could be no doubt, however, of the fact, for the lamps grew larger and brighter every moment, and I even fancied I could already see the dark outline of the carriage between them. It was coming up very fast, and quite noiselessly, the snow being nearly a foot deep under the wheels.

And now the body of the vehicle became distinctly visible behind the lamps. It looked strangely lofty. A sudden suspicion flashed upon me. Was it possible that I had passed the cross-roads in the dark without observing the sign-post, and could this be the very coach which I had come to meet?

No need to ask myself that question a second time, for here it came round the bend of the road, guard and driver, one outside passenger, and four steaming greys, all wrapped in a soft haze of light, through which the lamps blazed out, like a pair of fiery meteors.

I jumped forward, waved my hat, and shouted. The mail came down at full speed, and passed me. For a moment I feared that I had not been seen or heard, but it was only for a moment. The coachman pulled up; the guard, muffled to the eyes in capes and comforters, and apparently sound asleep in the rumble,* neither answered my hail nor made the slightest effort to dismount; the outside passenger did not even turn his head. I opened the door for myself, and looked in. There were but three travellers inside, so I stepped in, shut the door, slipped into the vacant corner, and congratulated myself on my good fortune.

The atmosphere of the coach seemed, if possible, colder than that of the outer air, and was pervaded by a singularly damp and disagreeable smell. I looked round at my fellow-passengers. They were all three, men, and all silent. They did not seem to be asleep, but each leaned back in his corner of the vehicle, as if absorbed in his own reflections. I attempted to open a conversation.

"How intensely cold it is to-night," I said, addressing my opposite neighbour.

He lifted his head, looked at me, but made no reply.

"The winter," I added, "seems to have begun in earnest."

Although the corner in which he sat was so dim that I could distinguish none of his features very clearly, I saw that his eyes were still turned full upon me. And yet he answered never a word.

At any other time I should have felt, and perhaps expressed, some annoyance, but at the moment I felt too ill to do either. The icy coldness of the night air had struck a chill to my very marrow, and the strange smell inside the coach was affecting me with an intolerable nausea. I shivered from head to foot, and, turning to my left-hand neighbour, asked if he had any objection to an open window?

He neither spoke nor stirred.

I repeated the question somewhat more loudly, but with the same result. Then I lost patience, and let the sash down. As I did so, the leather strap broke in my hand, and I observed that the glass was covered with a thick coat of mildew, the accumulation, apparently, of years. My attention being thus drawn to the condition of the coach, I examined it more narrowly, and saw by the uncertain light of the outer lamps that it was in the last stage of dilapidation. Every part of it was not only out of repair, but in a condition of decay. The sashes splintered at a touch. The leather fittings were crusted

---

* A seat at the rear of a coach.

over with mould, and literally rotting from the woodwork. The floor was almost breaking away beneath my feet. The whole machine, in short, was foul with damp, and had evidently been dragged from some outhouse in which it had been mouldering away for years, to do another day or two of duty on the road.

I turned to the third passenger, whom I had not yet addressed, and hazarded one more remark.

"This coach," I said, "is in a deplorable condition. The regular mail, I suppose, is under repair?"

He moved his head slowly, and looked me in the face, without speaking a word. I shall never forget that look while I live. I turned cold at heart under it. I turn cold at heart even now when I recall it. His eyes glowed with a fiery unnatural lustre. His face was livid as the face of a corpse. His bloodless lips were drawn back as if in the agony of death, and showed the gleaming teeth between.

The words that I was about to utter died upon my lips, and a strange horror—a dreadful horror—came upon me. My sight had by this time become used to the gloom of the coach, and I could see with tolerable distinctness. I turned to my opposite neighbour. He, too, was looking at me, with the same startling pallor in his face, and the same stony glitter in his eyes. I passed my hand across my brow. I turned to the passenger on the seat beside my own, and saw—oh Heaven! how shall I describe what I saw? I saw that he was no living man—that none of them were living men, like myself! A pale phosphorescent light—the light of putrefaction—played upon their awful faces; upon their hair, dank with the dews of the grave; upon their clothes, earth-stained and dropping to pieces; upon their hands, which were as the hands of corpses long buried. Only their eyes, their terrible eyes, were living; and those eyes were all turned menacingly upon me!

A shriek of terror, a wild unintelligible cry for help and mercy; burst from my lips as I flung myself against the door, and strove in vain to open it.

In that single instant, brief and vivid as a landscape beheld in the flash of summer lightning, I saw the moon shining down through a rift of stormy cloud—the ghastly sign-post rearing its warning finger by the wayside— the broken parapet—the plunging horses—the black gulf below. Then, the coach reeled like a ship at sea. Then, came a mighty crash—a sense of crushing pain—and then, darkness.

It seemed as if years had gone by when I awoke one morning from a deep sleep, and found my wife watching by my bedside I will pass over the scene that ensued, and give you, in half a dozen words, the tale she told me with tears of thanksgiving. I had fallen over a precipice, close against the junction of the old coach-road and the new, and had only been saved from certain death by lighting upon a deep snowdrift that had accumulated at the foot of the rock beneath. In this snowdrift I was discovered at daybreak, by a couple of shepherds, who carried me to the nearest shelter, and brought a surgeon to my aid. The surgeon found me in a state of raving delirium, with a broken arm and a compound fracture of the skull. The letters in my pocket-book showed my name and address; my wife was summoned to nurse me; and, thanks to youth and a fine constitution, I came out of danger at last. The place of my fall, I need scarcely say, was precisely that at which a frightful accident had happened to the north mail nine years before.

I never told my wife the fearful events which I have just related to you. I told the surgeon who attended me; but he treated the whole adventure as a mere dream born of the fever in my brain. We discussed the question over and over again, until we found that we could discuss it with temper no longer, and then we dropped it. Others may form what conclusions they please—I *know* that twenty years ago I was the fourth inside passenger in that Phantom Coach.

EDWARD PAGE MITCHELL *(1852–1927) was known chiefly for his journal-istic accomplishments during his lifetime, but he's now referred to (by the late author and genre expert Sam Moskowitz) as "the lost giant of Amer-ican science fiction." Mitchell spent most of his life working for* The Sun, *a daily newspaper in New York; first he wrote stories for the paper—many of which were fictitious, but presented as fact—and he eventually took over as editor-in-chief. Later science fiction standards that Mitchell was among the first to write about include time travel, computers, mutants, and faster-than-light travel. Mitchell wrote a number of supernatural stories as well, including this one, which first appeared in the March 30, 1879, issue of* The Sun.

AN UNCOMMON SORT OF SPECTRE

by Edward Page Mitchell

(1879)

T he ancient castle of Weinstein,* on the upper Rhine, was, as every-body knows, inhabited in the autumn of 1352 by the powerful Baron Kalbsbraten,† better known in those parts as Old Twenty Flasks, a sobriquet derived from his reputed daily capacity for the product of the vineyard. The baron had many other admirable qualities. He was a genial, whole-souled, public-spirited gentleman, and robbed, murdered, burned, pillaged, and drove up the steep sides of the Weinstein his neighbors' cattle, wives,

---

* There really is a Castle Weinstein in Switzerland, overlooking the Rhine. The castle dates back 600 years; today it operates as a restaurant and vineyard.

† Mitchell was fond of occasionally giving his characters deliberately silly names, likes "Kalbsbraten," which means "roast veal" in German.

and sisters, with a hearty bonhomie that won for him the unaffected esteem of his contemporaries.

One evening the good baron sat alone in the great hall of Weinstein, in a particularly happy mood. He had dined well, as was his habit, and twenty empty bottles stood before him in a row upon the table, like a train of delightful memories of the recent past. But the baron had another reason to be satisfied with himself and with the world. The consciousness that he had that day become a parent lit up his countenance with a tender glow that mere wine cannot impart.

"What ho! Without! Hi! Seneschal!'" he presently shouted, in a tone that made the twenty empty bottles ring as if they were musical glasses, while a score of suits of his ancestors' armor hanging around the walls gave out in accompaniment a deep metallic bass. The seneschal was speedily at his side.

"Seneschal," said Old Twenty Flasks, "you gave me to understand that the baroness was doing finely?"

"I am told," replied the seneschal, "that her ladyship is doing as well as could be expected."

The baron mused in silence for a moment, absently regarding the empty bottles. "You also gave me to understand," he continued, "that there were—"

"Four," said the seneschal, gravely. "I am credibly informed that there are four, all boys."

"That," exclaimed the baron, with a glow of honest pride, bringing a brawny fist down upon the table—"That, in these days, when the abominable doctrines of Malthus† are gaining ground among the upper classes, is what I call creditable—creditable, by Saint Christopher. If I do say it!" His eyes rested again upon the empty bottles. "I think, Seneschal," he added, after a brief pause, "that under the circumstances we may venture—"

---

* "Seneschal" is a title, and refers to the major-domo of a medieval great house.

† Of course, this is an anachronism, inserted for humorous effect: Thomas Robert Malthus (1766–1834) was a British economist who—400 years later—theorized that progress invariably led to unsustainable population growth.

"Nothing could be more eminently proper," rejoined the seneschal. "I will fetch another flask forthwith, and of the best. What says Your Excellency to the vintage of 1304, the year of the comet?*'"

"But," hesitated the baron, toying with his mustache, "I understood you to say that there were four of 'em—four boys?"

"True, my lord," replied the seneschal, snatching the idea with the readiness of a well-trained domestic. "I will fetch four more flasks."

As the excellent retainer deposited four fresh bottles upon the table within the radius of the baron's reach, he casually remarked, "A pious old man, a traveler, is in the castle yard, my lord, seeking shelter and a supper. He comes from beyond the Alps, and fares toward Cologne."

"I presume," said the baron, with an air of indifference, "that he has been duly searched for plunder."

"He passed this morning," replied the retainer, "through the domain of your well-born cousin, Count Conrad of Schwinkenfels.† Your lordship will readily understand that he has nothing now save a few beggarly Swiss coins of copper."

"My worthy cousin Conrad!" exclaimed the baron, affectionately. "It is the one great misfortune of my life that I live to the leeward of Schwinkenfels. But you relieved the pious man of his copper?"

"My lord," said the seneschal, with an apologetic smile, "it was not worth the taking."

"Now by my soul," roared the baron, "you exasperate me! Coin, and not worth the taking! Perhaps not for its intrinsic value, but you should have cleaned him out as a matter of principle, you fool!"

The seneschal hung his head and muttered an explanation. At the same time he opened the twenty-first bottle.

"Never," continued the baron, less violently but still severely, "if you value my esteem and your own paltry skin, suffer yourself to be swerved a hair's breadth from principle by the apparent insignificance of the loot. A

---

* Halley's Comet was actually seen over Europe in 1301, not 1304, although there was a large comet also witnessed in February 1304.

† This is a name completely made up by Mitchell which translates nonsensically as "waving rock."

conscientious attention to details is one of the fundamental elements of a prosperous career—in fact, it underlies all political economy."

The withdrawal of the cork from the twenty-second bottle emphasized this statement.

"However," the baron went on, somewhat mollified, "this is not a day on which I can consistently make a fuss over a trifle. Four, and all boys! This is a glorious day for Weinstein. Open the two remaining flasks, Seneschal, and show the pious stranger in. I fain would amuse myself with him."

II

Viewed through the baron's twenty-odd bottles, the stranger appeared to be an aged man—eighty years, if a day. He wore a shabby gray cloak and carried a palmer's staff,* and seemed an innocuous old fellow, cast in too commonplace a mold to furnish even a few minutes' diversion. The baron regretted sending for him, but being a person of unfailing politeness, when not upon the rampage, he bade his guest be seated and filled him a beaker of the comet wine.

After an obeisance, profound yet not servile, the pilgrim took the glass and critically tasted the wine. He held the beaker up athwart the light with trembling hand, and then tasted again. The trial seemed to afford him great satisfaction, and he stroked his long white beard.

"Perhaps you are a connoisseur. It pleases your palate, eh?" said the baron, winking at the full-length portrait of one of his ancestors.

"Proper well," replied the pilgrim, "though it is a trifle syrupy from too long keeping. By the bouquet and the tint, I should pronounce it of the vintage of 1304, grown on the steep slope south southeast of the castle, in the fork of the two pathways that lead to under the hill. The sun's rays reflected from the turret give a peculiar excellence to the growth of that particular spot. But your rascally varlets have shelved the bottle on the wrong side of the cellar. It should have been put on the dry side, near where

---

* Also known as a pilgrim's staff; commonly used by those on pilgrimages.

your doughty grandsire Sigismund von Weinstein, the Hairy Handed, walled up his third wife in preparation for a fourth."

The baron regarded his guest with a look of amazement. "Upon my life!" said he, "but you appear to be familiar with the ins and outs of this establishment."

"If I do," rejoined the stranger, composedly sipping his wine, "'tis no more than natural, for I lived more than sixty years under this roof and know its every leak. I happen to be a Von Weinstein myself."

The baron crossed himself and pulled his chair a little further away from the bottles and the stranger.

"Oh no," said the pilgrim, laughing; "quiet your fears. I am aware that every well-regulated castle has an ancestral ghost, but my flesh and blood are honest. I was lord of Weinstein till I went, twelve years ago, to study metaphysics in the Arabic schools, and the cursed scriveners wrote me out of the estate. Why, I know this hall from infancy! Yonder is the fireplace at which I used to warm my baby toes. There is the identical suit of armor into which I crawled when a boy of six and hid till my sainted mother—heaven rest her!—nigh died of fright. It seems but yesterday. There on the wall hangs the sharp two-handed sword of our ancestor, Franz, the One-Eared, with which I cut off the mustaches of my tipsy sire as he sat muddled over his twentieth bottle. There is the very casque—but perhaps these reminiscences weary you. You must pardon the garrulity of an old man who has come to revisit the home of his childhood and prime."

The baron pressed his hand to his forehead. "I have lived in this castle myself for half a century," said he, "and am tolerably familiar with the history of my immediate progenitors. But I can't say that I ever had the pleasure of your acquaintance. However, permit me to fill your glass."

"It is good wine," said the pilgrim, holding out his glass. "Except, perhaps, the vintage of 1392, when the grapes—"

The baron stared at his guest. "The grapes of 1392," said he dryly, "lack forty years of ripening. You are aged, my friend, and your mind wanders."

"Excuse me, worthy host," calmly replied the pilgrim. "The vintage of 1392 has been forty years cellared. You have no memory for dates."

"What call you this year?" demanded the baron.

"By the almanacs, and the stars, and precedent, and common consent, it is the year of grace 1433."

"By my soul and hope of salvation," ejaculated the baron, "it is the year of grace 1352."

"There is evidently a misunderstanding somewhere," remarked the venerable stranger. "I was born here in the year 1352, the year the Turks invaded Europe.*"

"No Turk has invaded Europe, thanks be to heaven," replied Old Twenty Flasks, recovering his self-control. "You are either a magician or an imposter. In either case I shall order you drawn and quartered as soon as we have finished this bottle. Pray proceed with your very interesting reminiscences, and do not spare the wine."

"I never practice magic," quietly replied the pilgrim, "and as to being an imposter, scan well my face. Don't you recognize the family nose, thick, short, and generously colored? How about the three lateral and two diagonal wrinkles on my brow? I see them there on yours. Are not my chaps Weinstein chaps?† Look closely. I court investigation."

"You do look damnably like us," the baron admitted.

"I was the youngest," the stranger went on, "of quadruplets. My three brothers were puny, sickly things, and did not long survive their birth. As a child I was the idol of my poor father, who had some traits worthy of respectful mention, guzzling old toper and unconscionable thief though he was."

The baron winced.

"They used to call him Old Twenty Flasks. It is my candid opinion, based on memory, that Old Forty Flasks would have been nearer the truth."

"It's a lie!" shouted the baron, "I rarely exceeded twenty bottles."

"And as for his standing in the community," the pilgrim went on, without taking heed of the interruption, "it must be confessed that nothing could be worse. He was the terror of honest folk for miles around. Property rights were extremely insecure in this neighborhood, for the rapacity of my lamented parent knew no bounds. Yet nobody dared to complain aloud,

---

* In 1352, the Byzantine civil war broke out and led to 10,000 Ottoman troops retaking the cities of Thrace.

† Chaps are the bones that form the mouth.

for lives were not much safer than sheep or ducats. How the people hated his shadow, and roundly cursed him behind his back! I remember well that, when I was about fourteen—it must have been in '66, the year the Grand Turk occupied Adrianople˙—tall Hugo, the miller, called me up to him, and said: 'Boy, thou has a right pretty nose.' 'It is a pretty nose, Hugo,' said I, straightening up. 'Is it on firm and strong?' asked Hugo, with a sneer. 'Firm enough, and strong enough, I dare say,' I answered; 'but why ask such a fool's question?' 'Well, well, boy,' said Hugo, turning away, "look sharp with thine eyes after thy nose when thy father is unoccupied, for he has just that conscience to steal the nose off his son's face in lack of better plunder.'"

"By Saint Christopher!" roared the baron, "tall Hugo, the miller, shall pay for this. I always suspected him. By Saint Christopher's burden, I'll break every bone in his villainous body."

"'Twould be an ignoble vengeance," replied the pilgrim, quietly, "for tall Hugo has been in his grave these sixty years."

"True," said the baron, putting both hands to his head, and gazing at his guest with a look of utter helplessness. "I forget that it is now next century—that is to say, if you be not a spectre."

"You will excuse me, my respected parent," returned the pilgrim, "if I subject your hypothesis to the test of logic, for it touches me upon a very tender spot, impugning, as it does, my physical verity and my status as an actual individualized ego. Now, what is our relative position? You acknowledge the date of my birth to have been the year of grace 1352. That is a matter in which your memory is not likely to be at fault. On the other hand, with a strange inconsistency, you maintain, in the face of almanacs, chronologies, and the march of events, that it is still the year of grace 1352. Were you one of the seven sleepers,[†] your hallucination [to use no harsher

---

* Adrianople (also known as Edirne) is a city in East Thrace that was captured by the Ottoman Empire in 1366 (although the year is often given as 1369), and served as the capital of the empire until 1453.

† The Seven Sleepers is a medieval legend of seven Christian men who, to escape Roman persecution circa 250 CE, fled to a cave; the emperor ordered the mouth of the cave sealed. When it was unsealed 300 years later, the seven were found to be asleep, but alive; upon waking, they believed they had slept only one day.

term] might be pardoned, but you are neither a sleeper nor a saint. Now, every one of the eighty years that are packed away in the carpet bag of my experience protests against your extraordinary error. It is I who have a prima facie right to question your physical existence, not you mine. Did you ever hear of a ghost, spectre, wraith, apparition, eidolon, or spook coming out of the future to haunt, annoy, or frighten individuals of an earlier generation?"

The baron was obliged to admit that he never had.

"But you have heard of instances where apparitions, ghosts, spooks, call them what you will, have invaded the present from out the limbo of the past?"

The baron crossed himself a second time and peered anxiously into the dark corners of the apartment. "If you are a genuine Von Weinstein," he whispered, "you already know that this castle is overrun with spectres of that sort. It is difficult to move about after nightfall without tumbling over half a dozen of them."

"Then," said the placid logician, "you surrender your case. You commit what, my revered preceptor in dialectics, the learned Arabian Ben Dusty,* used to style syllogistic suicide. For you allow that, while ghosts out of the future are unheard of, ghosts from the past are not infrequently encountered. Now I submit to you as a man, this proposition: That it is infinitely more probable that you are a ghost than that I am one!"

The baron turned very red. "Is this filial," he demanded, "to deny the flesh and blood of your own father?"

"Is it paternal," retorted the pilgrim, not losing his composure, "to insinuate the unrealness of the son of your own begetting?"

"By all the saints!" growled the baron, growing still redder, "this question shall be settled, and speedily. Halloo, there, Seneschal!" He called again and again, but in vain.

"Spare your lungs," calmly suggested the pilgrim. "The best-trained domestic in the world will not stir from beneath the sod for all your shouting."

Twenty Flasks sank back helplessly in his chair. He tried to speak, but his tongue and throat repudiated their functions. They only gurgled.

---

* Another of Mitchell's ridiculous fictitious names.

"That is right," said his guest, approvingly. "Conduct yourself as befits a venerable and respectable ghost from the last century. A well-behaved apparition neither blusters nor is violent. You can well afford to be peaceable in your deportment now; you were turbulent enough before your death."

"My death?" gasped the baron.

"Excuse me," apologized the pilgrim, "for referring to that unpleasant event."

"My death!" stammered the baron, his hair standing on end. "I should like to hear the particulars."

"I was hardly more than fifteen at the time," said the pilgrim musingly; "but I shall never forget the most trifling circumstances of the great popular arising that put an end to my worthy sire's career. Exasperated beyond endurance by your outrageous crimes, the people for miles around at last rose in a body, and, led by my old friend tall Hugo, the miller, flocked to Schwinkenfels and appealed to your cousin, Count Conrad, for protection against yourself, their natural protector. Von Schwinkenfels heard their complaints with great gravity. He replied that he had long watched your abominable actions with distress and consternation; that he had frequently remonstrated with you, but in vain; that he regarded you as the scourge of the neighborhood; that your castle was full of blood-stained treasure and shamefully acquired booty; and that he now regarded it as the personal duty of himself, the conservator of lawful order and good morals, to march against Weinstein and exterminate you for the common good."

"The hypocritical pirate!" exclaimed Twenty Flasks.

"Which he proceeded to do," continued the pilgrim, "supported not only by his retainers but by your own. I must say that you made a sturdy defense. Had not your rascally seneschal sold you out to Schwinkenfels and let down the drawbridge one evening when you were as usual fuddling your brains with your twenty bottles, perhaps Conrad never would have gained an entrance, and my young eyes would have been spared the horrid task of watching the body of my venerated parent dangling at the end of a rope from the topmost turret of the northwest tower."

The baron buried his face in his hands and began to cry like a baby. "They hanged me, did they?" he faltered.

"I am afraid no other construction can be put on it," said the pilgrim. "It was the inevitable termination of such a career as yours had been. They hanged you, they strangled you, they choked you to death with a rope; and the unanimous verdict of the community was Justifiable Homicide. You weep! Behold, Father, I also weep for the shame of the house of Von Weinstein! Come to my arms."

Father and son clasped each other in a long, affectionate embrace and mingled their tears over the disgrace of Weinstein. When the baron recovered from his emotion he found himself alone with his conscience and twenty-four empty bottles. The pilgrim had disappeared.

III

Meanwhile, in the apartments consecrated to the offices of maternity, all had been confusion, turmoil, and distress. In four huge armchairs sat four experienced matrons, each holding in her lap a pillow of swan's down. On each pillow had reposed an infinitesimal fraction of humanity, recently added to the sum total of Von Weinstein. One experienced matron had dozed over her charge; when she awoke the pillow in her lap was unoccupied. An immediate census taken by the alarmed attendants disclosed the startling fact that, although there were still four armchairs, and four sage women, and four pillows of swan's down, there were but three infants. The seneschal, as an expert in mathematics and accounts, was hastily summoned from below. His reckoning merely confirmed the appalling suspicion. One of the quadruplets was gone.

Prompt measures were taken in this fearful emergency. The corners of the rooms were ransacked in vain. Piles of bedclothing and baskets of linen were searched through and through. The hunt extended to other parts of the castle. The seneschal even sent out trusted and discreet retainers on horseback to scour the surrounding country. They returned with downcast countenances; no trace of the lost Von Weinstein had been found.

During one terrible hour the wails of the three neglected infants mingled with the screams of the hysterical mother, to whom the attention of the four sage women was exclusively directed. At the end of the hour her ladyship had sufficiently recovered to implore her attendants to make a last, though hopeless count. On three pillows lay three babies howling lustily in unison. On the fourth pillow reposed a fourth infant, with a mysterious smile upon his face, but cheeks that bore traces of recent tears.

MAN-SIZE IN MARBLE

by Edith Nesbit

(1887)

A lthough every word of this story is as true as despair, I do not expect people to believe it. Nowadays a "rational explanation" is required before belief is possible. Let me then, at once, offer the "rational explanation" which finds most favour among those who have heard the tale of my life's tragedy. It is held that we were "under a delusion," Laura and I, on that 31st of October; and that this supposition places the whole matter on a satisfactory and believable basis. The reader can judge, when he, too, has heard my story, how far this is an "explanation," and in what sense it is "rational." There were three who took part in this: Laura and I and another man. The other man still lives, and can speak to the truth of the least credible part of my story.

I never in my life knew what it was to have as much money as I required to supply the most ordinary needs—good colours, books, and cab-fares—and when we were married we knew quite well that we should only be able to live at all by "strict punctuality and attention to business."* I used to paint in those days, and Laura used to write, and we felt sure we could keep the pot at least simmering. Living in town was out of the question, so we went to look for a cottage in the country, which should be at once sanitary and picturesque. So rarely do these two qualities meet in one cottage that our search was for some time quite fruitless. We tried advertisements, but most of the desirable rural residences which we did look at proved to be lacking in both essentials, and when a cottage chanced to have drains it always had stucco as well and was shaped like a tea-caddy. And if we found a vine or rose-covered porch, corruption invariably lurked within. Our minds got so befogged by the eloquence of house-agents and the rival disadvantages of the fever-traps and outrages to beauty which we had seen and scorned, that I very much doubt whether either of us, on our wedding morning, knew the difference between a house and a haystack. But when we got away from friends and house-agents, on our honeymoon, our wits grew clear again, and we knew a pretty cottage when at last we saw one. It was at Brenzett†—a little village set on a hill over against the southern marshes. We had gone there, from the seaside village where we were staying, to see the church, and two fields from the church we found this cottage. It stood quite by itself, about two miles from the village. It was a long, low building, with rooms sticking out in unexpected places. There was a bit of stone-work—ivy-covered and moss-grown, just two old rooms, all that was left of a big house that had once stood there—and round this stone-work the house had grown up. Stripped of its roses and jasmine it would have been hideous. As it stood it was charming, and after a brief examination we took it. It was absurdly cheap. The rest of our honeymoon we spent in grubbing

---

* This was a popular saying in the nineteenth century, appearing in both newspapers and novels such as *Richard Hunne: A Story of Old London* by George E. Sargent.

† Brenzett is a real village located in Kent, approximately 8 miles from the coast.

about in second-hand shops in the county town, picking up bits of old oak and Chippendale chairs for our furnishing. We wound up with a run up to town and a visit to Liberty's, and soon the low oak-beamed lattice-windowed rooms began to be home. There was a jolly old-fashioned garden, with grass paths, and no end of hollyhocks and sunflowers, and big lilies. From the window you could see the marsh-pastures, and beyond them the blue, thin line of the sea. We were as happy as the summer was glorious, and settled down into work sooner than we ourselves expected. I was never tired of sketching the view and the wonderful cloud effects from the open lattice, and Laura would sit at the table and write verses about them, in which I mostly played the part of foreground.

We got a tall old peasant woman to do for us. Her face and figure were good, though her cooking was of the homeliest; but she understood all about gardening, and told us all the old names of the coppices* and corn-fields, and the stories of the smugglers and highwaymen, and, better still, of the "things that walked," and of the "sights" which met one in lonely glens of a starlight night. She was a great comfort to us, because Laura hated housekeeping as much as I loved folklore, and we soon came to leave all the domestic business to Mrs. Dorman, and to use her legends in little magazine stories which brought in the jingling guinea.

We had three months of married happiness, and did not have a single quarrel. One October evening I had been down to smoke a pipe with the doctor—our only neighbour—a pleasant young Irishman. Laura had stayed at home to finish a comic sketch of a village episode for the *Monthly Marplot*.† I left her laughing over her own jokes, and came in to find her a crumpled heap of pale muslin weeping on the window seat.

"Good heavens, my darling, what's the matter?" I cried, taking her in my arms. She leaned her little dark head against my shoulder and went on crying. I had never seen her cry before—we had always been so happy, you see—and I felt sure some frightful misfortune had happened.

"What is the matter? Do speak."

"It's Mrs. Dorman," she sobbed.

---

* A wooded area periodically cut back to produce new growth.

† A marplot is a busy-body or meddler.

"What has she done?" I inquired, immensely relieved.

"She says she must go before the end of the month, and she says her niece is ill; she's gone down to see her now, but I don't believe that's the reason, because her niece is always ill. I believe someone has been setting her against us. Her manner was so queer—"

"Never mind, Pussy," I said; "whatever you do, don't cry, or I shall have to cry too, to keep you in countenance, and then you'll never respect your man again!"

She dried her eyes obediently on my handkerchief, and even smiled faintly.

"But you see," she went on, "it is really serious, because these village people are so sheepy, and if one won't do a thing you may be quite sure none of the others will. And I shall have to cook the dinners, and wash up the hateful greasy plates; and you'll have to carry cans of water about, and clean the boots and knives—and we shall never have any time for work, or earn any money, or anything. We shall have to work all day, and only be able to rest when we are waiting for the kettle to boil!"

I represented to her that even if we had to perform these duties, the day would still present some margin for other toils and recreations. But she refused to see the matter in any but the greyest light. She was very unreasonable, my Laura, but I could not have loved her any more if she had been as reasonable as Whately.*

"I'll speak to Mrs. Dorman when she comes back, and see if I can't come to terms with her," I said. "Perhaps she wants a rise in her screw. It will be all right. Let's walk up to the church."

The church was a large and lonely one, and we loved to go there, especially upon bright nights. The path skirted a wood, cut through it once, and ran along the crest of the hill through two meadows, and round the churchyard wall, over which the old yews loomed in black masses of shadow. This path, which was partly paved, was called "the bier-balk," for it had long been the way by which the corpses had been carried to burial. The churchyard was richly treed, and was shaded by great elms which

---

* Richard Whately (1787–1863) was an English philosopher and economist known for the standard works *Elements of Logic* and *Elements of Rhetoric*.

stood just outside and stretched their majestic arms in benediction over the happy dead. A large, low porch let one into the building by a Norman doorway and a heavy oak door studded with iron. Inside, the arches rose into darkness, and between them the reticulated windows, which stood out white in the moonlight. In the chancel, the windows were of rich glass, which showed in faint light their noble colouring, and made the black oak of the choir pews hardly more solid than the shadows. But on each side of the altar lay a grey marble figure of a knight in full plate armour lying upon a low slab, with hands held up in everlasting prayer, and these figures, oddly enough, were always to be seen if there was any glimmer of light in the church.* Their names were lost, but the peasants told of them that they had been fierce and wicked men, marauders by land and sea, who had been the scourge of their time, and had been guilty of deeds so foul that the house they had lived in—the big house, by the way, that had stood on the site of our cottage—had been stricken by lightning and the vengeance of Heaven.† But for all that, the gold of their heirs had bought them a place in the church. Looking at the bad hard faces reproduced in the marble, this story was easily believed.

The church looked at its best and weirdest on that night, for the shadows of the yew trees fell through the windows upon the floor of the nave and touched the pillars with tattered shade. We sat down together without speaking, and watched the solemn beauty of the old church, with some of that awe which inspired its early builders. We walked to the chancel and looked at the sleeping warriors. Then we rested some time on the stone seat in the porch, looking out over the stretch of quiet moonlit meadows, feeling in every fibre of our being the peace of the night and of our happy love; and came away at last with a sense that even scrubbing and black-leading‡ were but small troubles at their worst.

---

* This is quite different from the monument to John Fagge and his son found in St. Eanswith's Church: In the real circumstance, both figures share the top of the monument; one, who is dressed in armor, is sculpted resting on an elbow; the other, who is fully reclining, is depicted in regular clothing.

† The real John Fagge was a seventeenth-century bailiff.

‡ To polish with graphite.

Mrs. Dorman had come back from the village, and I at once invited her to a tête-à-tête.

"Now, Mrs. Dorman," I said, when I had got her into my painting room, "what's all this about your not staying with us?"

"I should be glad to get away, sir, before the end of the month," she answered, with her usual placid dignity.

"Have you any fault to find, Mrs. Dorman?"

"None at all, sir; you and your lady have always been most kind, I'm sure—"

"Well, what is it? Are your wages not high enough?"

"No, sir, I gets quite enough."

"Then why not stay?"

"I'd rather not"—with some hesitation—"my niece is ill."

"But your niece has been ill ever since we came."

No answer. There was a long and awkward silence. I broke it.

"Can't you stay for another month?" I asked.

"No, sir. I'm bound to go by Thursday."

And this was Monday!

"Well, I must say, I think you might have let us know before. There's no time now to get any one else, and your mistress is not fit to do heavy housework. Can't you stay till next week?"

"I might be able to come back next week."

I was now convinced that all she wanted was a brief holiday, which we should have been willing enough to let her have, as soon as we could get a substitute.

"But why must you go this week?" I persisted. "Come, out with it."

Mrs. Dorman drew the little shawl, which she always wore, tightly across her bosom, as though she were cold. Then she said, with a sort of effort—

"They say, sir, as this was a big house in Catholic times, and there was a many deeds done here."

The nature of the "deeds" might be vaguely inferred from the inflection of Mrs. Dorman's voice—which was enough to make one's blood run cold. I was glad that Laura was not in the room. She was always nervous, as highly-strung natures are, and I felt that these tales about our house, told by this old peasant woman, with her impressive manner and contagious credulity, might have made our home less dear to my wife.

"Tell me all about it, Mrs. Dorman," I said; "you needn't mind about telling me. I'm not like the young people who make fun of such things."

Which was partly true.

"Well, sir"—she sank her voice—"you may have seen in the church, beside the altar, two shapes."

"You mean the effigies of the knights in armour," I said cheerfully.

"I mean them two bodies, drawed out man-size in marble," she returned, and I had to admit that her description was a thousand times more graphic than mine, to say nothing of a certain weird force and uncanniness about the phrase "drawed out man-size in marble."

"They do say, as on All Saints' Eve* them two bodies sits up on their slabs, and gets off of them, and then walks down the aisle, in their marble"— (another good phrase, Mrs. Dorman)—"and as the church clock strikes eleven they walks out of the church door, and over the graves, and along the bier-balk, and if it's a wet night there's the marks of their feet in the morning."

"And where do they go?" I asked, rather fascinated.

"They comes back here to their home, sir, and if any one meets them—"

"Well, what then?" I asked.

But no—not another word could I get from her, save that her niece was ill and she must go. After what I had heard I scorned to discuss the niece, and tried to get from Mrs. Dorman more details of the legend. I could get nothing but warnings.

"Whatever you do, sir, lock the door early on All Saints' Eve, and make the cross-sign over the doorstep and on the windows."

"But has any one ever seen these things?" I persisted.

"That's not for me to say. I know what I know, sir."

"Well, who was here last year?"

"No one, sir; the lady as owned the house only stayed here in summer, and she always went to London a full month afore the night. And I'm sorry to inconvenience you and your lady, but my niece is ill and I must go on Thursday."

---

* Halloween, in other words.

I could have shaken her for her absurd reiteration of that obvious fiction, after she had told me her real reasons.

She was determined to go, nor could our united entreaties move her in the least.

I did not tell Laura the legend of the shapes that "walked in their marble," partly because a legend concerning our house might perhaps trouble my wife, and partly, I think, from some more occult reason. This was not quite the same to me as any other story, and I did not want to talk about it till the day was over. I had very soon ceased to think of the legend, however. I was painting a portrait of Laura, against the lattice window, and I could not think of much else. I had got a splendid background of yellow and grey sunset, and was working away with enthusiasm at her lace. On Thursday Mrs. Dorman went. She relented, at parting, so far as to say—

"Don't you put yourself about too much, ma'am, and if there's any little thing I can do next week, I'm sure I shan't mind."

From which I inferred that she wished to come back to us after Hallowe'en.[*] Up to the last she adhered to the fiction of the niece with touching fidelity.

Thursday passed off pretty well. Laura showed marked ability in the matter of steak and potatoes, and I confess that my knives, and the plates, which I insisted upon washing, were better done than I had dared to expect.

Friday came. It is about what happened on that Friday that this is written. I wonder if I should have believed it, if any one had told it to me. I will write the story of it as quickly and plainly as I can. Everything that happened on that day is burnt into my brain. I shall not forget anything, nor leave anything out.

I got up early, I remember, and lighted the kitchen fire, and had just achieved a smoky success, when my little wife came running down, as sunny and sweet as the clear October morning itself. We prepared breakfast together, and found it very good fun. The housework was soon done, and when brushes and brooms and pails were quiet again, the house was

---

[*] Halloween (which is short for All Hallows' Eve or Evening) was spelled with an apostrophe until several decades into the twentieth century.

still indeed. It is wonderful what a difference one makes in a house. We really missed Mrs. Dorman, quite apart from considerations concerning pots and pans. We spent the day in dusting our books and putting them straight, and dined gaily on cold steak and coffee. Laura was, if possible, brighter and gayer and sweeter than usual, and I began to think that a little domestic toil was really good for her. We had never been so merry since we were married, and the walk we had that afternoon was, I think, the happiest time of all my life. When we had watched the deep scarlet clouds slowly pale into leaden grey against a pale-green sky, and saw the white mists curl up along the hedgerows in the distant marsh,* we came back to the house, silently, hand in hand.

"You are sad, my darling," I said, half-jestingly, as we sat down together in our little parlour. I expected a disclaimer, for my own silence had been the silence of complete happiness. To my surprise she said—

"Yes. I think I am sad, or rather I am uneasy. I don't think I'm very well. I have shivered three or four times since we came in, and it is not cold, is it?"

"No," I said, and hoped it was not a chill caught from the treacherous mists that roll up from the marshes in the dying light. No—she said, she did not think so. Then, after a silence, she spoke suddenly—

"Do you ever have presentiments of evil?"

"No," I said, smiling, "and I shouldn't believe in them if I had."

"I do," she went on; "the night my father died I knew it, though he was right away in the north of Scotland."† I did not answer in words.

She sat looking at the fire for some time in silence, gently stroking my hand. At last she sprang up, came behind me, and, drawing my head back, kissed me.

"There, it's over now," she said. "What a baby I am! Come, light the candles, and we'll have some of these new Rubinstein‡ duets."

And we spent a happy hour or two at the piano.

---

* Brenzett is one of a number of villages located around Romney Marsh, which is supposedly haunted by the ghosts of highwaymen and smugglers.

† Scottish believers in the paranormal would say that Laura possesses "second sight."

‡ Anton Rubinstein (1829–1894) was a Russian pianist and a prolific composer.

At about half-past ten I began to long for the good-night pipe, but Laura looked so white that I felt it would be brutal of me to fill our sitting-room with the fumes of strong cavendish.*

"I'll take my pipe outside," I said.

"Let me come, too."

"No, sweetheart, not to-night; you're much too tired. I shan't be long. Get to bed, or I shall have an invalid to nurse to-morrow as well as the boots to clean."

I kissed her and was turning to go, when she flung her arms round my neck, and held me as if she would never let me go again. I stroked her hair.

"Come, Pussy, you're over-tired. The housework has been too much for you."

She loosened her clasp a little and drew a deep breath.

"No. We've been very happy to-day, Jack, haven't we? Don't stay out too long."

"I won't, my dearie."

I strolled out of the front door, leaving it unlatched. What a night it was! The jagged masses of heavy dark cloud were rolling at intervals from horizon to horizon, and thin white wreaths covered the stars. Through all the rush of the cloud river, the moon swam, breasting the waves and disappearing again in the darkness. When now and again her light reached the woodlands they seemed to be slowly and noiselessly waving in time to the swing of the clouds above them. There was a strange grey light over all the earth; the fields had that shadowy bloom over them which only comes from the marriage of dew and moonshine, or frost and starlight.

I walked up and down, drinking in the beauty of the quiet earth and the changing sky. The night was absolutely silent. Nothing seemed to be abroad. There was no skurrying of rabbits, or twitter of the half-asleep birds. And though the clouds went sailing across the sky, the wind that drove them never came low enough to rustle the dead leaves in the woodland paths. Across the meadows I could see the church tower standing out black and grey against the sky. I walked there thinking over our three

---

* Cavendish tobacco has been treated by a process which brings out the natural sugars, making it somewhat sweet.

months of happiness—and of my wife, her dear eyes, her loving ways. Oh, my little girl! my own little girl; what a vision came then of a long, glad life for you and me together!

I heard a bell-beat from the church. Eleven already! I turned to go in, but the night held me. I could not go back into our little warm rooms yet. I would go up to the church. I felt vaguely that it would be good to carry my love and thankfulness to the sanctuary whither so many loads of sorrow and gladness had been borne by the men and women of the dead years.

I looked in at the low window as I went by. Laura was half lying on her chair in front of the fire. I could not see her face, only her little head showed dark against the pale blue wall. She was quite still. Asleep, no doubt. My heart reached out to her, as I went on. There must be a God, I thought, and a God who was good. How otherwise could anything so sweet and dear as she have ever been imagined?

I walked slowly along the edge of the wood. A sound broke the stillness of the night, it was a rustling in the wood. I stopped and listened. The sound stopped too. I went on, and now distinctly heard another step than mine answer mine like an echo. It was a poacher or a wood-stealer, most likely, for these were not unknown in our Arcadian neighbourhood. But whoever it was, he was a fool not to step more lightly. I turned into the wood, and now the footstep seemed to come from the path I had just left. It must be an echo, I thought. The wood looked perfect in the moonlight. The large dying ferns and the brushwood showed where through thinning foliage the pale light came down. The tree trunks stood up like Gothic columns all around me. They reminded me of the church, and I turned into the bier-balk, and passed through the corpse-gate between the graves to the low porch. I paused for a moment on the stone seat where Laura and I had watched the fading landscape. Then I noticed that the door of the church was open, and I blamed myself for having left it unlatched the other night. We were the only people who ever cared to come to the church except on Sundays, and I was vexed to think that through our carelessness the damp autumn airs had had a chance of getting in and injuring the old fabric. I went in. It will seem strange, perhaps, that I should have gone half-way up the aisle before I remembered—with a sudden chill, followed by as sudden a rush of self-contempt—that this was the very day and hour when, according to tradition, the "shapes drawed out man-size in marble" began to walk.

Having thus remembered the legend, and remembered it with a shiver, of which I was ashamed, I could not do otherwise than walk up towards the altar, just to look at the figures—as I said to myself; really what I wanted was to assure myself, first, that I did not believe the legend, and, secondly, that it was not true. I was rather glad that I had come. I thought now I could tell Mrs. Dorman how vain her fancies were, and how peacefully the marble figures slept on through the ghastly hour. With my hands in my pockets I passed up the aisle. In the grey dim light the eastern end of the church looked larger than usual, and the arches above the two tombs looked larger too. The moon came out and showed me the reason. I stopped short, my heart gave a leap that nearly choked me, and then sank sickeningly.

The "bodies drawed out man-size" were gone, and their marble slabs lay wide and bare in the vague moonlight that slanted through the east window.

Were they really gone? Or was I mad? Clenching my nerves, I stooped and passed my hand over the smooth slabs, and felt their flat unbroken surface. Had some one taken the things away? Was it some vile practical joke? I would make sure, anyway. In an instant I had made a torch of a newspaper, which happened to be in my pocket, and lighting it held it high above my head. Its yellow glare illumined the dark arches and those slabs. The figures were gone. And I was alone in the church; or was I alone?

And then a horror seized me, a horror indefinable and indescribable—an overwhelming certainty of supreme and accomplished calamity. I flung down the torch and tore along the aisle and out through the porch, biting my lips as I ran to keep myself from shrieking aloud. Oh, was I mad—or what was this that possessed me? I leaped the churchyard wall and took the straight cut across the fields, led by the light from our windows. Just as I got over the first stile, a dark figure seemed to spring out of the ground. Mad still with that certainty of misfortune, I made for the thing that stood in my path, shouting, "Get out of the way, can't you!"

But my push met with a more vigorous resistance than I had expected. My arms were caught just above the elbow and held as in a vice, and the raw-boned Irish doctor actually shook me.

"Would ye?" he cried, in his own unmistakable accents—"would ye, then?"

"Let me go, you fool," I gasped. "The marble figures have gone from the church; I tell you they've gone."

He broke into a ringing laugh. "I'll have to give ye a draught to-morrow, I see. Ye've bin smoking too much and listening to old wives' tales."

"I tell you, I've seen the bare slabs."

"Well, come back with me. I'm going up to old Palmer's—his daughter's ill; we'll look in at the church and let me see the bare slabs."

"You go, if you like," I said, a little less frantic for his laughter; "I'm going home to my wife."

"Rubbish, man," said he; "d'ye think I'll permit of that? Are ye to go saying all yer life that ye've seen solid marble endowed with vitality, and me to go all me life saying ye were a coward? No, sir—ye shan't do ut."

The night air—a human voice—and I think also the physical contact with this six feet of solid common sense, brought me back a little to my ordinary self, and the word "coward" was a mental shower-bath.

"Come on, then," I said sullenly; "perhaps you're right."

He still held my arm tightly. We got over the stile and back to the church. All was still as death. The place smelt very damp and earthy. We walked up the aisle. I am not ashamed to confess that I shut my eyes: I knew the figures would not be there. I heard Kelly strike a match.

"Here they are, ye see, right enough; ye've been dreaming or drinking, asking yer pardon for the imputation."

I opened my eyes. By Kelly's expiring vesta* I saw two shapes lying "in their marble" on their slabs. I drew a deep breath, and caught his hand.

"I'm awfully indebted to you," I said. "It must have been some trick of light, or I have been working rather hard, perhaps that's it. Do you know, I was quite convinced they were gone."

"I'm aware of that," he answered rather grimly; "ye'll have to be careful of that brain of yours, my friend, I assure ye."

He was leaning over and looking at the right-hand figure, whose stony face was the most villainous and deadly in expression.

---

* A kind of wax match.

"By Jove," he said, "something has been afoot here—this hand is broken."

And so it was. I was certain that it had been perfect the last time Laura and I had been there.

"Perhaps some one has tried to remove them," said the young doctor.

"That won't account for my impression," I objected.

"Too much painting and tobacco will account for that, well enough."

"Come along," I said, "or my wife will be getting anxious. You'll come in and have a drop of whisky and drink confusion to ghosts and better sense to me."

"I ought to go up to Palmer's, but it's so late now I'd best leave it till the morning," he replied. "I was kept late at the Union,* and I've had to see a lot of people since. All right, I'll come back with ye."

I think he fancied I needed him more than did Palmer's girl, so, discussing how such an illusion could have been possible, and deducing from this experience large generalities concerning ghostly apparitions, we walked up to our cottage. We saw, as we walked up the garden-path, that bright light streamed out of the front door, and presently saw that the parlour door was open too. Had she gone out?

"Come in," I said, and Dr. Kelly followed me into the parlour. It was all ablaze with candles, not only the wax ones, but at least a dozen guttering, glaring tallow dips, stuck in vases and ornaments in unlikely places. Light, I knew, was Laura's remedy for nervousness. Poor child! Why had I left her? Brute that I was.

We glanced round the room, and at first we did not see her. The window was open, and the draught set all the candles flaring one way. Her chair was empty and her handkerchief and book lay on the floor. I turned to the window. There, in the recess of the window, I saw her. Oh, my child, my love, had she gone to that window to watch for me? And what had come into the room behind her? To what had she turned with that look of frantic fear and horror? Oh, my little one, had she thought that it was I whose step she heard, and turned to meet—what?

She had fallen back across a table in the window, and her body lay half on it and half on the window-seat, and her head hung down over the table, the

---

* A workhouse or poorhouse.

brown hair loosened and fallen to the carpet. Her lips were drawn back, and her eyes wide, wide open. They saw nothing now. What had they seen last?

The doctor moved towards her, but I pushed him aside and sprang to her; caught her in my arms and cried—

"It's all right, Laura! I've got you safe, wifie."

She fell into my arms in a heap. I clasped her and kissed her, and called her by all her pet names, but I think I knew all the time that she was dead. Her hands were tightly clenched. In one of them she held something fast. When I was quite sure that she was dead, and that nothing mattered at all any more, I let him open her hand to see what she held.

It was a grey marble finger.

OSCAR WILDE *(1854–1900) was born into a family that had multiple connections to supernatural literature: His mother produced influential collections of Irish and Celtic folktales (under the name "Lady Jane"), and she was the niece of Charles Maturin, author of the Gothic classic* Melmoth the Wanderer. *Although Wilde began his own literary career with poetry, he found his greatest success as a novelist (he published the horror classic* The Picture of Dorian Gray *in 1890) and playwright (*The Importance of Being Earnest, Lady Windermere's Fan, *and* Salome *are among his theatrical works). Wilde also became the subject of infamy when his relationship with Lord Alfred Douglas (who introduced him to male prostitutes) eventually led to his arrest and conviction on charges of gross indecency, for which he received the maximum sentence of two years of hard labor. Upon his release in 1897, he immediately left Great Britain for France, where he died of meningitis at the age of forty-six. "The Canterville Ghost" was Wilde's first published fiction; it appeared in two parts in the February 23 and March 2, 1887, issues of the* Court and Society Review. *It has been adapted more than a dozen times to film and television, and has also served as the basis for radio shows, graphic novels, and operas.*

THE CANTERVILLE GHOST

by Oscar Wilde

(1887)

I

When Mr. Hiram B. Otis, the American Minister,* bought Canterville Chase, every one told him he was doing a very foolish thing, as there was no doubt at all that the place was haunted. Indeed, Lord Canterville himself,

---

* *See first footnote on the following page.*

who was a man of the most punctilious honour, had felt it his duty to mention the fact to Mr. Otis when they came to discuss terms.

"We have not cared to live in the place ourselves," said Lord Canterville, "since my grandaunt, the Dowager Duchess of Bolton, was frightened into a fit, from which she never really recovered, by two skeleton hands being placed on her shoulders as she was dressing for dinner, and I feel bound to tell you, Mr. Otis, that the ghost has been seen by several living members of my family, as well as by the rector of the parish, the Rev. Augustus Dampier, who is a Fellow of King's College, Cambridge. After the unfortunate accident to the Duchess, none of our younger servants would stay with us, and Lady Canterville often got very little sleep at night, in consequence of the mysterious noises that came from the corridor and the library."

"My Lord," answered the Minister, "I will take the furniture and the ghost at a valuation. I have come from a modern country, where we have everything that money can buy; and with all our spry young fellows painting the Old World red, and carrying off your best actors and primadonnas,* I reckon that if there were such a thing as a ghost in Europe, we'd have it at home in a very short time in one of our public museums, or on the road as a show."

"I fear that the ghost exists," said Lord Canterville, smiling, "though it may have resisted the overtures of your enterprising impresarios. It has been well known for three centuries, since 1584 in fact, and always makes its appearance before the death of any member of our family."

"Well, so does the family doctor for that matter, Lord Canterville. But there is no such thing, sir, as a ghost, and I guess the laws of Nature are not going to be suspended for the British aristocracy."

** *(from previous page)* This is likely a disguise for Edward John Phelps, who became the American ambassador (called minister at that time) in 1885 and served until 1889, when he was succeeded by Robert Todd Lincoln, the deceased President's son. Phelps, a lawyer from Vermont, founded the American Bar Association in 1878 and served as its president from 1880–81. Phelps's predecessor in the post was the poet James Russell Lowell, who served as minister from 1880 to 1885.

* The Jersey-born actress Lillie Langtry, a close friend of Wilde's and a paramour of the Prince of Wales, must be counted among them; she made frequent triumphant tours of the United States and lived in California for a while.

"You are certainly very natural in America," answered Lord Canterville, who did not quite understand Mr. Otis's last observation, "and if you don't mind a ghost in the house, it is all right. Only you must remember I warned you."

A few weeks after this, the purchase was concluded, and at the close of the season* the Minister and his family went down to Canterville Chase. Mrs. Otis, who, as Miss Lucretia R. Tappan, of West 53d Street, had been a celebrated New York belle, was now a very handsome, middle-aged woman, with fine eyes, and a superb profile.† Many American ladies on leaving their native land adopt an appearance of chronic ill-health, under the impression that it is a form of European refinement, but Mrs. Otis had never fallen into this error. She had a magnificent constitution, and a really wonderful amount of animal spirits. Indeed, in many respects, she was quite English, and was an excellent example of the fact that we have really everything in common with America nowadays, except, of course, language.‡ Her eldest son, christened Washington by his parents in a moment of patriotism, which he never ceased to regret, was a fair-haired, rather good-looking young man,§ who had qualified himself for American diplomacy by leading the German¶ at the Newport Casino** for three successive seasons, and even in London was well known as an excellent dancer. Gardenias and the peerage were his only weaknesses. Otherwise he was extremely sensible. Miss Virginia E. Otis was a little girl of fifteen, lithe

---

* The London "season" was a whirl of social affairs, parties, and balls that occupied the upper classes of England in the spring.

† Mary Haight Phelps married Edward Phelps in 1845, when she was eighteen.

‡ The remark "England and America are two countries divided by a common language" is often attributed to George Bernard Shaw, but it does not appear in any of his published work. By 1887, when this story appeared, none of Shaw's plays had been produced, and his literary output consisted of a few novels serialized between 1885 and 1887. Therefore, it is more likely that Wilde coined the phrase.

§ Charles Pierpont Phelps, Edward Phelps's youngest son, was born in 1861. His only daughter Mary was born in 1855.

¶ A popular mid-century dance.

** A popular resort in Newport, Rhode Island, that opened in 1881.

and lovely as a fawn, and with a fine freedom in her large blue eyes. She was a wonderful Amazon, and had once raced old Lord Bilton on her pony twice round the park, winning by a length and a half, just in front of the Achilles statue,* to the huge delight of the young Duke of Cheshire,† who proposed for her on the spot, and was sent back to Eton that very night by his guardians, in floods of tears. After Virginia came the twins, who were usually called "The Star and Stripes," as they were always getting swished.‡ They were delightful boys, and, with the exception of the worthy Minister, the only true republicans of the family.

As Canterville Chase is seven miles from Ascot,§ the nearest railway station, Mr. Otis had telegraphed for a waggonette to meet them, and they started on their drive in high spirits. It was a lovely July evening, and the air was delicate with the scent of the pinewoods. Now and then they heard a wood-pigeon brooding over its own sweet voice, or saw, deep in the rustling fern, the burnished breast of the pheasant. Little squirrels peered at them from the beech-trees as they went by, and the rabbits scudded away through the brushwood and over the mossy knolls, with their white tails in the air. As they entered the avenue of Canterville Chase, however, the sky became suddenly overcast with clouds, a curious stillness seemed to hold the atmosphere, a great flight of rooks passed silently over their heads, and, before they reached the house, some big drops of rain had fallen.

Standing on the steps to receive them was an old woman, neatly dressed in black silk, with a white cap and apron. This was Mrs. Umney, the housekeeper, whom Mrs. Otis, at Lady Canterville's earnest request, had consented to keep in her former position. She made them each a low curtsey as they alighted, and said in a quaint, old-fashioned manner, "I bid you welcome to Canterville Chase." Following her, they passed through the fine Tudor hall into the library, a long, low room, panelled in black oak, at the end of which was a large stained glass window. Here they found tea laid

---

* An eighteen-foot-tall statue of Achilles was erected in Hyde Park in 1822 as a memorial to Arthur Wellesley, the first Duke of Wellington.

† A fictional peer.

‡ "Swished" refers to flogging, especially at school (and hence the twins' "stripes").

§ Ascot is 25 miles west of London.

out for them, and, after taking off their wraps, they sat down and began to look round, while Mrs. Umney waited on them.

Suddenly Mrs. Otis caught sight of a dull red stain on the floor just by the fireplace, and, quite unconscious of what it really signified, said to Mrs. Umney, "I am afraid something has been spilt there."

"Yes, madam," replied the old housekeeper in a low voice, "blood has been spilt on that spot."

"How horrid!" cried Mrs. Otis; "I don't at all care for blood-stains in a sitting-room. It must be removed at once."

The old woman smiled, and answered in the same low, mysterious voice, "It is the blood of Lady Eleanore de Canterville, who was murdered on that very spot by her own husband, Sir Simon de Canterville, in 1575. Sir Simon survived her nine years, and disappeared suddenly under very mysterious circumstances. His body has never been discovered, but his guilty spirit still haunts the Chase. The blood-stain has been much admired by tourists and others, and cannot be removed."

"That is all nonsense," cried Washington Otis; "Pinkerton's Champion Stain Remover and Paragon Detergent will clean it up in no time," and before the terrified housekeeper could interfere, he had fallen upon his knees, and was rapidly scouring the floor with a small stick of what looked like a black cosmetic. In a few moments no trace of the blood-stain could be seen.

"I knew Pinkerton would do it," he exclaimed, triumphantly, as he looked round at his admiring family; but no sooner had he said these words than a terrible flash of lightning lit up the sombre room, a fearful peal of thunder made them all start to their feet, and Mrs. Umney fainted.

"What a monstrous climate!" said the American Minister, calmly, as he lit a long cheroot. "I guess the old country is so overpopulated that they have not enough decent weather for everybody. I have always been of opinion that emigration is the only thing for England."

"My dear Hiram," cried Mrs. Otis, "what can we do with a woman who faints?"

"Charge it to her like breakages,"* answered the Minister; "she won't faint after that;" and in a few moments Mrs. Umney certainly came to.

---

* That is, treat it as a "break"—a rest stop.

There was no doubt, however, that she was extremely upset, and she sternly warned Mr. Otis to beware of some trouble coming to the house.

"I have seen things with my own eyes, sir," she said, "that would make any Christian's hair stand on end, and many and many a night I have not closed my eyes in sleep for the awful things that are done here." Mr. Otis, however, and his wife warmly assured the honest soul that they were not afraid of ghosts, and, after invoking the blessings of Providence on her new master and mistress, and making arrangements for an increase of salary, the old housekeeper tottered off to her own room.

II

The storm raged fiercely all that night, but nothing of particular note occurred. The next morning, however, when they came down to break-fast, they found the terrible stain of blood once again on the floor. "I don't think it can be the fault of the Paragon Detergent," said Washington, "for I have tried it with everything. It must be the ghost." He accordingly rubbed out the stain a second time, but the second morning it appeared again. The third morning also it was there, though the library had been locked up at night by Mr. Otis himself, and the key carried up-stairs. The whole family were now quite interested; Mr. Otis began to suspect that he had been too dogmatic in his denial of the existence of ghosts, Mrs. Otis expressed her intention of joining the Psychical Society, and Washington prepared a long letter to Messrs. Myers and Podmore on the subject of the Permanence of Sanguineous Stains when connected with Crime.* That night all doubts about the objective existence of phantasmata were removed for ever.

The day had been warm and sunny; and, in the cool of the evening, the whole family went out to drive. They did not return home till nine o'clock, when they had a light supper. The conversation in no way turned

---

* The Society for Psychical Research was founded in 1883 and boasted many important members. Among the founders was Frederic W. H. Myers, who, along with Edwin Gurney and Frank Podmore, coauthored the two-volume *Phantasms of the Living* (1886), a detailed report of alleged sightings of ghosts and spirits. This reference confirms that the events took place after 1885, during Phelps's term as minister.

upon ghosts, so there were not even those primary conditions of receptive expectations which so often precede the presentation of psychical phenomena. The subjects discussed, as I have since learned from Mr. Otis, were merely such as form the ordinary conversation of cultured Americans of the better class, such as the immense superiority of Miss Fanny Devonport* over Sarah Bernhardt† as an actress; the difficulty of obtaining green corn, buckwheat cakes, and hominy, even in the best English houses; the importance of Boston in the development of the world-soul; the advantages of the baggage-check system in railway travelling; and the sweetness of the New York accent as compared to the London drawl. No mention at all was made of the supernatural, nor was Sir Simon de Canterville alluded to in any way. At eleven o'clock the family retired, and by half-past all the lights were out. Some time after, Mr. Otis was awakened by a curious noise in the corridor, outside his room. It sounded like the clank of metal, and seemed to be coming nearer every moment. He got up at once, struck a match, and looked at the time. It was exactly one o'clock. He was quite calm, and felt his pulse, which was not at all feverish. The strange noise still continued, and with it he heard distinctly the sound of footsteps. He put on his slippers, took a small oblong phial out of his dressing-case, and opened the door. Right in front of him he saw, in the wan moonlight, an old man of terrible aspect. His eyes were as red burning coals; long grey hair fell over his shoulders in matted coils; his garments, which were of antique cut, were soiled and ragged, and from his wrists and ankles hung heavy manacles and rusty gyves.‡

"My dear sir," said Mr. Otis, "I really must insist on your oiling those chains, and have brought you for that purpose a small bottle of the Tammany Rising Sun Lubricator. It is said to be completely efficacious upon one application, and there are several testimonials to that effect on the wrapper

---

* A celebrated actress of the day (1850–1898), born in England but raised in the United States; her greatest successes were roles in the plays of the French playwright Victorien Sardou, in many cases first performed in Europe by Sarah Bernhardt.

† The legendary French actress (1824–1923) who captivated European audiences, often in male roles. Bernhardt's name became synonymous with melodramatic acting. In her long career, she even appeared in films, beginning in 1898.

‡ Shackles.

from some of our most eminent native divines. I shall leave it here for you by the bedroom candles, and will be happy to supply you with more, should you require it." With these words the United States Minister laid the bottle down on a marble table, and, closing his door, retired to rest.

For a moment the Canterville ghost stood quite motionless in natural indignation; then, dashing the bottle violently upon the polished floor, he fled down the corridor, uttering hollow groans, and emitting a ghastly green light. Just, however, as he reached the top of the great oak staircase, a door was flung open, two little white-robed figures appeared, and a large pillow whizzed past his head! There was evidently no time to be lost, so, hastily adopting the Fourth dimension of Space* as a means of escape, he vanished through the wainscoting, and the house became quite quiet.

On reaching a small secret chamber in the left wing, he leaned up against a moonbeam to recover his breath, and began to try and realize his position. Never, in a brilliant and uninterrupted career of three hundred years, had he been so grossly insulted. He thought of the Dowager Duchess, whom he had frightened into a fit as she stood before the glass in her lace and diamonds; of the four housemaids, who had gone into hysterics when he merely grinned at them through the curtains on one of the spare bedrooms; of the rector of the parish, whose candle he had blown out as he was coming late one night from the library, and who had been under the care of Sir William Gull† ever since, a perfect martyr to nervous disorders; and of old Madame de Tremouillac, who, having wakened up one morning early and seen a skeleton seated in an armchair by the fire reading her diary, had been confined to her bed for six weeks with an attack of brain fever, and, on her recovery, had become reconciled to the Church, and broken off her connection with that notorious sceptic, Monsieur de Voltaire. He remembered the terrible night when the wicked Lord Canterville was found choking in his dressing-room, with the knave of diamonds half-way down his throat, and confessed, just before he died, that he had cheated Charles James Fox

---

* Four-dimensional space was hypothesized as early as 1754, by French mathematician Jean le Rond D'Alembert.

† One of the Court physicians (1816–1890) and, some have suggested, "Jack the Ripper"!

out of £50,000 at Crockford's* by means of that very card, and swore that the ghost had made him swallow it. All his great achievements came back to him again, from the butler who had shot himself in the pantry because he had seen a green hand tapping at the window-pane, to the beautiful Lady Stutfield, who was always obliged to wear a black velvet band round her throat to hide the mark of five fingers burnt upon her white skin, and who drowned herself at last in the carp-pond at the end of the King's Walk. With the enthusiastic egotism of the true artist, he went over his most celebrated performances, and smiled bitterly to himself as he recalled to mind his last appearance as "Red Reuben, or the Strangled Babe," his *début* as "Gaunt Gibeon, the Blood-sucker of Bexley Moor," and the *furore* he had excited one lovely June evening by merely playing ninepins with his own bones upon the lawn-tennis ground. And after all this some wretched modern Americans were to come and offer him the Rising Sun Lubricator, and throw pillows at his head! It was quite unbearable. Besides, no ghost in history had ever been treated in this manner. Accordingly, he determined to have vengeance, and remained till daylight in an attitude of deep thought.

III

The next morning, when the Otis family met at breakfast, they discussed the ghost at some length. The United States Minister was naturally a little annoyed to find that his present had not been accepted. "I have no wish," he said, "to do the ghost any personal injury, and I must say that, considering the length of time he has been in the house, I don't think it is at all polite to throw pillows at him,"—a very just remark, at which, I am sorry to say, the twins burst into shouts of laughter. "Upon the other hand," he continued, "if he really declines to use the Rising Sun Lubricator, we shall have to take his chains from him. It would be quite impossible to sleep, with such a noise going on outside the bedrooms."

---

* The nickname of William Crockford's St. James's Club, a gentlemen's club that flourished from 1823 to 1845 and was a gambling den. Today, Crockfords is a casino.

For the rest of the week, however, they were undisturbed, the only thing that excited any attention being the continual renewal of the blood-stain on the library floor. This certainly was very strange, as the door was always locked at night by Mr. Otis, and the windows kept closely barred. The chameleon-like colour, also, of the stain excited a good deal of comment. Some mornings it was a dull (almost Indian) red, then it would be vermilion, then a rich purple, and once when they came down for family prayers, according to the simple rites of the Free American Reformed Episcopalian Church, they found it a bright emerald-green. These kaleidoscopic changes naturally amused the party very much, and bets on the subject were freely made every evening. The only person who did not enter into the joke was little Virginia, who, for some unexplained reason, was always a good deal distressed at the sight of the blood-stain, and very nearly cried the morning it was emerald-green.

The second appearance of the ghost was on Sunday night. Shortly after they had gone to bed they were suddenly alarmed by a fearful crash in the hall. Rushing down-stairs, they found that a large suit of old armour had become detached from its stand, and had fallen on the stone floor, while seated in a high-backed chair was the Canterville ghost, rubbing his knees with an expression of acute agony on his face. The twins, having brought their pea-shooters with them, at once discharged two pellets on him, with that accuracy of aim which can only be attained by long and careful practice on a writing-master, while the United States Minister covered him with his revolver, and called upon him, in accordance with Californian etiquette, to hold up his hands! The ghost started up with a wild shriek of rage, and swept through them like a mist, extinguishing Washington Otis's candle as he passed, and so leaving them all in total darkness. On reaching the top of the staircase he recovered himself, and determined to give his celebrated peal of demoniac laughter. This he had on more than one occasion found extremely useful. It was said to have turned Lord Raker's wig grey in a single night, and had certainly made three of Lady Canterville's French governesses give warning before their month was up. He accordingly laughed his most horrible laugh, till the old vaulted roof rang and rang again, but hardly had the fearful echo died away when a door opened, and Mrs. Otis came out in a light blue dressing-gown. "I am afraid you are far from well," she said, "and have brought you a bottle of Doctor Dobell's tincture. If it is indigestion, you will find it a most excellent remedy." The ghost glared at her in fury, and began at once to make preparations for turning himself into a large black dog, an accomplishment for which he was justly renowned, and to which the family doctor always attributed the permanent idiocy of Lord Canterville's uncle, the Hon. Thomas Horton. The sound of approaching footsteps, however, made him hesitate in his fell purpose, so he contented himself with becoming faintly phosphorescent, and vanished with a deep churchyard groan, just as the twins had come up to him.

On reaching his room he entirely broke down, and became a prey to the most violent agitation. The vulgarity of the twins, and the gross materialism of Mrs. Otis, were naturally extremely annoying, but what really distressed him most was that he had been unable to wear the suit of mail. He had hoped that even modern Americans would be thrilled by the sight of a Spectre in armour, if for no more sensible reason, at least out of respect for their natural poet Longfellow,[*] over whose graceful and attractive poetry he himself had whiled away many a weary hour when the Cantervilles were up in town. Besides it was his own suit. He had worn it with great success at the Kenilworth tournament,[†] and had been highly complimented on it by no less a person than the Virgin Queen herself. Yet when he had put it on, he had been completely overpowered by the weight of the huge breastplate and steel casque, and had fallen heavily on the stone pavement, barking both his knees severely, and bruising the knuckles of his right hand.

For some days after this he was extremely ill, and hardly stirred out of his room at all, except to keep the blood-stain in proper repair. However, by taking great care of himself, he recovered, and resolved to make a third attempt to frighten the United States Minister and his family. He selected Friday, August 17th,[‡] for his appearance, and spent most of that day in

---

[*] Henry Wadsworth Longfellow wrote several famous poems about ghosts, especially "Haunted Houses."

[†] Kenilworth Castle in Warwickshire was a popular site for medieval jousting tournaments.

[‡] Unfortunately for our dating of the events of this story, August 17 was not a Friday until 1888.

looking over his wardrobe, ultimately deciding in favour of a large slouched hat with a red feather, a winding-sheet frilled at the wrists and neck, and a rusty dagger. Towards evening a violent storm of rain came on, and the wind was so high that all the windows and doors in the old house shook and rattled. In fact, it was just such weather as he loved. His plan of action was this. He was to make his way quietly to Washington Otis's room, gibber at him from the foot of the bed, and stab himself three times in the throat to the sound of low music. He bore Washington a special grudge, being quite aware that it was he who was in the habit of removing the famous Canterville blood-stain by means of Pinkerton's Paragon Detergent. Having reduced the reckless and foolhardy youth to a condition of abject terror, he was then to proceed to the room occupied by the United States Minister and his wife, and there to place a clammy hand on Mrs. Otis's forehead, while he hissed into her trembling husband's ear the awful secrets of the charnel-house. With regard to little Virginia, he had not quite made up his mind. She had never insulted him in any way, and was pretty and gentle. A few hollow groans from the wardrobe, he thought, would be more than sufficient, or, if that failed to wake her, he might grabble at the counterpane with palsy-twitching fingers. As for the twins, he was quite determined to teach them a lesson. The first thing to be done was, of course, to sit upon their chests, so as to produce the stifling sensation of nightmare. Then, as their beds were quite close to each other, to stand between them in the form of a green, icy-cold corpse, till they became paralyzed with fear, and finally, to throw off the winding-sheet, and crawl round the room, with white, bleached bones and one rolling eyeball, in the character of "Dumb Daniel, or the Suicide's Skeleton," a *rôle* in which he had on more than one occasion produced a great effect, and which he considered quite equal to his famous part of "Martin the Maniac, or the Masked Mystery."*

At half-past ten he heard the family going to bed. For some time he was disturbed by wild shrieks of laughter from the twins, who, with the light-hearted gaiety of schoolboys, were evidently amusing themselves before they retired to rest, but at a quarter-past eleven all was still, and,

---

* The ghost's roles parody titles of shilling shockers (penny dreadfuls), popular pulp novels of the day.

as midnight sounded, he sallied forth. The owl beat against the window-panes, the raven croaked from the old yew-tree, and the wind wandered moaning round the house like a lost soul; but the Otis family slept unconscious of their doom, and high above the rain and storm he could hear the steady snoring of the Minister for the United States. He stepped stealthily out of the wainscoting, with an evil smile on his cruel, wrinkled mouth, and the moon hid her face in a cloud as he stole past the great oriel window,* where his own arms and those of his murdered wife were blazoned in azure and gold. On and on he glided, like an evil shadow, the very darkness seeming to loathe him as he passed. Once he thought he heard something call, and stopped; but it was only the baying of a dog from the Red Farm, and he went on, muttering strange sixteenth-century curses, and ever and anon brandishing the rusty dagger in the midnight air. Finally he reached the corner of the passage that led to luckless Washington's room. For a moment he paused there, the wind blowing his long grey locks about his head, and twisting into grotesque and fantastic folds the nameless horror of the dead man's shroud. Then the clock struck the quarter, and he felt the time was come. He chuckled to himself, and turned the corner; but no sooner had he done so than, with a piteous wail of terror, he fell back, and hid his blanched face in his long, bony hands. Right in front of him was standing a horrible spectre, motionless as a carven image, and monstrous as a madman's dream! Its head was bald and burnished; its face round, and fat, and white; and hideous laughter seemed to have writhed its features into an eternal grin. From the eyes streamed rays of scarlet light, the mouth was a wide well of fire, and a hideous garment, like to his own, swathed with its silent snows the Titan form. On its breast was a placard with strange writing in antique characters, some scroll of shame it seemed, some record of wild sins, some awful calendar of crime, and, with its right hand, it bore aloft a falchion of gleaming steel.

Never having seen a ghost before, he naturally was terribly frightened, and, after a second hasty glance at the awful phantom, he fled back to his room, tripping up in his long winding-sheet as he sped down the corridor,

---

* A bay window projecting from an upper story. One is prominently mentioned in Horace Walpole's gothic novel *The Castle of Otranto* (1764).

and finally dropping the rusty dagger into the Minister's jack-boots, where it was found in the morning by the butler. Once in the privacy of his own apartment, he flung himself down on a small pallet-bed, and hid his face under the clothes. After a time, however, the brave old Canterville spirit asserted itself, and he determined to go and speak to the other ghost as soon as it was daylight. Accordingly, just as the dawn was touching the hills with silver, he returned towards the spot where he had first laid eyes on the grisly phantom, feeling that, after all, two ghosts were better than one, and that, by the aid of his new friend, he might safely grapple with the twins. On reaching the spot, however, a terrible sight met his gaze. Something had evidently happened to the spectre, for the light had entirely faded from its hollow eyes, the gleaming falchion had fallen from its hand, and it was leaning up against the wall in a strained and uncomfortable attitude. He rushed forward and seized it in his arms, when, to his horror, the head slipped off and rolled on the floor, the body assumed a recumbent posture, and he found himself clasping a white dimity bed-curtain, with a sweeping-brush, a kitchen cleaver, and a hollow turnip lying at his feet! Unable to understand this curious transformation, he clutched the placard with feverish haste, and there, in the grey morning light, he read these fearful words—

YE OTIS GHOSTE
Ye Onlie True and Originale Spook,
Beware of Ye Imitationes.
All others are counterfeite.

The whole thing flashed across him. He had been tricked, foiled, and out-witted! The old Canterville look came into his eyes; he ground his toothless gums together; and, raising his withered hands high above his head, swore according to the picturesque phraseology of the antique school, that, when Chanticleer* had sounded twice his merry horn, deeds of blood would be wrought, and murder walk abroad with silent feet.

---

* A proud rooster depicted in Chaucer's *Canterbury Tales* (1387–1400).

Hardly had he finished this awful oath when, from the red-tiled roof of a distant homestead, a cock crew. He laughed a long, low, bitter laugh, and waited. Hour after hour he waited, but the cock, for some strange reason, did not crow again. Finally, at half-past seven, the arrival of the housemaids made him give up his fearful vigil, and he stalked back to his room, thinking of his vain oath and baffled purpose. There he consulted several books of ancient chivalry, of which he was exceedingly fond, and found that, on every occasion on which this oath had been used, Chanticleer had always crowed a second time. "Perdition seize the naughty fowl," he muttered, "I have seen the day when, with my stout spear, I would have run him through the gorge, and made him crow for me an 'twere in death!" He then retired to a comfortable lead coffin, and stayed there till evening.

IV

The next day the ghost was very weak and tired. The terrible excitement of the last four weeks was beginning to have its effect. His nerves were completely shattered, and he started at the slightest noise. For five days he kept his room, and at last made up his mind to give up the point of the blood-stain on the library floor. If the Otis family did not want it, they clearly did not deserve it. They were evidently people on a low, material plane of existence, and quite incapable of appreciating the symbolic value of sensuous phenomena. The question of phantasmic apparitions, and the development of astral bodies, was of course quite a different matter, and really not under his control. It was his solemn duty to appear in the corridor once a week, and to gibber from the large oriel window on the first and third Wednesdays in every month, and he did not see how he could honourably escape from his obligations. It is quite true that his life had been very evil, but, upon the other hand, he was most conscientious in all things connected with the supernatural. For the next three Saturdays, accordingly, he traversed the corridor as usual between midnight and three o'clock, taking every possible precaution against being either heard or seen. He removed his boots, trod as lightly as possible on the old worm-eaten boards, wore a large black velvet cloak, and was careful to use the Rising

Sun Lubricator for oiling his chains. I am bound to acknowledge that it was with a good deal of difficulty that he brought himself to adopt this last mode of protection. However, one night, while the family were at dinner, he slipped into Mr. Otis's bedroom and carried off the bottle. He felt a little humiliated at first, but afterwards was sensible enough to see that there was a great deal to be said for the invention, and, to a certain degree, it served his purpose. Still in spite of everything he was not left unmolested. Strings were continually being stretched across the corridor, over which he tripped in the dark, and on one occasion, while dressed for the part of "Black Isaac, or the Huntsman of Hogley Woods," he met with a severe fall, through treading on a butter-slide, which the twins had constructed from the entrance of the Tapestry Chamber to the top of the oak staircase. This last insult so enraged him, that he resolved to make one final effort to assert his dignity and social position, and determined to visit the insolent young Etonians the next night in his celebrated character of "Reckless Rupert, or the Headless Earl."

He had not appeared in this disguise for more than seventy years; in fact, not since he had so frightened pretty Lady Barbara Modish by means of it, that she suddenly broke off her engagement with the present Lord Canterville's grandfather, and ran away to Gretna Green with handsome Jack Castletown, declaring that nothing in the world would induce her to marry into a family that allowed such a horrible phantom to walk up and down the terrace at twilight. Poor Jack was afterwards shot in a duel by Lord Canterville on Wandsworth Common, and Lady Barbara died of a broken heart at Tunbridge Wells before the year was out, so, in every way, it had been a great success. It was, however an extremely difficult "make-up," if I may use such a theatrical expression in connection with one of the greatest mysteries of the supernatural, or, to employ a more scientific term, the higher-natural world, and it took him fully three hours to make his preparations. At last everything was ready, and he was very pleased with his appearance. The big leather riding-boots that went with the dress were just a little too large for him, and he could only find one of the two horse-pistols, but, on the whole, he was quite satisfied, and at a quarter-past one he glided out of the wainscoting and crept down the corridor. On reaching the room occupied by the twins, which I should mention was called the Blue Bed Chamber, on account of the colour of its hangings, he found the door just ajar. Wishing to make an effective entrance, he flung it wide open, when a heavy jug of water fell right down on him, wetting him to the skin, and just missing his left shoulder by a couple of inches. At the same moment he heard stifled shrieks of laughter proceeding from the four-post bed. The shock to his nervous system was so great that he fled back to his room as hard as he could go, and the next day he was laid up with a severe cold. The only thing that at all consoled him in the whole affair was the fact that he had not brought his head with him, for, had he done so, the consequences might have been very serious.

He now gave up all hope of ever frightening this rude American family, and contented himself, as a rule, with creeping about the passages in list slippers, with a thick red muffler round his throat for fear of draughts, and a small arquebuse,* in case he should be attacked by the twins. The final blow he received occurred on the 19th of September. He had gone down-stairs to the great entrance-hall, feeling sure that there, at any rate, he would be quite unmolested, and was amusing himself by making satirical remarks on the large Saroni photographs† of the United States Minister and his wife which had now taken the place of the Canterville family pictures. He was simply but neatly clad in a long shroud, spotted with churchyard mould, had tied up his jaw with a strip of yellow linen, and carried a small lantern and a sexton's spade. In fact, he was dressed for the character of "Jonas the Graveless, or the Corpse-Snatcher of Chertsey Barn," one of his most remarkable impersonations, and one which the Cantervilles had every reason to remember, as it was the real origin of their quarrel with their neighbour, Lord Rufford. It was about a quarter-past two o'clock in

---

* A fifteenth-century gun.

† Napoleon Sarony was a famous American photographer of the day, especially known for portraits. In the late nineteenth century, photographers usually paid the subject for the right to take the subject's photograph and then sold copies for a profit. Oscar Wilde was one of Sarony's subjects before this story was first published. When an American publisher copied one of Sarony's photographs of Wilde in an advertisement, Sarony sued. The case went to the US Supreme Court (*Burrow-Giles Lithographic Co. v. Sarony*) and, ruling for Sarony, the court established the principle that copyright protection extended to photographs.

the morning, and, as far as he could ascertain, no one was stirring. As he was strolling towards the library, however, to see if there were any traces left of the blood-stain, suddenly there leaped out on him from a dark corner two figures, who waved their arms wildly above their heads, and shrieked out "BOO!" in his ear.

Seized with a panic, which, under the circumstances, was only natural, he rushed for the staircase, but found Washington Otis waiting for him there with the big garden-syringe, and being thus hemmed in by his enemies on every side, and driven almost to bay, he vanished into the great iron stove, which, fortunately for him, was not lit, and had to make his way home through the flues and chimneys, arriving at his own room in a terrible state of dirt, disorder, and despair.

After this he was not seen again on any nocturnal expedition. The twins lay in wait for him on several occasions, and strewed the passages with nutshells every night to the great annoyance of their parents and the servants, but it was of no avail. It was quite evident that his feelings were so wounded that he would not appear. Mr. Otis consequently resumed his great work on the history of the Democratic Party, on which he had been engaged for some years; Mrs. Otis organized a wonderful clam-bake, which amazed the whole county; the boys took to lacrosse, euchre, poker, and other American national games, and Virginia rode about the lanes on her pony, accompanied by the young Duke of Cheshire, who had come to spend the last week of his holidays at Canterville Chase. It was generally assumed that the ghost had gone away, and, in fact, Mr. Otis wrote a letter to that effect to Lord Canterville, who, in reply, expressed his great pleasure at the news, and sent his best congratulations to the Minister's worthy wife.

The Otises, however, were deceived, for the ghost was still in the house, and though now almost an invalid, was by no means ready to let matters rest, particularly as he heard that among the guests was the young Duke of Cheshire, whose grand-uncle, Lord Francis Stilton, had once bet a hundred guineas with Colonel Carbury that he would play dice with the Canterville ghost, and was found the next morning lying on the floor of the card-room in such a helpless paralytic state that, though he lived on to a great age, he was never able to say anything again but "Double Sixes." The story was well known at the time, though, of course, out of respect to the feelings of the two noble families, every attempt was made to hush it up, and a full account of all the circumstances connected with it will be found in the third volume of Lord Tattle's *Recollections of the Prince Regent and his Friends.* The ghost, then, was naturally very anxious to show that he had not lost his influence over the Stiltons, with whom, indeed, he was distantly connected, his own first cousin having been married *en secondes noces** to the Sieur de Bulkeley, from whom, as every one knows, the Dukes of Cheshire are lineally descended. Accordingly, he made arrangements for appearing to Virginia's little lover in his celebrated impersonation of "The Vampire Monk, or the Bloodless Benedictine," a performance so horrible that when old Lady Startup saw it, which she did on one fatal New Year's Eve, in the year 1764, she went off into the most piercing shrieks, which culminated in violent apoplexy, and died in three days, after disinheriting the Cantervilles, who were her nearest relations, and leaving all her money to her London apothecary. At the last moment, however, his terror of the twins prevented his leaving his room, and the little Duke slept in peace under the great feathered canopy in the Royal Bedchamber, and dreamed of Virginia.

V

A few days after this, Virginia and her curly-haired cavalier went out riding on Brockley meadows, where she tore her habit† so badly in getting through a hedge that, on their return home, she made up her mind to go up by the back staircase so as not to be seen. As she was running past the Tapestry Chamber, the door of which happened to be open, she fancied she saw some one inside, and thinking it was her mother's maid, who sometimes used to bring her work there, looked in to ask her to mend her habit. To her immense surprise, however, it was the Canterville Ghost himself! He was sitting by the window, watching the ruined gold of the yellowing trees fly through the air, and the red leaves dancing madly down the long

---

* A second marriage.

† A woman's riding-dress.

avenue. His head was leaning on his hand, and his whole attitude was one of extreme depression. Indeed, so forlorn, and so much out of repair did he look, that little Virginia, whose first idea had been to run away and lock herself in her room, was filled with pity, and determined to try and comfort him. So light was her footfall, and so deep his melancholy, that he was not aware of her presence till she spoke to him.

"I am so sorry for you," she said, "but my brothers are going back to Eton to-morrow, and then, if you behave yourself, no one will annoy you."

"It is absurd asking me to behave myself," he answered, looking round in astonishment at the pretty little girl who had ventured to address him, "quite absurd. I must rattle my chains, and groan through keyholes, and walk about at night, if that is what you mean. It is my only reason for existing."

"It is no reason at all for existing, and you know you have been very wicked. Mrs. Umney told us, the first day we arrived here, that you had killed your wife."

"Well, I quite admit it," said the Ghost, petulantly, "but it was a purely family matter, and concerned no one else."

"It is very wrong to kill any one," said Virginia, who at times had a sweet puritan gravity, caught from some old New England ancestor.

"Oh, I hate the cheap severity of abstract ethics! My wife was very plain, never had my ruffs properly starched, and knew nothing about cookery. Why, there was a buck I had shot in Hogley Woods, a magnificent pricket,* and do you know how she had it sent to table? However, it is no matter now, for it is all over, and I don't think it was very nice of her brothers to starve me to death, though I did kill her."

"Starve you to death? Oh, Mr. Ghost—I mean Sir Simon, are you hungry? I have a sandwich in my case. Would you like it?"

"No, thank you, I never eat anything now; but it is very kind of you, all the same, and you are much nicer than the rest of your horrid, rude, vulgar, dishonest family."

"Stop!" cried Virginia, stamping her foot, "it is you who are rude, and horrid, and vulgar, and as for dishonesty, you know you stole the paints out of my box to try and furbish up that ridiculous blood-stain in the library.

---

* A young male deer with straight, unbranched antlers.

First you took all my reds, including the vermilion, and I couldn't do any more sunsets, then you took the emerald-green and the chrome-yellow, and finally I had nothing left but indigo and Chinese white,* and could only do moonlight scenes, which are always depressing to look at, and not at all easy to paint. I never told on you, though I was very much annoyed, and it was most ridiculous, the whole thing; for who ever heard of emerald-green blood?"

"Well, really," said the Ghost, rather meekly, "what was I to do? It is a very difficult thing to get real blood nowadays, and, as your brother began it all with his Paragon Detergent, I certainly saw no reason why I should not have your paints. As for colour, that is always a matter of taste: the Cantervilles have blue blood, for instance, the very bluest in England; but I know you Americans don't care for things of this kind."

"You know nothing about it, and the best thing you can do is to emigrate and improve your mind. My father will be only too happy to give you a free passage, and though there is a heavy duty on spirits of every kind,† there will be no difficulty about the Custom House, as the officers are all Democrats. Once in New York, you are sure to be a great success. I know lots of people there who would give a hundred thousand dollars to have a grandfather, and much more than that to have a family ghost."

"I don't think I should like America."

"I suppose because we have no ruins and no curiosities," said Virginia, satirically.

"No ruins! No curiosities!" answered the Ghost; "you have your navy and your manners."

"Good evening; I will go and ask papa to get the twins an extra week's holiday."

"Please don't go, Miss Virginia," he cried; "I am so lonely and so unhappy, and I really don't know what to do. I want to go to sleep and I cannot."

"That's quite absurd! You have merely to go to bed and blow out the candle. It is very difficult sometimes to keep awake, especially at church, but there is no difficulty at all about sleeping. Why, even babies know how to do that, and they are not very clever."

---

* A white color with a blue undertone.

† She is joking: There was a heavy duty on alcoholic spirits.

"I have not slept for three hundred years," he said sadly, and Virginia's beautiful blue eyes opened in wonder; "for three hundred years I have not slept, and I am so tired."

Virginia grew quite grave, and her little lips trembled like rose-leaves. She came towards him, and kneeling down at his side, looked up into his old withered face.

"Poor, poor Ghost," she murmured; "have you no place where you can sleep?"

"Far away beyond the pine-woods," he answered, in a low, dreamy voice, "there is a little garden. There the grass grows long and deep, there are the great white stars of the hemlock flower, there the nightingale sings all night long. All night long he sings, and the cold crystal moon looks down, and the yew-tree spreads out its giant arms over the sleepers."

Virginia's eyes grew dim with tears, and she hid her face in her hands.

"You mean the Garden of Death," she whispered.

"Yes, death. Death must be so beautiful. To lie in the soft brown earth, with the grasses waving above one's head, and listen to silence. To have no yesterday, and no to-morrow. To forget time, to forget life, to be at peace. You can help me. You can open for me the portals of death's house, for love is always with you, and love is stronger than death is."

Virginia trembled, a cold shudder ran through her, and for a few moments there was silence. She felt as if she was in a terrible dream.

Then the ghost spoke again, and his voice sounded like the sighing of the wind.

"Have you ever read the old prophecy on the library window?"

"Oh, often," cried the little girl, looking up; "I know it quite well. It is painted in curious black letters, and is difficult to read. There are only six lines:

"'When a golden girl can win
Prayer from out the lips of sin,
When the barren almond bears,
And a little child gives away its tears,
Then shall all the house be still
And peace come to Canterville.'
But I don't know what they mean."

"They mean," he said, sadly, "that you must weep with me for my sins, because I have no tears, and pray with me for my soul, because I have no faith, and then, if you have always been sweet, and good, and gentle, the angel of death will have mercy on me. You will see fearful shapes in darkness, and wicked voices will whisper in your ear, but they will not harm you, for against the purity of a little child the powers of Hell cannot prevail."

Virginia made no answer, and the ghost wrung his hands in wild despair as he looked down at her bowed golden head. Suddenly she stood up, very pale, and with a strange light in her eyes. "I am not afraid," she said firmly, "and I will ask the angel to have mercy on you."

He rose from his seat with a faint cry of joy, and taking her hand bent over it with old-fashioned grace and kissed it. His fingers were as cold as ice, and his lips burned like fire, but Virginia did not falter, as he led her across the dusky room. On the faded green tapestry were broidered little huntsmen. They blew their tasselled horns and with their tiny hands waved to her to go back. "Go back! little Virginia," they cried, "go back!" but the ghost clutched her hand more tightly, and she shut her eyes against them. Horrible animals with lizard tails and goggle eyes blinked at her from the carven chimneypiece, and murmured, "Beware! little Virginia, beware! we may never see you again," but the Ghost glided on more swiftly, and Virginia did not listen. When they reached the end of the room he stopped, and muttered some words she could not understand. She opened her eyes, and saw the wall slowly fading away like a mist, and a great black cavern in front of her. A bitter cold wind swept round them, and she felt something pulling at her dress. "Quick, quick," cried the Ghost, "or it will be too late," and in a moment the wainscoting had closed behind them, and the Tapestry Chamber was empty.

VI

About ten minutes later, the bell rang for tea, and, as Virginia did not come down, Mrs. Otis sent up one of the footmen to tell her. After a little time he returned and said that he could not find Miss Virginia anywhere. As she was in the habit of going out to the garden every evening to get flowers for the dinner-table, Mrs. Otis was not at all alarmed at first, but when six o'clock struck, and Virginia did not appear, she became really agitated, and sent the boys out to look for her, while she herself and Mr. Otis searched every room in the house. At half-past six the boys came back and said that they could find no trace of their sister anywhere. They were all now in the greatest state of excitement, and did not know what to do, when Mr. Otis suddenly remembered that, some few days before, he had given a band of gipsies permission to camp in the park. He accordingly at once set off for Blackfell Hollow, where he knew they were, accompanied by his eldest son and two of the farm-servants. The little Duke of Cheshire, who was perfectly frantic with anxiety, begged hard to be allowed to go too, but Mr. Otis would not allow him, as he was afraid there might be a scuffle. On arriving at the spot, however, he found that the gipsies had gone, and it was evident that their departure had been rather sudden, as the fire was still burning, and some plates were lying on the grass. Having sent off Washington and the two men to scour the district, he ran home, and despatched telegrams to all the police inspectors in the county, telling them to look out for a little girl who had been kidnapped by tramps or gipsies. He then ordered his horse to be brought round, and, after insisting on his wife and the three boys sitting down to dinner, rode off down the Ascot road with a groom. He had hardly, however, gone a couple of miles, when he heard somebody galloping after him, and, looking round, saw the little Duke coming up on his pony, with his face very flushed, and no hat. "I'm awfully sorry, Mr. Otis," gasped out the boy, "but I can't eat any dinner as long as Virginia is lost. Please don't be angry with me; if you had let us be engaged last year, there would never have been all this trouble. You won't send me back, will you? I can't go! I won't go!"

The Minister could not help smiling at the handsome young scapegrace, and was a good deal touched at his devotion to Virginia, so leaning down from his horse, he patted him kindly on the shoulders, and said, "Well, Cecil, if you won't go back, I suppose you must come with me, but I must get you a hat at Ascot."

"Oh, bother my hat! I want Virginia!" cried the little Duke, laughing, and they galloped on to the railway station. There Mr. Otis inquired of the station-master if any one answering to the description of Virginia had been seen on the platform, but could get no news of her. The station-master, however, wired up and down the line, and assured him that a strict watch would be kept for her, and, after having bought a hat for the little Duke from a linen-draper, who was just putting up his shutters, Mr. Otis rode off to Bexley, a village about four miles away, which he was told was a well-known haunt of the gipsies, as there was a large common next to it. Here they roused up the rural policeman, but could get no information from him, and, after riding all over the common, they turned their horses' heads homewards, and reached the Chase about eleven o'clock, dead-tired and almost heart-broken. They found Washington and the twins waiting for them at the gate-house with lanterns, as the avenue was very dark. Not the slightest trace of Virginia had been discovered. The gipsies had been caught on Brockley meadows, but she was not with them, and they had explained their sudden departure by saying that they had mistaken the date of Chorton Fair, and had gone off in a hurry for fear they should be late. Indeed, they had been quite distressed at hearing of Virginia's disappearance, as they were very grateful to Mr. Otis for having allowed them to camp in his park, and four of their number had stayed behind to help in the search. The carp-pond had been dragged, and the whole Chase thoroughly gone over, but without any result. It was evident that, for that night at any rate, Virginia was lost to them; and it was in a state of the deepest depression that Mr. Otis and the boys walked up to the house, the groom following behind with the two horses and the pony. In the hall they found a group of frightened servants, and lying on a sofa in the library was poor Mrs. Otis, almost out of her mind with terror and anxiety, and having her forehead bathed with eau de cologne by the old housekeeper. Mr. Otis at once insisted on her having something to eat, and ordered up supper for the whole party. It was a melancholy meal, as hardly any one spoke, and even the twins were awestruck and subdued, as they were very fond of their sister. When they had finished, Mr. Otis, in spite of the entreaties of the little Duke, ordered them all to bed, saying that nothing more could be done that night, and that he would telegraph in the morning to Scotland Yard for some detectives to be sent down immediately. Just as they were passing out of the dining-room, midnight began to boom from the clock tower, and when the last stroke sounded they heard a crash and a sudden shrill cry; a dreadful peal of thunder shook the house, a strain of unearthly music floated through the air, a panel at the top of the staircase flew back with a loud noise, and out on the landing, looking very pale and white, with a little casket in her hand, stepped Virginia. In a moment they had all rushed up to her. Mrs. Otis clasped her passionately in her arms, the Duke smothered her with violent kisses, and the twins executed a wild war-dance round the group.

"Good heavens! Child, where have you been?" said Mr. Otis, rather angrily, thinking that she had been playing some foolish trick on them. "Cecil and I have been riding all over the country looking for you, and your mother has been frightened to death. You must never play these practical jokes any more."

"Except on the Ghost! Except on the Ghost!" shrieked the twins, as they capered about.

"My own darling, thank God you are found; you must never leave my side again," murmured Mrs. Otis, as she kissed the trembling child, and smoothed the tangled gold of her hair.

"Papa," said Virginia, quietly, "I have been with the Ghost. He is dead, and you must come and see him. He had been very wicked, but he was really sorry for all that he had done, and he gave me this box of beautiful jewels before he died."

The whole family gazed at her in mute amazement, but she was quite grave and serious; and, turning round, she led them through the opening in the wainscoting down a narrow secret corridor, Washington following with a lighted candle, which he had caught up from the table. Finally, they came to a great oak door, studded with rusty nails. When Virginia touched it, it swung back on its heavy hinges, and they found themselves in a little low room, with a vaulted ceiling, and one tiny grated window. Imbedded in the wall was a huge iron ring, and chained to it was a gaunt skeleton, that was stretched out at full length on the stone floor, and seemed to be trying to grasp with its long fleshless fingers an old-fashioned trencher and ewer, that were placed just out of its reach. The jug had evidently been once filled with water, as it was covered inside with green mould. There was nothing on the trencher but a pile of dust. Virginia knelt down beside the skeleton, and, folding her little hands together, began to pray silently, while the rest of the party looked on in wonder at the terrible tragedy whose secret was now disclosed to them.

"Hallo!" suddenly exclaimed one of the twins, who had been looking out of the window to try and discover in what wing of the house the room was situated. "Hallo! The old withered almond-tree has blossomed. I can see the flowers quite plainly in the moonlight."

"God has forgiven him," said Virginia, gravely, as she rose to her feet, and a beautiful light seemed to illumine her face.

"What an angel you are!" cried the young Duke, and he put his arm round her neck, and kissed her.

VII

Four days after these curious incidents, a funeral started from Canterville Chase at about eleven o'clock at night. The hearse was drawn by eight black horses, each of which carried on its head a great tuft of nodding ostrich-plumes, and the leaden coffin was covered by a rich purple pall, on which was embroidered in gold the Canterville coat-of-arms. By the side of the hearse and the coaches walked the servants with lighted torches, and the whole procession was wonderfully impressive. Lord Canterville was the chief mourner, having come up specially from Wales to attend the funeral, and sat in the first carriage along with little Virginia. Then came the United States Minister and his wife, then Washington and the three boys, and in the last carriage was Mrs. Umney. It was generally felt that, as she had been frightened by the ghost for more than fifty years of her life, she had a right to see the last of him. A deep grave had been dug in the corner of the churchyard, just under the old yew-tree, and the service was read in the most impressive manner by the Rev. Augustus Dampier. When the ceremony was over, the servants, according to an old custom observed in the Canterville family, extinguished their torches, and, as the coffin was being lowered into the grave, Virginia stepped forward, and laid on it a large cross made of white and pink almond-blossoms. As she did so, the moon came out from behind a cloud, and flooded with its silent silver the little churchyard, and from a distant copse a nightingale began to sing. She thought of the ghost's description of the Garden of

Death, her eyes became dim with tears, and she hardly spoke a word during the drive home.

The next morning, before Lord Canterville went up to town, Mr. Otis had an interview with him on the subject of the jewels the ghost had given to Virginia. They were perfectly magnificent, especially a certain ruby necklace with old Venetian setting, which was really a superb specimen of sixteenth-century work, and their value was so great that Mr. Otis felt considerable scruples about allowing his daughter to accept them.

"My lord," he said, "I know that in this country mortmain* is held to apply to trinkets as well as to land, and it is quite clear to me that these jewels are, or should be, heirlooms in your family. I must beg you, accordingly, to take them to London with you, and to regard them simply as a portion of your property which has been restored to you under certain strange conditions. As for my daughter, she is merely a child, and has as yet, I am glad to say, but little interest in such appurtenances of idle luxury. I am also informed by Mrs. Otis, who, I may say, is no mean authority upon Art—having had the privilege of spending several winters in Boston when she was a girl—that these gems are of great monetary worth, and if offered for sale would fetch a tall price. Under these circumstances, Lord Canterville, I feel sure that you will recognize how impossible it would be for me to allow them to remain in the possession of any member of my family; and, indeed, all such vain gauds and toys, however suitable or necessary to the dignity of the British aristocracy, would be completely out of place among those who have been brought up on the severe, and I believe immortal, principles of Republican simplicity. Perhaps I should mention that Virginia is very anxious that you should allow her to retain the box, as a memento of your unfortunate but misguided ancestor. As it is extremely old, and consequently a good deal out of repair, you may perhaps think fit to comply with her request. For my own part, I confess I am a good deal surprised to find a child of mine expressing sympathy with mediævalism in any form, and can only account for it by the fact that Virginia was born in one of your London suburbs shortly after Mrs. Otis had returned from a trip to Athens."

---

* This is not an accurate use of the term, but figuratively, mortmain means post-mortem control over property by a testator.

Lord Canterville listened very gravely to the worthy Minister's speech, pulling his grey moustache now and then to hide an involuntary smile, and when Mr. Otis had ended, he shook him cordially by the hand, and said: "My dear sir, your charming little daughter rendered my unlucky ancestor, Sir Simon, a very important service, and I and my family are much indebted to her for her marvellous courage and pluck. The jewels are clearly hers, and, egad, I believe that if I were heartless enough to take them from her, the wicked old fellow would be out of his grave in a fortnight, leading me the devil of a life. As for their being heirlooms, nothing is an heirloom that is not so mentioned in a will or legal document, and the existence of these jewels has been quite unknown. I assure you I have no more claim on them than your butler, and when Miss Virginia grows up, I dare say she will be pleased to have pretty things to wear. Besides, you forget, Mr. Otis, that you took the furniture and the ghost at a valuation, and anything that belonged to the ghost passed at once into your possession, as, whatever activity Sir Simon may have shown in the corridor at night, in point of law he was really dead, and you acquired his property by purchase."

Mr. Otis was a good deal distressed at Lord Canterville's refusal, and begged him to reconsider his decision, but the good-natured peer was quite firm, and finally induced the Minister to allow his daughter to retain the present the ghost had given her, and when, in the spring of 1890, the young Duchess of Cheshire was presented at the Queen's first drawing-room on the occasion of her marriage, her jewels were the universal theme of admiration. For Virginia received the coronet, which is the reward of all good little American girls, and was married to her boy-lover as soon as he came of age. They were both so charming, and they loved each other so much, that every one was delighted at the match, except the old Marchioness of Dumbleton, who had tried to catch the Duke for one of her seven unmarried daughters, and had given no less than three expensive dinner-parties for that purpose, and, strange to say, Mr. Otis himself. Mr. Otis was extremely fond of the young Duke personally, but, theoretically, he objected to titles, and, to use his own words, "was not without apprehension lest, amid the enervating influences of a pleasure-loving aristocracy, the true principles of Republican simplicity should be forgotten." His objections, however, were completely overruled, and I believe that when he walked up the aisle of St. George's, Hanover Square, with his daughter leaning on his arm, there was not a prouder man in the whole length and breadth of England.

The Duke and Duchess, after the honeymoon was over, went down to Canterville Chase, and on the day after their arrival they walked over in the afternoon to the lonely churchyard by the pine-woods. There had been a great deal of difficulty at first about the inscription on Sir Simon's tombstone, but finally it had been decided to engrave on it simply the initials of the old gentleman's name, and the verse from the library window. The Duchess had brought with her some lovely roses, which she strewed upon the grave, and after they had stood by it for some time they strolled into the ruined chancel of the old abbey. There the Duchess sat down on a fallen pillar, while her husband lay at her feet smoking a cigarette and looking up at her beautiful eyes. Suddenly he threw his cigarette away, took hold of her hand, and said to her, "Virginia, a wife should have no secrets from her husband."

"Dear Cecil! I have no secrets from you."

"Yes, you have," he answered, smiling, "you have never told me what happened to you when you were locked up with the ghost."

"I have never told any one, Cecil," said Virginia, gravely.

"I know that, but you might tell me."

"Please don't ask me, Cecil, I cannot tell you. Poor Sir Simon! I owe him a great deal. Yes, don't laugh, Cecil, I really do. He made me see what Life is, and what Death signifies, and why Love is stronger than both."

The Duke rose and kissed his wife lovingly.

"You can have your secret as long as I have your heart," he murmured.

"You have always had that, Cecil."

"And you will tell our children some day, won't you?"

Virginia blushed.

ROSA MULHOLLAND *(1841–1921) was an Irish author and poet whose work, like her 1872 novel* The Wicked Woods of Toberevil, *often incorporates elements of Irish folklore. She was born into a prosperous family and, in 1891, married the eminent historian John T. Gilbert, who was knighted in 1897. Rosa achieved her greatest success writing for Charles Dickens; she became one of the select stable of authors—which also included Elizabeth Gaskell and Amelia B. Edwards—who provided the ghost stories for the annual Christmas issues of his magazines. "The Haunted Organist of Hurly Burly" first appeared in the September 1886 magazine the* Irish Monthly.

THE HAUNTED ORGANIST
OF HURLY BURLY

by Rosa Mulholland

(1891)

There had been a thunderstorm in the village of Hurly Burly.* Every door was shut, every dog in his kennel, every rut and gutter a flowing river after the deluge of rain that had fallen. Up at the great house, a mile from the town, the rooks were calling to one another about the fright they had been in, the fawns in the deer-park were venturing their timid heads from behind the trunks of trees, and the old woman at the gate-lodge had risen from her knees, and was putting back her prayer-book on the shelf. In the garden, July roses, unwieldy with their full-blown richness, and saturated

---

* A fictitious place name. Colloquially, this means a commotion or tumultuous gathering. The origin of the phrase is unknown, though it may be traced back to the 15th century. Here, it is used comically, as derived from the family name.

with rain, hung their heads heavily to the earth; others, already fallen, lay flat upon their blooming faces on the path, where Bess, Mistress Hurly's maid, would find them, when going on her morning quest of rose-leaves for her lady's pot-pourri. Ranks of white lilies, just brought to perfection by today's sun, lay dabbled in the mire of flooded mould. Tears ran down the amber cheeks of the plums on the south wall, and not a bee had ventured out of the hives, though the scent of the air was sweet enough to tempt the laziest drone. The sky was still lurid behind the boles of the upland oaks, but the birds had begun to dive in and out of the ivy that wrapped up the home of the Hurlys of Hurly Burly.

This thunderstorm took place more than half a century ago, and we must remember that Mistress Hurly was dressed in the fashion of that time as she crept out from behind the squire's chair, now that the lightning was over, and, with many nervous glances towards the window, sat down before her husband, the tea-urn, and the muffins. We can picture her fine lace cap, with its peachy ribbons, the frill on the hem of her cambric* gown just touching her ankles, the embroidered clocks on her stockings, the rosettes on her shoes, but not so easily the lilac shade of her mild eyes, the satin skin, which still kept its delicate bloom, though wrinkled with advancing age, and the pale, sweet, puckered mouth, that time and sorrow had made angelic while trying vainly to deface its beauty.

The squire was as rugged as his wife was gentle, his skin as brown as hers was white, his grey hair as bristling as hers was glossed; the years had ploughed his face into ruts and channels; a bluff, choleric, noisy man he had been; but of late a dimness had come on his eyes, a hush on his loud voice, and a check on the spring of his hale step. He looked at his wife often, and very often she looked at him. She was not a tall woman, and he was only a head higher. They were a quaintly well-matched couple, despite their differences. She turned to you with nervous sharpness and revealed her tender voice and eye; he spoke and glanced roughly, but the turn of his head was courteous. Of late they fitted one another better than they had ever done in the heyday of their youthful love. A common sorrow had developed a singular likeness between them. In former years the cry from the wife had been, "Don't curb my son too much!" and from the

---

* Cambric is a dense but lightweight linen or cotton fabric.

husband, "You ruin the lad with softness." But now the idol that had stood between them was removed, and they saw each other better.

The room in which they sat was a pleasant old-fashioned drawing-room, with a general spider-legged character about the fittings; spinnet* and guitar in their places, with a great deal of copied music beside them; carpet, tawny wreaths on the pale blue; blue flutings on the walls, and faint gilding on the furniture. A huge urn, crammed with roses, in the open bay-window, through which came delicious airs from the garden, the twittering of birds settling to sleep in the ivy close by, and occasionally the pattering of a flight of rain-drops, swept to the ground as a bough bent in the breeze. The urn on the table was ancient silver, and the china rare. There was nothing in the room for luxurious ease of the body, but everything of delicate refinement for the eye.

There was a great hush all over Hurly Burly, except in the neighbourhood of the rooks. Every living thing had suffered from heat for the past month, and now, in common with all Nature, was receiving the boon of refreshed air in silent peace. The mistress and master of Hurly Burly shared the general spirit that was abroad, and were not talkative over their tea.

"Do you know," said Mistress Hurly, at last, "when I heard the first of the thunder beginning I thought it was—it was—"

The lady broke down, her lips trembling, and the peachy ribbons of her cap stirring with great agitation.

"Pshaw!" cried the old squire, making his cup suddenly ring upon the saucer, "we ought to have forgotten that. Nothing has been heard for three months."

At this moment a rolling sound struck upon the ears of both. The lady rose from her seat trembling, and folded her hands together, while the tea-urn flooded the tray.

"Nonsense, my love," said the squire; "that is the noise of wheels. Who can be arriving?"

"Who, indeed?" murmured the lady, reseating herself in agitation.

Presently pretty Bess of the rose-leaves appeared at the door in a flutter of blue ribbons.

---

* A spinet or spinnet is a keyed instrument like a harpsichord, though usually smaller.

"Please, madam, a lady has arrived, and says she is expected. She asked for her apartment, and I put her into the room that was got ready for Miss Calderwood. And she sends her respects to you, madam, and she'll be down with you presently."

The squire looked at his wife, and his wife looked at the squire.

"It is some mistake," murmured madam. "Some visitor for Calderwood or the Grange.* It is very singular."

Hardly had she spoken when the door again opened, and the stranger appeared—a small creature, whether girl or woman it would be hard to say—dressed in a scanty black silk dress, her narrow shoulders covered with a white muslin pelerine.† Her hair was swept up to the crown of her head, all but a little fringe hanging over her low forehead within an inch of her brows. Her face was brown and thin, eyes black and long, with blacker settings, mouth large, sweet, and melancholy. She was all head, mouth, and eyes; her nose and chin were nothing.

This visitor crossed the floor hastily, dropped a courtesy in the middle of the room, and approached the table, saying abruptly, with a soft Italian accent:

"Sir and madam, I am here. I am come to play your organ."

"The organ!" gasped Mistress Hurly.

"The organ!" stammered the squire.

"Yes, the organ," said the little stranger lady, playing on the back of a chair with her fingers, as if she felt notes under them. "It was but last week that the handsome signor, your son, came to my little house, where I have lived teaching music since my English father and my Italian mother and brothers and sisters died and left me so lonely."

Here the fingers left off drumming, and two great tears were brushed off, one from each eye with each hand, child's fashion. But the next moment the fingers were at work again, as if only whilst they were moving the tongue could speak.

---

* Although there was a Calderwood in Scotland until the mid-twentieth century, these are likely more fictitious names.

† A woman's short cape.

"The noble signor, your son," said the little woman, looking trustfully from one to the other of the old couple, while a bright blush shone through her brown skin, "he often came to see me before that, always in the evening, when the sun was warm and yellow all through my little studio, and the music was swelling my heart, and I could play out grand with all my soul; then he used to come and say, 'Hurry, little Lisa, and play better, better still. I have work for you to do by-and-by.' Sometimes he said, 'Brava!' and sometimes he said 'Eccellentissima!' but one night last week he came to me and said, 'It is enough. Will you swear to do my bidding, whatever it may be?' Here the black eyes fell. And I said, 'Yes.' And he said, 'Now you are my betrothed.' And I said, 'Yes.' And he said, 'Pack up your music, little Lisa, and go off to England to my English father and mother, who have an organ in their house which must be played upon. If they refuse to let you play, tell them I sent you, and they will give you leave. You must play all day, and you must get up in the night and play. You must never tire. You are my betrothed, and you have sworn to do my work.' I said, 'Shall I see you there, signor?' And he said, 'Yes, you shall see me there.' I said, 'I will keep my vow, Signor.' And so, sir and madam, I am come."

The soft foreign voice left off talking, the fingers left off thrumming on the chair, and the little stranger gazed in dismay at her auditors, both pale with agitation.

"You are deceived. You make a mistake," said they in one breath.

"Our son—" began Mistress Hurly, but her mouth twitched, her voice broke, and she looked piteously towards her husband.

"Our son," said the squire, making an effort to conquer the quavering in his voice, "our son is long dead."

"Nay, nay," said the little foreigner. "If you have thought him dead have good cheer, dear sir and madam. He is alive; he is well, and strong, and handsome. But one, two, three, four, five" (on the fingers) "days ago he stood by my side."

"It is some strange mistake, some wonderful coincidence!" said the mistress and master of Hurly Burly.

"Let us take her to the gallery," murmured the mother of this son who was thus dead and alive.

"There is yet light to see the pictures. She will not know his portrait."

The bewildered wife and husband led their strange visitor away to a long gloomy room at the west side of the house, where the faint gleams from the darkening sky still lingered on the portraits of the Hurly family.

"Doubtless he is like this," said the squire, pointing to a fair-haired young man with a mild face, a brother of his own who had been lost at sea.

But Lisa shook her head, and went softly on tiptoe from one picture to another, peering into the canvas, and still turning away troubled. But at last a shriek of delight startled the shadowy chamber.

"Ah, here he is! See, here he is, the noble signor, the beautiful signor, not half so handsome as he looked five days ago, when talking to poor little Lisa! Dear sir and madam, you are now content. Now take me to the organ, that I may commence to do his bidding at once."

The mistress of Hurly Burly clung fast by her husband's arm. "How old are you, girl?" she said faintly.

"Eighteen," said the visitor impatiently, moving towards the door.

"And my son has been dead for twenty years!" said his mother, and swooned on her husband's breast.

"Order the carriage at once," said Mistress Hurly, recovering from her swoon; "I will take her to Margaret Calderwood. Margaret will tell her the story. Margaret will bring her to reason. No, not tomorrow; I cannot bear tomorrow, it is so far away. We must go tonight."

The little signora thought the old lady mad, but she put on her cloak again obediently, and took her seat beside Mistress Hurly in the Hurly family coach. The moon that looked in at them through the pane as they lumbered along was not whiter than the aged face of the squire's wife, whose dim faded eyes were fixed upon it in doubt and awe too great for tears or words. Lisa, too, from her corner gloated upon the moon, her black eyes shining with passionate dreams.

A carriage rolled away from the Calderwood door as the Hurly coach drew up at the steps.

Margaret Calderwood had just returned from a dinner-party, and at the open door a splendid figure was standing, a tall woman dressed in brown velvet, the diamonds on her bosom glistening in the moonlight that revealed her, pouring, as it did, over the house from eaves to basement. Mistress Hurly fell into her outstretched arms with a groan, and the strong woman carried her aged friend, like a baby, into the house. Little Lisa was over-looked, and sat down contentedly on the threshold to gloat awhile longer on the moon, and to thrum imaginary sonatas on the doorstep.

There were tears and sobs in the dusk, moonlit room into which Margaret Calderwood carried her friend. There was a long consultation, and then Margaret, having hushed away the grieving woman into some quiet corner, came forth to look for the little dark-faced stranger, who had arrived, so unwelcome, from beyond the seas, with such wild communication from the dead.

Up the grand staircase of handsome Calderwood the little woman followed the tall one into a large chamber where a lamp burned, showing Lisa, if she cared to see it, that this mansion of Calderwood was fitted with much greater luxury and richness than was that of Hurly Burly. The appointments of this room announced it the sanctum of a woman who depended for the interest of her life upon resources of intellect and taste. Lisa noticed nothing but a morsel of biscuit that was lying on a plate.

"May I have it?" said she eagerly. "It is so long since I have eaten. I am hungry."

Margaret Calderwood gazed at her with a sorrowful, motherly look, and, parting the fringing hair on her forehead, kissed her. Lisa, staring at her in wonder, returned the caress with ardour.

Margaret's large fair shoulders, Madonna face, and yellow braided hair, excited a rapture within her. But when food was brought her, she flew to it and ate.

"It is better than I have ever eaten at home!" she said gratefully. And Margaret Calderwood murmured, "She is physically healthy, at least."

"And now, Lisa," said Margaret Calderwood, "come and tell me the whole history of the grand signor who sent you to England to play the organ."

Then Lisa crept in behind a chair, and her eyes began to burn and her fingers to thrum, and she repeated word for word her story as she had told it at Hurly Burly.

When she had finished, Margaret Calderwood began to pace up and down the floor with a very troubled face. Lisa watched her, fascinated, and, when she bade her listen to a story which she would relate to her, folded her restless hands together meekly, and listened.

"Twenty years ago, Lisa, Mr. and Mrs. Hurly had a son. He was handsome, like that portrait you saw in the gallery, and he had brilliant talents. He was idolized by his father and mother, and all who knew him felt obliged to love him. I was then a happy girl of twenty. I was an orphan, and Mrs. Hurly, who had been my mother's friend, was like a mother to me. I, too, was petted and caressed by all my friends, and I was very wealthy; but I only valued admiration, riches—every good gift that fell to my share—just in proportion as they seemed of worth in the eyes of Lewis Hurly. I was his affianced wife, and I loved him well.

"All the fondness and pride that were lavished on him could not keep him from falling into evil ways, nor from becoming rapidly more and more abandoned to wickedness, till even those who loved him best despaired of seeing his reformation. I prayed him with tears, for my sake, if not for that of his grieving mother, to save himself before it was too late. But to my horror I found that my power was gone, my words did not even move him; he loved me no more. I tried to think that this was some fit of madness that would pass, and still clung to hope. At last his own mother forbade me to see him."

Here Margaret Calderwood paused, seemingly in bitter thought, but resumed:

"He and a party of his boon companions, named by themselves the 'Devil's Club', were in the habit of practising all kinds of unholy pranks in the country. They had midnight carousings on the tomb-stones in the village graveyard; they carried away helpless old men and children, whom they tortured by making believe to bury them alive; they raised the dead and placed them sitting round the tombstones at a mock feast. On one occasion there was a very sad funeral from the village. The corpse was carried into the church, and prayers were read over the coffin, the chief mourner, the aged father of the dead man, standing weeping by. In the midst of this solemn scene the organ suddenly pealed forth a profane tune, and a number of voices shouted a drinking chorus. A groan of execration burst from the crowd, the clergyman turned pale and closed his book, and the old man, the father of the dead, climbed the altar steps, and, raising his arms above his head, uttered a terrible curse. He cursed Lewis Hurly to all eternity, he cursed the organ he played, that it might be dumb henceforth, except under the fingers that had now profaned it, which, he prayed, might be forced to labour upon it till they stiffened in death. And the curse seemed to work, for the organ stood dumb in the church from that day, except when touched by Lewis Hurly.

"For a bravado he had the organ taken down and conveyed to his father's house, where he had it put up in the chamber where it now stands. It was also for a bravado that he played on it every day. But, by-and-by, the amount of time which he spent at it daily began to increase rapidly. We wondered long at this whim, as we called it, and his poor mother thanked God that he had set his heart upon an occupation which would keep him out of harm's way. I was the first to suspect that it was not his own will that kept him hammering at the organ so many laborious hours, while his boon companions tried vainly to draw him away. He used to lock himself up in the room with the organ, but one day I hid myself among the curtains, and saw him writhing on his seat, and heard him groaning as he strove to wrench his hands from the keys, to which they flew back like a needle to a magnet. It was soon plainly to be seen that he was an involuntary slave to the organ; but whether through a madness that had grown within himself, or by some supernatural doom, having its cause in the old man's curse, we did not dare to say. By-and-by there came a time when we were wakened out of our sleep at nights by the rolling of the organ. He wrought now night and day. Food and rest were denied him. His face got haggard, his beard grew long, his eyes started from their sockets. His body became wasted, and his cramped fingers like the claws of a bird. He groaned piteously as he stooped over his cruel toil. All save his mother and I were afraid to go near him. She, poor, tender woman, tried to put wine and food between his lips, while the tortured fingers crawled over the keys; but he only gnashed his teeth at her with curses, and she retreated from him in terror, to pray. At last, one dreadful hour, we found him a ghastly corpse on the ground before the organ.

"From that hour the organ was dumb to the touch of all human fingers. Many, unwilling to believe the story, made persevering endeavours to draw sound from it, in vain. But when the darkened empty room was locked up and left, we heard as loud as ever the well-known sounds humming and rolling through the walls. Night and day the tones of the organ boomed on as before. It seemed that the doom of the wretched man was not yet fulfilled, although his tortured body had been worn out in the terrible struggle to accomplish it. Even his own mother was afraid to go near the room then. So the time went on, and the curse of this perpetual music was not removed from the house. Servants refused to stay about the place. Visitors shunned it. The squire and his wife left their home for years, and returned; left it, and returned again, to find their ears still tortured and their hearts wrung by the unceasing persecution of terrible sounds. At last, but a few months ago, a holy man was found, who locked himself up in the cursed chamber for many days, praying and wrestling with the demon. After he came forth and went away the sounds ceased, and the organ was heard no more. Since then there has been peace in the house. And now, Lisa, your strange appearance and your strange story convince us that you are a victim of a ruse of the Evil One. Be warned in time, and place your-self under the protection of God, that you may be saved from the fearful influences that are at work upon you. Come—"

Margaret Calderwood turned to the corner where the stranger sat, as she had supposed, listening intently. Little Lisa was fast asleep, her hands spread before her as if she played an organ in her dreams.

Margaret took the soft brown face to her motherly breast, and kissed the swelling temples, too big with wonder and fancy.

"We will save you from a horrible fate!" she murmured, and carried the girl to bed.

In the morning Lisa was gone. Margaret Calderwood, coming early from her own chamber, went into the girl's room and found the bed empty.

"She is just such a wild thing," thought Margaret, "as would rush out at sunrise to hear the larks!" and she went forth to look for her in the meadows, behind the beech hedges and in the home park. Mistress Hurly, from the breakfast-room window, saw Margaret Calderwood, large and fair in her white morning gown, coming down the garden-path between the rose bushes, with her fresh draperies dabbled by the dew, and a look of trouble on her calm face. Her quest had been unsuccessful. The little foreigner had vanished.

A second search after breakfast proved also fruitless, and towards eve-ning the two women drove back to Hurly Burly together. There all was panic and distress. The squire sat in his study with the doors shut, and his hands over his ears. The servants, with pale faces, were huddled together in whispering groups. The haunted organ was pealing through the house as of old.

Margaret Calderwood hastened to the fatal chamber, and there, sure enough, was Lisa, perched upon the high seat before the organ, beating the keys with her small hands, her slight figure swaying, and the evening sunshine playing about her weird head. Sweet unearthly music she wrung from the groaning heart of the organ—wild melodies, mounting to rapturous heights and falling to mournful depths. She wandered from Mendelssohn to Mozart, and from Mozart to Beethoven. Margaret stood fascinated awhile by the ravishing beauty of the sounds she heard, but, rousing herself quickly, put her arms round the musician and forced her away from the chamber. Lisa returned next day, however, and was not so easily coaxed from her post again.

Day after day she laboured at the organ, growing paler and thinner and more weird-looking as time went on.

"I work so hard," she said to Mrs Hurly. "The signor, your son, is he pleased? Ask him to come and tell me himself if he is pleased."

Mistress Hurly got ill and took to her bed. The squire swore at the young foreign baggage, and roamed abroad. Margaret Calderwood was the only one who stood by to watch the fate of the little organist. The curse of the organ was upon Lisa; it spoke under her hand, and her hand was its slave.

At last she announced rapturously that she had had a visit from the brave signor, who had commended her industry, and urged her to work yet harder. After that she ceased to hold any communication with the living. Time after time Margaret Calderwood wrapped her arms about the frail thing, and carried her away by force, locking the door of the fatal chamber. But locking the chamber and burying the key were of no avail. The door stood open again, and Lisa was labouring on her perch.

One night, wakened from her sleep by the well-known humming and moaning of the organ, Margaret dressed hurriedly and hastened to the unholy room. Moonlight was pouring down the staircase and passages of Hurly Burly. It shone on the marble bust of the dead Lewis Hurly, that stood in the niche above his mother's sitting-room door. The organ room was full of it when Margaret pushed open the door and entered—full of the pale green moonlight from the window, mingled with another light, a dull lurid glare which seemed to centre round a dark shadow, like the figure of a man standing by the organ, and throwing out in fantastic relief the slight form of Lisa writhing, rather than swaying, back and forward, as if in agony. The sounds that came from the organ were broken and meaningless, as if the hands of the player lagged and stumbled on the keys. Between the intermittent chords low moaning cries broke from Lisa, and the dark figure bent towards her with menacing gestures. Trembling with the sickness of supernatural fear, yet strong of will, Margaret Calderwood crept forward within the lurid light, and was drawn into its influence. It grew and intensified upon her, it dazzled and blinded her at first; but presently, by a daring effort of will, she raised her eyes, and beheld Lisa's face convulsed with torture in the burning glare, and bending over her the figure and the features of Lewis Hurly! Smitten with horror, Margaret did not even then lose her presence of mind. She wound her strong arms around the wretched girl and dragged her from her seat and out of the influence of the lurid light, which immediately paled away and vanished. She carried her to her own bed, where Lisa lay, a wasted wreck, raving about the cruelty of the pitiless signor who would not see that she was labouring her best. Her poor cramped hands kept beating the coverlet, as though she were still at her agonizing task.

Margaret Calderwood bathed her burning temples, and placed fresh flowers upon her pillow.

She opened the blinds and windows, and let in the sweet morning air and sunshine, and then, looking up at the newly awakened sky with its fair promise of hope for the day, and down at the dewy fields, and afar off at the dark green woods with the purple mists still hovering about them, she prayed that a way might be shown her by which to put an end to this curse. She prayed for Lisa, and then, thinking that the girl rested somewhat, stole from the room. She thought that she had locked the door behind her.

She went downstairs with a pale, resolved face, and, without consulting anyone, sent to the village for a bricklayer. Afterwards she sat by Mistress Hurly's bedside, and explained to her what was to be done. Presently she went to the door of Lisa's room, and hearing no sound, thought the girl slept, and stole away. By-and-by she went downstairs, and found that the bricklayer had arrived and already begun his task of building up the organ-room door. He was a swift workman, and the chamber was soon sealed safely with stone and mortar.

Having seen this work finished, Margaret Calderwood went and listened again at Lisa's door; and still hearing no sound, she returned, and took her seat at Mrs Hurly's bedside once more. It was towards evening that she at last entered her room to assure herself of the comfort of Lisa's sleep. But the bed and room were empty. Lisa had disappeared.

Then the search began, upstairs and downstairs, in the garden, in the grounds, in the fields and meadows. No Lisa. Margaret Calderwood ordered the carriage and drove to Calderwood to see if the strange little Will-o'-the-wisp* might have made her way there; then to the village, and to many other places in the neighbourhood which it was not possible she could have reached. She made enquiries everywhere; she pondered and puzzled over the matter. In the weak, suffering state that the girl was in, how far could she have crawled?

After two days' search, Margaret returned to Hurly Burly. She was sad and tired, and the evening was chill. She sat over the fire wrapped in her shawl when little Bess came to her, weeping behind her muslin apron.

"If you'd speak to Mistress Hurly about it, please, ma'am," she said. "I love her dearly, and it breaks my heart to go away, but the organ haven't done yet, ma'am, and I'm frightened out of my life, so I can't stay."

"Who has heard the organ, and when?" asked Margaret Calderwood, rising to her feet.

"Please, ma'am, I heard it the night you went away—the night after the door was built up!"

"And not since?"

"No, ma'am," hesitatingly, "not since. Hist! hark, ma'am! Is not that like the sound of it now?"

"No," said Margaret Calderwood; "it is only the wind." But pale as death she flew down the stairs and laid her ear to the yet damp mortar of the

---

* In folklore, a will-o'-the-wisp is a light encountered in bogs or marshes that often leads unwary travelers astray.

newly built wall. All was silent. There was no sound but the monotonous sough of the wind in the trees outside. Then Margaret began to dash her soft shoulder against the strong wall, and to pick the mortar away with her white fingers, and to cry out for the bricklayer who had built up the door.

It was midnight, but the bricklayer left his bed in the village, and obeyed the summons to Hurly Burly. The pale woman stood by and watched him undo all his work of three days ago, and the servants gathered about in trembling groups, wondering what was to happen next.

What happened next was this: When an opening was made the man entered the room with a light, Margaret Calderwood and others following. A heap of something dark was lying on the ground at the foot of the organ. Many groans arose in the fatal chamber. Here was little Lisa dead!

When Mistress Hurly was able to move, the squire and his wife went to live in France, where they remained till their death. Hurly Burly was shut up and deserted for many years. Lately it has passed into new hands. The organ has been taken down and banished, and the room is a bed-chamber, more luxuriously furnished than any in the house. But no one sleeps in it twice.

Margaret Calderwood was carried to her grave the other day a very aged woman.

MARY E. WILKINS FREEMAN *(1852–1930) was a prolific American writer of poems, novels, and short stories for children and adults. Born in Massachusetts to a strict religious family, she married at the age of forty and moved to New Jersey. Primarily known for her depictions of New England life, she penned a dozen novels and as many short story collections, and much of her work explored the changing role of women, especially in rural settings. Wilkins Freeman also wrote of things supernatural, including ghosts and vampires. In 1926, she became the first recipient of the William Dean Howells Medal for Distinction in Fiction from the American Academy of Arts and Letters. "Death" first appeared as the last in a quartet of prose poems under the umbrella title "Pastels in Prose" (*Harpers New Monthly Magazine, *December 1892).*

DEATH

by Mary E. Wilkins Freeman

(1892)

There is a little garden full of white flowers before this house, before this little house, which is sunken in a green hillock to the lintel of its door. The white flowers are full of honey; yellow butterflies and bees suck at them. The unseen wind comes rushing like a presence and a power which the heart feels only. The white flowers press together before it in a soft tumult, and shake out fragrance like censers; but the bees and the butterflies cling to them blowing. The crickets chirp in the green roof of the house unceasingly, like clocks which have told off the past, and will tell off the future.

I pray you, friend, who dwells in this little house sunken in the green hillock, with the white flower-garden before the door?

A dead man.

Passes he ever out of his little dwelling and down the path between his white flower-bushes?

He never passes out.

There is no chimney in that grassy roof. How fares he when the white flowers are gone and the white storm drives?

He feels it not.

Had he happiness?

His heart broke for it.

Does his heart pain him in there?

He has forgot.

Comes ever anybody here to visit him?

His widow comes in her black veil, and weeps here, and sometimes his old mother, wavering out in the sun like a black shadow.

And he knows it not?

He knows it not.

He knows not of his little prison-house in the green hillock, of his white flower-garden, of the winter storm, of his broken heart, and his beloved who yet bear the pain of it, and send out their thoughts to watch with him in the wintry nights?

He knows it not.

Only the living know?

Only the living.

Then, then the tombs be not for the dead, but the living! I would, I would, I would that I were dead, that I might be free from the tomb, and sorrow, and death!

The American writer **WILLIAM CHARLES MORROW** *(1854–1923) was born in Alabama but gave up managing his family's hotel and moved to California in 1879. There, he was introduced by Ambrose Bierce to Frank Somers, publisher of the* Argonaut, *an influential San Francisco weekly newspaper, where some of Morrow's early work appeared. Subsequently, probably at Bierce's behest, he wrote for William Randolph Hearst's San Francisco Examiner. Though Morrow wrote several novels, he is best remembered today as a writer of horror and suspense. The following tale of a haunting may have appeared in the 1880s in the* Argonaut *with some of his other early stories, including the oft-reprinted "His Unconquerable Foe," but it was definitely included in his collection* The Ape, the Idiot & Other People, *first published in 1897.*

AN ORIGINAL REVENGE

by W. C. Morrow

(1897)

O n a certain day I received a letter from a private soldier, named Gratmar, attached to the garrison of San Francisco.* I had known him but slightly, the acquaintance having come about through his interest in some stories which I had published, and which he had a way of calling "psychological studies." He was a dreamy, romantic, fine-grained lad, proud as a tiger-lily

---

* The Presidio of San Francisco was an active military base until 1989, when Congress terminated its military status. The property itself was transferred to the National Park Service in 1994. It was used by the Spanish until 1846, when it was seized by the US in the US-Mexican War and converted to a US Army base. It became the home of an important military medical center in the 1890s and was used as such and as an important command post until its closure.

and sensitive as a blue-bell. What mad caprice led him to join the army I never knew; but I did know that there he was wretchedly out of place, and I foresaw that his rude and repellant environment would make of him in time a deserter, or a suicide, or a murderer. The letter at first seemed a wild outpouring of despair, for it informed me that before it should reach me its author would be dead by his own hand. But when I had read farther I understood its spirit, and realized how coolly formed a scheme it disclosed and how terrible its purport was intended to be. The worst of the contents was the information that a certain officer (whom he named) had driven him to the deed, and that *he was committing suicide for the sole purpose of gaining thereby the power to revenge himself upon his enemy*! I learned afterward that the officer had received a similar letter.

This was so puzzling that I sat down to reflect upon the young man's peculiarities. He had always seemed somewhat uncanny, and had I proved more sympathetic he doubtless would have gone farther and told me of certain problems which he professed to have solved concerning the life beyond this. One thing that he had said came back vividly: "If I could only overcome that purely gross and animal love of life that makes us all shun death, I would kill myself, for I know how far more powerful I could be in spirit than in flesh."

The manner of the suicide was startling, and that was what might have been expected from this odd character. Evidently scorning the flummery of funerals, he had gone into a little canyon near the military reservation and blown himself into a million fragments with dynamite, so that all of him that was ever found was some minute particles of flesh and bone.

I kept the letter a secret, for I desired to observe the officer without rousing his suspicion of my purpose; it would be an admirable test of a dead man's power and deliberate intention to haunt the living, for so I interpreted the letter. The officer thus to be punished was an oldish man, short, apoplectic, overbearing, and irascible. Generally he was kind to most of the men in a way; but he was gross and mean, and that explained sufficiently his harsh treatment of young Gratmar, whom he could not understand, and his efforts to break that flighty young man's spirit.

Not very long after the suicide certain modifications in the officer's conduct became apparent to my watchful oversight. His choler,* though none the less sporadic, developed a quality which had some of the characteristics of senility; and yet he was still in his prime, and passed for a sound man. He was a bachelor, and had lived always alone; but presently he began to shirk solitude at night and court it in daylight. His brother-officers chaffed him, and thereupon he would laugh in rather a forced and silly fashion, quite different from the ordinary way with him, and would sometimes, on these occasions, blush so violently that his face would become almost purple. His soldierly alertness and sternness relaxed surprisingly at some times and at others were exaggerated into unnecessary acerbity, his conduct in this regard suggesting that of a drunken man who knows that he is drunk and who now and then makes a brave effort to appear sober. All these things, and more, indicating some mental strain, or some dreadful apprehension, or perhaps something worse than either, were observed partly by me and partly by an intelligent officer whose watch upon the man had been secured by me.

To be more particular, the afflicted man was observed often to start suddenly and in alarm, look quickly round, and make some unintelligent monosyllabic answer, seemingly to an inaudible question that no visible person had asked. He acquired the reputation, too, of having taken lately to nightmares, for in the middle of the night he would shriek in the most dreadful fashion, alarming his roommates prodigiously. After these attacks he would sit up in bed, his ruddy face devoid of color, his eyes glassy and shining, his breathing broken with gasps, and his body wet with a cold perspiration.

Knowledge of these developments and transformations spread throughout the garrison; but the few (mostly women) who dared to express sympathy or suggest a tonic encountered so violent rebuffs that they blessed Heaven for escaping alive from his word-volleys. Even the garrison surgeon, who had a kindly manner, and the commanding general, who was constructed on dignified and impressive lines, received little thanks for their solicitude. Clearly the doughty old officer, who had fought like a bulldog in two wars

---

* Anger, rage, or ill temper.

and a hundred battles, was suffering deeply from some undiscoverable malady.

The next extraordinary thing which he did was to visit one evening (not so clandestinely as to escape my watch) a spirit medium—extraordinary, because he always had scoffed at the idea of spirit communications. I saw him as he was leaving the medium's rooms. His face was purple, his eyes were bulging and terrified, and he tottered in his walk. A policeman, seeing his distress, advanced to assist him; whereupon the soldier hoarsely begged—

"Call a hack."

Into it he fell, and asked to be driven to his quarters. I hastily ascended to the medium's rooms, and found her lying unconscious on the floor. Soon, with my aid, she recalled her wits, but her conscious state was even more alarming than the other. At first she regarded me with terror, and cried—

"It is horrible for you to hound him so!"

I assured her that I was hounding no one.

"Oh, I thought you were the spir—I mean—I—oh, but it was standing exactly where you are!" she exclaimed.

"I suppose so," I agreed, "but you can see that I am not the young man's spirit. However, I am familiar with this whole case, madam, and if I can be of any service in the matter I should be glad if you would inform me. I am aware that our friend is persecuted by a spirit, which visits him frequently, and I am positive that through you it has informed him that the end is not far away, and that our elderly friend's death will assume some terrible form. Is there anything that I can do to avert the tragedy?"

The woman stared at me in a horrified silence. "How did you know these things?" she gasped.

"That is immaterial. When will the tragedy occur? Can I prevent it?"

"Yes, yes!" she exclaimed. "It will happen this very night! But no earthly power can prevent it!"

She came close to me and looked at me with an expression of the most acute terror.

"Merciful God! what will become of me? He is to be murdered, you understand—murdered in cold blood by a spirit—and he knows it and *I know it*! If he is spared long enough he will tell them at the garrison, and they will all think that I had something to do with it! Oh, this is terrible,

terrible, and yet I dare not say a word in advance—nobody there would believe in what the spirits say, and they will think that I had a hand in the murder!" The woman's agony was pitiful.

"Be assured that he will say nothing about it," I said; "and if you keep your tongue from wagging you need fear nothing."

With this and a few other hurried words of comfort, I soothed her and hastened away.

For I had interesting work on hand: it is not often that one may be in at such a murder as that! I ran to a livery stable, secured a swift horse, mounted him, and spurred furiously for the reservation. The hack, with its generous start, had gone far on its way, but my horse was nimble, and his legs felt the pricking of my eagerness. A few miles of this furious pursuit brought me within sight of the hack just as it was crossing a dark ravine near the reservation. As I came nearer I imagined that the hack swayed somewhat, and that a fleeing shadow escaped from it into the tree-banked further wall of the ravine. I certainly was not in error with regard to the swaying, for it had roused the dull notice of the driver. I saw him turn, with an air of alarm in his action, and then pull up with a heavy swing upon the reins. At this moment I dashed up and halted.

"Anything the matter?" I asked.

"I don't know," he answered, getting down. "I felt the carriage sway, and I see that the door's wide open. Guess my load thought he'd sobered up enough to get out and walk, without troubling me or his pocket-book."

Meanwhile I too had alighted; then struck a match, and by its light we discovered, through the open door, the "load" huddled confusedly on the floor of the hack, face upward, his chin compressed upon his breast by his leaning against the further door, and looking altogether vulgar, misshapen, and miserably unlike a soldier. He neither moved nor spoke when we called. We hastily clambered within and lifted him upon the seat, but his head rolled about with an awful looseness and freedom, and another match disclosed a ghastly dead face and wide eyes that stared horribly at nothing.

"You would better drive the body to headquarters," I said.

Instead of following, I cantered back to town, housed my horse, and went straightway to bed; and this will prove to be the first information that I was the "mysterious man on a horse," whom the coroner could never find.

About a year afterwards I received the following letter (which is observed to be in fair English) from Stockholm, Sweden:

"Dear Sir—For some years I have been reading your remarkable psychological studies with great interest, and I take the liberty to suggest a theme for your able pen. I have just found in a library here a newspaper, dated about a year ago, in which is an account of the mysterious death of a military officer in a hack."

Then followed the particulars, as I have already detailed them, and the very theme of post-mortem revenge which I have adopted in this setting out of facts. Some persons may regard the coincidence between my correspondent's suggestion and my private and exclusive knowledge as being a very remarkable thing; but there are likely even more wonderful things in the world, and at none of them do I longer marvel. More extraordinary still is his suggestion that in the dynamite explosion a dog or a quarter of beef might as well have been employed as a suicide-minded man; that, in short, the man may not have killed himself at all, but might have employed a presumption of such an occurrence to render more effective a physical persecution ending in murder by the living man who had posed as a spirit. The letter even suggested an arrangement with a spirit medium, and I regard that also as a queer thing.

The declared purpose of this letter was to suggest material for another of my "psychological studies"; but I submit that the whole affair is of too grave a character for treatment in the levity of fiction. And if the facts and coincidences should prove less puzzling to others than to me, a praiseworthy service might be done to humanity by the presentation of whatever solution a better understanding than mine might evolve.

The only remaining disclosure which I am prepared now to make is that my correspondent signed himself "Ramtarg,"*—an odd-sounding name, but for all I know it may be respectable in Sweden. And yet there is something about the name that haunts me unceasingly, much as does some strange dream which we know we have dreamt and yet which it is impossible to remember.

---

* Even the least observant reader will see that the name is "Gratmar" in reverse.

HESKETH VERNON PRICHARD *(who would write as "Hesketh-Prichard" and was known as "Hex") (1876–1922) was an adventurer, explorer, and writer in many genres. His father died before he was born, and so he developed a close relationship with his mother* KATE PRICHARD. *She encouraged him to write, and they cowrote many books, generally credited to the son alone. After a summer of travel, Hex returned to London in 1896, and he and his mother wrote a number of stories together under the pseudonyms "H. Heron" and "E. Heron." These saw publication in several journals, including the prestigious* Cornhill Magazine. *Most popular were the stories collected as* The Chronicles of Don Q *(1904), about a Zorro-like figure,* The New Chronicles of Don Q *(1906),* Don Q's Love Story *(1909), which became the basis for a "Zorro" film starring Douglas Fairbanks, and* November Joe *(1913), about a backwoodsman detective, written by Hex alone. In 1897, J. M. Barrie, part of the circle of writers to which Prichard belonged (along with Sir Arthur Conan Doyle), introduced the Prichards to the publisher Cyril Arthur Pearson, who encouraged them to write a series of stories that Pearson would, to their dismay, label "Real Ghost Stories." The Prichards invented the character of Flaxman Low, the world's first detective specializing in psychic matters, and the following tale, the first of the series, appeared in* Pearson's Magazine #25 for January 1898. *The entire series of twelve tales was published as* Ghosts: Being the Experiences of Flaxman Low *in 1899.*

THE STORY OF THE SPANIARDS, HAMMERSMITH

by E. and H. Heron

(1898)

H ave ghosts any existence outside our own fancy and emotions? This is the question with which the end of the century concerns itself more and more, for, though a vast amount of evidence with regard to occult phenomena already exists, the ultimate answer has yet to be supplied.* In this connection it may not generally be known that, as one of the first steps towards reducing Psychology to the lines of an exact science, an attempt has been made to classify spirits and ghosts, with the result that some very bizarre and terrible theories have been put forward—things undreamt of outside the circle of the select few.†

With a view to meeting the widespread interest in these matters, the following series of ghost stories is laid before the public. They have been gathered out of a large number of supernatural experiences with which Mr. Flaxman Low—under the thin disguise of which name many are sure to recognise one of the leading scientists of the day, with whose works on Psychology and kindred subjects they are familiar—has been more or less connected. He is, moreover, the first student in this field of inquiry who has had the boldness and originality to break free from old and conventional methods, and to approach the elucidation of so-called supernatural problems on the lines of natural law.

The details of these stories have been supplied by the narratives of those most concerned, supplemented by the clear and ample notes which Mr. Flaxman Low has had the courtesy to place in our hands.

For obvious reasons, the exact localities where these events are said to have happened are in every case merely indicated.

No. I.—THE STORY OF THE SPANIARDS, HAMMERSMITH.

LIEUTENANT RODERICK HOUSTON, of H.M.S. *Sphinx*,‡ had practically nothing beyond his pay, and he was beginning to be very tired

---

* The author refers to Spiritualism, the great religious movement that gained popularity in Europe and America and espoused the beliefs that the afterlife existed and that it was possible to communicate with those who had passed over. By 1897, it was said to have over eight million followers.

† At the time this story was written, psychology was a very different field of study, focusing more on human consciousness than behavior. William James, often considered "the father of modern psychology," was also an ardent Spiritualist and sought early on to integrate the two systems.

‡ The HMS Sphinx was a real ship, launched in 1882 and classified as a composite paddle vehicle.

of the West African station,* when he received the pleasant intelligence that a relative had left him a legacy. This consisted of a satisfactory sum in ready money and a house in Hammersmith,† which was rated at over £200 a year, and was said in addition to be comfortably furnished. Houston, therefore, counted on its rental to bring his income up to a fairly desirable figure. Further information from home, however, showed him that he had been rather premature in his expectations, whereupon, being a man of action, he applied for two months' leave, and came home to look after his affairs himself.

When he had been a week in London he arrived at the conclusion that he could not possibly hope single-handed to tackle the difficulties which presented themselves. He accordingly wrote the following letter to his friend, Flaxman Low:

"The Spaniards, Hammersmith, 23-3-1892.

"DEAR LOW—Since we parted some three years ago, I have heard very little of you. It was only yesterday that I met our mutual friend, Sammy Smith ('Silkworm' of our schooldays) who told me that your studies have developed in a new direction, and that you are now a good deal interested in psychical subjects. If this be so, I hope to induce you to come and stay with me here for a few days by promising to introduce you to a problem in your own line. I am just now living at 'The Spaniards,' a house that has lately been left to me, and which in the first instance was built by an old fellow named Van Nuysen, who married a great-aunt of mine. It is a good house, but there is said to be 'something wrong' with it. It lets easily, but unluckily the tenants cannot be persuaded to remain above a week or two. They complain that the place is haunted by something—presumably a ghost—because its vagaries bear just that brand of inconsequence which stamps the common run of manifestations.

"It occurs to me that you may care to investigate the matter with me. If so, send me a wire when to expect you.

---

* The West Coast of Africa Station, the base for the British Navy's squadron charged with capturing slave ships and freeing the captive slaves, was merged in 1867 with the Cape of Good Hope Station.

† A district of London.

"Yours ever.

"RODERICK HOUSTON."

Houston waited in some anxiety for an answer. Low was the sort of man one could rely on in almost any emergency. Sammy Smith had told him a characteristic anecdote of Low's career at Oxford, where, although his intellectual triumphs may be forgotten, he will always be remembered by the story that when Sands, of Queen's,* fell ill on the day before the Varsity sports, a telegram was sent to Low's rooms: "Sands ill. You must do the hammer for us." Low's reply was pithy: "I'll be there." Thereupon he finished the treatise upon which he was engaged, and next day his strong, lean figure was to be seen swinging the hammer amidst vociferous cheering, for that was the occasion on which he not only won the event, but beat the record.

On the fifth day Low's answer came from Vienna. As he read it, Houston recalled the high forehead, long neck—with its accompanying low collar—and thin moustache of his scholarly, athletic friend, and smiled. There was so much more in Flaxman Low than anyone gave him credit for.

"MY DEAR HOUSTON—Very glad to hear of you again. In response to your kind invitation, I thank you for the opportunity of meeting the ghost, and still more for the pleasure of your companionship. I came here to inquire into a somewhat similar affair. I hope, however, to be able to leave to-morrow, and will be with you some time on Friday evening.

"Very sincerely yours.

"FLAXMAN LOW."

"P.S.—By the way, will it be convenient to give your servants a holiday during the term of my visit, as, if my investigations are to be of any value, not a grain of dust must be disturbed in your house, excepting by ourselves?—F.L."

"The Spaniards" was within some fifteen minutes' walk of Hammersmith Bridge. Set in the midst of a fairly respectable neighbourhood, it presented an odd contrast to the commonplace dullness of the narrow streets crowded about it. As Flaxman Low drove up in the evening light,

---

* The Queen's College, that is, founded in 1341.

he reflected that the house might have come from the back of beyond—it gave an impression of something old-world and something exotic.

It was surrounded by a ten-foot wall, above which the upper storey was visible, and Low decided that this intensely English house still gave some curious suggestion of the tropics. The interior of the house carried out the same idea, with its sense of space and air, cool tints and wide, matted passages.

"So you have seen something yourself since you came?" Low said, as they sat at dinner, for Houston had arranged that meals should be sent in for them from a hotel.

"I've heard tapping up and down the passage upstairs. It is an uncarpeted landing which runs the whole length of the house. One night, when I was quicker than usual, I saw what looked like a bladder* disappear into one of the bedrooms—your room it is to be, by the way—and the door closed behind it," replied Houston discontentedly. "The usual meaningless antics of a ghost."

"What had the tenants who lived here to say about it?" went on Low.

"Most of the people saw and heard just what I have told you, and promptly went away. The only one who stood out for a little while was old Filderg—you know the man? Twenty years ago he made an effort to cross the Australian deserts—he stopped for eight weeks. When he left he saw the house-agent, and said he was afraid he had done a little shooting practice in the upper passage, and he hoped it wouldn't count against him in the bill, as it was done in defence of his life. He said something had jumped on to the bed and tried to strangle him. He described it as cold and glutinous, and he pursued it down the passage, firing at it. He advised the owner to have the house pulled down; but, of course, my cousin did nothing of the kind. It's a very good house, and he did not see the sense of spoiling his property."

"That's very true," replied Flaxman Low, looking round. "Mr. Van Nuysen had been in the West Indies, and kept his liking for spacious rooms."

"Where did you hear anything about him?" asked Houston in surprise.

---

* Here meaning the prepared airbag of an animal, inflated like a ball.

"I have heard nothing beyond what you told me in your letter; but I see a couple of bottles of Gulf weed* and a lace-plant† ornament, such as people used to bring from the West Indies in former days."

"Perhaps I should tell you the history of the old man," said Houston doubtfully; "but we aren't proud of it!"

Flaxman Low considered a moment.

"When was the ghost seen for the first time?"

"When the first tenant took the house. It was let after old Van Nuysen's time."

"Then it may clear the way if you will tell me something of him."

"He owned sugar plantations in Trinidad, where he passed the greater part of his life, while his wife mostly remained in England—incompatibility of temper it was said. When he came home for good and built this house they still lived apart, my aunt declaring that nothing on earth would persuade her to return to him. In course of time he became a confirmed invalid, and he then insisted on my aunt joining him. She lived here for perhaps a year, when she was found dead in bed one morning—in your room."

"What caused her death?"

"She had been in the habit of taking narcotics, and it was supposed that she smothered herself while under their influence."‡

"That doesn't sound very satisfactory," remarked Flaxman Low.

"Her husband was satisfied with it anyhow, and it was no one else's business. The family were only too glad to have the affair hushed up."

"And what became of Mr. Van Nuysen?"

"That I can't tell you. He disappeared a short time after. Search was made for him in the usual way, but nobody knows to this day what became of him."

"Ah, that was strange, as he was such an invalid," said Low, and straightway fell into a long fit of abstraction, from which he was roused by

---

* A coarse, olive-brown seaweed found in the waters of the Gulf of Mexico.

† Another aquatic plant, now used in aquariums.

‡ This does not imply criminal conduct; opium, cocaine, heroin, and other narcotics were freely available at this time for pain relief and sleep aid. Their addictive nature was little understood.

hearing Houston curse the incurable foolishness and imbecility of ghostly behaviour. Flaxman woke up at this. He broke a walnut thoughtfully and began in a gentle voice:

"My dear fellow, we are apt to be hasty in our condemnation of the general behaviour of ghosts. It may appear incalculably foolish in our eyes, and I admit there often seems to be a total absence of any apparent object or intelligent action. But remember that what appears to us to be foolishness may be wisdom in the spirit world, since our unready senses can only catch broken glimpses of what is, I have not the slightest doubt, a coherent whole, if we could trace the connection."

"There may be something in that," replied Houston indifferently. "People naturally say that this ghost is the ghost of old Van Nuysen. But what connection can possibly exist between what I have told you of him and the manifestations—a tapping up and down the passage and the drawing about of a bladder like a child at play? It sounds idiotic!"

"Certainly. Yet it need not necessarily be so. There are isolated facts, we must look for the links which lie between. Suppose a saddle and a horse-shoe were to be shown to a man who had never seen a horse, I doubt whether he, however intelligent, could evolve the connecting idea! The ways of spirits are strange to us simply because we need further data to help us to interpret them."

"It's a new point of view," returned Houston, "but upon my word, you know, Low, I think you're wasting your time!"

Flaxman Low smiled slowly; his grave, melancholy face brightened.

"I have," said he, "gone somewhat deeply into the subject. In other sciences one reasons by analogy. Psychology is unfortunately a science with a future but without a past, or more probably it is a lost science of the ancients. However that may be, we stand to-day on the frontier of an unknown world, and progress is the result of individual effort; each solution of difficult phenomena forms a step towards the solution of the next problem. In this case, for example, the bladder-like object may be the key to the mystery."

Houston yawned.

"It all seems pretty senseless, but perhaps you may be able to read reason into it. If it were anything tangible, anything a man could meet with his fists, it would be easier."

"I entirely agree with you. But suppose we deal with this affair as it stands, on similar lines, I mean on prosaic, rational lines, as we should deal with a purely human mystery."

"My dear fellow," returned Houston, pushing his chair back from the table wearily, "you shall do just as you like, only get rid of the ghost!"

For some time after Low's arrival nothing very special happened. The tappings continued, and more than once Low had been in time to see the bladder disappear into the closing door of his bedroom, though, unluckily, he never chanced to be inside the room on these occasions, and however quickly he followed the bladder, he never succeeded in seeing anything further. He made a thorough examination of the house, and left no space unaccounted for in his careful measurement. There were no cellars, and the foundation of the house consisted of a thick layer of concrete.

At length, on the sixth night, an event took place, which, as Flaxman Low remarked, came very near to putting an end to the investigations as far as he was concerned. For the preceding two nights he and Houston had kept watch in the hope of getting a glimpse of the person or thing which tapped so persistently up and down the passage. But they were disappointed, for there were no manifestations. On the third evening, therefore, Low went off to his room a little earlier than usual, and fell asleep almost immediately.

He says he was awakened by feeling a heavy weight upon his feet, something that seemed inert and motionless. He recollected that he had left the gas burning, but the room was now in darkness.

Next he was aware that the thing on the bed had slowly shifted, and was gradually travelling up towards his chest. How it came on the bed he had no idea. Had it leaped or climbed? The sensation he experienced as it moved was of some ponderous, pulpy body, not crawling or creeping, but spreading! It was horrible! He tried to move his lower limbs, but could not because of the deadening weight. A feeling of drowsiness began to overpower him, and a deadly cold, such as he said he had before felt at sea when in the neighbourhood of icebergs, chilled upon the air.

With a violent struggle he managed to free his arms, but the thing grew more irresistible as it spread upwards. Then he became conscious of a pair of glassy eyes, with livid, everted* lids, looking into his own. Whether they were human eyes or beast eyes, he could not tell, but they were watery, like the eyes of a dead fish, and gleamed with a pale, internal lustre.

Then he owns he grew afraid. But he was still cool enough to notice one peculiarity about this ghastly visitant—although the head was within a few inches of his own, he could detect no breathing. It dawned on him that he was about to be suffocated, for, by the same method of extension, the thing was now coming over his face! It felt cold and clammy, like a mass of mucilage or a monstrous snail. And every instant the weight became greater. He is a powerful man, and he struck with his fists again and again at the head. Some substance yielded under the blows with a sickening sensation of bruised flesh.

With a lucky twist he raised himself in the bed and battered away with all the force he was capable of in his cramped position. The only effect was an occasional shudder or quake that ran through the mass as his half-arm blows rained upon it. At last, by chance, his hand knocked against the candle beside him. In a moment he recollected the matches. He seized the box, and struck a light.

As he did so, the lump slid to the floor. He sprang out of bed, and lit the candle. He felt a cold touch upon his leg, but when he looked down there was nothing to be seen. The door, which he had locked overnight, was now open, and he rushed out into the passage. All was still and silent with the throbbing vacancy of night time.

After searching round, he returned to his room. The bed still gave ample proof of the struggle that had taken place, and by his watch he saw the hour to be between two and three.

As there seemed nothing more to be done, he put on his dressing-gown, lit his pipe, and sat down to write an account of the experience he had just passed through for the Psychical Research Society†—from which paper the above is an abstract.

---

* Turned outward or inside-out. It's hard to understand what "everted lids" means.

† The Society for Psychical Research was founded in 1882 in England and was devoted to the study of parapsychology; when the American branch was formed, William James became its first president. Although many of its members were Spiritualists, when the society exposed William Hope and others as fraudulent mediums, Arthur Conan Doyle led a mass exodus of Spiritualists in protest of what they perceived to be an anti-Spiritualist bias.

He is a man of strong nerves, but he could not disguise from himself that he had been at handgrips with some grotesque form of death. What might be the nature of his assailant he could not determine, but his experience was supported by the attack which had been made on Filderg, and also—it was impossible to avoid the conclusion—by the manner of Mrs. Van Nuysen's death.

He thought the whole situation over carefully in connection with the tapping and the disappearing bladder, but, turn these events how he would, he could make nothing of them. They were entirely incongruous. A little later he went and made a shakedown* in Houston's room.

"What was the thing?" asked Houston, when Low had ended his story of the encounter.

Low shrugged his shoulders.

"At least it proves that Filderg did not dream," he said.

"But this is monstrous! We are more in the dark than ever. There's nothing for it but to have the house pulled down. Let us leave to-day."

"Don't be in a hurry, my dear fellow. You would rob me of a very great pleasure; besides, we may be on the verge of some valuable discovery. This series of manifestations is even more interesting than the Vienna mystery I was telling you of."

"Discovery or not," replied the other, "I don't like it."

The first thing next morning Low went out for a quarter of an hour. Before breakfast a man with a barrowful of sand came into the garden. Low looked up from his paper, leant out of the window, and gave some order.

When Houston came down a few minutes later he saw the yellowish heap on the lawn with some surprise.

"Hullo! What's this?" he asked.

"I ordered it," replied Low.

"All right. What's it for?"

"To help us in our investigations. Our visitor is capable of being felt, and he or it left a very distinct impression on the bed. Hence I gather it can also leave an impression on sand. It would be an immense advance if we could arrive at any correct notion of what sort of feet the ghost walks on. I

---

* A makeshift bed.

propose to spread a layer of this sand in the upper passage, and the result should be footmarks if the tapping comes to-night."

That evening the two men made a fire in Houston's bedroom, and sat there smoking and talking, to leave the ghost "a free run for once," as Houston phrased it. The tapping was heard at the usual hour, and presently the accustomed pause at the other end of the passage and the quiet closing of the door.

Low heaved a long sigh of satisfaction as he listened.

"That's my bedroom door," he said; "I know the sound of it perfectly. In the morning, and with the help of daylight, we shall see what we shall see."

As soon as there was light enough for the purpose of examining the footprints, Low roused Houston.

Houston was full of excitement as a boy, but his spirits fell by the time he had passed from end to end of the passage.

"There are marks," he said, "but they are as perplexing as everything else about this haunting brute, whatever it is. I suppose you think this is the print left by the thing which attacked you the night before last?"

"I fancy it is," said Low, who was still bending over the floor eagerly. "What do you make of it, Houston?"

"The brute has only one leg, to start with," replied Houston, "and that leaves the mark of a large, clawless pad! It's some animal—some ghoulish monster!"

"On the contrary," said Low, "I think we have now every reason to conclude that it is a man."

"A man? What man ever left footmarks like these?"

"Look at these hollows and streaks at the sides; they are the traces of the sticks we have heard tapping."

"You don't convince me," returned Houston doggedly.

"Let us wait another twenty-four hours, and to-morrow night, if nothing further occurs, I will give you my conclusions. Think it over. The tapping, the bladder, and the fact that Mr. Van Nuysen had lived in Trinidad. Add to these things this single pad-like print. Does nothing strike you by way of a solution?"

Houston shook his head.

"Nothing. And I fail to connect any of these things with what happened both to you and Filderg."

"Ah! now," said Flaxman Low, his face clouding a little, "I confess you lead me into a somewhat different region, though to me the connection is perfect."

Houston raised his eyebrows and laughed.

"If you can unravel this tangle of hints and events and diagnose the ghost, I shall be extremely astonished," he said. "What can you make of the footless impression?"

"Something, I hope. In fact, that mark may be a clue—an outrageous one, perhaps, but still a clue."

That evening the weather broke, and by night the storm had risen to a gale, accompanied by sharp bursts of rain.

"It's a noisy night," remarked Houston; "I don't suppose we'll hear the ghost, supposing it does turn up."

This was after dinner, as they were about to go into the smoking-room. Houston, finding the gas low in the hall, stopped to run it higher; at the same time asking Low to see if the jet on the upper landing was also alight.

Flaxman Low glanced up and uttered a slight exclamation, which brought Houston to his side.

Looking down at them from over the banisters was a face—a blotched, yellowish face, flanked by two swollen, protruding ears, the whole aspect being strangely leonine. It was but a glimpse, a clash of meeting glances, as it were, a glare of defiance, and the face was quickly withdrawn as the two men literally leapt up the stairs.

"There's nothing here," exclaimed Houston, after a search had been carried out through every room above.

"I didn't suppose we'd find anything," returned Low.

"This fairly knots up the thread," said Houston. "You can't pretend to unravel it now."

"Come down," said Low briefly; "I'm ready to give you my opinion, such as it is."

Once in the smoking-room, Houston busied himself in turning on all the light he could procure, then he saw to securing the windows, and piled up an immense fire, while Flaxman Low, who, as usual, had a cigarette in his mouth, sat on the edge of the table and watched him with some amusement.

"You saw that abominable face?" cried Houston, as he threw himself into a chair. "It was as material as yours or mine. But where did he go to? He must be somewhere about."

"We saw him clearly. That is sufficient for our purpose."

"You are very good at enumerating points, Low. Now just listen to my list. The difficulties grow with every fresh discovery. We're at a deadlock now, I take it? The sticks and the tapping point to an old man, the playing with a bladder to a child; the footmark might be the pad of a tiger minus claws, yet the thing that attacked you at night was cold and pulpy. And, lastly, by way of a wind-up, we see a lion-like, human face! If you can make all these items square with each other, I'll be happy to hear what you have got to say."

"You must first allow me to ask you a question. I understood you to say that no blood relationship existed between you and old Mr. Van Nuysen?"

"Certainly not. He was quite an outsider," answered Houston brusquely.

"In that case you are welcome to my conclusions. All the things you have mentioned point to one explanation. This house is haunted by the ghost of Mr. Van Nuysen, and he was a leper."

Houston stood up and stared at his companion.

"What a horrible notion! I must say I fail to see how you have arrived at such a conclusion."

"Take the chain of evidence in rather different order," said Low. "Why should a man tap with a stick?"

"Generally because he's blind."

"In cases of blindness, one stick is used for guidance. Here we have two for support."

"A man who has lost the use of his feet."

"Exactly; a man who has from some cause partially lost the use of his feet."

"But the bladder and the lion-like face?" went on Houston.

"The bladder, or what seemed to us to resemble a bladder, was one of his feet, contorted by the disease and probably swathed in linen, which foot he dragged rather than used; consequently, in passing through a door, for example, he would in the habit of drawing it in after him. Now, as regards the single footmark we saw. In one form of leprosy, the smaller bones of the extremities frequently fall away. The pad-like impression was, as I believe, the mark of the other foot—a toeless foot which he used, because in a more advanced stage of the disease the maimed hand or foot heals and becomes callous."

"Go on," said Houston; "it sounds as if it might be true. And the lion-like face I can account for myself. I have been in China, and have seen it before in lepers."

"Mr. Van Nuysen had been in Trinidad for many years, as we know, and while there he probably contracted the disease."

"I suppose so. After his return," added Houston, "he shut himself up almost entirely, and gave out that he was a martyr to rheumatic gout, this awful thing being the true explanation."

"It also accounts for Mrs. Van Nuysen's determination not to return to her husband."

Houston appeared much disturbed.

"We can't drop it here, Low," he said, in a constrained voice. "There is a good deal more to be cleared up yet. Can you tell me more?"

"From this point I find myself on less certain ground," replied Low unwillingly. "I merely offer a suggestion, remember—I don't ask you to accept it. I believe Mrs. Van Nuysen was murdered!"

"What?" exclaimed Houston. "By her husband?"

"Indications tend that way."

"But, my good fellow—"

"He suffocated her and then made away with himself. It is a pity that his body was not recovered. The condition of the remains would be the only really satisfactory test of my theory. If the skeleton could even now be found, the fact that he was a leper would be finally settled."

There was a prolonged pause until Houston put another question.

"Wait a minute, Low," he said. "Ghosts are admittedly immaterial. In this instance our spook has an extremely palpable body. Surely this is rather unusual? You have made everything else more or less plain. Can you tell me why this dead leper should have tried to murder you and old Filderg? And also how he came to have the actual physical power to do so?"

Low removed his cigarette to look thoughtfully at the end of it. "Now I lapse into the purely theoretical," he answered. "Cases have been known where the assumption of diabolical agency is apparently justifiable."

"Diabolical agency?—I don't follow you."

"I will try to make myself clear, though the subject is still in a stage of vagueness and immaturity. Van Nuysen committed a murder of exceptional atrocity, and afterwards killed himself. Now, bodies of suicides are known to be peculiarly susceptible to spiritual influences, even to the point of arrested corruption. Add to this our knowledge that the highest aim of an evil spirit is to gain possession of a material body. If I carried out my theory to its logical conclusion, I should say that Van Nuysen's body is hidden somewhere on these premises—that this body is intermittently animated by some spirit, which at certain points is forced to re-enact the gruesome tragedy of the Van Nuysens. Should any living person chance to occupy the position of the first victim, so much the worse for him!"

For some minutes Houston made no remark on this singular expression of opinion.

"But have you ever met with anything of the sort before?" he said at last.

"I can recall," replied Flaxman Low thoughtfully, "quite a number of cases which would seem to bear out this hypothesis. Among them a curious problem of haunting exhaustively examined by Busner in the early part of 1888, at which I was myself lucky enough to assist. Indeed, I may add that the affair which I have recently engaged upon in Vienna offers some rather similar features. There, however, we had to stop short of excavation, by which alone any specific results might have been attained."

"Then you are of the opinion," said Houston, "that pulling the house to pieces might cast some further light upon this affair?"

"I cannot see any better course," said Mr. Low.

Then Houston closed the discussion by a very definite declaration.

"This house shall come down!"

So "The Spaniards" was pulled down.

Such is the story of "The Spaniards," Hammersmith, and it has been given the first place in this series because, although it may not be of so strange a nature as some that will follow it, yet it seems to us to embody in a high degree the peculiar methods by which Mr. Flaxman Low is wont to approach these cases.

The work of demolition, begun at the earliest possible moment, did not occupy very long, and during its early stages, under the boarding at an angle of the landing was found a skeleton. Several of the phalanges were missing, and other indications also established beyond a doubt the fact that the remains were the remains of a leper.

The skeleton is now in the museum of one of our city hospitals. It bears a scientific ticket, and is the only evidence extant of the correctness of Mr. Flaxman Low's methods and the possible truth of his extraordinary theories.

HERBERT GEORGE WELLS *(1866–1946) is one of the towering figures of English literature of the twentieth century. Best remembered today as an author of science fiction (*War of the Worlds, The Time Machine, The Island of Dr. Moreau, *and* The Invisible Man *are timeless classics), Wells was incredibly prolific, penning several dozen novels, numerous short stories, and works of social commentary, history, satire, biography and autobiography. Educated as a biologist, he styled himself a "futurist" and was an outspoken critic of the government and its military, often expressing Socialist or pacifist views. Wells is credited with fostering the style dubbed "Wells's law," later characterized by H. P. Lovecraft as crafting a "hoax"—creating an utterly realistic tale with a single extraordinary assumption (e.g., an invasion from Mars). The following story, while humorous, may also be seen as a poke at the serious Spiritualist movement that was afoot in England. It first appeared in the* Strand Magazine *in March 1902.*

THE STORY OF THE
INEXPERIENCED GHOST

by H. G. Wells

(1902)

The scene amidst which Clayton told his last story comes back very vividly to my mind. There he sat, for the greater part of the time, in the corner of the authentic settle* by the spacious open fire, and Sanderson sat beside

---

* A long wooden bench, usually with a box under the seat.

him smoking the Broseley clay* that bore his name. There was Evans, and that marvel among actors, Wish, who is also a modest man. We had all come down to the Mermaid Club† that Saturday morning, except Clayton, who had slept there overnight—which indeed gave him the opening of his story. We had golfed until golfing was invisible; we had dined, and we were in that mood of tranquil kindliness when men will suffer a story. When Clayton began to tell one, we naturally supposed he was lying. It may be that indeed he was lying—of that the reader will speedily be able to judge as well as I. He began, it is true, with an air of matter-of-fact anecdote, but that we thought was only the incurable artifice of the man.

"I say!" he remarked, after a long consideration of the upward rain of sparks from the log that Sanderson had thumped, "you know I was alone here last night?"

"Except for the domestics," said Wish.

"Who sleep in the other wing," said Clayton. "Yes. Well—" He pulled at his cigar for some little time as though he still hesitated about his confidence. Then he said, quite quietly, "I caught a ghost!"

"Caught a ghost, did you?" said Sanderson. "Where is it?"

And Evans, who admires Clayton immensely and has been four weeks in America, shouted, "CAUGHT a ghost, did you, Clayton? I'm glad of it! Tell us all about it right now."

Clayton said he would in a minute, and asked him to shut the door.

He looked apologetically at me. "There's no eavesdropping of course, but we don't want to upset our very excellent service with any rumours of ghosts in the place. There's too much shadow and oak panelling to trifle with that. And this, you know, wasn't a regular ghost. I don't think it will come again—ever."

"You mean to say you didn't keep it?" said Sanderson.

"I hadn't the heart to," said Clayton.

---

* Broseley is a town in Shropshire famous for its manufacture of clay pipes; this was evidently a custom-made pipe, with the owner's name affixed.

† Named after the original Mermaid Club, an Elizabethan literary society affiliated with London's Mermaid Tavern that included John Donne, Ben Jonson, and allegedly (though unlikely) William Shakespeare. The tavern itself was destroyed in the Great Fire in 1666.

And Sanderson said he was surprised.

We laughed, and Clayton looked aggrieved. "I know," he said, with the flicker of a smile, "but the fact is it really WAS a ghost, and I'm as sure of it as I am that I am talking to you now. I'm not joking. I mean what I say."

Sanderson drew deeply at his pipe, with one reddish eye on Clayton, and then emitted a thin jet of smoke more eloquent than many words.

Clayton ignored the comment. "It is the strangest thing that has ever happened in my life. You know, I never believed in ghosts or anything of the sort, before, ever; and then, you know, I bag one in a corner; and the whole business is in my hands."

He meditated still more profoundly, and produced and began to pierce a second cigar with a curious little stabber he affected.

"You talked to it?" asked Wish.

"For the space, probably, of an hour."

"Chatty?" I said, joining the party of the sceptics.

"The poor devil was in trouble," said Clayton, bowed over his cigar-end and with the very faintest note of reproof.

"Sobbing?" some one asked.

Clayton heaved a realistic sigh at the memory. "Good Lord!" he said; "yes." And then, "Poor fellow! yes."

"Where did you strike it?" asked Evans, in his best American accent.

"I never realised," said Clayton, ignoring him, "the poor sort of thing a ghost might be," and he hung us up again for a time, while he sought for matches in his pocket and lit and warmed to his cigar.

"I took an advantage," he reflected at last.

We were none of us in a hurry. "A character," he said, "remains just the same character for all that it's been disembodied. That's a thing we too often forget. People with a certain strength or fixity of purpose may have ghosts of a certain strength and fixity of purpose—most haunting ghosts, you know, must be as one-idea'd as monomaniacs and as obstinate as mules to come back again and again. This poor creature wasn't." He suddenly looked up rather queerly, and his eye went round the room. "I say it," he said, "in all kindliness, but that is the plain truth of the case. Even at the first glance he struck me as weak."

He punctuated with the help of his cigar.

"I came upon him, you know, in the long passage. His back was towards me and I saw him first. Right off I knew him for a ghost. He was transparent and whitish; clean through his chest I could see the glimmer of the little window at the end. And not only his physique but his attitude struck me as being weak. He looked, you know, as though he didn't know in the slightest whatever he meant to do. One hand was on the panelling and the other fluttered to his mouth. Like—SO!"

"What sort of physique?" said Sanderson.

"Lean. You know that sort of young man's neck that has two great flutings down the back, here and here—so! And a little, meanish head with scrubby hair—And rather bad ears. Shoulders bad, narrower than the hips; turn-down collar, ready-made short jacket, trousers baggy and a little frayed at the heels. That's how he took me. I came very quietly up the staircase. I did not carry a light, you know—the candles are on the landing table and there is that lamp—and I was in my list* slippers, and I saw him as I came up. I stopped dead at that—taking him in. I wasn't a bit afraid. I think that in most of these affairs one is never nearly so afraid or excited as one imagines one would be. I was surprised and interested. I thought, 'Good Lord! Here's a ghost at last! And I haven't believed for a moment in ghosts during the last five-and-twenty years.'"

"Um," said Wish.

"I suppose I wasn't on the landing a moment before he found out I was there. He turned on me sharply, and I saw the face of an immature young man, a weak nose, a scrubby little moustache, a feeble chin. So for an instant we stood—he looking over his shoulder at me and regarded one another. Then he seemed to remember his high calling. He turned round, drew himself up, projected his face, raised his arms, spread his hands in approved ghost fashion—came towards me. As he did so his little jaw dropped, and he emitted a faint, drawn-out 'Boo.' No, it wasn't—not a bit dreadful. I'd dined. I'd had a bottle of champagne, and being all alone, perhaps two or three—perhaps even four or five—whiskies, so I was as solid as rocks and no more frightened than if I'd been assailed by a frog. 'Boo!' I said. 'Nonsense. You don't belong to THIS place. What are you doing here?'

---

* Cotton.

"I could see him wince. 'Boo-oo,' he said.

"'Boo—be hanged! Are you a member?' I said; and just to show I didn't care a pin for him I stepped through a corner of him and made to light my candle. 'Are you a member?' I repeated, looking at him sideways.

"He moved a little so as to stand clear of me, and his bearing became crestfallen. 'No,' he said, in answer to the persistent interrogation of my eye; 'I'm not a member—I'm a ghost.'

"'Well, that doesn't give you the run of the Mermaid Club. Is there any one you want to see, or anything of that sort?' and doing it as steadily as possible for fear that he should mistake the carelessness of whisky for the distraction of fear, I got my candle alight. I turned on him, holding it. 'What are you doing here?' I said.

"He had dropped his hands and stopped his booing, and there he stood, abashed and awkward, the ghost of a weak, silly, aimless young man. 'I'm haunting,' he said.

"'You haven't any business to,' I said in a quiet voice.

"'I'm a ghost,' he said, as if in defence.

"'That may be, but you haven't any business to haunt here. This is a respectable private club; people often stop here with nursemaids and children, and, going about in the careless way you do, some poor little mite could easily come upon you and be scared out of her wits. I suppose you didn't think of that?'

"'No, sir,' he said, 'I didn't.'

"'You should have done. You haven't any claim on the place, have you? Weren't murdered here, or anything of that sort?'

"'None, sir; but I thought as it was old and oak-panelled—'

"'That's NO excuse.' I regarded him firmly. 'Your coming here is a mistake,' I said, in a tone of friendly superiority. I feigned to see if I had my matches, and then looked up at him frankly. 'If I were you I wouldn't wait for cock-crow—I'd vanish right away.'

"He looked embarrassed. 'The fact IS, sir—' he began.

"'I'd vanish,' I said, driving it home.

"'The fact is, sir, that—somehow—I can't.'

"'You CAN'T?'

"'No, sir. There's something I've forgotten. I've been hanging about here since midnight last night, hiding in the cupboards of the empty bedrooms and things like that. I'm flurried. I've never come haunting before, and it seems to put me out.'

"'Put you out?'

"'Yes, sir. I've tried to do it several times, and it doesn't come off. There's some little thing has slipped me, and I can't get back.'

"That, you know, rather bowled me over. He looked at me in such an abject way that for the life of me I couldn't keep up quite the high, hectoring vein I had adopted. 'That's queer,' I said, and as I spoke I fancied I heard some one moving about down below. 'Come into my room and tell me more about it,' I said. 'I didn't, of course, understand this,' and I tried to take him by the arm. But, of course, you might as well have tried to take hold of a puff of smoke! I had forgotten my number, I think; anyhow, I remember going into several bedrooms—it was lucky I was the only soul in that wing—until I saw my traps.* 'Here we are,' I said, and sat down in the arm-chair; 'sit down and tell me all about it. It seems to me you have got yourself into a jolly awkward position, old chap.'

"Well, he said he wouldn't sit down! He'd prefer to flit up and down the room if it was all the same to me. And so he did, and in a little while we were deep in a long and serious talk. And presently, you know, something of those whiskies and sodas evaporated out of me, and I began to realise just a little what a thundering rum and weird business it was that I was in. There he was, semi-transparent—the proper conventional phantom, and noiseless except for his ghost of a voice—flitting to and fro in that nice, clean, chintz-hung old bedroom. You could see the gleam of the copper candlesticks through him, and the lights on the brass fender, and the corners of the framed engravings on the wall—and there he was telling me all about this wretched little life of his that had recently ended on earth. He hadn't a particularly honest face, you know, but being transparent, of course, he couldn't avoid telling the truth."

"Eh?" said Wish, suddenly sitting up in his chair.

"What?" said Clayton.

---

* Traps in this sense refers to baggage or suitcases.

"Being transparent—couldn't avoid telling the truth—I don't see it," said Wish.

"*I* don't see it," said Clayton, with inimitable assurance. "But it IS so, I can assure you nevertheless. I don't believe he got once a nail's breadth off the Bible truth. He told me how he had been killed—he went down into a London basement with a candle to look for a leakage of gas—and described himself as a senior English master in a London private school when that release occurred."

"Poor wretch!" said I.

"That's what I thought, and the more he talked the more I thought it. There he was, purposeless in life and purposeless out of it. He talked of his father and mother and his schoolmaster, and all who had ever been anything to him in the world, meanly. He had been too sensitive, too nervous; none of them had ever valued him properly or understood him, he said. He had never had a real friend in the world, I think; he had never had a success. He had shirked games and failed examinations. 'It's like that with some people,' he said; 'whenever I got into the examination-room or anywhere everything seemed to go.' Engaged to be married of course—to another over-sensitive person, I suppose—when the indiscretion with the gas escape ended his affairs. 'And where are you now?' I asked. 'Not in—?'

"He wasn't clear on that point at all. The impression he gave me was of a sort of vague, intermediate state, a special reserve for souls too non-existent for anything so positive as either sin or virtue. *I* don't know. He was much too egotistical and unobservant to give me any clear idea of the kind of place, kind of country, there is on the Other Side of Things. Wherever he was, he seems to have fallen in with a set of kindred spirits: ghosts of weak Cockney young men, who were on a footing of Christian names, and among these there was certainly a lot of talk about 'going haunting' and things like that. Yes—going haunting! They seemed to think 'haunting' a tremendous adventure, and most of them funked it all the time. And so primed, you know, he had come."

"But really!" said Wish to the fire.

"These are the impressions he gave me, anyhow," said Clayton, modestly. "I may, of course, have been in a rather uncritical state, but that was the sort of background he gave to himself. He kept flitting up and down, with his thin voice going talking, talking about his wretched self, and never a word of clear, firm statement from first to last. He was thinner and sillier and more pointless than if he had been real and alive. Only then, you know, he would not have been in my bedroom here—if he HAD been alive. I should have kicked him out."

"Of course," said Evans, "there ARE poor mortals like that."

"And there's just as much chance of their having ghosts as the rest of us," I admitted.

"What gave a sort of point to him, you know, was the fact that he did seem within limits to have found himself out. The mess he had made of haunting had depressed him terribly. He had been told it would be a 'lark'; he had come expecting it to be a 'lark,' and here it was, nothing but another failure added to his record! He proclaimed himself an utter out-and-out failure. He said, and I can quite believe it, that he had never tried to do anything all his life that he hadn't made a perfect mess of—and through all the wastes of eternity he never would. If he had had sympathy, perhaps—. He paused at that, and stood regarding me. He remarked that, strange as it might seem to me, nobody, not any one, ever, had given him the amount of sympathy I was doing now. I could see what he wanted straight away, and I determined to head him off at once. I may be a brute, you know, but being the Only Real Friend, the recipient of the confidences of one of these egotistical weaklings, ghost or body, is beyond my physical endurance. I got up briskly. 'Don't you brood on these things too much,' I said. 'The thing you've got to do is to get out of this—sharp. You pull yourself together and TRY.' 'I can't,' he said. 'You try,' I said, and try he did."

"Try!" said Sanderson. "HOW?"

"Passes," said Clayton.

"Passes?"

"Complicated series of gestures and passes with the hands. That's how he had come in and that's how he had to get out again. Lord! what a business I had!"

"But how could ANY series of passes—?" I began.

"My dear man," said Clayton, turning on me and putting a great emphasis on certain words, "you want EVERYTHING clear. *I* don't know

HOW. All I know is that you DO—that HE did, anyhow, at least. After a fearful time, you know, he got his passes right and suddenly disappeared."

"Did you," said Sanderson, slowly, "observe the passes?"

"Yes," said Clayton, and seemed to think. "It was tremendously queer," he said. "There we were, I and this thin vague ghost, in that silent room, in this silent, empty inn, in this silent little Friday-night town. Not a sound except our voices and a faint panting he made when he swung. There was the bedroom candle, and one candle on the dressing-table alight, that was all—sometimes one or other would flare up into a tall, lean, astonished flame for a space. And queer things happened. 'I can't,' he said; 'I shall never—!' And suddenly he sat down on a little chair at the foot of the bed and began to sob and sob. Lord! what a harrowing, whimpering thing he seemed!

"'You pull yourself together,' I said, and tried to pat him on the back, and . . . my confounded hand went through him! By that time, you know, I wasn't nearly so—massive as I had been on the landing. I got the queerness of it full. I remember snatching back my hand out of him, as it were, with a little thrill, and walking over to the dressing-table. 'You pull yourself together,' I said to him, 'and try.' And in order to encourage and help him I began to try as well."

"What!" said Sanderson, "the passes?"

"Yes, the passes."

"But—" I said, moved by an idea that eluded me for a space.

"This is interesting," said Sanderson, with his finger in his pipe-bowl. "You mean to say this ghost of yours gave away—"

"Did his level best to give away the whole confounded barrier? YES."

"He didn't," said Wish; "he couldn't. Or you'd have gone there too."

"That's precisely it," I said, finding my elusive idea put into words for me.

"That IS precisely it," said Clayton, with thoughtful eyes upon the fire.

For just a little while there was silence.

"And at last he did it?" said Sanderson.

"At last he did it. I had to keep him up to it hard, but he did it at last—rather suddenly. He despaired, we had a scene, and then he got up abruptly and asked me to go through the whole performance, slowly, so that he might see. 'I believe,' he said, 'if I could SEE I should spot what was wrong at once.' And he did. 'I know,' he said. 'What do you know?' said I. 'I know,' he repeated. Then he said, peevishly, 'I CAN'T do it if you look at me—I really CAN'T; it's been that, partly, all along. I'm such a nervous fellow that you put me out.' Well, we had a bit of an argument. Naturally I wanted to see; but he was as obstinate as a mule, and suddenly I had come over as tired as a dog—he tired me out. 'All right,' I said, 'I won't look at you,' and turned towards the mirror, on the wardrobe, by the bed.

"He started off very fast. I tried to follow him by looking in the looking-glass, to see just what it was had hung. Round went his arms and his hands, so, and so, and so, and then with a rush came to the last gesture of all—you stand erect and open out your arms—and so, don't you know, he stood. And then he didn't! He didn't! He wasn't! I wheeled round from the looking-glass to him. There was nothing, I was alone, with the flaring candles and a staggering mind. What had happened? Had anything happened? Had I been dreaming? . . . And then, with an absurd note of finality about it, the clock upon the landing discovered the moment was ripe for striking ONE. So!—Ping! And I was as grave and sober as a judge, with all my champagne and whisky gone into the vast serene. Feeling queer, you know—confoundedly QUEER! Queer! Good Lord!"

He regarded his cigar-ash for a moment. "That's all that happened," he said.

"And then you went to bed?" asked Evans.

"What else was there to do?"

I looked Wish in the eye. We wanted to scoff, and there was something, something perhaps in Clayton's voice and manner, that hampered our desire.

"And about these passes?" said Sanderson.

"I believe I could do them now."

"Oh!" said Sanderson, and produced a pen-knife and set himself to grub the dottel* out of the bowl of his clay.

"Why don't you do them now?" said Sanderson, shutting his pen-knife with a click.

"That's what I'm going to do," said Clayton.

---

* The half-burnt tobacco at the bottom of the pipe bowl.

"They won't work," said Evans.

"If they do—" I suggested.

"You know, I'd rather you didn't," said Wish, stretching out his legs.

"Why?" asked Evans.

"I'd rather he didn't," said Wish.

"But he hasn't got 'em right," said Sanderson, plugging too much tobacco in his pipe.

"All the same, I'd rather he didn't," said Wish.

We argued with Wish. He said that for Clayton to go through those gestures was like mocking a serious matter. "But you don't believe—?" I said. Wish glanced at Clayton, who was staring into the fire, weighing something in his mind. "I do—more than half, anyhow, I do," said Wish.

"Clayton," said I, "you're too good a liar for us. Most of it was all right. But that disappearance . . . happened to be convincing. Tell us, it's a tale of cock and bull."

He stood up without heeding me, took the middle of the hearthrug, and faced me. For a moment he regarded his feet thoughtfully, and then for all the rest of the time his eyes were on the opposite wall, with an intent expression. He raised his two hands slowly to the level of his eyes and so began. . . .

Now, Sanderson is a Freemason, a member of the lodge of the Four Kings,* which devotes itself so ably to the study and elucidation of all the mysteries of Masonry past and present, and among the students of this lodge Sanderson is by no means the least. He followed Clayton's motions with a singular interest in his reddish eye. "That's not bad," he said, when it was done. "You really do, you know, put things together, Clayton, in a most amazing fashion. But there's one little detail out."

"I know," said Clayton. "I believe I could tell you which."

"Well?"

"This," said Clayton, and did a queer little twist and writhing and thrust of the hands.

"Yes."

---

* There were several lodges of Freemasons in London, but this does not appear to have been one of them.

"That, you know, was what HE couldn't get right," said Clayton. "But how do YOU—?"

"Most of this business, and particularly how you invented it, I don't understand at all," said Sanderson, "but just that phase—I do." He reflected. "These happen to be a series of gestures—connected with a certain branch of esoteric Masonry. Probably you know. Or else—HOW?" He reflected still further. "I do not see I can do any harm in telling you just the proper twist. After all, if you know, you know; if you don't, you don't."

"I know nothing," said Clayton, "except what the poor devil let out last night."

"Well, anyhow," said Sanderson, and placed his churchwarden* very carefully upon the shelf over the fireplace. Then very rapidly he gesticulated with his hands.

"So?" said Clayton, repeating.

"So," said Sanderson, and took his pipe in hand again.

"Ah, NOW," said Clayton, "I can do the whole thing—right."

He stood up before the waning fire and smiled at us all. But I think there was just a little hesitation in his smile. "If I begin—" he said.

"I wouldn't begin," said Wish.

"It's all right!" said Evans. "Matter is indestructible. You don't think any jiggery-pokery of this sort is going to snatch Clayton into the world of shades. Not it! You may try, Clayton, so far as I'm concerned, until your arms drop off at the wrists."

"I don't believe that," said Wish, and stood up and put his arm on Clayton's shoulder. "You've made me half believe in that story somehow, and I don't want to see the thing done!"

"Goodness!" said I, "here's Wish frightened!"

"I am," said Wish, with real or admirably feigned intensity. "I believe that if he goes through these motions right he'll GO."

"He'll not do anything of the sort," I cried. "There's only one way out of this world for men, and Clayton is thirty years from that. Besides . . . And such a ghost! Do you think—?"

---

* A long-stemmed pipe.

Wish interrupted me by moving. He walked out from among our chairs and stopped beside the tole and stood there. "Clayton," he said, "you're a fool."

Clayton, with a humorous light in his eyes, smiled back at him. "Wish," he said, "is right and all you others are wrong. I shall go. I shall get to the end of these passes, and as the last swish whistles through the air, Presto!— this hearthrug will be vacant, the room will be blank amazement, and a respectably dressed gentleman of fifteen stone* will plump into the world of shades. I'm certain. So will you be. I decline to argue further. Let the thing be tried."

"NO," said Wish, and made a step and ceased, and Clayton raised his hands once more to repeat the spirit's passing.

By that time, you know, we were all in a state of tension—largely because of the behaviour of Wish. We sat all of us with our eyes on Clayton—I, at least, with a sort of tight, stiff feeling about me as though from the back of my skull to the middle of my thighs my body had been changed to steel. And there, with a gravity that was imperturbably serene, Clayton bowed and swayed and waved his hands and arms before us. As he drew towards the end one piled up, one tingled in one's teeth. The last gesture, I have said, was to swing the arms out wide open, with the face held up. And when at last he swung out to this closing gesture I ceased even to breathe. It was ridiculous, of course, but you know that ghost-story feeling. It was after dinner, in a queer, old shadowy house. Would he, after all—?

There he stood for one stupendous moment, with his arms open and his upturned face, assured and bright, in the glare of the hanging lamp. We hung through that moment as if it were an age, and then came from all of us something that was half a sigh of infinite relief and half a reassuring "NO!" For visibly—he wasn't going. It was all nonsense. He had told an idle story, and carried it almost to conviction, that was all! . . . And then in that moment the face of Clayton, changed.

It changed. It changed as a lit house changes when its lights are suddenly extinguished. His eyes were suddenly eyes that were fixed, his smile

---

* Or 210 pounds.

was frozen on his lips, and he stood there still. He stood there, very gently swaying.

That moment, too, was an age. And then, you know, chairs were scraping, things were falling, and we were all moving. His knees seemed to give, and he fell forward, and Evans rose and caught him in his arms. . . .

It stunned us all. For a minute I suppose no one said a coherent thing. We believed it, yet could not believe it. . . . I came out of a muddled stupefaction to find myself kneeling beside him, and his vest and shirt were torn open, and Sanderson's hand lay on his heart. . . .

Well—the simple fact before us could very well wait our convenience; there was no hurry for us to comprehend. It lay there for an hour; it lies athwart my memory, black and amazing still, to this day. Clayton had, indeed, passed into the world that lies so near to and so far from our own, and he had gone thither by the only road that mortal man may take. But whether he did indeed pass there by that poor ghost's incantation, or whether he was stricken suddenly by apoplexy* in the midst of an idle tale—as the coroner's jury would have us believe—is no matter for my judging; it is just one of those inexplicable riddles that must remain unsolved until the final solution of all things shall come. All I certainly know is that, in the very moment, in the very instant, of concluding those passes, he changed, and staggered, and fell down before us—dead!

---

* What we now call a stroke.

Koizumi Yakumo, born **PATRICK LAFCADIO HEARN** *(1850–1904), was a writer of Greek-Irish descent. At the age of nineteen, he emigrated to the United States and began writing for newspapers. He moved to the West Indies and eventually to Japan, where he immersed himself in its culture and heritage, eventually adopting Japan as his home. Hearn married a Japanese woman and had four children. When he accepted a teaching position in Tokyo in 1896, he changed his name, eventually becoming a Japanese citizen. Hearn wrote extensively about Japanese culture and is probably best remembered for his tales of Japanese ghosts. The following appeared in his collection* Kwaidan: Stories and Studies of Strange Things *(1904).*

JIKININKI

by Lafcadio Hearn

(1904)

O nce, when Muso Kokushi, a priest of the Zen sect, was journeying alone through the province of Mino,* he lost his way in a mountain-district where there was nobody to direct him. For a long time he wandered about helplessly; and he was beginning to despair of finding shelter for the night, when he perceived, on the top of a hill lighted by the last rays of the sun, one of those little hermitages, called anjitsu, which are built for solitary priests. It seemed to be in ruinous condition; but he hastened to it eagerly, and found that it was inhabited by an aged priest, from whom he begged the favor of a night's lodging. This the old man harshly refused; but he

---

* [Author's note:] The southern part of present-day Gifu Prefecture [on the island of Honshu].

directed Muso to a certain hamlet, in the valley adjoining where lodging and food could be obtained.

Muso found his way to the hamlet, which consisted of less than a dozen farm-cottages; and he was kindly received at the dwelling of the headman. Forty or fifty persons were assembled in the principal apartment, at the moment of Muso's arrival; but he was shown into a small separate room, where he was promptly supplied with food and bedding. Being very tired, he lay down to rest at an early hour; but a little before midnight he was roused from sleep by a sound of loud weeping in the next apartment. Presently the sliding-screens were gently pushed apart; and a young man, carrying a lighted lantern, entered the room, respectfully saluted him, and said—

"Reverend Sir, it is my painful duty to tell you that I am now the responsible head of this house. Yesterday I was only the eldest son. But when you came here, tired as you were, we did not wish that you should feel embarrassed in any way: therefore we did not tell you that father had died only a few hours before. The people whom you saw in the next room are the inhabitants of this village: they all assembled here to pay their last respects to the dead; and now they are going to another village, about three miles off—for by our custom, no one of us may remain in this village during the night after a death has taken place. We make the proper offerings and prayers—then we go away, leaving the corpse alone. Strange things always happen in the house where a corpse has thus been left: so we think that it will be better for you to come away with us. We can find you good lodging in the other village. But perhaps, as you are a priest, you have no fear of demons or evil spirits; and, if you are not afraid of being left alone with the body, you will be very welcome to the use of this poor house. However, I must tell you that nobody, except a priest, would dare to remain here tonight."

Muso made answer—

"For your kind intention and your generous hospitality, I am deeply grateful. But I am sorry that you did not tell me of your father's death when I came—for, though I was a little tired, I certainly was not so tired that I should have found difficulty in doing my duty as a priest. Had you told me, I could have performed the service before your departure. As it is, I shall perform the service after you have gone away; and I shall stay by the body until morning. I do not know what you mean by your words about the danger of staying here alone; but I am not afraid of ghosts or demons: therefore please to feel no anxiety on my account."

The young man appeared to be rejoiced by these assurances, and expressed his gratitude in fitting words. Then the other members of the family, and the folk assembled in the adjoining room, having been told of the priest's kind promises, came to thank him—after which the master of the house said—

"Now, reverend Sir, much as we regret to leave you alone, we must bid you farewell. By the rule of our village, none of us can stay here after midnight. We beg, kind Sir, that you will take every care of your honorable body, while we are unable to attend upon you. And if you happen to hear or see anything strange during our absence, please tell us of the matter when we return in the morning."

All then left the house, except the priest, who went to the room where the dead body was lying. The usual offerings had been set before the corpse; and a small Buddhist lamp—tomyo—was burning. The priest recited the service, and performed the funeral ceremonies—after which he entered into meditation. So meditating he remained through several silent hours; and there was no sound in the deserted village. But, when the hush of the night was at its deepest, there noiselessly entered a Shape, vague and vast; and in the same moment Muso found himself without power to move or speak. He saw that Shape lift the corpse, as with hands, devour it, more quickly than a cat devours a rat—beginning at the head, and eating everything: the hair and the bones and even the shroud. And the monstrous Thing, having thus consumed the body, turned to the offerings, and ate them also. Then it went away, as mysteriously as it had come.

When the villagers returned next morning, they found the priest awaiting them at the door of the headman's dwelling. All in turn saluted him; and when they had entered, and looked about the room, no one expressed any surprise at the disappearance of the dead body and the offerings. But the master of the house said to Muso—

"Reverent Sir, you have probably seen unpleasant things during the night: all of us were anxious about you. But now we are very happy to find you alive and unharmed. Gladly we would have stayed with you, if it had been possible. But the law of our village, as I told you last evening, obliges us to quit our houses after a death has taken place, and to leave the corpse alone. Whenever this law has been broken, heretofore, some great misfortune has followed. Whenever it is obeyed, we find that the corpse and the offerings disappear during our absence. Perhaps you have seen the cause."

Then Muso told of the dim and awful Shape that had entered the death-chamber to devour the body and the offerings. No person seemed to be surprised by his narration; and the master of the house observed—

"What you have told us, reverend Sir, agrees with what has been said about this matter from ancient time."

Muso then inquired—

"Does not the priest on the hill sometimes perform the funeral service for your dead?"

"What priest?" the young man asked.

"The priest who yesterday evening directed me to this village," answered Muso. "I called at his anjitsu on the hill yonder. He refused me lodging, but told me the way here."

The listeners looked at each other, as in astonishment; and, after a moment of silence, the master of the house said—

"Reverend Sir, there is no priest and there is no anjitsu on the hill. For the time of many generations there has not been any resident-priest in this neighborhood."

Muso said nothing more on the subject; for it was evident that his kind hosts supposed him to have been deluded by some goblin. But after having bidden them farewell, and obtained all necessary information as to his road, he determined to look again for the hermitage on the hill, and so to ascertain whether he had really been deceived. He found the anjitsu without any difficulty; and, this time, its aged occupant invited him to enter. When he had done so, the hermit humbly bowed down before him, exclaiming—"Ah! I am ashamed!—I am very much ashamed!—I am exceedingly ashamed!"

"You need not be ashamed for having refused me shelter," said Muso. "You directed me to the village yonder, where I was very kindly treated; and I thank you for that favor."

"I can give no man shelter," the recluse made answer—"and it is not for the refusal that I am ashamed. I am ashamed only that you should have seen me in my real shape—for it was I who devoured the corpse and the offerings last night before your eyes . . . Know, reverend Sir, that I am a jikininki,*—an eater of human flesh. Have pity upon me, and suffer me to confess the secret fault by which I became reduced to this condition.

"A long, long time ago, I was a priest in this desolate region. There was no other priest for many leagues around. So, in that time, the bodies of the mountain-folk who died used to be brought here—sometimes from great distances—in order that I might repeat over them the holy service. But I repeated the service and performed the rites only as a matter of business— I thought only of the food and the clothes that my sacred profession enabled me to gain. And because of this selfish impiety I was reborn, immediately after my death, into the state of a jikininki. Since then I have been obliged to feed upon the corpses of the people who die in this district: every one of them I must devour in the way that you saw last night . . . Now, reverend Sir, let me beseech you to perform a Segaki-service† for me: help me by your prayers, I entreat you, so that I may be soon able to escape from this horrible state of existence . . ."

No sooner had the hermit uttered this petition than he disappeared; and the hermitage also disappeared at the same instant. And Muso Kokushi found himself kneeling alone in the high grass, beside an ancient and moss-grown tomb of the form called go-rin-ishi,‡ which seemed to be the tomb of a priest.

---

* [Author's note:] Literally, a man-eating goblin. The Japanese narrator gives also the Sanscrit term, "Rakshasa;" but this word is quite as vague as jikininki, since there are many kinds of Rakshasas. Apparently the word jikininki signifies here one of the Baramon-Rasetsu-Gaki—forming the twenty-sixth class of pretas ("hungry ghosts") enumerated in the old Buddhist books.

† [Author's note:] A Segaki-service is a special Buddhist service performed on behalf of beings supposed to have entered into the condition of gaki (pretas), or hungry spirits. For a brief account of such a service, see my *Japanese Miscellany.*

‡ [Author's note:] Literally, "five-circle [or five-zone] stone." A funeral monument consisting of five parts superimposed—each of a different form—symbolizing the five mystic elements: Ether, Air, Fire, Water, Earth.

JOSEPH RUDYARD KIPLING *(1865–1936), though born in India, was the quintessential English writer. Though decried today as a propagandist for the worst aspects of the British Empire, his work was among the most popular of its day. In 1907, he was the youngest person to date to receive the Nobel Prize in Literature; he was also the first English-language writer to be so honored.* The Jungle Book *(1894) is a classic, as is* Kim *(1901), and his numerous short stories are frequently filmed and retold. Perhaps because of his fascination with Eastern civilization, he wrote much speculative fiction, including ghost stories. His writing for children, including a sequel to* The Jungle Book, *as well as poetry, brought him much joy, including extensive correspondence with child readers. Sadly, only one of his three children lived to adulthood—Kipling's beloved daughter Josephine died in 1899 at the age of six and his son John died in 1918. The following, which first appeared in* Scribner's Magazine *for August 1904, is heartbreakingly beautiful.*

THEY

by Rudyard Kipling

(1904)

One view called me to another; one hill top to its fellow, half across the county, and since I could answer at no more trouble than the snapping forward of a lever, I let the country flow under my wheels. The orchid-studded flats of the East gave way to the thyme, ilex, and grey grass of the Downs; these again to the rich cornland and fig-trees of the lower coast, where you carry the beat of the tide on your left hand for fifteen level miles; and when at last I turned inland through a huddle of rounded hills and woods I had run myself clean out of my known marks. Beyond that precise hamlet which stands godmother to the capital of the United States,[*] I found hidden villages where bees, the only things awake, boomed in eighty-foot lindens that overhung grey Norman churches; miraculous brooks diving under stone bridges built for heavier traffic than would ever vex them again; tithe-barns[†] larger than their churches, and an old smithy that cried out aloud how it had once been a hall of the Knights of the Temple. Gipsies I found on a common where the gorse, bracken, and heath fought it out together up a mile of Roman road; and a little farther on I disturbed a red fox rolling dog-fashion in the naked sunlight.

As the wooded hills closed about me I stood up in the car to take the bearings of that great Down whose ringed head is a landmark for fifty miles across the low countries. I judged that the lie of the country would bring me across some westward running road that went to his feet, but I did not allow for the confusing veils of the woods. A quick turn plunged me first into a green cutting brimful of liquid sunshine, next into a gloomy tunnel where last year's dead leaves whispered and scuffled about my tyres. The strong hazel stuff meeting overhead had not been cut for a couple of generations at least, nor had any axe helped the moss-cankered oak and beech to spring above them. Here the road changed frankly into a carpetted ride on whose brown velvet spent primrose-clumps showed like jade, and a few sickly, white-stalked bluebells nodded together. As the slope favoured I shut off the power and slid over the whirled leaves, expecting every moment to meet a keeper; but I only heard a jay, far off, arguing against the silence under the twilight of the trees.

Still the track descended. I was on the point of reversing and working my way back on the second speed ere I ended in some swamp, when I saw sunshine through the tangle ahead and lifted the brake.

It was down again at once. As the light beat across my face my fore-wheels took the turf of a great still lawn from which sprang horsemen ten feet high with levelled lances, monstrous peacocks, and sleek round-headed

---

[*] This locational clue points to Washington, a small town near Newcastle-upon-Tyne near the northeast coast of England, but this is belied by the subsequent reference to the Downs (located in southeast England).

[†] A tithe-barn is a structure used for storing tithes received in the form of produce.

maids of honour—blue, black, and glistening—all of clipped yew. Across the lawn—the marshalled woods besieged it on three sides—stood an ancient house of lichened and weather-worn stone, with mullioned windows and roofs of rose-red tile. It was flanked by semi-circular walls, also rose-red, that closed the lawn on the fourth side, and at their feet a box hedge grew man-high. There were doves on the roof about the slim brick chimneys, and I caught a glimpse of an octagonal dove-house behind the screening wall.

Here, then, I stayed; a horseman's green spear laid at my breast; held by the exceeding beauty of that jewel in that setting.

"If I am not packed off for a trespasser, or if this knight does not ride a wallop at me," thought I, "Shakespeare and Queen Elizabeth at least must come out of that half-open garden door and ask me to tea."

A child appeared at an upper window, and I thought the little thing waved a friendly hand. But it was to call a companion, for presently another bright head showed. Then I heard a laugh among the yew-peacocks, and turning to make sure (till then I had been watching the house only) I saw the silver of a fountain behind a hedge thrown up against the sun. The doves on the roof cooed to the cooing water; but between the two notes I caught the utterly happy chuckle of a child absorbed in some light mischief.

The garden door—heavy oak sunk deep in the thickness of the wall—opened further: a woman in a big garden hat set her foot slowly on the time-hollowed stone step and as slowly walked across the turf. I was forming some apology when she lifted up her head and I saw that she was blind.

"I heard you," she said. "Isn't that a motor car?"

"I'm afraid I've made a mistake in my road. I should have turned off up above—I never dreamed"—I began.

"But I'm very glad. Fancy a motor car coming into the garden! It will be such a treat—" She turned and made as though looking about her. "You—you haven't seen any one have you—perhaps?"

"No one to speak to, but the children seemed interested at a distance."

"Which?"

"I saw a couple up at the window just now, and I think I heard a little chap in the grounds."

"Oh, lucky you!" she cried, and her face brightened. "I hear them, of course, but that's all. You've seen them and heard them?"

"Yes," I answered. "And if I know anything of children one of them's having a beautiful time by the fountain yonder. Escaped, I should imagine."

"You're fond of children?"

I gave her one or two reasons why I did not altogether hate them.

"Of course, of course," she said. "Then you understand. Then you won't think it foolish if I ask you to take your car through the gardens, once or twice—quite slowly. I'm sure they'd like to see it. They see so little, poor things. One tries to make their life pleasant, but—" she threw out her hands towards the woods. "We're so out of the world here."

"That will be splendid," I said. "But I can't cut up your grass."

She faced to the right. "Wait a minute," she said. "We're at the South gate, aren't we? Behind those peacocks there's a flagged path. We call it the Peacock's Walk. You can't see it from here, they tell me, but if you squeeze along by the edge of the wood you can turn at the first peacock and get on to the flags."

It was sacrilege to wake that dreaming house-front with the clatter of machinery, but I swung the car to clear the turf, brushed along the edge of the wood and turned in on the broad stone path where the fountain-basin lay like one star-sapphire.

"May I come too?" she cried. "No, please don't help me. They'll like it better if they see me."

She felt her way lightly to the front of the car, and with one foot on the step she called: "Children, oh, children! Look and see what's going to happen!"

The voice would have drawn lost souls from the Pit, for the yearning that underlay its sweetness, and I was not surprised to hear an answering shout behind the yews. It must have been the child by the fountain, but he fled at our approach, leaving a little toy boat in the water. I saw the glint of his blue blouse among the still horsemen.

Very disposedly we paraded the length of the walk and at her request backed again. This time the child had got the better of his panic, but stood far off and doubting.

"The little fellow's watching us," I said. "I wonder if he'd like a ride."

"They're very shy still. Very shy. But, oh, lucky you to be able to see them! Let's listen."

I stopped the machine at once, and the humid stillness, heavy with the scent of box, cloaked us deep. Shears I could hear where some gardener was clipping; a mumble of bees and broken voices that might have been the doves.

"Oh, unkind!" she said weariedly.

"Perhaps they're only shy of the motor. The little maid at the window looks tremendously interested."

"Yes?" She raised her head. "It was wrong of me to say that. They are really fond of me. It's the only thing that makes life worth living—when they're fond of you, isn't it? I daren't think what the place would be without them. By the way, is it beautiful?"

"I think it is the most beautiful place I have ever seen."

"So they all tell me. I can feel it, of course, but that isn't quite the same thing."

"Then have you never—?" I began, but stopped abashed.

"Not since I can remember. It happened when I was only a few months old, they tell me. And yet I must remember something, else how could I dream about colours. I see light in my dreams, and colours, but I never see *them*. I only hear them just as I do when I'm awake."

"It's difficult to see faces in dreams. Some people can, but most of us haven't the gift," I went on, looking up at the window where the child stood all but hidden.

"I've heard that too," she said. "And they tell me that one never sees a dead person's face in a dream. Is that true?"

"I believe it is—now I come to think of it."

"But how is it with yourself—yourself?" The blind eyes turned towards me.

"I have never seen the faces of my dead in any dream," I answered.

"Then it must be as bad as being blind."

The sun had dipped behind the woods and the long shades were possessing the insolent horsemen one by one. I saw the light die from off the top of a glossy-leaved lance and all the brave hard green turn to soft black. The house, accepting another day at end, as it had accepted an hundred thousand gone, seemed to settle deeper into its rest among the shadows.

"Have you ever wanted to?" she said after the silence.

"Very much sometimes," I replied. The child had left the window as the shadows closed upon it.

"Ah! So've I, but I don't suppose it's allowed. . . . Where d'you live?"

"Quite the other side of the county—sixty miles and more, and I must be going back. I've come without my big lamp."

"But it's not dark yet. I can feel it."

"I'm afraid it will be by the time I get home. Could you lend me someone to set me on my road at first? I've utterly lost myself."

"I'll send Madden with you to the cross-roads. We are so out of the world, I don't wonder you were lost! I'll guide you round to the front of the house; but you will go slowly, won't you, till you're out of the grounds? It isn't foolish, do you think?"

"I promise you I'll go like this," I said, and let the car start herself down the flagged path.

We skirted the left wing of the house, whose elaborately cast lead guttering alone was worth a day's journey; passed under a great rose-grown gate in the red wall, and so round to the high front of the house which in beauty and stateliness as much excelled the back as that all others I had seen.

"Is it so very beautiful?" she said wistfully when she heard my raptures. "And you like the lead-figures too? There's the old azalea garden behind. They say that this place must have been made for children. Will you help me out, please? I should like to come with you as far as the cross-roads, but I mustn't leave them. Is that you, Madden? I want you to show this gentleman the way to the cross-roads. He has lost his way but—he has seen them."

A butler appeared noiselessly at the miracle of old oak that must be called the front door, and slipped aside to put on his hat. She stood looking at me with open blue eyes in which no sight lay, and I saw for the first time that she was beautiful.

"Remember," she said quietly, "if you are fond of them you will come again," and disappeared within the house.

The butler in the car said nothing till we were nearly at the lodge gates, where catching a glimpse of a blue blouse in a shrubbery I swerved amply lest the devil that leads little boys to play should drag me into child-murder.

"Excuse me," he asked of a sudden, "but why did you do that, Sir?"

"The child yonder."

"Our young gentleman in blue?"

"Of course."

"He runs about a good deal. Did you see him by the fountain, Sir?"

"Oh, yes, several times. Do we turn here?"

"Yes, Sir. And did you 'appen to see them upstairs too?"

"At the upper window? Yes."

"Was that before the mistress come out to speak to you, Sir?"

"A little before that. Why d'you want to know?"

He paused a little. "Only to make sure that—that they had seen the car, Sir, because with children running about, though I'm sure you're driving particularly careful, there might be an accident. That was all, Sir. Here are the cross-roads. You can't miss your way from now on. Thank you, Sir, but that isn't *our* custom, not with—"

"I beg your pardon," I said, and thrust away the British silver.

"Oh, it's quite right with the rest of 'em as a rule. Goodbye, Sir."

He retired into the armour-plated conning tower of his caste and walked away. Evidently a butler solicitous for the honour of his house, and interested, probably through a maid, in the nursery.

Once beyond the signposts at the cross-roads I looked back, but the crumpled hills interlaced so jealously that I could not see where the house had lain. When I asked its name at a cottage along the road, the fat woman who sold sweetmeats there gave me to understand that people with motor cars had small right to live—much less to "go about talking like carriage folk." They were not a pleasant-mannered community.

When I retraced my route on the map that evening I was little wiser. Hawkin's Old Farm appeared to be the survey title of the place, and the old *County Gazetteer*, generally so ample, did not allude to it. The big house of those parts was Hodnington Hall, Georgian with early Victorian embellishments, as an atrocious steel engraving attested. I carried my difficulty to a neighbour—a deep-rooted tree of that soil—and he gave me a name of a family which conveyed no meaning.

A month or so later—I went again, or it may have been that my car took the road of her own volition. She over-ran the fruitless Downs, threaded every turn of the maze of lanes below the hills, drew through the high-walled woods, impenetrable in their full leaf, came out at the cross roads where the butler had left me, and a little further on developed an internal trouble which forced me to turn her in on a grass way-waste that cut into a summer-silent hazel wood. So far as I could make sure by the sun and a six-inch Ordnance map, this should be the road flank of that wood which I had first explored from the heights above. I made a mighty serious business of my repairs and a glittering shop of my repair kit, spanners, pump, and the like, which I spread out orderly upon a rug. It was a trap to catch all childhood, for on such a day, I argued, the children would not be far off. When I paused in my work I listened, but the wood was so full of the noises of summer (though the birds had mated) that I could not at first distinguish these from the tread of small cautious feet stealing across the dead leaves. I rang my bell in an alluring manner, but the feet fled, and I repented, for to a child a sudden noise is very real terror. I must have been at work half an hour when I heard in the wood the voice of the blind woman crying: "Children, oh children, where are you?" and the stillness made slow to close on the perfection of that cry. She came towards me, half feeling her way between the tree boles, and though a child it seemed clung to her skirt, it swerved into the leafage like a rabbit as she drew nearer.

"Is that you?" she said, "from the other side of the county?"

"Yes, it's me from the other side of the county."

"Then why didn't you come through the upper woods? They were there just now."

"They were here a few minutes ago. I expect they knew my car had broken down, and came to see the fun."

"Nothing serious, I hope? How do cars break down?"

"In fifty different ways. Only mine has chosen the fifty first."

She laughed merrily at the tiny joke, cooed with delicious laughter, and pushed her hat back.

"Let me hear," she said.

"Wait a moment," I cried, "and I'll get you a cushion."

She set her foot on the rug all covered with spare parts, and stooped above it eagerly. "What delightful things!" The hands through which she saw glanced in the chequered sunlight. "A box here—another box! Why you've arranged them like playing shop!"

"I confess now that I put it out to attract them. I don't need half those things really."

"How nice of you! I heard your bell in the upper wood. You say they were here before that?"

"I'm sure of it. Why are they so shy? That little fellow in blue who was with you just now ought to have got over his fright. He's been watching me like a Red Indian."

"It must have been your bell," she said. "I heard one of them go past me in trouble when I was coming down. They're shy—so shy even with me." She turned her face over her shoulder and cried again: "Children! Oh, children! Look and see!"

"They must have gone off together on their own affairs," I suggested, for there was a murmur behind us of lowered voices broken by the sudden squeaking giggles of childhood. I returned to my tinkerings and she leaned forward, her chin on her hand, listening interestedly.

"How many are they?" I said at last. The work was finished, but I saw no reason to go.

Her forehead puckered a little in thought. "I don't quite know," she said simply. "Sometimes more—sometimes less. They come and stay with me because I love them, you see."

"That must be very jolly," I said, replacing a drawer, and as I spoke I heard the inanity of my answer.

"You—you aren't laughing at me," she cried. "I—I haven't any of my own. I never married. People laugh at me sometimes about them because—because—"

"Because they're savages," I returned. "It's nothing to fret for. That sort laugh at everything that isn't in their own fat lives."

"I don't know. How should I? I only don't like being laughed at about *them*. It hurts; and when one can't see . . . . I don't want to seem silly," her chin quivered like a child's as she spoke, "but we blindies have only one skin, I think. Everything outside hits straight at our souls. It's different with you. You've such good defences in your eyes—looking out—before anyone can really pain you in your soul. People forget that with us."

I was silent reviewing that inexhaustible matter—the more than inherited (since it is also carefully taught) brutality of the Christian peoples, beside which the mere heathendom of the West Coast nigger is clean and restrained.* It led me a long distance into myself.

"Don't do that!" she said of a sudden, putting her hands before her eyes.

"What?"

She made a gesture with her hand.

"That! It's—it's all purple and black. Don't! That colour hurts."

"But, how in the world do you know about colours?" I exclaimed, for here was a revelation indeed.

"Colours as colours?" she asked.

"No. *Those* Colours which you saw just now."

"You know as well as I do," she laughed, "else you wouldn't have asked that question. They aren't in the world at all. They're in *you*—when you went so angry."

"D'you mean a dull purplish patch, like port-wine mixed with ink?" I said.

"I've never seen ink or port-wine, but the colours aren't mixed. They are separate—all separate."

"Do you mean black streaks and jags across the purple?"

She nodded. "Yes—if they are like this," and zigzagged her finger again, "but it's more red than purple—that bad colour."

"And what are the colours at the top of the—whatever you see?"

Slowly she leaned forward and traced on the rug the figure of the Egg itself.†

"I see them so," she said, pointing with a grass stem, "white, green, yellow, red, purple, and when people are angry or bad, black across the red—as you were just now."

"Who told you anything about it—in the beginning?" I demanded.

"About the colours? No one. I used to ask what colours were when I was little—in table-covers and curtains and carpets, you see—because some colours hurt me and some made me happy. People told me; and when I got

---

* Though the language may be deplorable, this is a rare glimpse of the humanity that occasionally appears in Kipling's much-maligned stories of the empire.

† The narrator refers here to auras, often described as an egg-shaped oval of color around the human body. The concept of auras was first popularized by Charles Webster Leadbeater, a member of the Theosophical Society founded by Madame Blavatsky. Kipling, a lifelong student of the Orient, may have come across the concept of auras in India.

older that was how I saw people." Again she traced the outline of the Egg which it is given to very few of us to see.

"All by yourself?" I repeated.

"All by myself. There wasn't anyone else. I only found out afterwards that other people did not see the Colours."

She leaned against the tree-hole plaiting and unplaiting chance-plucked grass stems. The children in the wood had drawn nearer. I could see them with the tail of my eye frolicking like squirrels.

"Now I am sure you will never laugh at me," she went on after a long silence. "Nor at *them*."

"Goodness! No!" I cried, jolted out of my train of thought. "A man who laughs at a child—unless the child is laughing too—is a heathen!"

"I didn't mean that of course. You'd never laugh *at* children, but I thought—I used to think—that perhaps you might laugh about *them*. So now I beg your pardon. . . . What are you going to laugh at?"

I had made no sound, but she knew.

"At the notion of your begging my pardon. If you had done your duty as a pillar of the state and a landed proprietress you ought to have summoned me for trespass when I barged through your woods the other day. It was disgraceful of me—inexcusable."

She looked at me, her head against the tree trunk—long and steadfastly—this woman who could see the naked soul.

"How curious," she half whispered. "How very curious."

"Why, what have I done?"

"You don't understand . . . and yet you understood about the Colours. Don't you understand?"

She spoke with a passion that nothing had justified, and I faced her bewilderedly as she rose. The children had gathered themselves in a roundel behind a bramble bush. One sleek head bent over something smaller, and the set of the little shoulders told me that fingers were on lips. They, too, had some child's tremendous secret. I alone was hopelessly astray there in the broad sunlight.

"No," I said, and shook my head as though the dead eyes could note. "Whatever it is, I don't understand yet. Perhaps I shall later—if you'll let me come again."

"You will come again," she answered. "You will surely come again and walk in the wood."

"Perhaps the children will know me well enough by that time to let me play with them—as a favour. You know what children are like."

"It isn't a matter of favour but of right," she replied, and while I wondered what she meant, a dishevelled woman plunged round the bend of the road, loose-haired, purple, almost lowing with agony as she ran. It was my rude, fat friend of the sweetmeat shop. The blind woman heard and stepped forward. "What is it, Mrs. Madehurst?" she asked.

The woman flung her apron over her head and literally grovelled in the dust, crying that her grandchild was sick to death, that the local doctor was away fishing, that Jenny the mother was at her wits end, and so forth, with repetitions and bellowings.

"Where's the next nearest doctor?" I asked between paroxysms.

"Madden will tell you. Go round to the house and take him with you. I'll attend to this. Be quick!" She half-supported the fat woman into the shade. In two minutes I was blowing all the horns of Jericho under the front of the House Beautiful, and Madden, in the pantry, rose to the crisis like a butler and a man.

A quarter of an hour at illegal speeds caught us a doctor five miles away. Within the half-hour we had decanted him, much interested in motors, at the door of the sweetmeat shop, and drew up the road to await the verdict.

"Useful things cars," said Madden, all man and no butler. "If I'd had one when mine took sick she wouldn't have died."

"How was it?" I asked.

"Croup.* Mrs. Madden was away. No one knew what to do. I drove eight miles in a tax cart† for the doctor. She was choked when we came back. This car 'd ha' saved her. She'd have been close on ten now."

"I'm sorry," I said. "I thought you were rather fond of children from what you told me going to the cross-roads the other day."

"Have you seen 'em again, Sir—this mornin'?"

---

* An inflammatory disease that is frequently identified by a specific cough and often proves fatal.

† A spring cart, formerly subject to a low tax in England.

"Yes, but they're well broke to cars. I couldn't get any of them within twenty yards of it."

He looked at me carefully as a scout considers a stranger—not as a menial should lift his eyes to his divinely appointed superior.

"I wonder why," he said just above the breath that he drew.

We waited on. A light wind from the sea wandered up and down the long lines of the woods, and the wayside grasses, whitened already with summer dust, rose and bowed in sallow waves.

A woman, wiping the suds off her arms, came out of the cottage next the sweetmeat shop.

"I've be'n listenin' in de back-yard," she said cheerily. "He says Arthur's unaccountable bad. Did ye hear him shruck just now? Unaccountable bad. I reckon t'will come Jenny's turn to walk in de wood nex' week along, Mr. Madden."

"Excuse me, Sir, but your lap-robe is slipping," said Madden deferentially. The woman started, dropped a curtsey, and hurried away.

"What does she mean by 'walking in the wood'?" I asked.

"It must be some saying they use hereabouts. I'm from Norfolk myself," said Madden. "They're an independent lot in this county. She took you for a chauffeur, Sir."

I saw the Doctor come out of the cottage followed by a draggle-tailed wench who clung to his arm as though he could make treaty for her with Death. "Dat sort," she wailed—"dey're just as much to us dat has 'em as if dey was lawful born. Just as much—just as much! An' God he'd be just as pleased if you saved 'un, Doctor. Don't take it from me. Miss Florence will tell ye de very same. Don't leave 'im, Doctor!"

"I know. I know," said the man, "but he'll be quiet for a while now. We'll get the nurse and the medicine as fast as we can." He signalled me to come forward with the car, and I strove not to be privy to what followed; but I saw the girl's face, blotched and frozen with grief, and I felt the hand without a ring clutching at my knees when we moved away.

The Doctor was a man of some humour, for I remember he claimed my car under the Oath of Æsculapius,* and used it and me without mercy.

---

* Also known as the Hippocratic Oath, a historic oath made by doctors to act ethically. It's sometimes called the Oath of Æsculapius because Asclepius was a Greek god of medicine.

First we convoyed Mrs. Madehurst and the blind woman to wait by the sick bed till the nurse should come. Next we invaded a neat county town for prescriptions (the Doctor said the trouble was cerebro-spinal meningitis),* and when the County Institute, banked and flanked with scared market cattle, reported itself out of nurses for the moment we literally flung ourselves loose upon the county. We conferred with the owners of great houses—magnates at the ends of overarching avenues whose big-boned womenfolk strode away from their tea-tables to listen to the imperious Doctor. At last a white-haired lady sitting under a cedar of Lebanon and surrounded by a court of magnificent Borzois—all hostile to motors—gave the Doctor, who received them as from a princess, written orders which we bore many miles at top speed, through a park, to a French nunnery, where we took over in exchange a pallid-faced and trembling Sister. She knelt at the bottom of the tonneau† telling her beads without pause till, by short cuts of the Doctor's invention, we had her to the sweetmeat shop once more. It was a long afternoon crowded with mad episodes that rose and dissolved like the dust of our wheels; cross-sections of remote and incomprehensible lives through which we raced at right angles; and I went home in the dusk, wearied out, to dream of the clashing horns of cattle; round-eyed nuns walking in a garden of graves; pleasant tea-parties beneath shaded trees; the carbolic-scented, grey-painted corridors of the County Institute; the steps of shy children in the wood, and the hands that clung to my knees as the motor began to move.

⚬—⁌—ᵒ

I had intended to return in a day or two, but it pleased Fate to hold me from that side of the county, on many pretexts, till the elder and the wild rose had fruited. There came at last a brilliant day, swept clear from the south-west, that brought the hills within hand's reach—a day of unstable

---

* Meningitis is an inflammation of the fluid and membranes surrounding the brain and spinal cord; in modern times it can be treated with antibiotics, but in the time of this story it often proved fatal.

† The tonneau is the part of a car open at the top.

airs and high filmy clouds. Through no merit of my own I was free, and set the car for the third time on that known road. As I reached the crest of the Downs I felt the soft air change, saw it glaze under the sun; and, looking down at the sea, in that instant beheld the blue of the Channel turn through polished silver and dulled steel to dingy pewter. A laden collier* hugging the coast steered outward for deeper water and, across copper-coloured haze, I saw sails rise one by one on the anchored fishing-fleet. In a deep dene† behind me an eddy of sudden wind drummed through shel-tered oaks, and spun aloft the first day sample of autumn leaves. When I reached the beach road the sea-fog fumed over the brickfields, and the tide was telling all the groins of the gale beyond Ushant. In less than an hour summer England vanished in chill grey. We were again the shut island of the North, all the ships of the world bellowing at our perilous gates; and between their outcries ran the piping of bewildered gulls. My cap dripped moisture, the folds of the rug held it in pools or sluiced it away in runnels, and the salt-rime stuck to my lips.

Inland the smell of autumn loaded the thickened fog among the trees, and the drip became a continuous shower. Yet the late flowers—mallow of the wayside, scabious of the field, and dahlia of the garden—showed gay in the mist, and beyond the sea's breath there was little sign of decay in the leaf. Yet in the villages the house doors were all open, and bare-legged, bare-headed children sat at ease on the damp doorsteps to shout "pip-pip" at the stranger.

I made bold to call at the sweetmeat shop, where Mrs. Madehurst met me with a fat woman's hospitable tears. Jenny's child, she said, had died two days after the nun had come. It was, she felt, best out of the way, even though insurance offices, for reasons which she did not pretend to follow, would not willingly insure such stray lives. "Not but what Jenny didn't tend to Arthur as though he'd come all proper at de end of de first year—like Jenny herself." Thanks to Miss Florence, the child had been buried with a pomp which, in Mrs. Madehurst's opinion, more than covered the small

---

* A coal-carrying ship.

† A dene is a vale or valley.

irregularity of its birth. She described the coffin, within and without, the glass hearse, and the evergreen lining of the grave.

"But how's the mother?" I asked.

"Jenny? Oh, she'll get over it. I've felt dat way with one or two o' my own. She'll get over. She's walkin' in de wood now."

"In this weather?"

Mrs. Madehurst looked at me with narrowed eyes across the counter.

"I dunno but it opens de 'eart like. Yes, it opens de 'eart. Dat's where losin' and bearin' comes so alike in de long run, we do say."

Now the wisdom of the old wives is greater than that of all the Fathers, and this last oracle sent me thinking so extendedly as I went up the road, that I nearly ran over a woman and a child at the wooded corner by the lodge gates of the House Beautiful.

"Awful weather!" I cried, as I slowed dead for the turn.

"Not so bad," she answered placidly out of the fog. "Mine's used to 'un. You'll find yours indoors, I reckon."

Indoors, Madden received me with professional courtesy, and kind inquiries for the health of the motor, which he would put under cover.

I waited in a still, nut-brown hall, pleasant with late flowers and warmed with a delicious wood fire—a place of good influence and great peace. (Men and women may sometimes, after great effort, achieve a creditable lie; but the house, which is their temple, cannot say anything save the truth of those who have lived in it.) A child's cart and a doll lay on the black-and-white floor, where a rug had been kicked back. I felt that the children had only just hurried away—to hide themselves, most like—in the many turns of the great adzed staircase that climbed statelily out of the hall, or to crouch at gaze behind the lions and roses of the carven gallery above. Then I heard her voice above me, singing as the blind sing—from the soul—

In the pleasant orchard-closes.

And all my early summer came back at the call.

In the pleasant orchard-closes,

God bless all our gains say we—

But may God bless all our losses,

Better suits with our degree,

She dropped the marring fifth line, and repeated—

Better suits with our degree!

I saw her lean over the gallery, her linked hands white as pearl against the oak.

"Is that you—from the other side of the county?" she called.

"Yes, me—from the other side of the county," I answered laughing.

"What a long time before you had to come here again." She ran down the stairs, one hand lightly touching the broad rail. "It's two months and four days. Summer's gone!"

"I meant to come before, but Fate prevented."

"I knew it. Please do something to that fire. They won't let me play with it, but I can feel it's behaving badly. Hit it!"

I looked on either side of the deep fireplace, and found but a half-charred hedge-stake with which I punched a black log into flame.

"It never goes out, day or night," she said, as though explaining. "In case any one comes in with cold toes, you see."

"It's even lovelier inside than it was out," I murmured. The red light poured itself along the age-polished dusky panels till the Tudor roses and lions of the gallery took colour and motion. An old eagle-topped convex mirror gathered the picture into its mysterious heart, distorting afresh the distorted shadows, and curving the gallery lines into the curves of a ship. The day was shutting down in half a gale as the fog turned to stringy scud. Through the uncurtained mullions of the broad window I could see valiant horsemen of the lawn rear and recover against the wind that taunted them with legions of dead leaves. "Yes, it must be beautiful," she said. "Would you like to go over it? There's still light enough upstairs."

I followed her up the unflinching, wagon-wide staircase to the gallery whence opened the thin fluted Elizabethan doors.

"Feel how they put the latch low down for the sake of the children." She swung a light door inward.

"By the way, where are they?" I asked. "I haven't even heard them to-day."

She did not answer at once. Then, "I can only hear them," she replied softly. "This is one of their rooms—everything ready, you see."

She pointed into a heavily-timbered room. There were little low gate tables and children's chairs. A doll's house, its hooked front half open, faced a great dappled rocking-horse, from whose padded saddle it was but a child's scramble to the broad window-seat overlooking the lawn. A toy gun lay in a corner beside a gilt wooden cannon.

"Surely they've only just gone," I whispered. In the failing light a door creaked cautiously. I heard the rustle of a frock and the patter of feet—quick feet through a room beyond.

"I heard that," she cried triumphantly. "Did you? Children, O children, where are you?"

The voice filled the walls that held it lovingly to the last perfect note, but there came no answering shout such as I had heard in the garden. We hurried on from room to oak-floored room; up a step here, down three steps there; among a maze of passages; always mocked by our quarry. One might as well have tried to work an unstopped warren with a single ferret. There were bolt-holes innumerable—recesses in walls, embrasures of deep slitten windows now darkened, whence they could start up behind us; and abandoned fireplaces, six feet deep in the masonry, as well as the tangle of communicating doors. Above all, they had the twilight for their helper in our game. I had caught one or two joyous chuckles of evasion, and once or twice had seen the silhouette of a child's frock against some darkening window at the end of a passage; but we returned empty-handed to the gallery, just as a middle-aged woman was setting a lamp in its niche.

"No, I haven't seen her either this evening, Miss Florence," I heard her say, "but that Turpin he says he wants to see you about his shed."

"Oh, Mr. Turpin must want to see me very badly. Tell him to come to the hall, Mrs. Madden."

I looked down into the hall whose only light was the dulled fire, and deep in the shadow I saw them at last. They must have slipped down while we were in the passages, and now thought themselves perfectly hidden behind an old gilt leather screen. By child's law, my fruitless chase was as good as an introduction, but since I had taken so much trouble I resolved to force them to come forward later by the simple trick, which children detest, of pretending not to notice them. They lay close, in a little huddle, no more than shadows except when a quick flame betrayed an outline.

"And now we'll have some tea," she said. "I believe I ought to have offered it you at first, but one doesn't arrive at manners somehow when one lives alone and is considered—h'm—peculiar." Then with very pretty scorn, "would you like a lamp to see to eat by?"

"The firelight's much pleasanter, I think." We descended into that delicious gloom and Madden brought tea.

I took my chair in the direction of the screen ready to surprise or be surprised as the game should go, and at her permission, since a hearth is always sacred, bent forward to play with the fire.

"Where do you get these beautiful short faggots from?" I asked idly. "Why, they are tallies!"*

"Of course," she said. "As I can't read or write I'm driven back on the early English tally for my accounts.† Give me one and I'll tell you what it meant."

I passed her an unburned hazel-tally, about a foot long, and she ran her thumb down the nicks.

"This is the milk-record for the home farm for the month of April last year, in gallons," said she. "I don't know what I should have done without tallies. An old forester of mine taught me the system. It's out of date now for every one else; but my tenants respect it. One of them's coming now to see me. Oh, it doesn't matter. He has no business here out of office hours. He's a greedy, ignorant man—very greedy or—he wouldn't come here after dark."

"Have you much land then?"

"Only a couple of hundred acres in hand, thank goodness. The other six hundred are nearly all let to folk who knew my folk before me, but this Turpin is quite a new man—and a highway robber."

"But are you sure I sha'n't be—?"

"Certainly not. You have the right. He hasn't any children."

"Ah, the children!" I said, and slid my low chair back till it nearly touched the screen that hid them. "I wonder whether they'll come out for me."

There was a murmur of voices—Madden's and a deeper note—at the low, dark side door, and a ginger-headed, canvas-gaitered giant of the unmistakable tenant farmer type stumbled or was pushed in.

"Come to the fire, Mr. Turpin," she said.

---

* Tallies, used in olden England, were marked with notches to keep records of debt.

† This is a woman who has intentionally turned her back on "new-fangled" notions, for Braille was in widespread use in England by the 1880s.

"If—if you please, Miss, I'll—I'll be quite as well by the door." He clung to the latch as he spoke like a frightened child. Of a sudden I realised that he was in the grip of some almost overpowering fear.

"Well?"

"About that new shed for the young stock—that was all. These first autumn storms settin' in . . . but I'll come again, Miss." His teeth did not chatter much more than the door latch.

"I think not," she answered levelly. "The new shed—m'm. What did my agent write you on the 15th?"

"I—fancied p'raps that if I came to see you—ma—man to man like, Miss. But—"

His eyes rolled into every corner of the room wide with horror. He half opened the door through which he had entered, but I noticed it shut again—from without and firmly.

"He wrote what I told him," she went on. "You are overstocked already. Dunnett's Farm never carried more than fifty bullocks—even in Mr. Wright's time. And *he* used cake.* You've sixty-seven and you don't cake. You've broken the lease in that respect. You're dragging the heart out of the farm."

"I'm—I'm getting some minerals—superphosphates—next week. I've as good as ordered a truck-load already. I'll go down to the station to-morrow about 'em. Then I can come and see you man to man like, Miss, in the daylight. . . . That gentleman's not going away, is he?" He almost shrieked.

I had only slid the chair a little further back, reaching behind me to tap on the leather of the screen, but he jumped like a rat.

"No. Please attend to me, Mr. Turpin." She turned in her chair and faced him with his back to the door. It was an old and sordid little piece of scheming that she forced from him—his plea for the new cowshed at his landlady's expense, that he might with the covered manure pay his next year's rent out of the valuation after, as she made clear, he had bled the enriched pastures to the bone. I could not but admire the intensity of his greed, when I saw him out-facing for its sake whatever terror it was that ran wet on his forehead.

---

* A fibrous substance formed out of pressed seeds, nuts, or beans to feed livestock, used to produce manure.

I ceased to tap the leather—was, indeed, calculating the cost of the shed—when I felt my relaxed hand taken and turned softly between the soft hands of a child. So at last I had triumphed. In a moment I would turn and acquaint myself with those quick-footed wanderers. . . .

The little brushing kiss fell in the centre of my palm—as a gift on which the fingers were, once, expected to close: as the all faithful half-reproachful signal of a waiting child not used to neglect even when grown-ups were busiest—a fragment of the mute code devised very long ago.

Then I knew. And it was as though I had known from the first day when I looked across the lawn at the high window.

I heard the door shut. The woman turned to me in silence, and I felt that she knew.

What time passed after this I cannot say. I was roused by the fall of a log, and mechanically rose to put it back. Then I returned to my place in the chair very close to the screen.

"Now you understand," she whispered, across the packed shadows.

"Yes, I understand—now. Thank you."

"I—I only hear them." She bowed her head in her hands. "I have no right, you know—no other right. I have neither borne nor lost—neither borne nor lost!"

"Be very glad then," said I, for my soul was torn open within me.

"Forgive me!"

She was still, and I went back to my sorrow and my joy.

"It was because I loved them so," she said at last, brokenly. "*That* was why it was, even from the first—even before I knew that they—they were all I should ever have. And I loved them so!"

She stretched out her arms to the shadows and the shadows within the shadow.

"They came because I loved them—because I needed them. I—I must have made them come. Was that wrong, think you?"

"No—no."

"I—I grant you that the toys and—and all that sort of thing were nonsense, but—but I used to so hate empty rooms myself when I was little." She pointed to the gallery. "And the passages all empty . . .And how could I ever bear the garden door shut? Suppose—"

"Don't! For pity's sake, don't!" I cried. The twilight had brought a cold rain with gusty squalls that plucked at the leaded windows.

"And the same thing with keeping the fire in all night. *I* don't think it so foolish—do you?"

I looked at the broad brick hearth, saw, through tears I believe, that there was no unpassable iron* on or near it, and bowed my head.

"I did all that and lots of other things—just to make believe. Then they came. I heard them, but I didn't know that they were not mine by right till Mrs. Madden told me——"

"The butler's wife? What?"

"One of them—I heard—she saw. And knew. Hers! *Not* for me. I didn't know at first. Perhaps I was jealous. Afterwards, I began to understand that it was only because I loved them, not because—Oh, you *must* bear or lose," she said piteously. "There is no other way—and yet they love me. They must! Don't they?"

There was no sound in the room except the lapping voices of the fire, but we two listened intently, and she at least took comfort from what she heard. She recovered herself and half rose. I sat still in my chair by the screen.

"Don't think me a wretch to whine about myself like this, but—but I'm all in the dark, you know, and *you* can see."

In truth I could see, and my vision confirmed me in my resolve, though that was like the very parting of spirit and flesh. Yet a little longer I would stay since it was the last time.

"You think it is wrong, then?" she cried sharply, though I had said nothing.

"Not for you. A thousand times no. For you it is right . . . I am grateful to you beyond words. For me it would be wrong. For me only . . . "

"Why?" she said, but passed her hand before her face as she had done at our second meeting in the wood. "Oh, I see," she went on simply as a child. "For you it would be wrong." Then with a little indrawn laugh, "and, d'you remember, I called you lucky—once—at first. You who must never come here again!"

She left me to sit a little longer by the screen, and I heard the sound of her feet die out along the gallery above.

---

* Iron has traditionally been used to repel fairies and ghosts.

EDWARD FREDERIC BENSON *(1867–1940) was the child of an English headmaster, later Bishop of Truro, and seemed to be predestined to be a writer. His brothers were a well-known hymn writer and a novelist, and his sister was known as a writer and Egyptologist. Educated at Marlborough College and Cambridge University, Benson's first success was* Sketches from Marlborough, *published when he was twenty-one; it was followed by a popular novel,* Dodo (1893), *beginning a flood of fiction, including novels (especially the beloved Mapp and Lucia series) and short stories, as well as biographies, autobiographies, and essays that continued until his death. Lovecraft spoke highly of his ventures into supernatural literature, and the following story, which first appeared in the* Pall Mall Magazine *for December 1906, was adapted for the classic 1944 horror film* Dead of Night *as well as a 1961* Twilight Zone *episode. Is it a ghost story? Or time travel? Or . . . ?*

THE BUS-CONDUCTOR

by E. F. Benson

(1906)

M y friend, Hugh Grainger, and I had just returned from a two days' visit in the country, where we had been staying in a house of sinister repute which was supposed to be haunted by ghosts of a peculiarly fearsome and truculent sort. The house itself was all that such a house should be, Jacobean* and oak-panelled, with long dark passages and high vaulted rooms. It stood, also, very remote, and was encompassed by a wood of sombre pines that muttered and whispered in the dark, and all the time that we were

---

* Dating from the reign of King James I of England, 1603–1625.

there a southwesterly gale with torrents of scolding rain had prevailed, so that by day and night weird voices moaned and fluted in the chimneys, a company of uneasy spirits held colloquy among the trees, and sudden tattoos and tappings beckoned from the window-panes. But in spite of these surroundings, which were sufficient in themselves, one would almost say, to spontaneously generate occult phenomena, nothing of any description had occurred. I am bound to add, also, that my own state of mind was peculiarly well adapted to receive or even to invent the sights and sounds we had gone to seek, for I was, I confess, during the whole time that we were there, in a state of abject apprehension, and lay awake both nights through hours of terrified unrest, afraid of the dark, yet more afraid of what a lighted candle might show me.

Hugh Grainger, on the evening after our return to town, had dined with me, and after dinner our conversation, as was natural, soon came back to these entrancing topics.

"But why you go ghost-seeking I cannot imagine," he said, "because your teeth were chattering and your eyes starting out of your head all the time you were there, from sheer fright."

"Or do you like being frightened?"

Hugh, though generally intelligent, is dense in certain ways; this is one of them.

"Why, of course, I like being frightened," I said. "I want to be made to creep and creep and creep. Fear is the most absorbing and luxurious of emotions. One forgets all else if one is afraid."

"Well, the fact that neither of us saw anything," he said, "confirms what I have always believed."

"And what have you always believed?"

"That these phenomena are purely objective, not subjective, and that one's state of mind has nothing to do with the perception that perceives them, nor have circumstances or surroundings anything to do with them either. Look at Osburton.* It has had the reputation of being a haunted house for years, and it certainly has all the accessories of one. Look at

---

* There is in fact an Osberton Hall, in Nottinghamshire, dating from medieval times and much improved over the centuries.

yourself, too, with all your nerves on edge, afraid to look round or light a candle for fear of seeing something! Surely there was the right man in the right place then, if ghosts are subjective."

He got up and lit a cigarette, and looking at him—Hugh is about six feet high, and as broad as he is long—I felt a retort on my lips, for I could not help my mind going back to a certain period in his life, when, from some cause which, as far as I knew, he had never told anybody, he had become a mere quivering mass of disordered nerves. Oddly enough, at the same moment and for the first time, he began to speak of it himself.

"You may reply that it was not worth my while to go either," he said, "because I was so clearly the wrong man in the wrong place. But I wasn't. You for all your apprehensions and expectancy have never seen a ghost. But I have, though I am the last person in the world you would have thought likely to do so, and, though my nerves are steady enough again now, it knocked me all to bits."

He sat down again in his chair.

"No doubt you remember my going to bits," he said, "and since I believe that I am sound again now, I should rather like to tell you about it. But before I couldn't; I couldn't speak of it at all to anybody. Yet there ought to have been nothing frightening about it; what I saw was certainly a most useful and friendly ghost. But it came from the shaded side of things; it looked suddenly out of the night and the mystery with which life is surrounded.

"I want first to tell you quite shortly my theory about ghost-seeing," he continued, "and I can explain it best by a simile, an image. Imagine then that you and I and everybody in the world are like people whose eye is directly opposite a little tiny hole in a sheet of cardboard which is continually shifting and revolving and moving about. Back to back with that sheet of cardboard is another, which also, by laws of its own, is in perpetual but independent motion. In it too there is another hole, and when, fortuitously it would seem, these two holes, the one through which we are always looking, and the other in the spiritual plane, come opposite one another, we see through, and then only do the sights and sounds of the spiritual world become visible or audible to us. With most people these holes never come opposite each other during their life. But at the hour of death they do, and then they remain stationary. That, I fancy, is how we 'pass over.'

"Now, in some natures, these holes are comparatively large, and are constantly coming into opposition. Clairvoyants, mediums are like that. But, as far as I knew, I had no clairvoyant or mediumistic powers at all. I therefore am the sort of person who long ago made up his mind that he never would see a ghost. It was, so to speak, an incalculable chance that my minute spy-hole should come into opposition with the other. But it did: and it knocked me out of time."

I had heard some such theory before, and though Hugh put it rather picturesquely, there was nothing in the least convincing or practical about it. It might be so, or again it might not.

"I hope your ghost was more original than your theory," said I, in order to bring him to the point.

"Yes, I think it was. You shall judge."

I put on more coal and poked up the fire. Hugh has got, so I have always considered, a great talent for telling stories, and that sense of drama which is so necessary for the narrator. Indeed, before now, I have suggested to him that he should take this up as a profession, sit by the fountain in Piccadilly Circus, when times are, as usual, bad, and tell stories to the passers-by in the street, Arabian fashion, for reward. The most part of mankind, I am aware, do not like long stories, but to the few, among whom I number myself, who really like to listen to lengthy accounts of experiences, Hugh is an ideal narrator. I do not care for his theories, or for his similes, but when it comes to facts, to things that happened, I like him to be lengthy.

"Go on, please, and slowly," I said. "Brevity may be the soul of wit, but it is the ruin of story-telling. I want to hear when and where and how it all was, and what you had for lunch and where you had dined and what—"

Hugh began:

"It was the 24th of June, just eighteen months ago," he said. "I had let my flat, you may remember, and came up from the country to stay with you for a week. We had dined alone here—"

I could not help interrupting.

"Did you see the ghost here?" I asked. "In this square little box of a house in a modern street?"

"I was in the house when I saw it."

I hugged myself in silence.

"We had dined alone here in Graeme Street," he said, "and after dinner I went out to some party, and you stopped at home. At dinner your man did not wait, and when I asked where he was, you told me he was ill, and, I thought, changed the subject rather abruptly.

"You gave me your latch-key when I went out, and on coming back, I found you had gone to bed. There were, however, several letters for me, which required answers. I wrote them there and then, and posted them at the pillar-box opposite. So I suppose it was rather late when I went upstairs.

"You had put me in the front room, on the third floor, overlooking the street, a room which I thought you generally occupied yourself. It was a very hot night, and though there had been a moon when I started to my party, on my return the whole sky was cloud-covered, and it both looked and felt as if we might have a thunderstorm before morning. I was feeling very sleepy and heavy, and it was not till after I had got into bed that I noticed by the shadows of the window-frames on the blind that only one of the windows was open. But it did not seem worth while to get out of bed in order to open it, though I felt rather airless and uncomfortable, and I went to sleep.

"What time it was when I awoke I do not know, but it was certainly not yet dawn, and I never remember being conscious of such an extraordinary stillness as prevailed. There was no sound either of foot-passengers or wheeled traffic; the music of life appeared to be absolutely mute. But now, instead of being sleepy and heavy, I felt, though I must have slept an hour or two at most, since it was not yet dawn, perfectly fresh and wide-awake, and the effort which had seemed not worth making before, that of getting out of bed and opening the other window, was quite easy now and I pulled up the blind, threw it wide open, and leaned out, for somehow I parched and pined for air. Even outside the oppression was very noticeable, and though, as you know, I am not easily given to feel the mental effects of climate, I was aware of an awful creepiness coming over me. I tried to analyse it away, but without success; the past day had been pleasant, I looked forward to another pleasant day to-morrow, and yet I was full of some nameless apprehension. I felt, too, dreadfully lonely in this stillness before the dawn.

"Then I heard suddenly and not very far away the sound of some approaching vehicle; I could distinguish the tread of two horses walking at a slow foot's pace. They were, though not yet visible, coming up the street, and yet this indication of life did not abate that dreadful sense of loneliness which I have spoken of. Also in some dim unformulated way that which was coming seemed to me to have something to do with the cause of my oppression.

"Then the vehicle came into sight. At first I could not distinguish what it was. Then I saw that the horses were black and had long tails, and that what they dragged was made of glass, but had a black frame. It was a hearse. Empty.

"It was moving up this side of the street. It stopped at your door.

"Then the obvious solution struck me. You had said at dinner that your man was ill, and you were, I thought, unwilling to speak more about his illness. No doubt, so I imagined now, he was dead, and for some reason, perhaps because you did not want me to know anything about it, you were having the body removed at night. This, I must tell you, passed through my mind quite instantaneously, and it did not occur to me how unlikely it really was, before the next thing happened.

"I was still leaning out of the window, and I remember also wondering, yet only momentarily, how odd it was that I saw things—or rather the one thing I was looking at—so very distinctly. Of course, there was a moon behind the clouds, but it was curious how every detail of the hearse and the horses was visible. There was only one man, the driver, with it, and the street was otherwise absolutely empty. It was at him I was looking now. I could see every detail of his clothes, but from where I was, so high above him, I could not see his face. He had on grey trousers, brown boots, a black coat buttoned all the way up, and a straw hat. Over his shoulder there was a strap, which seemed to support some sort of little bag. He looked exactly like—well, from my description what did he look exactly like?"

"Why—a bus-conductor," I said instantly.

"So I thought, and even while I was thinking this, he looked up at me. He had a rather long thin face, and on his left cheek there was a mole with a growth of dark hair on it. All this was as distinct as if it had been noonday, and as if I was within a yard of him. But—so instantaneous was all that takes so long in the telling—I had not time to think it strange that the driver of a hearse should be so unfunereally dressed.

"Then he touched his hat to me, and jerked his thumb over his shoulder.

"'Just room for one inside, sir,' he said.

"There was something so odious, so coarse, so unfeeling about this that I instantly drew my head in, pulled the blind down again, and then, for what reason I do not know, turned on the electric light in order to see what time it was. The hands of my watch pointed to half-past eleven.

"It was then for the first time, I think, that a doubt crossed my mind as to the nature of what I had just seen. But I put out the light again, got into bed, and began to think. We had dined; I had gone to a party, I had come back and written letters, had gone to bed and had slept. So how could it be half-past eleven? . . . Or—what half-past eleven was it?

"Then another easy solution struck me; my watch must have stopped. But it had not; I could hear it ticking.

"There was stillness and silence again. I expected every moment to hear muffled footsteps on the stairs, footsteps moving slowly and smally under the weight of a heavy burden, but from inside the house there was no sound whatever. Outside, too, there was the same dead silence, while the hearse waited at the door. And the minutes ticked on and ticked on, and at length I began to see a difference in the light in the room, and knew that the dawn was beginning to break outside. But how had it happened, then, that if the corpse was to be removed at night it had not gone, and that the hearse still waited, when morning was already coming?

"Presently I got out of bed again, and with the sense of strong physical shrinking I went to the window and pulled back the blind. The dawn was coming fast; the whole street was lit by that silver hueless light of morning. But there was no hearse there.

"Once again I looked at my watch. It was just a quarter-past four. But I would swear that not half an hour had passed since it had told me that it was half-past eleven.

"Then a curious double sense, as if I was living in the present and at the same moment had been living in some other time, came over me. It was dawn on June 25th, and the street, as natural, was empty. But a little while ago the driver of a hearse had spoken to me, and it was half-past eleven. What was that driver, to what plane did he belong? And again what half-past eleven was it that I had seen recorded on the dial of my watch?

"And then I told myself that the whole thing had been a dream. But if you ask me whether I believed what I told myself, I must confess that I did not.

"Your man did not appear at breakfast next morning, nor did I see him again before I left that afternoon. I think if I had, I should have told you about all this, but it was still possible, you see, that what I had seen was a real hearse, driven by a real driver, for all the ghastly gaiety of the face that had looked up to mine, and the levity of his pointing hand. I might possibly have fallen asleep soon after seeing him, and slumbered through the removal of the body and the departure of the hearse. So I did not speak of it to you."

There was something wonderfully straight-forward and prosaic in all this; here were no Jacobean houses oak-panelled and surrounded by weeping pine-trees, and somehow the very absence of suitable surroundings made the story more impressive. But for a moment a doubt assailed me.

"Don't tell me it was all a dream," I said.

"I don't know whether it was or not. I can only say that I believe myself to have been wide awake. In any case the rest of the story is—odd.

"I went out of town again that afternoon," he continued, "and I may say that I don't think that even for a moment did I get the haunting sense of what I had seen or dreamed that night out of my mind. It was present to me always as some vision unfulfilled. It was as if some clock had struck the four quarters, and I was still waiting to hear what the hour would be.

"Exactly a month afterwards I was in London again, but only for the day. I arrived at Victoria about eleven, and took the underground to Sloane Square in order to see if you were in town and would give me lunch. It was a baking hot morning, and I intended to take a bus from the King's Road as far as Graeme Street. There was one standing at the corner just as I came out of the station, but I saw that the top was full, and the inside appeared to be full also. Just as I came up to it the conductor, who, I suppose, had been inside, collecting fares or what not, came out on to the step within a few feet of me. He wore grey trousers, brown boots, a black coat buttoned, a straw hat, and over his shoulder was a strap on which hung his little machine for punching tickets. I saw his face, too; it was the face of the driver of the hearse, with a mole on the left cheek. Then he spoke to me, jerking his thumb over his shoulder.

"'Just room for one inside, sir,' he said.

"At that a sort of panic-terror took possession of me, and I knew I gesticulated wildly with my arms, and cried, 'No, no!' But at that moment I was living not in the hour that was then passing, but in that hour which had passed a month ago, when I leaned from the window of your bedroom here just before the dawn broke. At this moment too I knew that my spy-hole had been opposite the spy-hole into the spiritual world. What I had seen there had some significance, now being fulfilled, beyond the significance of the trivial happenings of to-day and to-morrow. The Powers of which we know so little were visibly working before me. And I stood there on the pavement shaking and trembling.

"I was opposite the post-office at the corner, and just as the bus started my eye fell on the clock in the window there. I need not tell you what the time was.

"Perhaps I need not tell you the rest, for you probably conjecture it, since you will not have forgotten what happened at the corner of Sloane Square at the end of July, the summer before last. The bus pulled out from the pavement into the street in order to get round a van that was standing in front of it. At the moment there came down the King's Road a big motor going at a hideously dangerous pace. It crashed full into the bus, burrowing into it as a gimlet* burrows into a board."

He paused.

"And that's my story," he said.

---

* A gimlet is a tool for drilling holes.

H. P. Lovecraft, *in his 1927 essay "Supernatural Horror in Literature,"
hailed as a "modern master . . . the inspired and prolific* **ALGERNON
BLACKWOOD**, *amidst whose voluminous and uneven work may be found
some of the finest spectral literature of this or any age." Blackwood (1869–
1951) was born in the Shooter's Hill area, now part of southeast London.
He traveled extensively, pursuing a variety of careers, until he returned to
England at the turn of the century and began writing supernatural tales.
He wrote ten collections of stories and fourteen novels, as well as plays
and children's books, and he became a popular narrator of his own work
on radio. An enthusiastic skier and mountain-climber, Blackwood was also
an intense student of the occult. The following, which first appeared in the
December 1908 issue of* Pall Mall Magazine, *makes no effort to explain
the horror experienced by a young man on the eve of his departure for a
skiing vacation.*

THE KIT-BAG

by Algernon Blackwood

(1908)

W hen the words "Not Guilty" sounded through the crowded courtroom
that dark December afternoon, Arthur Wilbraham, the great criminal
KC,* and leader for the triumphant defence, was represented by his junior;
but Johnson, his private secretary, carried the verdict across to his chambers
like lightning.

---

* King's Counsel—a barrister who prosecutes criminal cases for the Crown in the United
Kingdom's system.

"It's what we expected, I think," said the barrister, without emotion; "and, personally, I am glad the case is over." There was no particular sign of pleasure that his defence of John Turk, the murderer, on a plea of insanity, had been successful, for no doubt he felt, as everybody who had watched the case felt, that no man had ever better deserved the gallows.

"I'm glad too," said Johnson. He had sat in the court for ten days watching the face of the man who had carried out with callous detail one of the most brutal and cold-blooded murders of recent years.

The counsel glanced up at his secretary. They were more than employer and employed; for family and other reasons, they were friends. "Ah, I remember; yes," he said with a kind smile, "and you want to get away for Christmas? You're going to skate and ski in the Alps, aren't you? If I was your age I'd come with you.'

Johnson laughed shortly. He was a young man of twenty-six, with a delicate face like a girl's. "I can catch the morning boat now," he said; "but that's not the reason I'm glad the trial is over. I'm glad it's over because I've seen the last of that man's dreadful face. It positively haunted me. Bat white skin, with the black hair brushed low over the forehead, is a thing I shall never forget, and the description of the way the dismembered body was crammed and packed with lime into that—"

"Don't dwell on it, my dear fellow," interrupted the other, looking at him curiously out of his keen eyes, "don't think about it. Such pictures have a trick of coming back when one least wants them." He paused a moment. "Now go," he added presently, "and enjoy your holiday. I shall want all your energy for my Parliamentary work when you get back. And don't break your neck skiing."

Johnson shook hands and took his leave. At the door he turned suddenly. "I knew there was something I wanted to ask you," he said. "Would you mind lending me one of your kit-bags? It's too late to get one tonight, and I leave in the morning before the shops are open."

"Of course; I'll send Henry over with it to your rooms. You shall have it the moment I get home."

"I promise to take great care of it," said Johnson gratefully, delighted to think that within thirty hours he would be nearing the brilliant sunshine of the high Alps in winter. The thought of that criminal court was like an evil dream in his mind.

He dined at his club and went on to Bloomsbury, where he occupied the top floor in one of those old, gaunt houses in which the rooms are large and lofty. The floor below his own was vacant and unfurnished, and below that were other lodgers whom he did not know. It was cheerless, and he looked forward heartily to a change. The night was even more cheerless: it was miserable, and few people were about. A cold, sleety rain was driving down the streets before the keenest east wind he had ever felt. It howled dismally among the big, gloomy houses of the great squares, and when he reached his rooms he heard it whistling and shouting over the world of black roofs beyond his windows.

In the hall he met his landlady, shading a candle from the draughts with her thin hand. "This come by a man from Mr. Wilbr'im's, sir."

She pointed to what was evidently the kit-bag, and Johnson thanked her and took it upstairs with him. "I shall be going abroad in the morning for ten days, Mrs. Monks," he said. "I'll leave an address for letters."

"And I hope you'll 'ave a merry Christmas, sir," she said, in a raucous, wheezy voice that suggested spirits, "and better weather than this."

"I hope so too," replied her lodger, shuddering a little as the wind went roaring down the street outside.

When he got upstairs he heard the sleet volleying against the window panes. He put his kettle on to make a cup of hot coffee, and then set about putting a few things in order for his absence. "And now I must pack—such as my packing is," he laughed to himself, and set to work at once.

He liked the packing, for it brought the snow mountains so vividly before him, and made him forget the unpleasant scenes of the past ten days. Besides, it was not elaborate in nature. His friend had lent him the very thing—a stout canvas kit-bag, sack-shaped, with holes round the neck for the brass bar and padlock. It was a bit shapeless, true, and not much to look at, but its capacity was unlimited, and there was no need to pack carefully. He shoved in his waterproof coat, his fur cap and gloves, his skates and climbing boots, his sweaters, snow-boots, and ear-caps; and then on the top of these he piled his woolen shirts and underwear, his thick socks, puttees,* and knickerbockers. The dress suit came next, in case the hotel people dressed for dinner, and then, thinking of the best way to pack his white shirts, he paused a moment to reflect. "That's the worst of these kit-bags," he mused vaguely, standing in the centre of the sitting-room, where he had come to fetch some string.

It was after ten o'clock. A furious gust of wind rattled the windows as though to hurry him up, and he thought with pity of the poor Londoners whose Christmas would be spent in such a climate, whilst he was skimming over snowy slopes in bright sunshine, and dancing in the evening with rosy-cheeked girls—Ah! that reminded him; he must put in his dancing-pumps and evening socks. He crossed over from his sitting-room to the cupboard on the landing where he kept his linen.

And as he did so he heard someone coming softly up the stairs.

He stood still a moment on the landing to listen. It was Mrs. Monks's step, he thought; she must be coming up with the last post. But then the steps ceased suddenly, and he heard no more. They were at least two flights down, and he came to the conclusion they were too heavy to be those of his bibulous† landlady. No doubt they belonged to a late lodger who had mistaken his floor. He went into his bedroom and packed his pumps and dress-shirts as best he could.

The kit-bag by this time was two-thirds full, and stood upright on its own base like a sack of flour. For the first time he noticed that it was old and dirty, the canvas faded and worn, and that it had obviously been subjected to rather rough treatment. It was not a very nice bag to have sent him—certainly not a new one, or one that his chief valued. He gave the matter a passing thought, and went on with his packing. Once or twice, however, he caught himself wondering who it could have been wandering down below, for Mrs. Monks had not come up with letters, and the floor was empty and unfurnished. From time to time, moreover, he was almost certain he heard a soft tread of someone padding about over the bare

---

* Strips of cloth wrapped around the legs for protection.

† Addicted to drinking.

boards—cautiously, stealthily, as silently as possible—and, further, that the sounds had been lately coming distinctly nearer.

For the first time in his life he began to feel a little creepy. Then, as though to emphasize this feeling, an odd thing happened: as he left the bedroom, having just packed his recalcitrant white shirts, he noticed that the top of the kit-bag lopped over towards him with an extraordinary resemblance to a human face. The canvas fell into a fold like a nose and forehead, and the brass rings for the padlock just filled the position of the eyes. A shadow—or was it a travel stain? for he could not tell exactly—looked like hair. It gave him rather a turn, for it was so absurdly, so outrageously, like the face of John Turk the murderer.

He laughed, and went into the front room, where the light was stronger.

"That horrid case has got on my mind," he thought; "I shall be glad of a change of scene and air." In the sitting-room, however, he was not pleased to hear again that stealthy tread upon the stairs, and to realize that it was much closer than before, as well as unmistakably real. And this time he got up and went out to see who it could be creeping about on the upper staircase at so late an hour.

But the sound ceased; there was no one visible on the stairs. He went to the floor below, not without trepidation, and turned on the electric light to make sure that no one was hiding in the empty rooms of the unoccupied suite. There was not a stick of furniture large enough to hide a dog. Then he called over the banisters to Mrs. Monks, but there was no answer, and his voice echoed down into the dark vault of the house, and was lost in the roar of the gale that howled outside. Everyone was in bed and asleep—everyone except himself and the owner of this soft and stealthy tread.

"My absurd imagination, I suppose," he thought. "It must have been the wind after all, although—it seemed so *very* real and close, I thought."

He went back to his packing. It was by this time getting on towards midnight. He drank his coffee up and lit another pipe—the last before turning in.

It is difficult to say exactly at what point fear begins, when the causes of that fear are not plainly before the eyes. Impressions gather on the surface of the mind, film by film, as ice gathers upon the surface of still water, but often so lightly that they claim no definite recognition from the consciousness. Then a point is reached where the accumulated impressions become a definite emotion, and the mind realizes that something has happened. With something of a start, Johnson suddenly recognized that he felt nervous—oddly nervous; also, that for some time past the causes of this feeling had been gathering slowly in his mind, but that he had only just reached the point where he was forced to acknowledge them.

It was a singular and curious malaise that had come over him, and he hardly knew what to make of it. He felt as though he were doing something that was strongly objected to by another person, another person, moreover, who had some right to object. It was a most disturbing and disagreeable feeling, not unlike the persistent promptings of conscience: almost, in fact, as if he were doing something he knew to be wrong. Yet, though he searched vigorously and honestly in his mind, he could nowhere lay his finger upon the secret of this growing uneasiness, and it perplexed him. More, it distressed and frightened him.

"Pure nerves, I suppose," he said aloud with a forced laugh. "Mountain air will cure all that! Ah," he added, still speaking to himself, "and that reminds me—my snow-glasses."

He was standing by the door of the bedroom during this brief soliloquy, and as he passed quickly towards the sitting-room to fetch them from the cupboard he saw out of the corner of his eye the indistinct outline of a figure standing on the stairs, a few feet from the top. It was someone in a stooping position, with one hand on the banisters, and the face peering up towards the landing. And at the same moment he heard a shuffling footstep. The person who had been creeping about below all this time had at last come up to his own floor. Who in the world could it be? And what in the name of Heaven did he want?

Johnson caught his breath sharply and stood stock still. Then, after a few seconds' hesitation, he found his courage, and turned to investigate. The stairs, he saw to his utter amazement, were empty; there was no one.

He felt a series of cold shivers run over him, and something about the muscles of his legs gave a little and grew weak. For the space of several minutes he peered steadily into the shadows that congregated about the top of the staircase where he had seen the figure, and then he walked fast—almost ran, in fact—into the light of the front room; but hardly had he passed inside the doorway when he heard someone come up the stairs behind him with a quick bound and go swiftly into his bedroom. It was a heavy, but at the same time a stealthy footstep—the tread of somebody who did not wish to be seen. And it was at this precise moment that the nervousness he had hitherto experienced leaped the boundary line, and entered the state of fear, almost of acute, unreasoning fear. Before it turned into terror there was a further boundary to cross, and beyond that again lay the region of pure horror. Johnson's position was an unenviable one.

"By Jove! That was someone on the stairs, then," he muttered, his flesh crawling all over; "and whoever it was has now gone into my bedroom." His delicate, pale face turned absolutely white, and for some minutes he hardly knew what to think or do. Then he realized intuitively that delay only set a premium upon fear; and he crossed the landing boldly and went straight into the other room, where, a few seconds before, the steps had disappeared.

"Who's there? Is that you, Mrs. Monks?" he called aloud, as he went, and heard the first half of his words echo down the empty stairs, while the second half fell dead against the curtains in a room that apparently held no other human figure than his own.

"Who's there?" he called again, in a voice unnecessarily loud and that only just held firm. "What do you want here?"

The curtains swayed very slightly, and, as he saw it, his heart felt as if it almost missed a beat; yet he dashed forward and drew them aside with a rush. A window, streaming with rain, was all that met his gaze. He continued his search, but in vain; the cupboards held nothing but rows of clothes, hanging motionless; and under the bed there was no sign of anyone hiding. He stepped backwards into the middle of the room, and, as he did so, something all but tripped him up. Turning with a sudden spring of alarm he saw—the kit-bag.

"Odd!" he thought. "That's not where I left it!" A few moments before it had surely been on his right, between the bed and the bath; he did not remember having moved it. It was very curious. What in the world was the matter with everything? Were all his senses gone queer? A terrific gust of wind tore at the windows, dashing the sleet against the glass with the force of small gunshot, and then fled away howling dismally over the waste of Bloomsbury roofs. A sudden vision of the Channel next day rose in his mind and recalled him sharply to realities.

"There's no one here at any rate; that's quite clear!" he exclaimed aloud. Yet at the time he uttered them he knew perfectly well that his words were not true and that he did not believe them himself. He felt exactly as though someone was hiding close about him, watching all his movements, trying to hinder his packing in some way. "And two of my senses," he added, keeping up the pretence, "have played me the most absurd tricks: the steps I heard and the figure I saw were both entirely imaginary."

He went back to the front room, poked the fire into a blaze, and sat down before it to think. What impressed him more than anything else was the fact that the kit-bag was no longer where he had left it. It had been dragged nearer to the door.

What happened afterwards that night happened, of course, to a man already excited by fear, and was perceived by a mind that had not the full and proper control, therefore, of the senses. Outwardly, Johnson remained calm and master of himself to the end, pretending to the very last that everything he witnessed had a natural explanation, or was merely delusions of his tired nerves. But inwardly, in his very heart, he knew all along that someone had been hiding downstairs in the empty suite when he came in, that this person had watched his opportunity and then stealthily made his way up to the bedroom, and that all he saw and heard afterwards, from the moving of the kit-bag to—well, to the other things this story has to tell—were caused directly by the presence of this invisible person.

And it was here, just when he most desired to keep his mind and thoughts controlled, that the vivid pictures received day after day upon the mental plates exposed in the courtroom of the Old Bailey, came strongly to light and developed themselves in the dark room of his inner vision.

Unpleasant, haunting memories have a way of coming to life again just when the mind least desires them—in the silent watches of the night, on sleepless pillows, during the lonely hours spent by sick and dying beds.

And so now, in the same way, Johnson saw nothing but the dreadful face of John Turk, the murderer, lowering at him from every corner of his mental field of vision; the white skin, the evil eyes, and the fringe of black hair low over the forehead. All the pictures of those ten days in court crowded back into his mind unbidden, and very vivid.

"This is all rubbish and nerves," he exclaimed at length, springing with sudden energy from his chair. "I shall finish my packing and go to bed. I'm overwrought, overtired. No doubt, at this rate I shall hear steps and things all night!"

But his face was deadly white all the same. He snatched up his field-glasses and walked across to the bedroom, humming a music-hall song as he went—a trifle too loud to be natural; and the instant he crossed the threshold and stood within the room something turned cold about his heart, and he felt that every hair on his head stood up.

The kit-bag lay close in front of him, several feet nearer to the door than he had left it, and just over its crumpled top he saw a head and face slowly sinking down out of sight as though someone were crouching behind it to hide, and at the same moment a sound like a long-drawn sigh was distinctly audible in the still air about him between the gusts of the storm outside.

Johnson had more courage and will-power than the girlish indecision of his face indicated; but at first such a wave of terror came over him that for some seconds he could do nothing but stand and stare. A violent trembling ran down his back and legs, and he was conscious of a foolish, almost a hysterical, impulse to scream aloud. That sigh seemed in his very ear, and the air still quivered with it. It was unmistakably a human sigh.

"Who's there?" he said at length, finding his voice; but though he meant to speak with loud decision, the tones came out instead in a faint whisper, for he had partly lost the control of his tongue and lips.

He stepped forward, so that he could see all round and over the kit-bag. Of course there was nothing there, nothing but the faded carpet and the bulging canvas sides. He put out his hands and threw open the mouth of the sack where it had fallen over, being only three parts full, and then he saw for the first time that round the inside, some six inches from the top, there ran a broad smear of dull crimson. It was an old and faded blood stain. He uttered a scream, and drew back his hands as if they had been burnt. At the same moment the kit-bag gave a faint, but unmistakable, lurch forward towards the door.

Johnson collapsed backwards, searching with his hands for the support of something solid, and the door, being further behind him than he realized, received his weight just in time to prevent his falling, and shut to with a resounding bang. At the same moment the swinging of his left arm accidentally touched the electric switch, and the light in the room went out.

It was an awkward and disagreeable predicament, and if Johnson had not been possessed of real pluck he might have done all manner of foolish things. As it was, however, he pulled himself together, and groped furiously for the little brass knob to turn the light on again. But the rapid closing of the door had set the coats hanging on it a-swinging, and his fingers became entangled in a confusion of sleeves and pockets, so that it was some moments before he found the switch. And in those few moments of bewilderment and terror two things happened that sent him beyond recall over the boundary into the region of genuine horror—he distinctly heard the kit-bag shuffling heavily across the floor in jerks, and close in front of his face sounded once again the sigh of a human being.

In his anguished efforts to find the brass button on the wall he nearly scraped the nails from his fingers, but even then, in those frenzied moments of alarm—so swift and alert are the impressions of a mind keyed-up by a vivid emotion—he had time to realize that he dreaded the return of the light, and that it might be better for him to stay hidden in the merciful screen of darkness. It was but the impulse of a moment, however, and before he had time to act upon it he had yielded automatically to the original desire, and the room was flooded again with light.

But the second instinct had been right. It would have been better for him to have stayed in the shelter of the kind darkness. For there, close before him, bending over the half-packed kit-bag, clear as life in the merciless glare of the electric light, stood the figure of John Turk, the murderer. Not three feet from him the man stood, the fringe of black hair marked plainly against the pallor of the forehead, the whole horrible presentment of the scoundrel, as vivid as he had seen him day after day in the Old Bailey, when he stood there in the dock, cynical and callous, under the very shadow of the gallows.

In a flash Johnson realized what it all meant: the dirty and much-used bag; the smear of crimson within the top; the dreadful stretched condition of the bulging sides. He remembered how the victim's body had

been stuffed into a canvas bag for burial, the ghastly, dismembered fragments forced with lime into this very bag; and the bag itself produced as
evidence—it all came back to him as clear as day . . .

Very softly and stealthily his hand groped behind him for the handle of
the door, but before he could actually turn it the very thing that he most
of all dreaded came about, and John Turk lifted his devil's face and looked
at him. At the same moment that heavy sigh passed through the air of the
room, formulated somehow into words: "It's my bag. And I want it."

Johnson just remembered clawing the door open, and then falling in a
heap upon the floor of the landing, as he tried frantically to make his way
into the front room.

He remained unconscious for a long time, and it was still dark when he
opened his eyes and realized that he was lying, stiff and bruised, on the cold
boards. Then the memory of what he had seen rushed back into his mind,
and he promptly fainted again. When he woke the second time the wintry
dawn was just beginning to peep in at the windows, painting the stairs a
cheerless, dismal grey, and he managed to crawl into the front room, and
cover himself with an overcoat in the armchair, where at length he fell asleep.

A great clamour woke him. He recognized Mrs. Monks's voice, loud
and voluble.

"What! You ain't been to bed, sir! Are you ill, or has anything 'appened?
And there's an urgent gentleman to see you, though it ain't seven o'clock
yet, and—"

"Who is it?" he stammered. "I'm all right, thanks. Fell asleep in my
chair, I suppose."

"Someone from Mr. Wilb'rim's, and he says he ought to see you quick
before you go abroad, and I told him—"

"Show him up, please, at once," said Johnson, whose head was whirling,
and his mind was still full of dreadful visions.

Mr. Wilbraham's man came in with many apologies, and explained
briefly and quickly that an absurd mistake had been made, and that the
wrong kit-bag had been sent over the night before.

"Henry somehow got hold of the one that came over from the courtroom,
and Mr. Wilbraham only discovered it when he saw his own lying in his
room, and asked why it had not gone to you," the man said.

"Oh!" said Johnson stupidly.

"And he must have brought you the one from the murder case instead, sir, I'm afraid," the man continued, without the ghost of an expression on his face. "The one John Turk packed the dead body in. Mr. Wilbraham's awful upset about it, sir, and told me to come over first thing this morning with the right one, as you were leaving by the boat."

He pointed to a clean-looking kit-bag on the floor, which he had just brought. "And I was to bring the other one back, sir," he added casually.

For some minutes Johnson could not find his voice. At last he pointed in the direction of his bedroom. "Perhaps you would kindly unpack it for me. Just empty the things out on the floor."

The man disappeared into the other room, and was gone for five minutes. Johnson heard the shifting to and fro of the bag, and the rattle of the skates and boots being unpacked.

"Thank you, sir," the man said, returning with the bag folded over his arm. "And can I do anything more to help you, sir?"

"What is it?" asked Johnson, seeing that he still had something he wished to say.

The man shuffled and looked mysterious. "Beg pardon, sir, but knowing your interest in the Turk case, I thought you'd maybe like to know what's happened—"

"Yes."

"John Turk killed hisself last night with poison immediately on getting his release, and he left a note for Mr. Wilbraham saying as he'd be much obliged if they'd have him put away, same as the woman he murdered, in the old kit-bag."

"What time—did he do it?" asked Johnson.

"Ten o'clock last night, sir, the warder says."

FRANCIS MARION CRAWFORD *(1854–1909) was born in Tuscany to a family of artists, and received his education from various international universities. In 1879, he traveled to India, then to Boston to live with his aunt Julia Ward Howe. When it became clear that he would not have a career as a singer, he took up writing. His first novel, Mr. Isaacs (1882), was set in India, as was his next. He wrote a stream of successful novels, mostly set in Italy, where he returned in 1883 and would stay for the rest of his life. Crawford also wrote plays, several of which were filmed, and numerous short stories, many with supernatural or horror themes. In his 1929 article "Some Remarks on Ghost Stories," M. R. James singled out Crawford's work for praise, especially his frequently anthologized "The Upper Berth" (1885). While James called the following "some distance behind" Crawford's most popular story, the structure of the tale, which makes the reader a participant in the action, heightens the terror. It first appeared in Collier's on July 11, 1908.*

THE SCREAMING SKULL

by F. Marion Crawford

(1908)

I have often heard it scream. No, I am not nervous, I am not imaginative, and I never believed in ghosts, unless that thing is one. Whatever it is, it hates me almost as much as it hated Luke Pratt, and it screams at me.

If I were you, I would never tell ugly stories about ingenious ways of killing people, for you never can tell but that some one at the table may be tired of his or her nearest and dearest. I have always blamed myself for Mrs. Pratt's death, and I suppose I was responsible for it in a way, though heaven knows I never wished her anything but long life and happiness.

If I had not told that story she might be alive yet. That is why the thing screams at me, I fancy.

She was a good little woman, with a sweet temper, all things considered, and a nice gentle voice; but I remember hearing her shriek once when she thought her little boy was killed by a pistol that went off, though every one was sure that it was not loaded. It was the same scream; exactly the same, with a sort of rising quaver at the end; do you know what I mean? Unmistakable.

The truth is, I had not realised that the doctor and his wife were not on good terms. They used to bicker a bit now and then when I was here, and I often noticed that little Mrs. Pratt got very red and bit her lip hard to keep her temper, while Luke grew pale and said the most offensive things. He was that sort when he was in the nursery, I remember, and afterward at school. He was my cousin, you know; that is how I came by this house; after he died, and his boy Charley was killed in South Africa,* there were no relations left. Yes, it's a pretty little property, just the sort of thing for an old sailor like me who has taken to gardening.

One always remembers one's mistakes much more vividly than one's cleverest things, doesn't one? I've often noticed it. I was dining with the Pratts one night, when I told them the story that afterwards made so much difference. It was a wet night in November, and the sea was moaning. Hush!—if you don't speak you will hear it now. . . .

Do you hear the tide? Gloomy sound, isn't it? Sometimes, about this time of year—hallo!—there it is! Don't be frightened, man—it won't eat you—it's only a noise, after all! But I'm glad you've heard it, because there are always people who think it's the wind, or my imagination, or something. You won't hear it again to-night, I fancy, for it doesn't often come more than once. Yes—that's right. Put another stick on the fire, and a little more stuff into that weak mixture you're so fond of. Do you remember old Blauklot the carpenter, on that German ship that picked us up when the *Clontarf*†

---

* Almost surely in the Boer War, as the English styled it, fought from October 11, 1899, to May 31, 1902, between the United Kingdom and two Afrikaner republics.

† The *Clontarf* was a real ship that ran into trouble, but it didn't sink: it was a clipper carrying immigrants from England to New Zealand, and on its second run in 1859–1860 it lost forty-one passengers to a variety of diseases. It was dismissed from service after that.

went to the bottom? We were hove to in a howling gale one night, as snug as you please, with no land within five hundred miles, and the ship coming up and falling off as regularly as clockwork—"Biddy te boor beebles ashore tis night, poys!"* old Blauklot sang out, as he went off to his quarters with the sail-maker. I often think of that, now that I'm ashore for good and all.

Yes, it was on a night like this, when I was at home for a spell, waiting to take the *Olympia*† out on her first trip—it was on the next voyage that she broke the record, you remember—but that dates it. Ninety-two was the year, early in November.

The weather was dirty, Pratt was out of temper, and the dinner was bad, very bad indeed, which didn't improve matters, and cold, which made it worse. The poor little lady was very unhappy about it, and insisted on making a Welsh rarebit‡ on the table to counteract the raw turnips and the half-boiled mutton. Pratt must have had a hard day. Perhaps he had lost a patient. At all events, he was in a nasty temper.

"My wife is trying to poison me, you see!" he said. "She'll succeed some day." I saw that she was hurt, and I made believe to laugh, and said that Mrs. Pratt was much too clever to get rid of her husband in such a simple way; and then I began to tell them about Japanese tricks with spun glass and chopped horsehair and the like.

Pratt was a doctor, and knew a lot more than I did about such things, but that only put me on my mettle, and I told a story about a woman in Ireland who did for three husbands before any one suspected foul play.

Did you never hear that tale? The fourth husband managed to keep awake and caught her, and she was hanged. How did she do it? She drugged them, and poured melted lead into their ears through a little horn funnel when they were asleep§. . . . No—that's the wind whistling. It's backing

---

* "Pity the poor people ashore tonight, boys!"

† There was a famous ship called the *Olympia* that launched in November 1892, but it was a US Navy cruiser that remains the oldest steel warship still afloat.

‡ Cheese on toast.

§ This story was something of an urban legend, despite being reported in British newspapers circa 1847. That story—which claimed the lady in question had actually murdered six husbands before the seventh caught her—was based on the French legend of "La Corriveau."

up to the southward again. I can tell by the sound. Besides, the other thing doesn't often come more than once in an evening even at this time of year—when it happened. Yes, it was in November. Poor Mrs. Pratt died suddenly in her bed not long after I dined here. I can fix the date, because I got the news in New York by the steamer that followed the *Olympia* when I took her out on her first trip. You had the *Leofric** the same year? Yes, I remember. What a pair of old buffers we are coming to be, you and I. Nearly fifty years since we were apprentices together on the *Clontarf.* Shall you ever forget old Blauklot? "Biddy te boor beebles ashore, poys!" Ha, ha! Take a little more, with all that water. It's the old Hulstkamp† I found in the cellar when this house came to me, the same I brought Luke from Amsterdam five-and-twenty years ago. He had never touched a drop of it. Perhaps he's sorry now, poor fellow.

Where did I leave off? I told you that Mrs. Pratt died suddenly—yes. Luke must have been lonely here after she was dead, I should think; I came to see him now and then, and he looked worn and nervous, and told me that his practice was growing too heavy for him, though he wouldn't take an assistant on any account. Years went on, and his son was killed in South Africa, and after that he began to be queer. There was something about him not like other people. I believe he kept his senses in his profession to the end; there was no complaint of his having made bad mistakes in cases, or anything of that sort, but he had a look about him—

Luke was a red-headed man with a pale face when he was young, and he was never stout; in middle age he turned a sandy grey, and after his son died he grew thinner and thinner, till his head looked like a skull with parchment stretched over it very tight, and his eyes had a sort of glare in them that was very disagreeable to look at.

He had an old dog that poor Mrs. Pratt had been fond of, and that used to follow her everywhere. He was a bull-dog, and the sweetest tempered beast you ever saw, though he had a way of hitching his upper lip

---

* Although there's no record of a ship by this name, Leofric was a real historical person: he was the Earl of Mercia in the 11th century and is now best known as the husband of Lady Godiva.

† A Rotterdam distillery, subsequently taken over by Bols.

behind one of his fangs that frightened strangers a good deal. Sometimes, of an evening, Pratt and Bumble—that was the dog's name—used to sit and look at each other a long time, thinking about old times, I suppose, when Luke's wife used to sit in that chair you've got. That was always her place, and this was the doctor's, where I'm sitting. Bumble used to climb up by the footstool—he was old and fat by that time, and could not jump much, and his teeth were getting shaky. He would look steadily at Luke, and Luke looked steadily at the dog, his face growing more and more like a skull with two little coals for eyes; and after about five minutes or so, though it may have been less, old Bumble would suddenly begin to shake all over, and all on a sudden he would set up an awful howl, as if he had been shot, and tumble out of the easy-chair and trot away, and hide himself under the sideboard, and lie there making odd noises.

Considering Pratt's looks in those last months, the thing is not surprising, you know. I'm not nervous or imaginative, but I can quite believe he might have sent a sensitive woman into hysterics—his head looked so much like a skull in parchment.

At last I came down one day before Christmas, when my ship was in dock and I had three weeks off. Bumble was not about, and I said casually that I supposed the old dog was dead.

"Yes," Pratt answered, and I thought there was something odd in his tone even before he went on after a little pause. "I killed him," he said presently. "I could not stand it any longer."

I asked what it was that Luke could not stand, though I guessed well enough.

"He had a way of sitting in her chair and glaring at me, and then howling." Luke shivered a little. "He didn't suffer at all, poor old Bumble," he went on in a hurry, as if he thought I might imagine he had been cruel. "I put dionine* into his drink to make him sleep soundly, and then I chloroformed him gradually, so that he could not have felt suffocated even if he was dreaming. It's been quieter since then."

I wondered what he meant, for the words slipped out as if he could not help saying them. I've understood since. He meant that he did not hear

---

* Also known as ethyl morphine or codethyline, an opioid anesthetic.

that noise so often after the dog was out of the way. Perhaps he thought at first that it was old Bumble in the yard howling at the moon, though it's not that kind of noise, is it? Besides, I know what it is, if Luke didn't. It's only a noise, after all, and a noise never hurt anybody yet. But he was much more imaginative than I am. No doubt there really is something about this place that I don't understand; but when I don't understand a thing, I call it a phenomenon, and I don't take it for granted that it's going to kill me, as he did. I don't understand everything, by long odds, nor do you, nor does any man who has been to sea. We used to talk of tidal waves, for instance, and we could not account for them; now we account for them by calling them submarine earthquakes, and we branch off into fifty theories, any one of which might make earthquakes quite comprehensible if we only knew what they are. I fell in with one of them once, and the inkstand flew straight up from the table against the ceiling of my cabin. The same thing happened to Captain Lecky—I dare say you've read about it in his "Wrinkles."* Very good. If that sort of thing took place ashore, in this room for instance, a nervous person would talk about spirits and levitation and fifty things that mean nothing, instead of just quietly setting it down as a "phenomenon" that has not been explained yet. My view of that voice, you see.

Besides, what is there to prove that Luke killed his wife? I would not even suggest such a thing to any one but you. After all, there was nothing but the coincidence that poor little Mrs. Pratt died suddenly in her bed a few days after I told that story at dinner. She was not the only woman who ever died like that. Luke got the doctor over from the next parish, and they agreed that she had died of something the matter with her heart. Why not? It's common enough.†

Of course, there was the ladle. I never told anybody about that, and it made me start when I found it in the cupboard in the bedroom. It was new, too—a little tinned iron ladle that had not been in the fire more than once

---

* Squire Thornton Stratford ("S.T.S.") Lecky's *Wrinkles in Practical Navigation* (1884) does indeed recount such an instance, though he doesn't say whether it was his own inkstand. Lecky renames tidal waves as "Great Sea Waves," pointing out that earthquakes, not tides, are the cause of such waves.

† Luke must have talked the doctor out of an autopsy or even a cursory examination of the body; lead poured into her ear would have left obvious traces.

or twice, and there was some lead in it that had been melted, and stuck to the bottom of the bowl, all grey, with hardened dross on it. But that proves nothing. A country doctor is generally a handy man, who does everything for himself, and Luke may have had a dozen reasons for melting a little lead in a ladle. He was fond of sea-fishing, for instance, and he may have cast a sinker for a night-line; perhaps it was a weight for the hall clock, or something like that. All the same, when I found it I had a rather queer sensation, because it looked so much like the thing I had described when I told them the story. Do you understand? It affected me unpleasantly, and I threw it away; it's at the bottom of the sea a mile from the Spit, and it will be jolly well rusted beyond recognising if it's ever washed up by the tide.

You see, Luke must have bought it in the village, years ago, for the man sells just such ladles still. I suppose they are used in cooking. In any case, there was no reason why an inquisitive housemaid should find such a thing lying about, with lead in it, and wonder what it was, and perhaps talk to the maid who heard me tell the story at dinner—for that girl married the plumber's son in the village, and may remember the whole thing.

You understand me, don't you? Now that Luke Pratt is dead and gone, and lies buried beside his wife, with an honest man's tombstone at his head, I should not care to stir up anything that could hurt his memory. They are both dead, and their son, too. There was trouble enough about Luke's death, as it was.

How? He was found dead on the beach one morning, and there was a coroner's inquest. There were marks on his throat, but he had not been robbed. The verdict was that he had come to his end "by the hands or teeth of some person or animal unknown," for half the jury thought it might have been a big dog that had thrown him down and gripped his windpipe, though the skin of his throat was not broken. No one knew at what time he had gone out, nor where he had been. He was found lying on his back above high-water mark, and an old cardboard bandbox* that had belonged to his wife lay under his hand, open. The lid had fallen off. He seemed to have been carrying home a skull in the box—doctors are fond of collecting such things. It had rolled out and lay near his head, and it was a remarkably

---

* A hatbox.

fine skull, rather small, beautifully shaped and very white, with perfect teeth. That is to say, the upper jaw was perfect, but there was no lower one at all, when I first saw it.

Yes, I found it here when I came. You see, it was very white and polished, like a thing meant to be kept under a glass case, and the people did not know where it came from, nor what to do with it; so they put it back into the bandbox and set it on the shelf of the cupboard in the best bedroom, and of course they showed it to me when I took possession. I was taken down to the beach, too, to be shown the place where Luke was found, and the old fisherman explained just how he was lying, and the skull beside him. The only point he could not explain was why the skull had rolled up the sloping sand toward Luke's head instead of rolling downhill to his feet. It did not seem odd to me at the time, but I have often thought of it since, for the place is rather steep. I'll take you there to-morrow if you like—I made a sort of cairn of stones there afterward.

When he fell down, or was thrown down—whichever happened—the bandbox struck the sand, and the lid came off, and the thing came out and ought to have rolled down. But it didn't. It was close to his head, almost touching it, and turned with the face toward it. I say it didn't strike me as odd when the man told me; but I could not help thinking about it afterward, again and again, till I saw a picture of it all when I closed my eyes; and then I began to ask myself why the plaguey thing had rolled up instead of down, and why it had stopped near Luke's head instead of anywhere else, a yard away, for instance.

You naturally want to know what conclusion I reached, don't you? None that at all explained the rolling, at all events. But I got something else into my head, after a time, that made me feel downright uncomfortable.

Oh, I don't mean as to anything supernatural! There may be ghosts, or there may not be. If there are, I'm not inclined to believe that they can hurt living people except by frightening them, and, for my part, I would rather face any shape of ghost than a fog in the Channel when it's crowded. No. What bothered me was just a foolish idea, that's all, and I cannot tell how it began, nor what made it grow till it turned into a certainty.

I was thinking about Luke and his poor wife one evening over my pipe and a dull book, when it occurred to me that the skull might possibly be hers, and I have never got rid of the thought since. You'll tell me there's no sense in it, no doubt; that Mrs. Pratt was buried like a Christian and is lying in the churchyard where they put her, and that it's perfectly monstrous to suppose her husband kept her skull in her old bandbox in his bedroom. All the same, in the face of reason, and common sense, and probability, I'm convinced that he did. Doctors do all sorts of queer things that would make men like you and me feel creepy, and those are just the things that don't seem probable, nor logical, nor sensible to us.

Then, don't you see?—if it really was her skull, poor woman, the only way of accounting for his having it is that he really killed her, and did it in that way, as the woman killed her husbands in the story, and that he was afraid there might be an examination some day which would betray him. You see, I told that too, and I believe it had really happened some fifty or sixty years ago. They dug up the three skulls, you know, and there was a small lump of lead rattling about in each one. That was what hanged the woman. Luke remembered that, I'm sure. I don't want to know what he did when he thought of it; my taste never ran in the direction of horrors, and I don't fancy you care for them either, do you? No. If you did, you might supply what is wanting to the story.

It must have been rather grim, eh? I wish I did not see the whole thing so distinctly, just as everything must have happened. He took it the night before she was buried, I'm sure, after the coffin had been shut, and when the servant girl was asleep. I would bet anything, that when he'd got it, he put something under the sheet in its place, to fill up and look like it. What do you suppose he put there, under the sheet?

I don't wonder you take me up on what I'm saying! First I tell you that I don't want to know what happened, and that I hate to think about horrors, and then I describe the whole thing to you as if I had seen it. I'm quite sure that it was her work-bag that he put there. I remember the bag very well, for she always used it of an evening; it was made of brown plush, and when it was stuffed full it was about the size of—you understand. Yes, there I am, at it again! You may laugh at me, but you don't live here alone, where it was done, and you didn't tell Luke the story about the melted lead. I'm not nervous, I tell you, but sometimes I begin to feel that I understand why some people are. I dwell on all this when I'm alone, and I dream of it, and when that thing screams—well, frankly, I don't like the noise any more than you do, though I should be used to it by this time.

I ought not to be nervous. I've sailed in a haunted ship. There was a Man in the Top,* and two-thirds of the crew died of the West Coast fever[†] inside of ten days after we anchored; but I was all right, then and afterward. I have seen some ugly sights, too, just as you have, and all the rest of us. But nothing ever stuck in my head in the way this does.

You see, I've tried to get rid of the thing, but it doesn't like that. It wants to be there in its place, in Mrs. Pratt's bandbox in the cupboard in the best bedroom. It's not happy anywhere else. How do I know that? Because I've tried it. You don't suppose that I've not tried, do you? As long as it's there it only screams now and then, generally at this time of year, but if I put it out of the house it goes on all night, and no servant will stay here twenty-four hours. As it is, I've often been left alone and have been obliged to shift for myself for a fortnight at a time. No one from the village would ever pass a night under the roof now, and as for selling the place, or even letting it, that's out of the question. The old women say that if I stay here I shall come to a bad end myself before long.

I'm not afraid of that. You smile at the mere idea that any one could take such nonsense seriously. Quite right. It's utterly blatant nonsense, I agree with you. Didn't I tell you that it's only a noise after all when you started and looked round as if you expected to see a ghost standing behind your chair?

I may be all wrong about the skull, and I like to think that I am—when I can. It may be just a fine specimen which Luke got somewhere long ago, and what rattles about inside when you shake it may be nothing but a pebble, or a bit of hard clay, or anything. Skulls that have lain long in the ground generally have something inside them that rattles, don't they? No, I've never tried to get it out, whatever it is; I'm afraid it might be lead, don't you see? And if it is, I don't want to know the fact, for I'd much rather not be sure. If it really is lead, I killed her quite as much as if I had

---

* It's unknown why Crawford has capitalized this phrase, although there are many sailing legends of ghosts in the rigging and masts of ships.

† "West Coast fever" may be African trypanosomiasis, also known as African sleeping sickness, which is carried by tsetse flies in wet areas and resulted in an epidemic that ravaged Uganda in 1901.

done the deed myself. Anybody must see that, I should think. As long as I don't know for certain, I have the consolation of saying that it's all utterly ridiculous nonsense, that Mrs. Pratt died a natural death and that the beautiful skull belonged to Luke when he was a student in London. But if I were quite sure, I believe I should have to leave the house; indeed I do, most certainly. As it is, I had to give up trying to sleep in the best bedroom where the cupboard is.

You ask me why I don't throw it into the pond—yes, but please don't call it a "confounded bugbear"—it doesn't like being called names.

There! Lord, what a shriek! I told you so! You're quite pale, man. Fill up your pipe and draw your chair nearer to the fire, and take some more drink. Old Hollands* never hurt anybody yet. I've seen a Dutchman in Java drink half a jug of Hulstkamp in a morning without turning a hair. I don't take much rum myself, because it doesn't agree with my rheumatism, but you are not rheumatic and it won't damage you. Besides, it's a very damp night outside. The wind is howling again, and it will soon be in the southwest; do you hear how the windows rattle? The tide must have turned too, by the moaning.

We should not have heard the thing again if you had not said that. I'm pretty sure we should not. Oh yes, if you choose to describe it as a coincidence, you are quite welcome, but I would rather that you should not call the thing names again, if you don't mind. It may be that the poor little woman hears, and perhaps it hurts her, don't you know? Ghost? No! You don't call anything a ghost that you can take in your hands and look at in broad daylight, and that rattles when you shake it. Do you, now? But it's something that hears and understands; there's no doubt about that.

I tried sleeping in the best bedroom when I first came to the house, just because it was the best and the most comfortable, but I had to give it up. It was their room, and there's the big bed she died in, and the cupboard is in the thickness of the wall, near the head, on the left. That's where it likes to be kept, in its bandbox. I only used the room for a fortnight after I came, and then I turned out and took the little room downstairs, next to the surgery, where Luke used to sleep when he expected to be called to a patient during the night.

---

* That is, spirits distilled in Holland.

I was always a good sleeper ashore; eight hours is my dose, eleven to seven when I'm alone, twelve to eight when I have a friend with me. But I could not sleep after three o'clock in the morning in that room—a quarter past, to be accurate—as a matter of fact, I timed it with my old pocket chronometer, which still keeps good time, and it was always at exactly seventeen minutes past three. I wonder whether that was the hour when she died?

It was not what you have heard. If it had been that I could not have stood it two nights. It was just a start and a moan and hard breathing for a few seconds in the cupboard, and it could never have waked me under ordinary circumstances, I'm sure. I suppose you are like me in that, and we are just like other people who have been to sea. No natural sounds disturb us at all, not all the racket of a square-rigger hove to in a heavy gale, or rolling on her beam ends before the wind. But if a lead pencil gets adrift and rattles in the drawer of your cabin table you are awake in a moment. Just so—you always understand. Very well, the noise in the cupboard was no louder than that, but it waked me instantly.

I said it was like a "start." I know what I mean, but it's hard to explain without seeming to talk nonsense. Of course you cannot exactly "hear" a person "start"; at the most, you might hear the quick drawing of the breath between the parted lips and closed teeth, and the almost imperceptible sound of clothing that moved suddenly though very slightly. It was like that.

You know how one feels what a sailing vessel is going to do, two or three seconds before she does it, when one has the wheel. Riders say the same of a horse, but that's less strange, because the horse is a live animal with feelings of its own, and only poets and landsmen talk about a ship being alive, and all that. But I have always felt somehow that besides being a steaming machine or a sailing machine for carrying weights, a vessel at sea is a sensitive instrument, and a means of communication between nature and man, and most particularly the man at the wheel, if she is steered by hand. She takes her impressions directly from wind and sea, tide and stream, and transmits them to the man's hand, just as the wireless telegraph picks up the interrupted currents aloft and turns them out below in the form of a message.

You see what I am driving at; I felt that something started in the cupboard, and I felt it so vividly that I heard it, though there may have been nothing to hear, and the sound inside my head waked me suddenly. But I really heard the other noise. It was as if it were muffled inside a box, as far away as if it came through a long-distance telephone; and yet I knew that it was inside the cupboard near the head of my bed. My hair did not bristle and my blood did not run cold that time. I simply resented being waked up by something that had no business to make a noise, any more than a pencil should rattle in the drawer of my cabin table on board ship. For I did not understand; I just supposed that the cupboard had some communication with the outside air, and that the wind had got in and was moaning through it with a sort of very faint screech. I struck a light and looked at my watch, and it was seventeen minutes past three. Then I turned over and went to sleep on my right ear. That's my good one; I'm pretty deaf with the other, for I struck the water with it when I was a lad in diving from the foretopsail yard. Silly thing to do, it was, but the result is very convenient when I want to go to sleep when there's a noise.

That was the first night, and the same thing happened again and several times afterward, but not regularly, though it was always at the same time, to a second; perhaps I was sometimes sleeping on my good ear, and sometimes not. I overhauled the cupboard and there was no way by which the wind could get in, or anything else, for the door makes a good fit, having been meant to keep out moths, I suppose; Mrs. Pratt must have kept her winter things in it, for it still smells of camphor and turpentine.

After about a fortnight I had had enough of the noises. So far I had said to myself that it would be silly to yield to it and take the skull out of the room. Things always look differently by daylight, don't they? But the voice grew louder—I suppose one may call it a voice—and it got inside my deaf ear, too, one night. I realised that when I was wide awake, for my good ear was jammed down on the pillow, and I ought not to have heard a fog-horn in that position. But I heard that, and it made me lose my temper, unless it scared me, for sometimes the two are not far apart. I struck a light and got up, and I opened the cupboard, grabbed the bandbox and threw it out of the window, as far as I could.

Then my hair stood on end. The thing screamed in the air, like a shell from a twelve-inch gun. It fell on the other side of the road. The night was very dark, and I could not see it fall, but I know it fell beyond the road.

The window is just over the front door, it's fifteen yards to the fence, more or less, and the road is ten yards wide. There's a quickset hedge* beyond, along the glebe† that belongs to the vicarage.

I did not sleep much more that night. It was not more than half an hour after I had thrown the bandbox out when I heard a shriek outside—like what we've had to-night, but worse, more despairing, I should call it; and it may have been my imagination, but I could have sworn that the screams came nearer and nearer each time. I lit a pipe, and walked up and down for a bit, and then took a book and sat up reading, but I'll be hanged if I can remember what I read nor even what the book was, for every now and then a shriek came up that would have made a dead man turn in his coffin.

A little before dawn some one knocked at the front door. There was no mistaking that for anything else, and I opened my window and looked down, for I guessed that some one wanted the doctor, supposing that the new man had taken Luke's house. It was rather a relief to hear a human knock after that awful noise.

You cannot see the door from above, owing to the little porch. The knocking came again, and I called out, asking who was there, but nobody answered, though the knock was repeated. I sang out again, and said that the doctor did not live here any longer. There was no answer, but it occurred to me that it might be some old countryman who was stone deaf. So I took my candle and went down to open the door. Upon my word, I was not thinking of the thing yet, and I had almost forgotten the other noises. I went down convinced that I should find somebody outside, on the doorstep, with a message. I set the candle on the hall table, so that the wind should not blow it out when I opened. While I was drawing the old-fashioned bolt I heard the knocking again. It was not loud, and it had a queer, hollow sound, now that I was close to it, I remember, but I certainly thought it was made by some person who wanted to get in.

It wasn't. There was nobody there, but as I opened the door inward, standing a little on one side, so as to see out at once, something rolled across the threshold and stopped against my foot.

---

* Typically English hawthorn, planted as a boundary marker.

† A portion of land assigned by the church to a clergyman, as part of the clergy's benefice.

I drew back as I felt it, for I knew what it was before I looked down. I cannot tell you how I knew, and it seemed unreasonable, for I am still quite sure that I had thrown it across the road. It's a French window, that opens wide, and I got a good swing when I flung it out. Besides, when I went out early in the morning, I found the bandbox beyond the thickset hedge.

You may think it opened when I threw it, and that the skull dropped out; but that's impossible, for nobody could throw an empty cardboard box so far. It's out of the question; you might as well try to fling a ball of paper twenty-five yards, or a blown bird's egg.

To go back, I shut and bolted the hall door, picked the thing up carefully, and put it on the table beside the candle. I did that mechanically, as one instinctively does the right thing in danger without thinking at all—unless one does the opposite. It may seem odd, but I believe my first thought had been that somebody might come and find me there on the threshold while it was resting against my foot, lying a little on its side, and turning one hollow eye up at my face, as if it meant to accuse me. And the light and shadow from the candle played in the hollows of the eyes as it stood on the table, so that they seemed to open and shut at me. Then the candle went out quite unexpectedly, though the door was fastened and there was not the least draught; and I used up at least half a dozen matches before it would burn again.

I sat down rather suddenly, without quite knowing why. Probably I had been badly frightened, and perhaps you will admit there was no great shame in being scared. The thing had come home, and it wanted to go upstairs, back to its cupboard. I sat still and stared at it for a bit, till I began to feel very cold; then I took it and carried it up and set it in its place, and I remember that I spoke to it, and promised that it should have its bandbox again in the morning.

You want to know whether I stayed in the room till daybreak? Yes, but I kept a light burning, and sat up smoking and reading, most likely out of fright; plain, undeniable fear, and you need not call it cowardice either, for that's not the same thing. I could not have stayed alone with that thing in the cupboard; I should have been scared to death, though I'm not more timid than other people. Confound it all, man, it had crossed the road alone, and had got up the doorstep and had knocked to be let in.

When the dawn came, I put on my boots and went out to find the bandbox. I had to go a good way round, by the gate near the highroad, and I found the box open and hanging on the other side of the hedge. It had caught on the twigs by the string, and the lid had fallen off and was lying on the ground below it. That shows that it did not open till it was well over; and if it had not opened as soon as it left my hand, what was inside it must have gone beyond the road too.

That's all. I took the box upstairs to the cupboard, and put the skull back and locked it up. When the girl brought me my breakfast she said she was sorry, but that she must go, and she did not care if she lost her month's wages. I looked at her, and her face was a sort of greenish, yellowish white. I pretended to be surprised, and asked what was the matter; but that was of no use, for she just turned on me and wanted to know whether I meant to stay in a haunted house, and how long I expected to live if I did, for though she noticed I was sometimes a little hard of hearing, she did not believe that even I could sleep through those screams again—and if I could, why had I been moving about the house and opening and shutting the front door, between three and four in the morning? There was no answering that, since she had heard me, so off she went, and I was left to myself. I went down to the village during the morning and found a woman who was willing to come and do the little work there is and cook my dinner, on condition that she might go home every night. As for me, I moved downstairs that day, and I have never tried to sleep in the best bedroom since. After a little while I got a brace of middle-aged Scotch servants from London, and things were quiet enough for a long time. I began by telling them that the house was in a very exposed position, and that the wind whistled round it a good deal in the autumn and winter, which had given it a bad name in the village, the Cornish people being inclined to superstition and telling ghost stories.* The two hard-faced, sandy-haired sisters almost smiled, and they answered with great contempt that they had no great opinion of any Southern bogey whatever, having been in service in two English haunted houses, where

---

* The location of the village in Cornwall is confirmed in the newspaper account at the end of the tale.

they had never seen so much as the Boy in Gray, whom they reckoned no very particular rarity in Forfarshire.*

They stayed with me several months, and while they were in the house we had peace and quiet. One of them is here again now, but she went away with her sister within the year. This one—she was the cook—married the sexton, who works in my garden. That's the way of it. It's a small village and he has not much to do, and he knows enough about flowers to help me nicely, besides doing most of the hard work; for though I'm fond of exercise, I'm getting a little stiff in the hinges. He's a sober, silent sort of fellow, who minds his own business, and he was a widower when I came here—Trehearn is his name, James Trehearn. The Scotch sisters would not admit that there was anything wrong about the house, but when November came they gave me warning that they were going, on the ground that the chapel was such a long walk from here, being in the next parish, and that they could not possibly go to our church. But the younger one came back in the spring, and as soon as the banns could be published† she was married to James Trehearn by the vicar, and she seems to have had no scruples about hearing him preach since then. I'm quite satisfied, if she is! The couple live in a small cottage that looks over the churchyard.

I suppose you are wondering what all this has to do with what I was talking about. I'm alone so much that when an old friend comes to see me, I sometimes go on talking just for the sake of hearing my own voice. But in this case there is really a connection of ideas. It was James Trehearn who buried poor Mrs. Pratt, and her husband after her in the same grave, and it's not far from the back of his cottage. That's the connection in my mind, you see. It's plain enough. He knows something; I'm quite sure that he does, by his manner, though he's such a reticent beggar.

Yes, I'm alone in the house at night now, for Mrs. Trehearn does everything herself, and when I have a friend the sexton's niece comes in to wait on the table. He takes his wife home every evening in winter, but

---

* A county in Scotland, now known as Angus. "The Boy in Gray" is apparently a local legend.

† A published notice of an upcoming wedding that provides an opportunity for any objections to be made.

in summer, when there's light, she goes by herself. She's not a nervous woman, but she's less sure than she used to be that there are no bogies in England worth a Scotchwoman's notice. Isn't it amusing, the idea that Scotland has a monopoly of the supernatural? Odd sort of national pride, I call that, don't you?

That's a good fire, isn't it? When driftwood gets started at last there's nothing like it, I think. Yes, we get lots of it, for I'm sorry to say there are still a great many wrecks about here. It's a lonely coast, and you may have all the wood you want for the trouble of bringing it in. Trehearn and I borrow a cart now and then, and load it between here and the Spit. I hate a coal fire when I can get wood of any sort. A log is company, even if it's only a piece of a deck-beam or timber sawn off, and the salt in it makes pretty sparks. See how they fly, like Japanese hand-fireworks! Upon my word, with an old friend and a good fire and a pipe, one forgets all about that thing upstairs, especially now that the wind has moderated. It's only a lull, though, and it will blow a gale before morning.

You think you would like to see the skull? I've no objection. There's no reason why you shouldn't have a look at it, and you never saw a more perfect one in your life, except that there are two front teeth missing in the lower jaw.

Oh yes—I had not told you about the jaw yet. Trehearn found it in the garden last spring when he was digging a pit for a new asparagus bed. You know we make asparagus beds six or eight feet deep here. Yes, yes—I had forgotten to tell you that. He was digging straight down, just as he digs a grave; if you want a good asparagus bed made, I advise you to get a sexton to make it for you. Those fellows have a wonderful knack at that sort of digging.

Trehearn had got down about three feet when he cut into a mass of white lime in the side of the trench. He had noticed that the earth was a little looser there, though he says it had not been disturbed for a number of years. I suppose he thought that even old lime might not be good for asparagus, so he broke it out and threw it up. It was pretty hard, he says, in biggish lumps, and out of sheer force of habit he cracked the lumps with his spade as they lay outside the pit beside him; the jawbone of a skull dropped out of one of the pieces. He thinks he must have knocked out the two front teeth in breaking up the lime, but he did not see them anywhere. He's a very experienced man in such things, as you may imagine, and he said at once that the jaw had probably belonged to a young woman, and that the teeth had been complete when she died. He brought it to me, and asked me if I wanted to keep it; if I did not, he said he would drop it into the next grave he made in the churchyard, as he supposed it was a Christian jaw, and ought to have decent burial, wherever the rest of the body might be. I told him that doctors often put bones into quicklime to whiten them nicely, and that I supposed Dr. Pratt had once had a little lime pit in the garden for that purpose, and had forgotten the jaw. Trehearn looked at me quietly.

"Maybe it fitted that skull that used to be in the cupboard upstairs, sir," he said. "Maybe Dr. Pratt had put the skull into the lime to clean it, or something, and when he took it out he left the lower jaw behind. There's some human hair sticking in the lime, sir."

I saw there was, and that was what Trehearn said. If he did not suspect something, why in the world should he have suggested that the jaw might fit the skull? Besides, it did. That's proof that he knows more than he cares to tell. Do you suppose he looked before she was buried? Or perhaps—when he buried Luke in the same grave—

Well, well, it's of no use to go over that, is it? I said I would keep the jaw with the skull, and I took it upstairs and fitted it into its place. There's not the slightest doubt about the two belonging together, and together they are.

Trehearn knows several things. We were talking about plastering the kitchen a while ago, and he happened to remember that it had not been done since the very week when Mrs. Pratt died. He did not say that the mason must have left some lime on the place, but he thought it, and that it was the very same lime he had found in the asparagus pit. He knows a lot. Trehearn is one of your silent beggars who can put two and two together. That grave is very near the back of his cottage, too, and he's one of the quickest men with a spade I ever saw. If he wanted to know the truth, he could, and no one else would ever be the wiser unless he chose to tell. In a quiet village like ours, people don't go and spend the night in the churchyard to see whether the sexton potters about by himself between ten o'clock and daylight.

What is awful to think of, is Luke's deliberation, if he did it; his cool certainty that no one would find him out; above all, his nerve, for that must have been extraordinary. I sometimes think it's bad enough to live in the place where it was done, if it really was done. I always put in the condition, you see, for the sake of his memory, and a little bit for my own sake, too.

I'll go upstairs and fetch the box in a minute. Let me light my pipe; there's no hurry! We had supper early, and it's only half-past nine o'clock. I never let a friend go to bed before twelve, or with less than three glasses—you may have as many more as you like, but you shan't have less, for the sake of old times.

It's breezing up again, do you hear? That was only a lull just now, and we are going to have a bad night.

A thing happened that made me start a little when I found that the jaw fitted exactly. I'm not very easily startled in that way myself, but I have seen people make a quick movement, drawing their breath sharply, when they had thought they were alone and suddenly turned and saw some one very near them. Nobody can call that fear. You wouldn't, would you? No. Well, just when I had set the jaw in its place under the skull, the teeth closed sharply on my finger. It felt exactly as if it were biting me hard, and I confess that I jumped before I realised that I had been pressing the jaw and the skull together with my other hand. I assure you I was not at all nervous. It was broad daylight, too, and a fine day, and the sun was streaming into the best bedroom. It would have been absurd to be nervous, and it was only a quick mistaken impression, but it really made me feel queer. Somehow it made me think of the funny verdict of the coroner's jury on Luke's death, "by the hand or teeth of some person or animal unknown." Ever since that I've wished I had seen those marks on his throat, though the lower jaw was missing then.

I have often seen a man do insane things with his hands that he does not realise at all. I once saw a man hanging on by an old awning stop with one hand, leaning backward, outboard, with all his weight on it, and he was just cutting the stop with the knife in his other hand when I got my arms round him. We were in mid-ocean, going twenty knots. He had not the smallest idea what he was doing; neither had I when I managed to pinch my finger between the teeth of that thing. I can feel it now. It was exactly as if it were alive and were trying to bite me. It would if it could, for I know it hates me, poor thing! Do you suppose that what rattles about inside is really a bit of lead? Well, I'll get the box down presently, and if whatever it is happens to drop out into your hands that's your affair. If it's only a clod of earth or a pebble, the whole matter would be off my mind, and I don't believe I should ever think of the skull again; but somehow I cannot bring myself to shake out the bit of hard stuff myself. The mere idea that it may be lead makes me confoundedly uncomfortable, yet I've got the conviction that I shall know before long. I shall certainly know. I'm sure Trehearn knows, but he's such a silent beggar.

I'll go upstairs now and get it. What? You had better go with me? Ha, ha! do you think I'm afraid of a bandbox and a noise? Nonsense!

Bother the candle, it won't light! As if the ridiculous thing understood what it's wanted for! Look at that—the third match. They light fast enough for my pipe. There, do you see? It's a fresh box, just out of the tin safe where I keep the supply on account of the dampness. Oh, you think the wick of the candle may be damp, do you? All right, I'll light the beastly thing in the fire. That won't go out, at all events. Yes, it sputters a bit, but it will keep lighted now. It burns just like any other candle, doesn't it? The fact is, candles are not very good about here. I don't know where they come from, but they have a way of burning low occasionally, with a greenish flame that spits tiny sparks, and I'm often annoyed by their going out of themselves. It cannot be helped, for it will be long before we have electricity in our village. It really is rather a poor light, isn't it?

You think I had better leave you the candle and take the lamp, do you? I don't like to carry lamps about, that's the truth. I never dropped one in my life, but I have always thought I might, and it's so confoundedly dangerous if you do. Besides, I am pretty well used to these rotten candles by this time.

You may as well finish that glass while I'm getting it, for I don't mean to let you off with less than three before you go to bed. You won't have to go upstairs, either, for I've put you in the old study next to the surgery—that's where I live myself. The fact is, I never ask a friend to sleep upstairs now. The last man who did was Crackenthorpe, and he said he was kept awake all night. You remember old Crack, don't you? He stuck to the Service, and they've just made him an admiral. Yes, I'm off now—unless the candle goes out. I couldn't help asking if you remembered Crackenthorpe. If any one had told us that the skinny little idiot he used to be was to turn out the most successful of the lot of us, we should have laughed at the idea, shouldn't we? You and I did not do badly, it's true—but I'm really going now. I don't mean to let you think that I've been putting it off by talking! As if there were anything to be afraid of! If I were scared, I should tell you so quite frankly, and get you to go upstairs with me.

Here's the box. I brought it down very carefully, so as not to disturb it, poor thing. You see, if it were shaken, the jaw might get separated from it again, and I'm sure it wouldn't like that. Yes, the candle went out as I was coming downstairs, but that was the draught from the leaky window on the landing. Did you hear anything? Yes, there was another scream. Am I pale, do you say? That's nothing. My heart is a little queer sometimes, and I went upstairs too fast. In fact, that's one reason why I really prefer to live altogether on the ground floor.

Wherever that shriek came from, it was not from the skull, for I had the box in my hand when I heard the noise, and here it is now; so we have proved definitely that the screams are produced by something else. I've no doubt I shall find out some day what makes them. Some crevice in the wall, of course, or a crack in a chimney, or a chink in the frame of a window. That's the way all ghost stories end in real life. Do you know, I'm jolly glad I thought of going up and bringing it down for you to see, for that last shriek settles the question. To think that I should have been so weak as to fancy that the poor skull could really cry out like a living thing!

Now I'll open the box, and we'll take it out and look at it under the bright light. It's rather awful to think that the poor lady used to sit there, in your chair, evening after evening, in just the same light, isn't it? But then—I've made up my mind that it's all rubbish from beginning to end, and that it's just an old skull that Luke had when he was a student; and perhaps he put it into the lime merely to whiten it, and could not find the jaw.

I made a seal on the string, you see, after I had put the jaw in its place, and I wrote on the cover. There's the old white label on it still, from the milliner's, addressed to Mrs. Pratt when the hat was sent to her, and as there was room I wrote on the edge: "A skull, once the property of the late

Luke Pratt, M.D." I don't quite know why I wrote that, unless it was with the idea of explaining how the thing happened to be in my possession. I cannot help wondering sometimes what sort of hat it was that came in the bandbox. What colour was it, do you think? Was it a gay spring hat with a bobbing feather and pretty ribands? Strange that the very same box should hold the head that wore the finery—perhaps. No—we made up our minds that it just came from the hospital in London where Luke did his time. It's far better to look at it in that light, isn't it? There's no more connection between that skull and poor Mrs. Pratt than there was between my story about the lead and—

Good Lord! Take the lamp—don't let it go out, if you can help it—I'll have the window fastened again in a second—I say, what a gale! There, it's out! I told you so! Never mind, there's the firelight—I've got the window shut—the bolt was only half down. Was the box blown off the table? Where the deuce is it? There! That won't open again, for I've put up the bar. Good dodge, an old-fashioned bar—there's nothing like it. Now, you find the bandbox while I light the lamp. Confound those wretched matches! Yes, a pipe spill* is better—it must light in the fire—I hadn't thought of it—thank you—there we are again. Now, where's the box? Yes, put it back on the table, and we'll open it.

That's the first time I have ever known the wind to burst that window open; but it was partly carelessness on my part when I last shut it. Yes, of course I heard the scream. It seemed to go all round the house before it broke in at the window. That proves that it's always been the wind and nothing else, doesn't it? When it was not the wind, it was my imagination. I've always been a very imaginative man: I must have been, though I did not know it. As we grow older we understand ourselves better, don't you know?

I'll have a drop of the Hulstkamp neat, by way of an exception, since you are filling up your glass. That damp gust chilled me, and with my rheumatic tendency I'm very much afraid of a chill, for the cold sometimes seems to stick in my joints all winter when it once gets in.

By George, that's good stuff! I'll just light a fresh pipe, now that every-thing is snug again, and then we'll open the box. I'm so glad we heard

---

* A twisted or folded piece of paper used for lighting a pipe.

that last scream together, with the skull here on the table between us, for a thing cannot possibly be in two places at the same time, and the noise most certainly came from outside, as any noise the wind makes must. You thought you heard it scream through the room after the window was burst open? Oh yes, so did I, but that was natural enough when everything was open. Of course we heard the wind. What could one expect?

Look here, please. I want you to see that the seal is intact before we open the box together. Will you take my glasses? No, you have your own. All right. The seal is sound, you see, and you can read the words of the motto easily. "Sweet and low"—that's it—because the poem goes on "Wind of the Western sea," and says, "blow him again to me," and all that.* Here is the seal on my watch-chain, where it's hung for more than forty years. My poor little wife gave it to me when I was courting, and I never had any other. It was just like her to think of those words—she was always fond of Tennyson.

It's of no use to cut the string, for its fastened to the box, so I'll just break the wax and untie the knot, and afterward we'll seal it up again. You see, I like to feel that the thing is safe in its place, and that nobody can take it out. Not that I should suspect Trehearn of meddling with it, but I always feel that he knows a lot more than he tells.

You see, I've managed it without breaking the string, though when I fastened it I never expected to open the bandbox again. The lid comes off easily enough. There! Now look!

What? Nothing in it? Empty? It's gone, man, the skull is gone!

---

* The first stanza of the poem "Sweet and Low" by Alfred Lord Tennyson (1850) is as follows:
Sweet and low, sweet and low,
Wind of the western sea,
Low, low, breathe and blow,
Wind of the western sea.
Over the rolling waters go;
Come from the dying moon, and blow;
Blow him again to me,
While my little one, while my pretty one sleeps.

No, there's nothing the matter with me. I'm only trying to collect my thoughts. It's so strange. I'm positively certain that it was inside when I put on the seal last spring. I can't have imagined that: it's utterly impossible. If I ever took a stiff glass with a friend now and then, I would admit that I might have made some idiotic mistake when I had taken too much. But I don't, and I never did. A pint of ale at supper and half a go of rum at bedtime was the most I ever took in my good days. I believe it's always we sober fellows who get rheumatism and gout! Yet there was my seal, and there is the empty bandbox. That's plain enough.

I say, I don't half like this. It's not right. There's something wrong about it, in my opinion. You needn't talk to me about supernatural manifestations, for I don't believe in them, not a little bit! Somebody must have tampered with the seal and stolen the skull. Sometimes, when I go out to work in the garden in summer, I leave my watch and chain, on the table. Trehearn must have taken the seal then, and used it, for he would be quite sure that I should not come in for at least an hour.

If it was not Trehearn—oh, don't talk to me about the possibility that the thing has got out by itself! If it has, it must be somewhere about the house, in some out-of-the-way corner, waiting. We may come upon it anywhere, waiting for us, don't you know?—just waiting in the dark. Then it will scream at me; it will shriek at me in the dark, for it hates me, I tell you!

The bandbox is quite empty. We are not dreaming, either of us. There, I turn it upside down.

What's that? Something fell out as I turned it over. It's on the floor, it's near your feet, I know it is, and we must find it. Help me to find it, man. Have you got it? For God's sake, give it to me, quickly!

Lead! I knew it when I heard it fall. I knew it couldn't be anything else by the little thud it made on the hearth-rug. So it was lead after all, and Luke did it.

I feel a little bit shaken up—not exactly nervous, you know, but badly shaken up, that's the fact. Anybody would, I should think. After all, you cannot say that it's fear of the thing, for I went up and brought it down—at least, I believed I was bringing it down, and that's the same thing, and by George, rather than give in to such silly nonsense, I'll take the box upstairs again and put it back in its place. It's not that. It's the certainty that the poor little woman came to her end in that way, by my fault, because I told the story. That's what is so dreadful. Somehow, I had always hoped that I should never be quite sure of it, but there is no doubting it now. Look at that!

Look at it! That little lump of lead with no particular shape. Think of what it did, man! Doesn't it make you shiver? He gave her something to make her sleep, of course, but there must have been one moment of awful agony. Think of having boiling lead poured into your brain. Think of it. She was dead before she could scream, but only think of—oh! there it is again—it's just outside—I know it's just outside—I can't keep it out of my head!—oh!—oh!

You thought I had fainted? No, I wish I had, for it would have stopped sooner. It's all very well to say that it's only a noise, and that a noise never hurt anybody—you're as white as a shroud yourself. There's only one thing to be done, if we hope to close an eye tonight. We must find it and put it back into its bandbox and shut it up in the cupboard, where it likes to be. I don't know how it got out, but it wants to get in again. That's why it screams so awfully tonight—it was never so bad as this—never since I first—

Bury it? Yes, if we can find it, we'll bury it, if it takes us all night. We'll bury it six feet deep and ram down the earth over it, so that it shall never get out again, and if it screams, we shall hardly hear it so deep down. Quick, we'll get the lantern and look for it. It cannot be far away; I'm sure it's just outside—it was coming in when I shut the window, I know it.

Yes, you're quite right. I'm losing my senses, and I must get hold of myself. Don't speak to me for a minute or two; I'll sit quite still and keep my eyes shut and repeat something I know. That's the best way.

"Add together the altitude, the latitude, and the polar distance, divide by two and subtract the altitude from the half-sum; then add the logarithm of the secant of the latitude, the cosecant of the polar distance, the cosine of the half-sum and the sine of the half-sum minus the altitude"—there! Don't say that I'm out of my senses, for my memory is all right, isn't it?

Of course, you may say that it's mechanical, and that we never forget the things we learned when we were boys and have used almost every day for a lifetime. But that's the very point. When a man is going crazy, it's the mechanical part of his mind that gets out of order and won't work right; he remembers things that never happened, or he sees things that aren't real, or he hears noises when there is perfect silence. That's not what is the matter with either of us, is it?

Come, we'll get the lantern and go round the house. It's not raining—only blowing like old boots, as we used to say. The lantern is in the cupboard under the stairs in the hall, and I always keep it trimmed in case of a wreck.

No use to look for the thing? I don't see how you can say that. It was nonsense to talk of burying it, of course, for it doesn't want to be buried; it wants to go back into its bandbox and be taken upstairs, poor thing! Trehearn took it out, I know, and made the seal over again. Perhaps he took it to the churchyard, and he may have meant well. I daresay he thought that it would not scream any more if it were quietly laid in consecrated ground, near where it belongs. But it has come home. Yes, that's it. He's not half a bad fellow, Trehearn, and rather religiously inclined, I think. Does not that sound natural, and reasonable, and well meant? He supposed it screamed because it was not decently buried—with the rest. But he was wrong. How should he know that it screams at me because it hates me, and because it's my fault that there was that little lump of lead in it?

No use to look for it, anyhow? Nonsense! I tell you it wants to be found—Hark! what's that knocking? Do you hear it? Knock—knock—knock—three times, then a pause, and then again. It has a hollow sound, hasn't it?

It has come home. I've heard that knock before. It wants to come in and be taken upstairs, in its box. It's at the front door.

Will you come with me? We'll take it in. Yes, I own that I don't like to go alone and open the door. The thing will roll in and stop against my foot, just as it did before, and the light will go out. I'm a good deal shaken by finding that bit of lead, and, besides, my heart isn't quite right—too much strong tobacco, perhaps. Besides, I'm quite willing to own that I'm a bit nervous to-night, if I never was before in my life.

That's right, come along! I'll take the box with me, so as not to come back. Do you hear the knocking? It's not like any other knocking I ever heard. If you will hold this door open, I can find the lantern under the stairs by the light from this room without bringing the lamp into the hall—it would only go out.

The thing knows we are coming—hark! It's impatient to get in. Don't shut the door till the lantern is ready, whatever you do. There will be the usual trouble with the matches, I suppose—no, the first one, by Jove! I tell you it wants to get in, so there's no trouble. All right with that door now; shut it, please. Now come and hold the lantern, for it's blowing so hard outside that I shall have to use both hands. That's it, hold the light low. Do you hear the knocking still? Here goes—I'll open just enough with my foot against the bottom of the door—now!

Catch it! It's only the wind that blows it across the floor, that's all—there's half a hurricane outside, I tell you! Have you got it? The bandbox is on the table. One minute, and I'll have the bar up. There!

Why did you throw it into the box so roughly? It doesn't like that, you know.

What do you say? Bitten your hand? Nonsense, man! You did just what I did. You pressed the jaws together with your other hand and pinched yourself. Let me see. You don't mean to say you have drawn blood? You must have squeezed hard, by Jove, for the skin is certainly torn. I'll give you some carbolic solution for it before we go to bed, for they say a scratch from a skull's tooth may go bad and give trouble.

Come inside again and let me see it by the lamp. I'll bring the bandbox—never mind the lantern, it may just as well burn in the hall, for I shall need it presently when I go up the stairs. Yes, shut the door if you will; it makes it more cheerful and bright. Is your finger still bleeding? I'll get you the carbolic in an instant; just let me see the thing.

Ugh! There's a drop of blood on the upper jaw. It's on the eye-tooth. Ghastly, isn't it? When I saw it running along the floor of the hall, the strength almost went out of my hands, and I felt my knees bending; then I understood that it was the gale, driving it over the smooth boards. You don't blame me? No, I should think not! We were boys together, and we've seen a thing or two, and we may just as well own to each other that we were both in a beastly funk when it slid across the floor at you. No wonder you pinched your finger picking it up, after that, if I did the same thing out of sheer nervousness, in broad daylight, with the sun streaming in on me.

Strange that the jaw should stick to it so closely, isn't it? I suppose it's the dampness, for it shuts like a vice—I have wiped off the drop of blood, for it was not nice to look at. I'm not going to try to open the jaws, don't be afraid! I shall not play any tricks with the poor thing, but I'll just seal the box again, and we'll take it upstairs and put it away where it wants to be. The wax is on the writing-table by the window. Thank you. It will be long before I leave my seal lying about again, for Trehearn to use, I can tell you. Explain? I don't explain natural phenomena, but if you choose to think that Trehearn had hidden it somewhere in the bushes, and that the gale blew it to the house against the door, and made it knock, as if it wanted to be let in, you're not thinking the impossible, and I'm quite ready to agree with you.

Do you see that? You can swear that you've actually seen me seal it this time, in case anything of the kind should occur again. The wax fastens the strings to the lid, which cannot possibly be lifted, even enough to get in one finger. You're quite satisfied, aren't you? Yes. Besides, I shall lock the cupboard and keep the key in my pocket hereafter.

Now we can take the lantern and go upstairs. Do you know? I'm very much inclined to agree with your theory that the wind blew it against the house. I'll go ahead, for I know the stairs; just hold the lantern near my feet as we go up. How the wind howls and whistles! Did you feel the sand on the floor under your shoes as we crossed the hall?

Yes—this is the door of the best bedroom. Hold up the lantern, please. This side, by the head of the bed. I left the cupboard open when I got the box. Isn't it queer how the faint odour of women's dresses will hang about an old closet for years? This is the shelf. You've seen me set the box there, and now you see me turn the key and put it into my pocket. So that's done!

⚬━═━⚬

Good-night. Are you sure you're quite comfortable? It's not much of a room, but I daresay you would as soon sleep here as upstairs tonight. If you want anything, sing out; there's only a lath and plaster partition between us. There's not so much wind on this side by half. There's the Hollands on the table, if you'll have one more nightcap. No? Well, do as you please. Goodnight again, and don't dream about that thing, if you can.

⊙━━┿━━⊙

The following paragraph appeared in the *Penraddon News*, 23rd November, 1906:

Mysterious Death of a Retired Sea Captain

"The village of Tredcombe* is much disturbed by the strange death of Captain Charles Braddock, and all sorts of impossible stories are circulating with regard to the circumstances, which certainly seem difficult of explanation. The retired captain, who had successfully commanded in his time the largest and fastest liners belonging to one of the principal transatlantic steamship companies, was found dead in his bed on Tuesday morning in his own cottage, a quarter of a mile from the village. An examination was made at once by the local practitioner, which revealed the horrible fact that the deceased had been bitten in the throat by a human assailant, with such amazing force as to crush the windpipe and cause death. The marks of the teeth of both jaws were so plainly visible on the skin that they could be counted, but the perpetrator of the deed had evidently lost the two lower middle incisors. It is hoped that this peculiarity may help to identify the murderer, who can only be a dangerous escaped maniac. The deceased, though over sixty-five years of age, is said to have been a hale man of considerable physical strength, and it is remarkable that no signs of any struggle were visible in the room, nor could it be ascertained how the murderer had entered the house. Warning has been sent to all the insane asylums in the United Kingdom, but as yet no information has been received regarding the escape of any dangerous patient.

---

* The town is fictitious, as is the newspaper in which the article appears.

"The coroner's jury returned the somewhat singular verdict that Captain Braddock came to his death 'by the hands or teeth of some person unknown.' The local surgeon is said to have expressed privately the opinion that the maniac is a woman, a view he deduces from the small size of the jaws, as shown by the marks of the teeth. The whole affair is shrouded in mystery. Captain Braddock was a widower, and lived alone. He leaves no children."

[*Note.*—Students of ghost lore and haunted houses will find the foundation of the foregoing story in the legends about a skull which is still preserved in the farm-house called Bettiscombe Manor, situated, I believe, on the Dorsetshire coast.]*

---

* Bettiscombe Manor, in west Dorset, is indeed known as "The House of the Screaming Skull"; this legend dates back to the nineteenth century, and the skull is said to have been that of a Jamaican slave who was brought to England, but asked for his body to be returned to his homeland burial. When his owner, Azariah Pinney, refused, the village was beset by bad fortune and screams were heard for some time. An examination in 1963 determined that the skull was actually several thousand years old and belonged to a woman. The skull remains in Bettiscombe Manor to this day.

VIRGINIA WOOLF *(1882–1941) was one of the leading English modernist writers of the twentieth century. A founder and spiritual leader of the Bohemian Bloomsbury Group of artists and writers, she lived, loved, and argued with other intellectuals like biographer Lytton Strachey, novelist E. M. Forster, and economist John Maynard Keynes. Woolf developed the stream-of-consciousness form of narrative to great success in her novels, especially her triumph,* Mrs. Dalloway *(1925). She also wrote numerous short stories as well as essays on the philosophy and craft of writing. On March 28, 1941, fearing the invasion of England and the ruin of civilization, suffering as well as from her own recurring self-doubts, she walked down from her home to the River Ouse, put stones in her pockets, and drowned herself. The following meditation on memory and death first appeared in her collection* Monday or Tuesday, *published in 1921 by the Hogarth Press operated by Woolf and her husband, Leonard.*

A HAUNTED HOUSE

by Virginia Woolf

(1921)

Whatever hour you woke there was a door shutting. From room to room they went, hand in hand, lifting here, opening there, making sure—a ghostly couple.

"Here we left it," she said. And he added, "Oh, but here too!" "It's upstairs," she murmured. "And in the garden," he whispered. "Quietly," they said, "or we shall wake them."

But it wasn't that you woke us. Oh, no. "They're looking for it; they're drawing the curtain," one might say, and so read on a page or two.

"Now they've found it," one would be certain, stopping the pencil on the margin. And then, tired of reading, one might rise and see for one-self, the house all empty, the doors standing open, only the wood pigeons bubbling with content and the hum of the threshing machine sounding from the farm.

"What did I come in here for? What did I want to find?" My hands were empty. "Perhaps it's upstairs then?" The apples were in the loft. And so down again, the garden still as ever, only the book had slipped into the grass.

But they had found it in the drawing room. Not that one could ever see them. The window panes reflected apples, reflected roses; all the leaves were green in the glass. If they moved in the drawing room, the apple only turned its yellow side.

Yet, the moment after, if the door was opened, spread about the floor, hung upon the walls, pendant from the ceiling—what? My hands were empty. The shadow of a thrush crossed the carpet; from the deepest wells of silence the wood pigeon drew its bubble of sound.

"Safe, safe, safe," the pulse of the house beat softly. "The treasure buried; the room . . ." the pulse stopped short. Oh, was that the buried treasure?

A moment later the light had faded. Out in the garden then? But the trees spun darkness for a wandering beam of sun. So fine, so rare, coolly sunk beneath the surface the beam I sought always burnt behind the glass.

Death was the glass; death was between us; coming to the woman first, hundreds of years ago, leaving the house, sealing all the windows; the rooms were darkened. He left it, left her, went North, went East, saw the stars turned in the Southern sky; sought the house, found it dropped beneath the Downs. "Safe, safe, safe," the pulse of the house beat gladly. "The Treasure yours."

The wind roars up the avenue. Trees stoop and bend this way and that. Moonbeams splash and spill wildly in the rain. But the beam of the lamp falls straight from the window.

The candle burns stiff and still. Wandering through the house, opening the windows, whispering not to wake us, the ghostly couple seek their joy.

"Here we slept," she says. And he adds, "Kisses without number." "Waking in the morning—" "Silver between the trees—" "Upstairs—" "In the garden—" "When summer came—" "In winter snowtime—" The doors go shutting far in the distance, gently knocking like the pulse of a heart.

Nearer they come; cease at the doorway. The wind falls, the rain slides silver down the glass. Our eyes darken; we hear no steps beside us; we see no lady spread her ghostly cloak. His hands shield the lantern. "Look," he breathes. "Sound asleep. Love upon their lips."

Stooping, holding their silver lamp above us, long they look and deeply. Long they pause. The wind drives straightly; the flame stoops slightly. Wild beams of moonlight cross both floor and wall, and, meeting, stain the faces bent; the faces pondering; the faces that search the sleepers and seek their hidden joy.

"Safe, safe, safe," the heart of the house beats proudly. "Long years—" he sighs. "Again you found me." "Here," she murmurs, "sleeping; in the garden reading; laughing, rolling apples in the loft. Here we left our treasure—"

Stooping, their light lifts the lids upon my eyes. "Safe! safe! safe!" the pulse of the house beats wildly. Waking, I cry, "Oh, is this your buried treasure? The light in the heart."

G. G. PENDARVES *was born Gladys Gordon Trenery in 1885. Although she was born in Liverpool, her family hailed from Cornwall and much of her work incorporated Cornish folklore and locations. She became one of the major female writers of the pulps (despite the fact that her gender was unknown to readers), but little is known of her life. She wrote under several pseudonyms, contributed to mystery and adventure pulps as well as* Weird Tales, *and died of a heart attack in 1938. "The Laughing Thing" first appeared in the May 1929 issue of* Weird Tales.

THE LAUGHING THING

by G. G. Pendarves

(1929)

Very well, Mr. Drewe! I'll sign the agreement, though no one but you would drive such a devil's bargain."

The speaker's tall, emaciated body vibrated with indignation, and his strange light eyes blazed like incandescent lamps. There was something of the brooding menace of the gray sea in the latter, and a note in his voice reminded me of the sullen mutter of the wind before a storm.

A little shiver of apprehension ran through me as I turned from him to my brother-in-law, Jason Drewe. Nothing could have been more utterly and infuriatingly complacent than the latter, who was leaning back in the most comfortable chair my office afforded, with an expensive cigar in his mouth, his big frame clad in the smartest of light tweeds, and an orchid in his buttonhole.

Jason was an extremely wealthy man, young enough to enjoy his money, and with a son to inherit his millions one day. The loss of Mavis, his wife, had been more of an annoyance than a grief to him; he felt that she had died merely to make things awkward for him—in fact, he added her death to the many grievances he treasured up against her.

I knew that if there is such a thing as a broken heart, he broke my sister's, and I hated him for it. I would have cut off all intercourse with him, only that I had promised Mavis to keep an eye on the boy, and counteract his father's influence as far as possible. Jason knew nothing of this; he believed I hung to him for the sake of his wealth and twitted me with it quite openly, in spite of the fact that I was never indebted to him for a single dime, and would have cleaned the streets, or sold "hot dogs" rather than owe him a penny.

It seemed absurd to pity him, especially at this moment of his triumph, when he had succeeded in getting the land he wanted at the price he wanted, and was sitting there before me as pink and pleased as a prize baby after its bottle.

Eldred Werne, whom Jason had just cornered so successfully, was the one whom most people would have pitied. But I had only admiration for anyone as determined and strong of soul as Werne. Poor and desperately ill though he was, he was not an object for pity.

As junior partner in the firm of Baxter and Baxter, real estate agents, I was present to witness the signatures and conclude the deal between Werne and Jason; and I wished a thousand times that Baxter and Baxter had never had this affair entrusted to them. It was a sordid, despicable business altogether.

"I'll sign," repeated Werne, drawing his chair closer to my desk, and taking up the parchments in his thin, blue-veined hands. "The land shall be yours at your own price—for the present!"

Anger and instant suspicion showed in Jason's small, heavy-lidded eyes.

"What the devil do you mean?" he said. "If you sign these papers the land is mine, and there's no power on earth can make me pay more for it than the sum set down there in black and white."

"I wasn't thinking of money." Werne's voice was strangely quiet and yet so full of menace that again I felt every nerve in my body thrill to it. "I am sure you will never pay more in money."

"You're right—dead right, Werne," Jason's resonant voice echoed through the room.

"And yet—I think you will pay more in the end. Yes, in the end you will pay more, Mr. Drewe."

Jason turned to me blustering and furious.

"Aren't these deeds water-tight? What does he mean? If there is any flaw in these agreements I'll stamp you and your fool firm out of existence!"

Before I could reply, Werne began to laugh. He sat there and laughed long and dreadfully, the bright color staining his thin cheeks, his gray eyes brilliant and malicious. He laughed until the cough seized him, and he leant back at last utterly exhausted, an ominous stain on the handkerchief he pressed to his lips.

"Let me relieve your natural anxiety, Mr. Drewe," he said at last, his hoarse voice still shaken with mirth. "You will pay more, but not in money! Not in any material sense at all."

"What in the name of common sense do you mean?" growled Jason.

"There is nothing common at all in the sense of which I speak. It is very uncommon indeed! I refer to payments which have no connection with money—nothing which can be reckoned in dollars and cents."

Jason looked uncertain whether to call police protection or medical aid, and he watched Werne narrowly as the latter signed the documents.

When the signatures were completed, Eldred Werne got to his feet and stood looking down at Jason—a long, strange, deep look, as if he meant to learn the other's every feature off by heart. Behind Werne's eyes once more a sudden terrifying flame of laughter danced—flickered—and was gone!

"You don't fear any payment that will not reduce your bank account, then?"

"What other payment is there?" asked Jason in genuine surprise.

"You're wonderful!" said Werne. "So complete a product of your age and kind. So logical and limited and—excuse me—so thoroughly stupid!"

Jason's fresh-colored face turned a deep purple.

"If you were not a sick man—" he began.

"And one, moreover, whom you have thoroughly and satisfactorily fleeced," interpolated Werne.

"I should resent your remarks," continued Jason pompously. "As it is, I see no use in prolonging this conversation."

"Stay!" cried Werne, as Jason put on his fur coat and prepared to depart. "It's only fair to warn you that if I die out there in Denver City,* I shall come back again! I shall be in a better position then, without this wretched body of mine. I shall come back—to make you pay—a more satisfactory price for my Tareytown† acres."

Jason stared, standing in the doorway with one plump well-manicured hand on the door-knob, looking like a great shaggy ox in his fur coat, and with that air of stupid bewilderment on his broad face.

"Wha-a-a-at?" he stammered. Then, as the other's meaning slowly dawned on him, he leaned up against the door and showed every tooth in his head in a perfect bellow of mirth. "Are you threatening to haunt me?" he choked, the veins on his forehead swelling dangerously. "Well, my good fellow, if it gives you any comfort to imagine that, don't let me discourage your little idea. You'll be welcome at Tareytown any old time! The Tareytown specter, eh? It'll give quite an air to the place! What kind of payment will you want—moonshine, eh?" Jason almost burst with the humor of this remark. "Moonshine and ghosts! Seems the right sort of mixture!"

With a last fatuous chuckle, Jason opened the door; and, through the window, I saw him get into his new coupé and drive off, his face still creased in enjoyment of his last sally.

"The descent of man," murmured Werne, half to himself. "There's no doubt that Jason Drewe has descended a considerable way from the apes! The fool—the blind, besotted fool!"

2

It was a perfect day in the late autumn of that same year, when, for the first time, I saw the Tareytown estate.

---

* There is a Denver located in New York about 50 miles from the Hudson River, but it's a hamlet, not a city.

† Probably a play on the name "Tarrytown," a real village located on the Hudson River near Sleepy Hollow.

I dismissed my taxi at the huge stone gateway, and walked slowly up through the woods. After the hectic rush and noise of New York, the golden stillness around me was deeply satisfying; and I thought of poor Eldred Werne, who would never know the beauty and healing peace of this place again. I had seen the notice of his death in Denver City, only a month after he had signed away his rights to these lovely Tareytown woods, and I had thought very often since of the lonely bitterness which must have clouded his last days.

Glimpses of the blue, shining Hudson shone between the trees, and beyond, the flaming russet of the Palisades.* On all sides the country stretched out to dim, misty horizons for which Werne's dying eyes must have longed in his exile.

Then, quite suddenly, a chill passed over me. I became aware of the ominous and unusual stillness of the brooding woods. Neither bird nor squirrel darted to and fro among the leaves and branches—not even a fly buzzed about in the hazy sunshine.

I looked around in gathering apprehension. What *was* it that began to oppress me more and more? Why did the tall trees seem to be listening?—why did I have the impulse to look over my shoulder?—why did my heart thump and my hands chill suddenly?

With a great effort I restrained myself from breaking into a run, as I continued upward toward the house. The path doubled back on itself across and across the shoulder of the hill on which the house, Red Gables, was built; and it was fully ten minutes before I arrived breathless in sight of its red roof and high old-fashioned chimney-stack.

In a corner of its wide porch, I caught a glimpse of a boy's figure and let out a loud halloo, glad of an excuse to break the queer, unnatural silence.

There was an answering hail, and my nephew, Tony, came running down the path to meet me.

"Hello, Uncle John! I was waiting for you! Did you walk up through the woods—alone?" The boy's voice held an awed note, which was emphasized by the look of fear in his dark eyes.

---

* The Palisades are a line of steep basalt cliffs that run for about 20 miles along the west bank of the Hudson River; they are directly opposite Tarrytown and Sleepy Hollow.

He was only eight years old, and exactly like his mother. Thank heaven, there was no trace of Jason's complacent materialism in his son . . . mind and body, Tony was an utterly different type. I loved the boy, and a real friendship had developed between us, despite the disparity of our years. He was curiously sensitive and mature for his age, and it was a great thing for a bachelor like myself to have a child make a little tin god of me, as Tony did.

"And why not walk alone through the woods?" I demanded, looking down at him as he rubbed his head against my arm like some friendly colt.

"I wouldn't," he replied simply.

"Why not, old man? There aren't any wolves or bears or even Indians left here, are there?"

"Don't laugh, Uncle." The boy's voice sank to a whisper. "There isn't time to tell you now, but there's something in those woods. Something you can't see—that—that is waiting!"

I stared at the boy, and once again the cold chill I had experienced during my walk up to the house crept over me.

"Look here, Tony," I began. "You mustn't get—"

"There is—there *is*, I tell you!" He was passionately in earnest. "Something that laughs—something that is waiting!"

"Laughs—waiting!" I echoed feebly.

"You'll hear it yourself," he answered. "Then you'll know. Father won't let me speak about it to him, and says if I'd play games instead of reading books, I'd only hear and see half what I do now."

"About as much as he hears and sees," I murmured to myself.

"I am sure Father hears it too, only he won't say so," continued Tony. "But I've noticed one thing—he won't let anyone knock at the doors. The servants even go into his study without knocking, and he was always so—so—"

"Exactly!" I said dryly; "I understand."

The small hand in mine gave a little warning pressure, and I saw Jason Drewe's big frame and massive head loom up in the comparative dimness of the interior, as Tony and I reached the entrance door of Red Gables.

"Well, John!" boomed my host, as he rose from the depths of a vast chair and came forward, cigar in hand. "Made your fortune yet?"

It was the form of greeting he invariably gave me; for he was that irritating type of man who uses a limited number of favorite witticisms and sticks to them persistently, in season and out of season.

Today, however, his complacent heartiness was obviously an immense effort to him, and I was quite startled by the change in his appearance. He seemed conscious of it himself, but there was a certain bravado in the sunken eyes he turned on me, which defied me to remark on his ill looks.

I was certainly shocked to notice how much thinner he was, how gray his skin, and how hunted and restless were his eyes, as he kept glancing from side to side with a quick upward jerk of his big head, as though he were listening for some expected and unwelcome summons.

He motioned me to a chair and poured out drinks with a fumbling sort of touch, which further indicated the change in him since I last saw him in the office of Baxter and Baxter.

Tony curled up at my side on the arm of my easy-chair, as quiet as a doormouse, taking no part in the conversation, but his precocious intelligence enabled him to follow the drift of it; that I could swear to. He annoyed his father, this silent observant child, and in the middle of a discussion Jason turned irritably to the boy.

"Why don't you go off and amuse yourself out of doors like any other boy of your age? You sit round the house like a little lap-dog and waste your time with books—always mooning about like someone in a dream! Just like your mother—just like her," he finished in an exasperated mutter.

When we were alone, Jason turned to me with a frown. "More like a girl than a boy!" he commented bitterly. "About as much pep as a soft drink! What's the use of building up a business and making a future for him, when he'll let it all slip through his fingers later on?"

He went on talking rather loudly and quickly on the subject, with no help at all from me, and it struck me he was talking in order to defeat his own clamorous unpleasant thoughts; working himself up into a pretense of anger to make the blood run more hot and swift in his veins.

As far as he was able, within the limited scope of his primitive nature, Jason loved the boy, and every hope and ambition he cherished was centered round Tony, and Tony's future. I just let him run on, and speculated with increasing bewilderment on the cause of my brother-in-law's obvious uneasiness of soul. It must be something tremendous to have shaken his colossal egotism, I argued to myself, and moreover it was something he was desperately anxious to hide—some unacknowledged fear which had pricked and wounded him deep beneath his tough skin.

"I'm not satisfied with that school of his—not at all satisfied!" he went on. "I ask you now, what's the use of filling a kid's head with all that imaginary stuff when he's got to live in a world of Jews and politicians and grafters? How's he going to grind his own* when his darned school has exchanged it for a silver butter knife? How's he going to—?"

He broke off with a queer strangled groan as a sudden clamorous knocking sounded—a loud tattoo like the sound of war-drums through the quiet house.

The big sunshiny room darkened suddenly and a puff of wind from an open window at my side breathed an icy chill on my cheek. The horror I had recently experienced in the woods swept over me again, and I saw Jason's face set in a mask of fear and loathing.

Silence held us bound for a perceptible moment, and in the quiet a loud, echoing laugh rang out.

It sounded as though someone were standing just outside the house, and I had a vivid mental image of a figure convulsed and rocking with mirth. But this figure of my imagination did not move me to laughter myself, although as a rule nothing is more contagious than laughter—but not this—not this hateful mirth!

I dashed to the window and looked out; then, making for the door in blind haste, stumbled out on the porch and ran round the house in a queer frenzy of desire to learn who—or *what*—had stood there laughing . . . laughing . . . laughing.

I only caught a glimpse of frightened faces in the servants' quarters at the back of the house as I dashed past, and saw windows and doors being hastily slammed.

When I got back to the living-room again Jason was gone, and I sat down breathless, and shaken to the very soul. I had stumbled on to the

---

* Jason has probably left out the word "axe" here.

secret—or part of it—with a vengeance; and I sat with my unlit pipe in my mouth for the better part of an hour, until the first overwhelming horror of the episode had faded a little.

Jason came in just as I was thinking of going up to my room to change for dinner, and any idea I might have entertained of asking him for explanations was foiled by the extraordinary change in him.

He was his old self again. Large, pink, and prosperous, he breezed into the room and stood with his hands in his pockets, grinning down at me from his massive six feet odd. If there was something defiant in the gleam of his blue eye, if his voice was harsh and his grin a trifle too wide, it needed someone who knew him as well as I did to detect it.

I never liked or admired him as much as I did at that moment; and the determination came to me, to stand by him in this trouble of his, to stay and fight it out, and give what help I could to him and the boy.

I am not a superstitious man, nor counted credulous by my friends or enemies. But here was something inexplicably evil which brooded over the lonely woods of Tareytown like some dark-winged genie.

I went slowly and thoughtfully up to my room, my mind heavy with doubt and perplexity, and as the night wore on and darkness closed in about the house, so did my mind grow darker and more fearful.

3

"Well, Soames! Rather a change from your roof-garden in New York—eh? How do you like it here?"

The old gardener folded his gnarled hands one over the other on the handle of his spade, and shook his head slowly from side to side.

"It was an unlucky day for the master when he came to Tareytown, sir—an unlucky day!"

"How's that? Won't your plants grow for you?"

"You know, sir! I see by your face that you know already!"

"I must confess there's something a bit depressing about the place," I answered. "It's just the time of year, no doubt. There's always something melancholy about the fall."

"There's nothing wrong about the time of year," said the old man. He leaned forward and his voice sank to a whisper. "Haven't you *heard* it yet?"

I gave an involuntary start, and he pursed up his mouth and nodded.

"Aye, I see you have!"

He came closer and peered up at me, his brown face with its faded blue eyes a network of anxious wrinkles.

"Sir, if you can help the master, for God's sake do it! He's a rare hard one, I know, but I've served him for thirty-five years, and I don't want to see no harm come to him. He won't own up that he hears anything amiss, nor go away from this accursed place with the boy, before any harm comes to either of them. He's that angry because he don't understand—*won't* understand there's something more than flesh and blood can hurt us sometimes!"

The old man's words came out in a flood, the result of long-suppressed anxiety, and I marveled that a man of Jason Drewe's type should command such solicitude from anyone.

"I'm all in the dark, Soames," I said slowly. "Who is it that knocks—that laughs?"

The gardener's eyes grew very somber. "No mortal man—no mortal man, sir."

"Why, Soames, you're as superstitious as they make them," I said, trying to make light of his words.

"See here, sir," he said, pulling me by the sleeve into the deeper shade of the shrubbery behind us, "I'll tell you what I've never spoken a word of yet. I'll tell you what I overheard one night when this—this *thing* first came here. I was pottering about late one evening, tying up bits of creeper against the wall outside the master's study. I heard the knock—loud and long as if the emperor of the world was a-knocking at the door, and I looks up to see who was there. The door was only three or four feet from where I was standing with bass* and scissors in my hand. And there was no one at all on the steps nor anywhere near the house. While I was a-staring and wondering I heard the laugh! My blood went cold, and I just stood there shaking like a poplar tree in a wind. And since then, night after night, that knock and that laugh comes as regular as the sun sets!"

---

* A length of fiber.

I stared at my companion in incredulous horror.

"And one time," he continued, "I heard the master call out. Terrible loud and fierce his voice was: '*Have you come for your moonshine, Eldred Werne?— take it!*' And with that, a bottle of whisky comes hurtling through the window and fell almost at my feet. I felt a wind blow across my face same as if it blew right off an iceberg; and as I stood there afraid to move hand or foot, I heard the laugh way down among the trees, getting fainter and fainter just as if someone was walking away down the path—and laughing and laughing to himself all the time!"

I listened aghast to the old man, and a vivid picture arose in my mind of Eldred Werne as I last saw him in life—the tall, emaciated figure, the arresting face with its beautifully chiseled features, and above all the strange gray eyes as they had dwelt in that last deep look on the burning mocking fire which lit them and the fathomless contempt of the strong mouth.

"You will pay—you will pay!" The words rang in my ears as if Werne were standing at my side speaking them at that very moment.

I sat down abruptly on a fallen tree, and lit a cigarette with unsteady fingers.

"Now look here, Soames," I said at last. "We mustn't let this thing get us scared out of all common sense and reason. I admit it's a beastly unpleasant business, but I can't—I won't believe yet that there is no natural explanation of these things. Someone who owes him a grudge may be putting one over on Mr. Drewe. It may be a deliberate plot to annoy and frighten him. There was a—er—well, a misunderstanding between your master and Mr. Werne over the purchase of this Tareytown estate, and Mr. Werne was quite capable of planning a neat little revenge to square his account a little. He was a very sick man, remember—and sick men are apt to be vindictive and unreasonable."

"I guessed as something had happened between the two," murmured Soames, "but I didn't rightly know what it was."

"You and I will watch the house from now on," I said. "We'll arrange to be outside, one or other or both of us, directly after sunset. And if—if we see nothing, if we find no one there—"

"Aye—you won't, sir!"

"Then I shall do my best to persuade Mr. Drewe to leave this place and return to the city."

"And that you'll never do. He'll never give in and go away, not if it means his death. The master is terrible obstinate, and he fair blazed up when I kind of suggested he wasn't looking just himself, and that maybe Tareytown didn't agree with him."

And remembering Jason's defiant eyes and the bluff he put up last evening for my benefit, I was inclined to agree with Soames.

"I'll do what I can," I said, getting up and brushing off twigs and leaves.

"I'm thankful to know you're here, sir. There was no one I dared say a word to until you came. The servants are in mortal terror, and never a week passes without one or more of them leaving. Soon we won't be able to get anyone to stay a night in the place!"

"If your master could be persuaded to send the boy away for the rest of his vacation—"

"He won't do that," was the lugubrious reply. "That would be sort of owning up that there *was* something here he was afraid of! He'll never admit that—never!"

4

Our first vigil took place that night.

The boy was safe indoors—he never went over the threshold of the house after dusk fell, I noticed. Jason had established himself with his favorite drink, a stack of newspapers, and a box of cigars, in his library. I left him looking as immovable as the Rock of Gibraltar—and as gray!

Soames and I planted ourselves in strategic positions on either side of the porch, where we could see both the big entrance door, and the whole of the front porch which ran in front of the library, dining-room, and sun-parlor.

A pale moon sailed serenely overhead, and I felt a passionate longing to be as far away from this evil haunted little piece of earth as was the moon itself. Revolt which was almost nausea seized me, as I looked around at the shadowy woods, and felt the unnamable creeping horror which waited there.

Slow minutes passed. The shadows grew denser, and the silence so profounded that the falling leaves rattled like metal things on the dry ground, and the creak of the great trees made my heart thump furiously against my ribs.

I could see Soames's small tense figure bent forward in a listening attitude, his face turned toward the entrance door. He looked like a terrier-dog straining eagerly on a leash.

My eyes roved restlessly to and fro, and fell at last on the long, uncut grass which grew about the tree-trunks. Quite suddenly I saw the reeds and grasses bend and quiver as if before a strong wind. In a long thin line they bent—a line advancing rapidly from the blackness of the trees out toward the open—toward the house—toward the entrance porch, with its broad steps gleaming silver in the moonlight.

My hand flew to my throat to stifle the cry that rose as I saw that sinister trail being blazed before my eyes. It advanced to the extreme edge of the tall grasses in a direct line with the entrance-door.

A moment of unendurable suspense—an agony of terrified expectant waiting! Then it came—loud—thunderous—awful as the stroke of doom! The knocker had been removed from the door, and on the bare wood itself beat that devil's tattoo.

I was paralyzed with the shock and thunder of it, and only when I saw Soames stumbling forward, and heard his hoarse cry, did I move—stiff and uncertainly as a man might move after a long illness.

We clutched each other like two terrified children when we arrived at the foot of the steps, and I felt Soames's body shaking against my own.

Then, abruptly, the infernal racket ceased; and in the momentary silence which ensued, a laugh broke out that sent our trembling hands over our ears, but we could not shut out the sound of that demoniac laughter. Uncontrolled and triumphant it rang out again and again, and the vision of someone rocking with mirth rose as before in my imagination.

But nothing was there on the porch in the moonlight!

The whole porch was visible in the clear white light. No one, no thing, could have escaped our staring, straining eyes. There was no one there, and yet almost within touch of our outstretched hands some invisible, intangible Thing stood laughing—laughing—laughing . . .

5

After that night the horror fell more and more darkly.

Soames, who was out all day working in the gardens and shrubberies, noticed increasingly sinister signs that our invisible enemy was marshaling his forces, and closing in on the last stages of the siege.

More and more frequently the old man would see the grasses bending and swaying around him in loops and circles, as though the laughing Thing moved to and fro in the mazes of some infernal dance. Often Soames felt the chill of the Thing's passing, and noted the shriveled, blighted foliage which marked its trail.

The woods grew darker with every passing day, despite the thinning of the leaves. The autumn mists which lay white and cloudlike in the valleys of the surrounding country, drifted in among the trees on the Tareytown estate like gray, choking smoke, dank and rotten with the breath of decay, shutting out the sunlit earth beyond, and the clear skies above, rolling up around the house with infinite menace and gloom.

Louder and more clamorous grew the nightly summons, and the laughter which followed echoed and reechoed about the house throughout the night, sounding at our very windows, then growing faint and ominous from the depths of the brooding woods.

6

At last, the boy's terror precipitated a crisis.

Jason, who had brought this cursed thing upon himself, it seemed, refused to acknowledge that he had been wrong, to make any amends which lay within his power, or even to move from the place which Eldred Werne had loved so passionately in the flesh, and haunted so persistently in the spirit.

Jason's courage, though I admired it in one way, was not of the highest order. I mean that his conduct was guided by no reason, but only by blind impulse.

I tackled him more than once about Tony, and only succeeded in rousing furious opposition.

"What the devil are you driving at?" he roared at me. "This is my house, isn't it? These are my woods and my lands. I paid for them according to my bond. No one is going to drive me out—no one, d'you hear?—neither man nor devil!"

"But Tony!" I protested. "You ought to consider him. He hears the servants talking. He hears whatever it is that comes knocking at your door, Jason—you know best what it is! The boy is almost beside himself with fear. Can't you see he is desperate? He doesn't eat or sleep properly. D'you want to kill him as you did his mother?" I added bitterly, remembrance of my sister's lonely, unhappy life with Jason goading me to speech.

But Jason was always impervious to anything he wished to ignore, and he brushed aside my last words and returned to Tony.

"The boy has got to learn—he's got to learn, I say! If this house is good enough for me, then it's good enough for him, too. Tony'll stay here with me to the end of his vacation. If I give in about this thing, it will be the thin end of the wedge. He'll expect me to indulge every girl's fad and fancy he has—and the Lord knows he's full of them! Here I stay, and here he stays, and that's all about it. Why on earth do you stay yourself, feeling as you do?" he added roughly. "If you're afraid, I'll excuse you the rest of your visit."

I didn't trouble to deny the fact that I was afraid, and went off cursing myself for interfering, and probably making Tony's relations with his father even more difficult.

7

That evening Jason seemed absolutely possessed. Whether he had been drinking heavily, or whether his endurance had reached the breaking point suddenly in the long, silent combat of wills with his invisible enemy, or whether the blind gray figure of Fate had written the last chapter, and he had no choice but to obey, I do not know.

Everything that happened that last fatal night seemed obscured and fogged with the waves of terror and desolation that swept over the house and the surrounding woods.

From early morning the attack on us strengthened perceptibly. Every hour I felt we were fighting a losing battle, and I had no comfort for Soames when he sought me out, and led me off to the potting-sheds after a pretense of breakfasting.

Tony had remained in bed, to his father's unbounded disgust. The boy had spent a sleepless night and I had given him a bromide* and persuaded him to stay in his room to rest.

"Making a mollycoddle of him!" growled Jason, his eyes light and dangerous as a wild boar's above his flabby, sallow cheeks. He put down his cup with a rattle on the saucer, and scraping his chair noisily on the polished flooring, he rose and strode heavily out of the room, and I heard the stairs creak under his weight as he went up to the boy.

Throughout the day, his evil mood grew on him, and Tony could do nothing right.

"Mark my words, sir," Soames had said to me as we stood in the potting-sheds that morning. "I've a feeling we've about come to the end. That Laughing Devil will knock for the last time tonight—for the last time! Mark my words!"

And as the day wore on I felt more assured that Soames was right.

Every hour the sense of imminent and immense danger grew heavier, and every hour Tony grew more and more nervous and Jason more brutally obstinate; for the sight of the boy's terror goaded his father into senseless anger.

The sun set that night in a bank of heavy dull cloud, which spread and darkened until thick impenetrable dusk closed about us.

With the coming of twilight we waited in fearful anticipation of our usual visitation; but dusk deepened to night and no summons sounded at the door, no mocking horror of laughter was heard at all.

Yet this silence brought no feeling of reprieve. Rather our expectancy grew more and more tense, and Tony sat by the fire with cold shaking hands

---

* A sedative.

thrust deep into his pockets, and tried to prevent his father noticing the ague of fear which shook his thin little body.

Jason did not send him to bed at his usual time—we all sat there waiting—just waiting!

The big logs smoldered dully and reluctantly on the hearthstone. Jason's face was a gray mask; his thick lips sneered; his eyes gleamed between their puffy lids. He was like a cornered animal of some primeval age—a great inert mass of flesh slumped down in his big chair by the dying fire.

Nine—ten—eleven! The torturing hours crept on and still we sat there like people under a spell, just waiting—waiting!

With the deep midnight chime of the clock in the library, the spell was broken with a hideous clamor that made Tony leap up with the shriek of a wild thing caught in a trap.

Jason got to his feet in one surprizing movement, and stood with feet apart and lowered head, as if about to do battle.

I sat clutching the arms of my chair, held by a blind terror that was like steel chains about me.

It was the Laughing Thing at last! Long and furiously the knock resounded, sinking to a low mutter and rising to a crescendo of blows that threatened to batter down the heavy door. And over and above the thunderous blows rose the high mocking laughter—triumphant, cruel, satisfied laughter!

I blame myself—I shall always blame myself for what happened then. I might have held the boy back—guarded him more closely when he was too frenzied with fear to guard himself. But I did not dream what he was about until it was too late! When he ran from the shelter of my arms, I thought he meant to seek another refuge!

But no—the boy was crazed beyond all reason and control, and ran desperately to the very horror which had driven him mad.

I heard his quick, light steps along the hall, and I thought he was making for the staircase, not the door—my God, not the door!

There was the quick rattle of a heavy chain, the groan of a bolt withdrawn—then a long, wailing shriek of terror!

With one accord Jason and I dashed out into the hall—Soames came rushing from the kitchen-quarters—and there stood the door flung wide, and from the porch without came a long exultant peal of laughter.

We flung ourselves forward and out into the night. In the distance among the trees we heard the dying echoes of that infernal laughter—then nothing more.

8

Until dawn we searched the woods of Tareytown, and as the first gray glimmer of light broke in the east we found him.

Have you ever seen anyone dead of a sudden violent poison—such as prussic acid*—with teeth showing in a terrible grin—the muscles of the face stiffened in inhuman laughter? It is the most dreadful of all masks which death can fix on human lineaments.

So we found Tony!

His eyes—awful contrast to his grinning mouth—mirrored a terror too profound for any words to convey. Eyes which had looked on the unnamable—the unthinkable; spawn of that outermost darkness which no human sight may endure.

That night was the end of my youth and happiness. Jason packed up and went for a prolonged tour of Europe with his fears and his memories, and I have never seen him since.

For myself, I live, and will always live, on the Tareytown estate, where perhaps Tony's spirit may wander lost and lonely, still possessed by that evil which caught him in its net.

I must remain at Red Gables, and perhaps here or hereafter I may atone for the selfish fear which made me fail Tony in that desperate crisis.

Somewhere—somehow, beyond the curtain of this life, I may meet the Thing which laughed—the evil, bitter Thing which once was Eldred Werne—the Thing which may still possess the boy and hold him earthbound and accurst.

I failed Tony once, but I will not do so a second time. I will offer my own soul to set him free—and perhaps the high god will hear me and accept the sacrifice.

---

* Cyanide.

ACKNOWLEDGMENTS

T hanks are due first and foremost to my brilliant partner Les Klinger, whose breadth of knowledge is a continual source of wonder. Thank you to Charles Dickens, whose work as both author and editor paved the way for so many others, and to Anne Lohrli, whose work *Household Words: A Weekly Journal 1850–1859 Conducted by Charles Dickens* led the way to the discovery of Dinah Mulock's remarkable "M. Anastasius." Thank you to our agent Donald Maass, and eternal gratitude to Claiborne Hancock, Maria Fernandez, and the entire Pegasus crew who always make the words look so good. Lastly, thank you to Kevin Cazares and Ricky Grove, who keep me entertained, informed, and alive.

—Lisa Morton

W ow, there are so many brilliant ghost stories to share! As usual, this book is the product of many hands. First and foremost, it is a thrill to again co-edit a book with my longtime pal Lisa Morton, whose work I constantly admire. This is our fourth collaboration, and I hope we have many more! Many thanks to my agent Don Maass, who is always supportive of my crazy-sounding ideas. Claiborne Hancock and the rest of the Pegasus team—Maria Fernandez and Victoria Wenzel in particular—lavished it with care and attention. I'm always grateful to my writer-friends, Laurie R. King, Neil Gaiman, Nicholas Meyer, Cornelia Funke, Bonnie MacBird, and Peter Straub and fellow horror lovers John Landis and Guillermo del Toro. My family is always understanding of my hiding in my office to do research and writing. In particular, I am blessed that my wife Sharon is my biggest fan and cheerleader, without whom none of my writing would ever happen. She has always been, and remains, "the woman."

—Leslie S. Klinger